The B↑ZARRO
STARTER KIT

AN INTRODUCTION TO THE BIZARRO GENRE

BIZARRO BOOKS
Portland * Seattle * Baltimore

A BIZARRO BOOK
www.bizarrocentral.com

BIZARRO BOOKS
P.O. Box 10065
Portland, OR 97269

IN COOPERATION WITH:

ERASERHEAD PRESS
LAZY FASCIST PRESS
FUNGASM PRESS
ROOSTER REPUBLIC PRESS
DEADITE PRESS

ISBN: 978-1-62105-187-9

Cover design by Carlton Mellick III

Edited by: Team Bizarro

Printed in the USA.

TABLE OF CONTENTS

DEFINING BIZARRO

1. Bizarro, simply put, is the genre of the weird.

2. Bizarro is the literary equivalent to the cult section at the video store.

3. Like cult movies, Bizarro is sometimes surreal, sometimes goofy, sometimes bloody, and sometimes borderline pornographic.

4. Bizarro often contains a certain cartoon logic that, when applied to the real world, creates an unstable universe where the bizarre becomes the norm and absurdities are made flesh.

5. Bizarro strives not only to be strange, but fascinating, thought-provoking, and, above all, fun to read.

6. Bizarro was created by a group of small press publishers in response to the increasing demand for (good) weird fiction and the increasing number of authors who specialize in it.

7. Bizarro is:

Franz Kafka meets Joe Bob Briggs

Dr. Seuss of the post-apocalypse

Alice in Wonderland for adults

Japanese animation directed by David Lynch

8. For more information on the bizarro genre, visit Bizarro Central at:

www.bizarrocentral.com

NICK ANTOSCA

LOCATION:
Los Angeles, CA

STYLE OF BIZARRO:
Sociopath Realism

BOOKS BY ANTOSCA:
Fires
Midnight Picnic
The Obese
The Girlfriend Game
The Hangman's Ritual

DESCRIPTION: Idle thoughts misbehave, go feral.

INTERESTS: TV writing, screenwriting, omokase, gluten-free pasta, apples, peanut butter.

INFLUENCES: Calvin & Hobbes, the Twilight Zone.

WEBSITE:
https://twitter.com/nickantosca

THE OBESE

My name is Nina Gilten, and I'm cutting pieces of hipbone off a beautiful South African girl called Behati van de Velde, a blond girl, a descendant of Boers. She's sixteen and her hips are bony, so they have to go. The gawky/provocative position she's in, kind of lying on her side on a brown velvet loveseat, facing the camera, head propped on her little fist, only makes the hip jut more egregiously. And even though she's thin and the convexity in her silhouette is *obviously* her hip, which is *obviously* just bone... *any* convexity in a girl's silhouette makes the mind think: FAT.

Which is why I'm cutting it off.

I also minimize her nasolabial folds and remove a tiny mole from the flume of her upper lip. I adjust her shoulder almost imperceptibly. I use a warping tool, which sort of fluffs up clusters of pixels to give the image a richer, more voluminous quality.

I'm 27 years old. I'm good at what I do. I've retouched images for *Redbook, Teen Vogue, Chic, Marie Claire,* and *Nylon,* as well as some famous fashion photographers you might know, like Peter Lindbergh and Terry Richardson. I don't look at photographs of myself anymore; it's too time-consuming. I avoid the mirror whenever possible. Because sometimes it's not possible, I've mastered the ability to look at myself as a collection of adequate segments.

In the guts of my bag, my iPhone vibrates. I dig it out and am intrigued to see a number I don't know. There are only two people I'd be interested in speaking to right now. One is my ex-boyfriend, Chris, who I broke up with seven weeks ago because he didn't seem to be putting any effort into our relationship. The fact that he didn't put any effort into persuading me not to break up with him suggests I made the right decision, but I still find it maddening that—if the news is true—he didn't waste a week before he started dating an emaciated ciliate named Molly Sweet, an F.I.T. student majoring in lingerie or somesuch. I consider it beyond dispute that the universe would be a better place if Chris realized how much he missed me and came begging for a second chance. I wouldn't give it to him, but I have a weird, persistent urge to communicate with him again and see how he's doing—an urge that, depressingly, has only been getting stronger even though I haven't run into him *once* since we broke up, despite us living two blocks apart.

Chris, though, is still in my phone, so unless he got a new number, this isn't him calling. That's okay, because I'm hoping it's the other person I'd like to hear from: the Handsome Stranger.

The Handsome Stranger's name is Leonardo or Gallardo or Armando, something like that—I'm not sure because I couldn't quite hear it two nights ago on the rainy block of Orchard Street where, like in a romantic comedy that slyly mocks meet-cute clichés in the process of brazenly employing one, this mesomorphic Adonis stopped to help me gather the suddenly soaked pages that had spilled from my tote and scattered on the sidewalk. In close proximity, I felt terribly self-conscious—off-balance and uncoordinated, as if all my limbs had suddenly ballooned to unmanageable proportions.

The Handsome Stranger was tall, and of course Handsome, with calm, faintly mocking blue eyes and cheekbones as high and nobly defined as cathedral arches. His accent: Italian or Spanish. He escorted me to the corner, his umbrella protecting us, and before he got in a cab, he took my number. I felt forward giving it to him, but I was afraid he wouldn't ask.

He seemed like the kind of guy I just don't usually meet in New York—handsome and masculine and exuding sex. Almost all the guys I meet are gay, and ninety percent of the ones who *are* straight either act gay to lower your defenses or prance around in horn-rimmed glasses prattling about the new Werner Herzog movie or how they just read the galley of Haruki Murakami's next book. The Pretentious Douchebag, perpetually on the prowl.

Anyway, I've been waiting for two days, and it's the Handsome Stranger's voice I expect to hear when I answer the phone call.

"Hi," says a female voice so burly it might as well have hair on its chest, "Nina?"

"Yes, who's this?" That sensation is hope shriveling up.

"It's Dora Hofflig." A long, crunchy pause. The connection is awful, as usual. Nudgingly, the voice says, "From high school?"

Oh, right. "Oh, right." God, why did I answer the phone? "Dora... what's up?"

Dora Hofflig was a girl I wouldn't have known in high school (or middle school, or elementary school) except that she grew up three houses down and we both went to Riverdale Country Prep. She was a slightly husky person with pretty eyes who could have made herself mildly attractive if she understood anything about anything. I think she played piano.

"Ha, you remember me!" she says, and perhaps there is a slight note of sarcasm in her voice. "Well, I've been in Washington, D.C., working for PETA, actually. But I'm visiting New York this week and I'd love to catch up."

"Okay," I hear myself say.

"Cool!" A hesitation. "Also, I was wondering—please tell me if I'm overstepping here, like if this isn't cool, but your mom told my mom that you might have room for me to stay at your place? I'm just going to be in town for three nights, or maybe four."

Oh, lovely. Another body in my space, *taking up* space, eating, needing attention. I could produce some excuse—apartment being painted, other guests in town, scarlet fever—but I both fear my mother's disapproval and am constantly on the lookout for chits I can use with her. If I accumulate enough, I may be able to get out of visiting on Thanksgiving.

"You can crash on my couch," I tell Dora.

As this is happening, my computer makes the autistic *bonk* that accompanies a Gmail chat message. It's Teresa Hollingsworth, the editor at *Chic* I'm working with on this job. She's 40-something, a legend in the industry. She gave me my first real job and I've known her for years.

Teresa: how's it goin? u still here?

My ears listen to Dora as my fingers communicate with Teresa.

me: about done

Teresa: whipped her into shape?

me: so to speak…lot of work but i did

Teresa: why do the girls even bother starving themselves when they have u?

me: ha well it's a matter of

principle also anorexia doesn't
get rid of hipbones

Teresa: i guess a good photo
requires computer wizardry *and*
an eating disorder starve away,
girls!

me: haha
poor behati

Teresa: poor nothing. skinny bitch
is blowing a billionaire

Dora's telling me she'll be in New
York to take notes for PETA on some
food producer's talk at a convention or
something, and I'm saying, "Uh-huh…
uh-huh… so when are you going to be
in the city?"

"I'm here right now."

"Oh."

"Are you at home? Your mom gave
me your address. I could just meet you
there in like fifteen minutes."

"I'll be home in forty."

I put the finishing touches on Behati
van de Velde, save the changes, and send
the file to Teresa. Outside, I hail a cab and
tell the driver to take me to 92nd Street and
Central Park West, where I live. It's night.
The scrolling news ticker on the CNN
building says: "Bioterror Experts to Meet
at U.N." On the Taxi TV I watch the news;
an "orange alert" is in effect due to "terrorist chatter," which seems depressing, so I
turn the TV off for the rest of the ride. I go
on Facebook using my iPhone, and I see
that Dora has friended me. I accept. Her
profile picture is an image of Audrey Hep-
burn in *Breakfast at Tiffany's*. Ha.

A homeless endomorph—his bul-
bously padded silhouette causing me to
think briefly of the Lorax—hunches outside my building, apparently studying the
tenant list beside the buzzer, a colorless
duffel bag at his feet.

"Excuse me," I mutter, trying to
squeeze past him and enter quickly in
case he's the type of homeless person
who likes to fumble at women's asses
while muttering horrible stuff like *I'd
eat that* or *Gimme the sugar*, but the
homeless guy *does* grab me—by my
shoulder—and says, "Nina?"

"Oh god—Dora?"

"Sorry, I've just been waiting here.
It's pretty nice out."

"No, it's not, Dora. It's hot and gross."

"Nina, you look *so* skinny! Are you
eating enough?"

Even though that's certainly one of the
more fraught and tone-deaf questions one
can ask a woman, Dora seems to mean it
sincerely, and I'm reminded of the afternoon in high school when she helpfully
pointed out to Mr. Thorpe, our forlorn cal-
culus teacher, that he had forgotten to wear
his wedding ring that day.

"Thanks, Dora," I say gamely. "I
actually eat by the shovelful. And how
are you? You look…"

Staggeringly corpulent. I'm forcing
myself to look only at her face, because
if I looked at any other part of her body,
I think I'd never stop staring. She's *ballooned*. I'm talking orders of magnitude.
How could anyone, anywhere, under any
circumstances, let her body go like this?
Maybe it's some glandular disorder?

"…so cute," I finish.

"Thanks!" Dora beams and her eyes
get a faraway look as she absorbs the compliment into the very fiber of her being.

We go inside. Walking up—I'm on the
fourth floor—her labored breathing almost
gives me a panic attack. I feel her presence
behind me on the stairs acutely; I can't *not*
be aware of it; the awareness provokes
incredible anxiety that radiates from my

chest up to my face and outward to my limbs, and I feel the desire to apologize for her to someone who isn't here.

I hate fat. I don't *want* to... I don't feel *malice* toward fat people... I just *hate fat*. I hate it so much, it's a physical reaction, a helpless nausea. I hate fat pasty bodies with the mottled skin and the splotching. I hate the way they look like they've half-melted, with *shelves* of blubber sliding down their frames. I hate how there's so little space in this city, and always getting less, and they take up *twice* their share. I hate the extra movement I have to make and discomfort I have to endure to accommodate them just so they can get into a subway car or sit in an airplane seat. I hate waddling. I hate jowls.

My apartment is a small renovated one bedroom that my grandparents were prescient or fortunate enough to buy in the 1960s. It features exposed brick, hardwood floors, California closets, original moldings, a marble countertop, and large windows allowing for natural light to stream in throughout the day.

"Oh, Nina, your place is *so* cute!"

"Thanks. I like it, too."

"In high school, I always knew you'd go off and live a glamorous life in New York. This is exactly the kind of apartment I would have pictured. This makes me so happy for you!"

"Wow. Thanks."

"So what do you *do*, exactly?"

"Oh, just... boring magazine stuff. So, let me know if you need anything."

When Dora takes off the coat she was inexplicably wearing despite the mugginess of the summer night, I see that her clothes—a cream-colored blouse with pintucks and anchor tabs, black pants, and little brown flats—are actually sort of cute in a hypothetical way, as in they *would* be cute on a proportional frame. At least she's trying.

As she continues a fawning initial inspection of my apartment—studying the framed Bruce Weber prints, reading the spines of my books (mostly fashion photography and biographies, a few feminist classics, Piers Paul Read's *Alive*), cooing over the little breakfast table in the kitchen—I'm opening my laptop on the coffee table, checking my email. Teresa, I see, approves of my work on Behati.

I also notice that Chris, my ex-boyfriend, is online. Of course, he will not message me, and I will not message him.

"Have you eaten dinner, Nina?" Dora asks from the kitchen. "There's literally no food in your fridge."

"I eat out a lot. You can order something if you want."

But Dora has brought dinner—a small, slightly damp-looking veggie sandwich, which she washes down with a glass of water from the Brita, which actually is the only thing in my fridge except for a bottle of Tabasco, some maple syrup, and a bag of lemons.

After she eats, she asks if she can use my shower—she is "funky" from the bus ride—and once I can hear the water roaring, I make dinner: two cups of room temperature water with a tablespoon each of maple syrup, a teaspoon each of Tabasco, and the juice of a squeezed lemon.

Gmail chat makes its useful-idiot *bonk*. Returning to my laptop, I am shocked to see that Chris has messaged me.

Chris: hey

me: hey

Chris: how have u been?

me: pretty great actually really busy

Chris: haha
i should have expected that
response

me: whats that supposed to
mean?

Chris: nothing just ur always
super busy!
and great
anything new in ur life

me: is that a compliment or
sarcasm

Chris: *not* /sarcasm

me: the 'and great' i mean whats
new is this weird girl i know from
highschool is crashing at my
place tonight and while she was
never acutally pretty she has
now become heartbreakingly fat
actually it's gross to be around.
it's like those nightmares i used
to have

Chris: why is she staying with
u?

me: dont know. honestly i
was mortified when i saw her.
mortified for her i mean. i think
she may have a glandular
condition

A heartfelt and melancholy whalesong floats from my bathroom. She's singing in the shower.

me: so how are things going with
molly
molly sweet, what a sweetheart

Chris: is that a compliment or
sarcasm we broke up it was hard
but i think it was probably the right
thing to do

me: oh sorry…didn't know

Chris: is that sympathy or
satisfaction

me: polite indifference?

Chris: if ur indifferent, why did u
ask

Annoyed, I wait a minute or so before I respond.

me: why did u message me

The shower stops. I hear Dora clomping around in there—it's a small room, with tiled ceramic walls, and I wonder if she feels cramped—and I wait and wait, but Chris does not respond. As Dora emerges from the bathroom, his status indicator goes grey; he has signed off.

"Your water pressure is really strong." She's red. She's lobstrous. She sits on the sofa next to me, then touches it cautiously with her palm. It's fake leather. "You must live a glamorous life, I guess. So, nine years. A lot to catch up on, right?"

I close my laptop. "Actually, Dora, I'm exhausted. I need sleep. Maybe we can catch up tomorrow?"

She looks a little crestfallen. (Do you know where the word crestfallen comes from? Donkeys have a crest on their necks that stores fat for cold winters, and if they're fed too much, they'll just keep eating until their necks can't hold the weight of the crest, which then slides off and sort of hangs to one side of the donkey's head. Thus, crestfallen. It's a serious medical condition, requiring veterinary surgery.)

"Oh. Okay."

"There are sheets and I think some pillows in the closet. The sofa's pretty… comfy. Um… let me know if you need anything."

"Do you mind if I check my email?"

Odd question. "Of course not." Only after I go into my bedroom and close the door do I realize she meant check her email on my laptop, which I left in the living room. She must not have a smartphone. Jesus. I literally don't have a single friend who can't get email on her phone.

Before I go to bed, I charge my iPhone beside the bed and turn the ring volume loud, just in case the Handsome Stranger calls while I'm asleep.

During the night I have terrible dreams: I'm a goose, a tube down my throat, held in some kind of claustrophobic cage that also seems to be an aisle seat on a Bolt bus. Then I'm a star, sunstorms breaking out all over my surface, now collapsing into a supermassive black hole, sucking in everything around, devouring the solar system. I wake unrested, eyes stingingly dry, shoulder sore from a strange sleep contortion. My dreams have been extremely disturbing and detailed lately.

The Handsome Stranger didn't call during the night. Chris didn't email. It's about 8:30 a.m. when I emerge from my bedroom. Dora's by the front door, fully dressed, wearing her ill-advised coat and stuffing yesterday's outfit in her duffel bag. Oddly, she doesn't look up.

"Do you ever die in your dreams?" I say. "I've been having the most intense dreams lately and I feel like I'm going to die in them. Oh, by the way, there's a vegan breakfast place a couple blocks over...."

I trail off as she zips her duffel bag. Something's wrong. Her face, yesterday so alive with bovine sincerity, has turned stony.

"Do you… want breakfast?" I say.

"No, thank you."

"Is everything okay?"

"Everything's fine."

"Any plans for today?"

She hefts her bag, slings it over her shoulder. "I just called Chantal. She says I can stay at her place the rest of the time I'm here."

"Who's Chantal?"

"Epstein. From high school."

I have absolutely no memory of any Chantal from high school. Sounds like a— "She's a successful model now," Dora says with a hint of triumph, as if staying with Chantal is superior to staying with me. "But not the dumb kind. She's actually posed for some PETA ads."

"Did you not sleep okay? What's wrong?"

"Nothing's wrong. How'd *you* sleep?"

She opens the door to go.

"Dora, seriously. What happened?"

"Nothing happened, and everything's *fine*, Nina. Enjoy your life here. With your… 'boring magazine stuff.'" She steps into the hallway, turns to look back. "Oh, by the way? I *do* have a glandular disorder."

As the door closes, I understand with horror that my Gmail window must have still been up last night when Dora checked her email on my laptop. I think I can safely assume that I never closed the chat with Chris. What did I say? I said she was *heartbreakingly fat*, didn't I? That was my phrase, wasn't it?

Fuck.

* * *

The casually awful exchange haunts my morning. I can't concentrate. Poor Behati. I'm removing a little more of her hipbone at Teresa Hollingsworth's request, but when I send the file, Teresa doesn't respond. On Gmail chat, her status indicator is gray. After an hour, an unusual amount of time to wait since she's constantly on Blackberry, I call her and get no answer. Weird.

For another hour, I sit around impatiently—I'm in the magazine's building for this job, using their software and computers, in a temporary office—screwing around on the internet, reading the *New York Times* online, ignoring all the front page stuff about terrorist cells and plots to release fatal toxins on the subway (one reason I prefer to take cabs now) and skipping to the Arts and Style pages.

Finally I go upstairs to her office. Her ectomorphic assistant, Ben—wispy, pale, in his late twenties but could pass for an adolescent—looks startled, then affronted, to see me.

"Is Teresa here? I'm just wondering if she'll want anything else done on Behati."

Ben leans back in his chair. "Um, Nina? Is that a serious question? I'm just *guessing* here, but I don't think we're going to run that picture anymore."

"She's killing it?"

He looks at me, shaking his head as if in disbelief. "*You* killed it."

His desk phone buzzes and he picks up. "Yes, Teresa, it *is* her. Okay." He hangs up. "She says… go in."

When I walk into Teresa's office, which looks down on 42nd Street from one wall-sized window, she's sitting behind her desk gripping a water bottle as if she wants to beat someone to death with it.

"Nina," she says.

Her mouth is a puckered dog's ass. Her eyes are slitted with anger, her tweezed eyebrows are rapiers.

"Um," I say. "Ben said you decided not to use Behati. Is it just the shot, or are you going to kill the whole editorial?"

She stands. She's rail-thin, Ichabod Crane in drag.

"I can't believe you have the nerve to come into my office. I can't believe you're even in the *building*. I hope you don't think you're ever going to work for a Conde Nast editor again."

I feel dizzy, like in the first couple days without eating.

"Hang on, I don't understand—"

"After all the jobs I've given you, and gotten you. Are you about to give me some lecture about body image? Is *this* going to be on Jezebel, too? Because I have a message for those bitches. We don't decide what's beautiful, okay. We reflect. There's a reason we put skinny girls with beautiful faces in magazines, okay? Because the clothes look better on them. *Because they're beautiful.* Name me a designer, a *real* designer, who makes clothes for fat girls. Name me a designer who wants to see his collection, that he worked months or *years* on, featured in *Vogue* all stretched out—"

"Teresa," I say desperately, "hold on. Jezebel, you mean that blog? I don't—"

"To those bitches I say, what do you want? Fat girls? Fat people? Everywhere, thundering around, eating everything?" She has tears in her eyes. "In muumuus? Is that what you want? Fat girls in muumuus, in every magazine? Let me tell you something! This industry employs tens of thousands of people. If we were to—"

"Teresa!" I yelp. "Just *wait a second*. I think there's been some—"

"Oh, just get out! Just *get out!!*" She's shouting now, actually weeping a little. Teresa, who's known for her passionate outbursts and cultivates a reputation for glamorous histrionics, has never actually cried in front of me before, and this seems more real than any fireworks I've witnessed in the past. Bewildered, I back out of the office. Ben gives me a *good riddance* sneer.

I rush back to the temporary office where I left my things. Everyone I pass steals a glance at me. Do I hear whispers? I have a nauseating suspicion that I know what's going on. Please let it not be true.

Using the temporary office computer, I open Firefox and go straight to Jezebel, the feminist blog Teresa referred to. I start to scroll down—but I don't even need to. The post I'm looking for is linked at the very top of the page, included in their banner of most popular posts. The title is *"Chic* Editor: 'Starve away, girls!'"

Oh, *fuck.*

We woke up to an interesting email this morning from Nina Gilten, a digital photo retoucher who's worked for *Chic, Teen Vogue, Marie Claire,* and *Nylon* (and who specifically asked that we use her name). Nina's become disgusted, understandably, by the tyrannical body image standards she has to enforce as part of her job. Along with her email, she included before and after images of 16-year-old model Behati van de Velde. Notice how van de Velde's hipbones and ribs are visible in the un-altered image, and how in the retouched one they disappear into a smooth, unblemished, biologically impossible silhouette, as if the already-emaciated model is simply being erased. At the end of her powerful email reproduced in full after the jump—Nina writes:

Convincing teenage girls that they have to starve themselves

to be beautiful... that they have to become skeletons in order to attract men... that the less space they take up in the world, the more valuable they are... I just can't do it anymore. What kind of person would I be if I kept helping promote diseased standards of beauty? As an example of the kind of casually vile attitudes that pervade the fashion industry, I reproduce a gmail chat exchange between Teresa Hollingsworth, an editor at Chic, *and myself. To be clear, I do not absolve myself in any way of promoting such attitudes for the past five years and participating in a cruel, sick industry that brings anguish and illness to women and girls everywhere. I am guilty.*

Teresa*: how's it goin? u still here?*

me*: about done*

Teresa*: whipped her into shape?*

And so on, just the short little exchange that includes me saying anorexia "doesn't get rid of hipbones" and Teresa saying "starve away, girls!" And then they have the files, the images of Behati, that I sent and received by email. The post went up on Jezebel a little over two hours ago and it already has 23,624 views and 79 comments, all things like, *Disgusting... just disgusting... amirite?,* and *Behold the queens of bodysnark,* and *If they have to whittle down a skinny girl like her, they'd have to cut my fat ass in half.*

As I read the whole, horrible post—which includes the entire in-depth, impassioned email from "me" trashing the industry that puts food in my mouth, so to speak—I'm imagining a storm growing outside the closed door of the temporary office. This stuff gets around fast… they'll all know it now, forwarding it via their Blackberries, texting about it, posting it on Facebook… it's just bad luck that I hadn't seen it already when I went to Teresa's office.

I've got to get out of here before the storm becomes a hurricane. I imagine them forming a mob, breaking down the door, holding me down, force-feeding me Alfredo sauce.

But first I go to my Gmail and open my sent mail folder. And there it is… an email sent by "me" to multiple email addresses with jezebel.com domain names, subject line: "I say goodbye to the Eating Disorder Industry."

Dora.

* * *

I gather my things and flee the building. It's raining a little. My career as I know it is over. In Times Square, I actually feel like I might pass out—I'm lightheaded, unsteady on my feet. The weather is more of a mist than a rain. Someone, a man, tries to help me, but I push him off without even looking at him, and he mutters, "Bitch," and disappears into the crowd. My mother will say I should have gone to law school in the first place. I buy an orange juice from a newspaper stand and, reluctantly, drink a third of it, hoping the hint of nutrition will ease my dizziness.

At first, as I walk north up Seventh Avenue, anonymous among the bobbing umbrellas—hurrying businessmen, husky tourists—I fear the ringing of my iPhone. But when I haven't heard anything after six blocks, I dig it out of my bag to make sure it's not on silent or vibrate. It's not. *No* missed calls. And the silence of the iPhone

is more frightening than any call could be.

I walk another few blocks—now I'm on 50th, passing steak houses and designer flagship stores, my hair matted and wet—before I summon the courage to check my emails. There are 56. About half from names I don't recognize. Others are from close friends, with subject lines like, "OMG WTF???" and "excuse me, who are you and what have you done with nina?"

The Jezebel post, when I access it on my iPhone, now has 28,146 views.

I open one of the emails from an unfamiliar sender, and read the following: "Dear Nina, As a proud Fat Girl, I just want to say you are a hero, and although we have a tough fight ahead of us, the stand you took today is a great stride in the struggle for Fat acceptance…"

Shuddering, I stuff the iPhone back in my bag and begin to weep piteously, the sobs taking over my whole body, shaking me as if I'm being rocked by waves in the ocean. I try to hail a cab so I can just go home and curl up, but they're *all* taken. The rain, I guess. I try to enter the subway but, bizarrely, there's a huge line snaking out of it.

"What the fuck is going *on*?" I wail, weeping now with frustration as well as self-pity. The burly Hispanic man in front of me says, "Police checking bags. That's what somebody up there said."

"What? Why?"

He shrugs. "You want to get on the train today, gotta get your bag checked."

I keep walking north, the mist clinging to me. I have to walk to the bottom of fucking Central Park before I spot a free cab and dive for it like a drowning man for a rowboat.

On the cab ride home, I go back into my Gmail via my iPhone and find the saved sent mail that Dora sent to Jezebel from my account. I click reply-all, and then type a quick message to Jezebel explaining that I didn't really send the email, it was a vindictive houseguest, I love the fashion and magazine industries, I support Teresa (a wonderful human being, I emphasize) and feel terrible for the public embarrassment I've caused her, and would they please, please take the post down?

The damage has already been done, I know, and I have no real hope they'll do as I ask, but at this point, is there anything else I can do?

Actually, there is.

Dora answers on the third ring.

"You fucking *bitch*," I say in a half-snarl, half-sob, causing the cab driver to glance over his shoulder, alarmed. "You *snake*. I let you into my house, and you—"

"You let her into your house and treated her like she was beneath you and told some guy she was a fat pig you were embarrassed to be around?" says a voice that's not Dora's. "This is Chantal. Remember me, from high school? Don't call this phone ever again, okay? Bye."

We pass a banner advertisement for a new show at the Met, *Models*, a history of fashion photography focusing on the models themselves. Christy Turlington's lovely visage overlooks the cab-clogged street—above it, but emphatically not *of* it. One block later, amusingly, there is another banner advertisement, this one for a different show running simultaneously at the Met, *Francis Bacon*. Beauties and the beast.

As I emerge from the cab outside my building, a reply to my Jezebel plea arrives. The email is terse: "Sorry, can't take the post down at this point, but we've just updated it."

Moaning involuntarily as I climb the stairs to my apartment, I go back to Jezebel on my iPhone and look again at the post (30,062 views), which now begins—

Update: We just received a bizarre follow-up email from Nina Gilten, defending Teresa Hollingsworth and disavowing her own earlier statements about the fashion industry. Gilten claims that this morning's email was sent by a vindictive houseguest who used her computer without permission. (She does not, however, deny the authenticity of the Gmail chat.) While we suppose it's possible she's telling the truth, it's hard not to wonder if she simply had second thoughts after sending the email (and facing the reactions of her colleagues in the industry?) and is hastily trying to cover her ass. If that's the case, shame on her. She had the courage to take a stand, and she should resist the cowardly impulse to disavow it when the fashion industry's fur, so to speak, starts flying. Gilten's follow-up email:

Dear Jezebel — Could you please, please take down the post about me from this morning? It was sent by a person who gained unauthorized access to my email account…

And so on, humiliatingly—they've posted my email, word for word. I briefly dare to peruse the new comments from readers, almost all of which express sentiments to the effect of, "Yeah, right." As angry as I am that they just posted my follow-up email—intended as private correspondence, a personal plea!—I don't dare email them again, because I know that at this point, anything I do will only be used to expose me further.

In my apartment, huddled on my couch behind locked door and closed curtains, my iPhone turned off, I'm momentarily seized by a desire never to go outside again. To disappear. To take an erasing tool and do to myself what I do every day (or used to do) to the Midwestern and South African and Eastern European girls who inhabit my hard drive, except do it completely, take it to the logical extreme, *erase* myself completely. Fuck *thinner*, I need to be *nonexistent*.

That feeling passes quickly. Fuck that... *that's* cowardice. That treacherous sea cow came into my home, took advantage of my hospitality, and then attempted to destroy my entire professional life (*and*, effectively, my social life, since the two are so interconnected) over a minor slight expressed in private correspondence that she had *no right* even to read. FUCK HER. I'm going to punish her. I'm not sure how yet, but I'm going to take my revenge.

I don't leave my apartment again for the rest of the day.

* * *

I wake up. It's around midnight. Everything seems weirdly vivid. Sensations are, somehow, both dull and acute. I have 19 voicemails, 41 texts, and 76 new emails. I napped fitfully throughout the afternoon and evening. Every time I *did* sleep I fell into dreams of being eaten or, worse, eating. I delete all the emails from people I don't know, and I archive all the others; I can read them later. One was from Chris, subject line: "damn. what happened?" Most of the texts are from friends or (former, I guess) colleagues, bursting with gleeful, barely contained curiosity about what could have prompted me to commit sudden and spectacular career suicide. The Jezebel post now has 59,414 views and 198 comments. I nearly put the phone away, intending to ignore the

voicemails, and then something occurs to me. I go through my visual voicemail box, looking for calls from unfamiliar numbers. There are seven. I listen to them. The third one is from the Handsome Stranger.

"*Hi Nina, it's Ferdinand... we met in the rain three nights ago and I mean to call you. You intrigued me a bit, I must say...* " This in his heavily, erotically accented European voice. "*... I would like you to have a drink with me tonight, I think nine tonight at Museum Bar. Give me a call if it is okay. My number is...* "

That's from over eight hours ago. It's after midnight now. Under normal circumstances I would be able to rationalize the merits of having missed the voicemail—*always keep them guessing! unavailability is the ultimate aphrodisiac!*—but now I'm simply seized by a fear that I've missed an opportunity.

I dial his number. It rings. It rings. Fuck... when he didn't hear from me, he probably just called one of twenty other girls in queue, and right now she's leaning on him, laughing, as they hail a cab outside Museum Bar...

You might think my Handsome Stranger infatuation would be distant past after today's disastrous events, something I can't believe I ever cared about. But it isn't. The thing is, he *doesn't even know* about the Jezebel shitstorm... he's a visitor from the time before my life collapsed.

I get his voicemail. I end the call without leaving a message. I slump on my sofa, right where Dora probably slumped while composing her toxic email. I can feel my heart eating itself. I think about getting up, drinking some water with Tabasco and maple syrup and lemon. I don't move. My iPhone rings.

"Hello?"

"Nina, I missed your call, sorry."

That *accent*. "I am at the gym."

"It's okay! Your gym… what gym is open this late?"

"The one on the top, on the roof, of my building."

"Where is your building, Ferdinand?"

"It is by 55th Street and Third Avenue."

"Would you still like to meet up tonight? I'm at 92nd Street on the west side of the park, but I could take a cab to Museum Bar. I could be there in twenty minutes."

Thirty minutes later, in skinny jeans and a loose, white button-down shirt, I step out of a cab into the thin drizzle outside Museum Bar. The drizzle quickly makes my white shirt a little indecent, which is the idea. In the spirit of forwardness, I'm wearing a black bra beneath.

Outside the bar, oddly, a little scene is in progress, two cops or private security guards trying to restrain an outrageously obese man—really, genuinely huge… *planetary*… he must be four hundred pounds—and the man making this weird, aggressive noise like *Num num num num num…* while flailing his arms. He smells like a rotten Halloween pumpkin. The whole thing fills me with profound uneasiness—you might even call it nascent terror—and I give them a wide berth as I hurry inside.

Museum Bar's an upscale, dark-lacquered-wood, golden-light-ambience kind of bar. Feels like the inside of a good dream. Everyone's well-dressed, and it's a point in the Handsome Stranger's favor that he suggested the place. I spot him at the bar.

He looks at me inscrutably as I take the soft leather seat beside him. He's beautiful, his eyes impossibly blue. The architecture of his face is classical, perfect. He could be the young Alain Delon. (Except for a small, irregular mole under his right eye. Mentally, I carve off the upper edge, making it symmetrical.)

"Something's going on outside," I say. "This huge guy is fighting with some cops. Anyway, sorry I'm late. Today's been just—the worst day."

"Still the fat man is fighting?"

"You saw him too?"

He purses his impossibly perfect lips, gesturing at the bartender to pour me one of what he's having—something bourbon-dark. "Yes, when I came in, I saw the—what's it called—hippopotamus man fighting with the cops, making a loud noise. A crazy man, and he smelled very bad. You know the hippopotamus? You think it is cute, but it is a most nasty animal. Attacking very sudden and with a terrible temper. Like many fat people. You think they are all jolly sweetness, but you are very, very wrong."

He says this so seriously, and it's so strikingly relevant to my recent experience, that I can't help melting into cathartic laughter. He stares at me.

"But you," he says, "you are not hiding anything, are you? You're a very skinny girl."

I swallow my laughter, recompose myself, and down half the strong dark drink that has materialized near my hand. "Where are you from, Ferdinand?"

"I was born in Portugal. But my parents raised us in Berlin and Paris. I don't talk to them in years. I grew up all over. Have you had the foie gras here? Are you hungry?"

"No, thanks—not hungry," I say. He nods approvingly. I ask, "And what do you do?"

"I'm a model. Also an actor."

"Oh! What? Like, do you do campaigns?" Jesus, is *that* why his face seems so familiar?

"I did Gap and Abercrombie, and I walked for Calvin Klein and Zac Posen."

And he was in an editorial in *Ny-*

lon—one I worked on six months ago. Jesus. I *already* carved off the upper edge of his mole to make it symmetrical. Vertigo comes over me. I've never fucked a model I've retouched before. Most are women, anyway. It's so weird to see him here, in real life, and not be able to adjust his earlobes or eliminate the slight sheen on his forehead. But I don't want to do those things. He's perfect.

Since he's in the industry—and I've personally retouched him—I guess I could worry he read the Jezebel piece. But somehow I know Ferdinand doesn't read blogs.

Also, as long as he never asks what I do—and I'm fairly confident he won't—I'm under no obligation to disclose my job, or even what industry I work in.

"Wow," I say. "So you're, like, a *successful* model."

"Very successful." He nods, solemn. He has that blank-slate model demeanor, always seductively bored and passionless. Even in bed, I know, he will have that face.

I want the conversation to go on for a while without any awkward pauses, and there's an easy way to make that happen. "So—tell me about yourself."

A quarter of an hour later, as he's describing the reality show he'd like to make, I flat-out ask if he wants to fuck. We sloppily make out in the cab back to my apartment. He can't kiss very well, but that's okay because his mouth is an *objet d'art*. We're stopped at a light when he says, "Look."

On the nearest corner, a morbidly obese man—if anything, even *bigger* than the one outside Museum Bar—is fighting with several young black men. It's not a normal fight. The obese man windmills his arms and charges at the young men, but they keep dodging him,

laughing. The obese man, however, looks unhinged, his mouth flapping in a constant babble. *Num num num num...* Anxious nausea fills me and I look away.

At my apartment, Ferdinand flops on the sofa and starts nonchalantly unbuttoning his shirt. Because I don't want to fuck where Dora slept, I say, "No, let's go in the bedroom." I unbutton my own shirt on the way there and he takes it off for me. Within what feels like two seconds, he's down to his black boxer briefs. I wriggle out of my jeans and I'm in black underwear and socks. We match. I start to take my socks off and he says, "Leave them on." I look at him, his smooth torso, his supernatural chest and abs.

"You're so... chiseled."

He touches his perfect stomach, contemplates it solemnly. He murmurs, "No fat." I laugh—at him, at myself, with the universe. He throws me on my bed and orders me: "Be naked." I obey. He gets on top and I yank his underwear down to grab his cock, which, unsurprisingly, is homicidally large. I'm very wet, and he's almost completely hard—I'm relieved—so while he sucks and bites my tits, I just lick my hand and massage his cock until it's all the way there, then let him shove his way inside me.

We fuck for a while, changing positions, taking breaks sometimes to give each other head. No condoms. He doesn't ask, and if he did, I'd say the thing I always say, which is, "I'm allergic to condoms." Jellyfish that smell like a doctor's office... I hate them.

I like that he doesn't mind me *hitting*, punching him as hard as I can in the shoulders and chest and even the face. He chokes me, which I also like, until it's a little too much and I tell him to stop.

He comes the first time after like

twenty minutes. Then we rest and drink some wine, and he gropes me, saying, "You're so skinny... I love your little tits," which gives me such a rush of lust and affection that I make him go down on me for a while, a dizzyingly pleasurable experience. I'm impressed and surprised by his abilities in this regard. Super handsome guys with large dicks are almost never good at it.

We fuck again around three a.m. and a third time around five, with breaks and fondling and lots of oral in between. (I'm a little suspicious of the frequency and consistency of the sex. I wonder if he's one of those physically healthy but insecure young guys who take Viagra for the extra edge.) During the breaks, he spends a lot of time casually admiring his own arms and abs and cock, like he's in a museum: the Museum of Himself. I'm covered in bite marks and gathering bruises by the time dawn is near. I feel dazed and drunk, although we only had a bottle of wine between us.

"What do you do today?" Ferdinand says, lying naked on my bed, the first thin sunlight just starting to filter in.

"You mean today as in the day that's about to start?"

"Yes. You don't have a job?"

I laugh. "Not anymore."

"What do you mean?"

I hesitate, and then I just tell him the whole Dora story. He listens intently, looking at me like he's watching a movie, eyes agleam. The first time all night his blank-slate model demeanor has disappeared. He grabs my arm.

"The fat bitch," he whispers. "She tries to destroy you."

"She overreacted, yeah."

"They hate us. They hate thin people because they want to be like us."

"Well, I don't know if *all* of them—"

"My mother," he says, passionate. "She was a fat woman. Huge. A Hindenburg. And always she hated me for my beauty. Do this, do this, clean the bathroom, clean the toilet. My fat little brothers and sisters, they get her love. Like little dumplings, sitting around, stuffing their faces with sauerbraten and kartoffelkloesse. And me, scrubbing away at the floor, all because I am handsome."

"Oh, no," I say. "That's terrible."

"You have to punish her, this fat Dora," he says coolly. "Have revenge. She can't get away with it."

"Believe me, I'd like to. But I don't know how."

"Get her to admit what she did. Get her to reveal the true motives, the hatred and jealousy of the fat girl for the thin girl. Record her. Then send the recording to this... blog."

I laugh. "She won't even talk to me. And even if she did, she'd never *say* that stuff to me."

"Not to you," he says. "To me."

* * *

As we go downstairs, dressed now, Ferdinand says, "A girl like this, she will do anything to fuck a man like me. If I seduce her, I can make her say anything, her deepest secrets, *anything*. And they all hate the skinny girls. They talk about it every time."

"Every time?"

He looks at me earnestly. "Every time I fuck a fat girl, then afterwards— in the afterglow, you know, when she is, what's the word, *blushed* and thinking I'm in love with her... she'll tell me how she hates the skinny girls. Sometimes she will weep."

"Do you... fuck many fat girls?"

"Oh yes. Because I hate them so much."

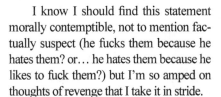

I know I should find this statement morally contemptible, not to mention factually suspect (he fucks them because he hates them? or... he hates them because he likes to fuck them?) but I'm so amped on thoughts of revenge that I take it in stride.

It's around nine a.m. when we step outside, a brilliantly sunny day beginning. We napped a little and fucked again after we hatched our plan. (I also checked his jeans pockets when he went to the bathroom and found two blank blue pills that I'm pretty sure were generic Viagra. Well, who cares. Okay, I do feel a little let down.)

Chantal Epstein, I found out via the high school alumni directory, actually lives just about ten blocks south. We're going to wait outside her building, and when Dora emerges, Ferdinand's going to bump into her and seduce her, take her back to his place, fuck her emotional defenses down, and then record her talking shit about me using the voice notes app on his Blackberry. Then, at the very least, I can send that recording to Teresa, and *maybe* she'll be more inclined to give me the benefit of the doubt.

"Ha. Look at that one."

Ferdinand points across the street as we walk south. A morbidly obese woman, probably around thirty but it's hard to tell, *sprints* up the sidewalk, every earthshaking footfall rippling up her nightgowned body, her eyes shining, face frozen in a greedy smile. Where is she running? To a feast, I imagine; to the world's most extraordinary feast. Ferdinand looks fascinated.

He notices my no-doubt-ashen face and quickly reverts to his default inscrutability. "I've never seen one run so fast. She is hungry."

"I guess so," I say. "Come on, let's walk."

We head south down Central Park West. Sirens scream in the distance, madly, like mental patients. It turns out not even to be necessary to stake out Chantal's building, because as we're passing French Toast, a bistro on 80th and CPW, I spot Dora. French Toast has three outdoor tables in a buttery square of sunlight, too perfect, like a painting of a Paris street scene. At one of them, Dora's eating breakfast with an astonishingly slender, elegant brunette—I've been around enough models to recognize one; there's *no way* she's anything but—who must be Chantal Epstein.

Actually, shit, I recognize Chantal. In high school she was a brace-faced girl who sat meekly in the back of class. The girl who would blush furiously when called on to answer any question, who had a terrible nervous stutter, so teachers took pity and left her alone. Between then and now, she transformed into the queen of swans.

Both she and Dora, bewilderingly, are tucking into plates of waffles laden with whipped cream and berries. The food looks disgusting, delicious. Does Dora look a little different? In the sun, smiling and happy, does she look almost... cute?

"*Stop.*" I turn quickly aside, leading Ferdinand across the street toward the park, my head lowered so they won't see me. "That's her—outside the bistro. Dora's the fat one, sitting with the model girl."

Ferdinand looks baffled. "Why are they together? How?"

"I don't know. But that's Dora."

He nods. One of the three outdoor tables is empty. "I will sit next to them."

Ferdinand's eyes remain locked on Dora. I'm unnerved by the intensity, the pure naked thirst of his gaze, and suddenly I know what maybe I already secretly suspected: He's into fat girls. That's why he had to use the Viagra with me. Fat girls are his sexual albatross.

With a strangled feeling I watch him cross Central Park West. I back into the park and watch from the shadow of an elm. More sirens wail in the distance. It isn't until Ferdinand reaches the empty table beside Dora and Chantal that I notice the couple sitting at the other occupied one: *Chris*, my ex-boyfriend, and Molly Sweet, the emaciated F.I.T. student he started dating right after we broke up. I'm frozen, stunned. For *weeks* I've been steeling myself to see him around in the neighborhood. So it happens *now*? And what are they doing together? He told me on chat that they broke up. I want to signal Ferdinand to abort, fall back, until I have a chance to figure out how to handle this, but it's too late. He's already sitting down.

A procession of police cars and ambulances screams up sunny Central Park West, blocking my view and distracting me, and when they've finally passed, I'm startled to see Chantal leaning away from Dora, speaking to Ferdinand with what seems like strange familiarity. I can't be sure, but it looks like *she* just initiated the interaction. Christ, she must *recognize* him. I guess if she's a model, too...

I feel dizzy. It just gets worse. Chris and Molly's body language tells me they're aware of the conversation sparking up beside them—of course they are, the three tables are arranged in a triangle—and then, surreally, I see Molly lean over and place her anorexic hand on Ferdinand's arm, tentatively interrupting, like a fan approaching a celebrity. She seems to ask a question, and then Ferdinand and Chantal both laugh warmly and turn their bodies slightly toward her, subtly accepting her into their orbit.

What the fuck is going on here. None of these people should know one another!

My ex-boyfriend Chris, neglected by the others, glances across the street—shielding his eyes from the sunlight—and suddenly straightens, peers intently, *sees me.*

I duck my head and turn away, just a random parkgoer deep in consultation with her iPhone. Face burning, I press the phone to my ear as if I've just received a call and, laughing breezily, stride deeper into the park, hoping that Chris will just think he saw someone who looked like me.

Birds caw, unseen; it's weirdly loud. The sky between the trees is a too-vivid blue. As I hurry down the oddly deserted path, passing only sinewy joggers thud-thud-thudding to the silent music of their iPods, I call Ferdinand. It rings until it goes to voicemail; he either hit Ignore or just really did ignore it. I'm unnerved. His plan to help me get revenge was a ploy to get me to lead him to Dora, wasn't it? His fat-girl fetish personified. In retrospect, I see it clearly: From the moment I told him about her, he was salivating with lust.

And if he wants to conceal his true sexual predilection from the world by fucking a skinny girl—or having one on his arm at parties—why waste time with *me* if he can have someone like Chantal? Because, from her body language, I'm pretty sure he can.

I've just been discarded.

Feet pound the path ahead of me, and around the bend comes a gangly young guy wearing a Columbia t-shirt and skinny corduroys. It's an outfit made for sitting in coffee shops and graduate seminars, but he's running at full speed. One hand clutches at his head; I see blood between his fingers.

"Are you okay?"

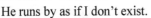

He runs by as if I don't exist.

I keep walking. Thirty seconds later, a second geeky-hip grad student type runs up the path.

"Go back," he shouts at me, not slowing. "They're in there!"

"What? Who's where?"

But he runs off, too.

Cautious but curious, I hurry onward, deeper into the park. My phone rings—Ferdinand!

"*Hello*?"

"Hi, Mother!" he says merrily. "How are you? Did you get the Mother's Day gift I sent you? Ha ha, yes, I know Mother's Day was last month… yes, I know I sent you something then, too… but I am just so fond of you, Mother!" I hear him speaking to his companions: "My Mother! She's so sweet."

"Ferdinand! What's going on?"

"Mother, I'm sitting at a little bistro in Manhattan, and I have met the loveliest people. There is Molly and her boyfriend Chris, and then also these beautiful girls Chantal and Dora. And guess what? Dora is a vegetarian, like me. You know how I like to meet vegetarian girls!"

"Ferdinand, cancel the plan and get out of there, okay?"

"And she works for an organization that protects the rights of animals. Isn't that so lovely? It is strange, I feel like I know her—we are getting along so well!"

I can almost see Dora blushing in the background. "Did you hear me, Ferdinand? I changed my mind… I don't want revenge anymore. Just… come meet me at my apartment. Spend the day with me, okay?"

"Oh, Mother—ha ha! You're so sweet, always joking with me. You know I can't visit you any time soon!"

I feel like I'm going to cry. "You used Viagra to fuck me," I shout crazily. "You can't get it up for an actual, pretty, thin girl! You like *fat* girls!"

He ends the call. The screaming of the birds is loud, alarmed. The sun is too bright. A hectic *clop-clop-clop* sound rushes up behind me. A horse-drawn carriage barrels up the path, one of those carriages that roam the park giving rides to couples and tourists. The coachman—he looks like a skinny Santa Claus—whips the horse. He's going too fast. I hardly have time to leap out of the way.

Someone's chasing it. *Another* hugely obese man, babbling just like those other ones: "*Num-num-num-num-num…*" Jowls bouncing and flushed, expression a goofy half-smile—a dog that wants to play.

He thunders past me—then trips spectacularly and takes a short, absurd, arcing flight through the air—arms and legs still moving—to slam the path face-first.

I hurry over. He smells absolutely awful, like a big rotting pumpkin, which is the first warning sign. He tries to get up but it's like a flipped-over potato bug trying to right itself. He's now making a weird, helpless, "*Munhmuh… muh… muh…*" through the mess of blood and teeth. The sight of blood makes me lightheaded. I try to help him up—but he heaves himself sideways, rolling over onto his back.

He's wearing jeans, loafers, and a button-down shirt with a nametag sticker, as if he just left a convention hall. The scribbled name begins with a "K"—"Keith" or "Kenneth."

"Don't move," I say. "I'm calling 911."

But K. gets up and hurries unsteadily on down the path, after the carriage. "Hey!" I shout, astonished. The path slopes upward toward a small ridge, and K. disappears over it. I chase him. When I come over the ridge, I see him lying beside the path, struggling where he's apparently fallen again.

The carriage is visible some distance ahead, following the path along the base of a rocky incline. Then, bewilderingly, three *more* obese people, a redheaded man and two redheaded women, come crashing down the incline. One of the women lunges at the horse, which tramples her and trips forward into the pavement—there's a leg-breaking crunch as the horse lands, and then the carriage smashes into it and the coachman, skinny Santa Claus, is thrown forward. He slams into the horse's hindquarters, which absorb his impact, then rolls onto the pavement, stunned.

Horrified, I run toward the accident.

The horse shrieks in a high, shaking, painful voice. I've always loved horses. The coachman touches the horse's head and says, "Oh no, oh no…" Then the redheaded obese man attacks him from behind, tearing at his head, biting at the back of his scalp—not biting but *gnawing*, a dog with a rawhide toy. The coachman screams and struggles free.

But the other redheaded woman blocks his escape. She and the redheaded man have the coachman trapped between them.

I've got my iPhone out, dialing 911, but I get a fucking *busy* signal. 911 can be *busy*?

For ten or fifteen seconds, helpless, I watch a horrible drama of feint and counterfeint. Finally they get him. They bend his head backward with a crunch. The back of his skull touches the spot between his shoulder blades. His body goes limp. They tear at the corpse.

I run, hyperventilating—off the path, across a grassy clearing. Screams come from different directions. I run south. A disheveled man with salt-and-pepper hair runs toward me, necktie flapping over his shoulder. He jabs his finger and says, "Do *not* go that way."

"Why?"

"It's a feeding frenzy! Times Square is full of fucking fat-ass tourists!"

He keeps running north. I stop and I just listen. Is this happening? Is this real? Screaming and sirens come from all directions, but more to the south. Not far away, there's an outcropping of dark rock, its surfaces smoothed by intrepid children. I claw my way up to the sun-warmed top, then look south, hand above my eyes like a mountaineer.

On the paths and fields further down, little nightmare vignettes unfold. An obese man pursues a red-faced little girl into a fountain. Three gigantic teenagers capture a collie. A huge girl, drenched in gore, carries the leg of her kill—which still wears a jogging shoe. (How did she *catch* him?)

The obese have gone rabid.

* * *

I escape the park around 70th Street and Central Park West and run north. The streets are calm—madness hasn't broken out here yet.

But not fifty feet ahead, at West 71st, an obese man covered, *drenched*, in blood runs joyfully from the west, crosses the busy street, and disappears into Central Park, chanting "*Num num num num…*" Pedestrians near me seem startled if not particularly scared, except for a bald man who shouts, "That was one of them! Get off the streets!"

Behind me, moments later, a woman shouts: "They're killing people in midtown! It's on Twitter! Get off the streets!"

Screaming erupts on 71st, and as I reach that street, five or six obese, gore-covered women come charging down it—toward me—like a pack of satanic hippopotami. One of the obese women gets flipped, smiling, like an enormous dough-filled bag, up and over a Lincoln Town Car's hood to bounce crunchingly on the road. Another one tackles a teenage girl. People scream. More obese appear; whale-wolves smelling a kill.

I run north. Police cars wail past. Behind me, the screaming falls away. On 75th Street, people aren't panicking yet… what seems to spook them most is the sight of *me*, a wild-eyed girl sprinting heedlessly up the street, obviously terrified.

Another five blocks and I'm at 80th. There's French Toast with its three outdoor tables. I see Ferdinand, his chair pulled up to Chantal and Dora's, regaling them with some story. Chris and Molly complete his audience—the five have become a little *group*… you'd think they'd known each other for years. Who says it's hard to make friends in Manhattan?

A waitress with a fashionable shag haircut (she *has* to be an aspiring actress) is emerging from the bistro, balancing a tray with five bright mimosas—five mimosas!

"HEY!" I scream.

Chris seems the most shocked to see me. "Nina?" Skinny Molly clutches his arm, possessive, when she realizes who I am. Chantal leans protectively toward Dora, who shrinks from me as if she fears a beating.

"Something's happening!" I pant. "Fat people! Going crazy—attacking everyone!"

"Nina, what are you doing here?" Chris says, just as Chantal snaps, "Is that supposed to be *funny*?"

"Not funny! Real—fat people, downtown—killing at random! Hear the

sirens?" I grab at Ferdinand's sleeve. "Ferdinand, we've got to get out of here—they're coming."

"Wait." Chantal sits forward, making a *hold on* gesture with her slender hands. "You guys know each other?"

Ferdinand shakes his head reproachfully. "Nina, please. What are you doing? Stop this… just leave."

"You *know* her?" Chris says to Ferdinand. "That's my ex-girlfriend."

"Wait, she's your ex?" Chantal says to Chris.

"He broke up with her like *months* ago," Molly says to Chantal.

"It was mutual!" I snap. "And it was seven *weeks* ago."

"Oh," Chris says to me, "wait, *you're* the girl Dora was staying with?"

"Wait," Dora says to Chris, "*you're* her ex-boyfriend Chris, from G-chat?"

"Your last relationship ended seven weeks ago?" Chantal asks Chris. "And you just got engaged?"

"Wait, WHAT?" I yelp. A rock glitters on Molly's finger. "*Engaged*? To her? Two nights ago you said you just broke up!"

Molly turns sharply to Chris. "You were talking to her?"

"On G-chat!"

"You got *engaged?* " I yell.

"Excuse me, please calm down?" says the perturbed waitress, who's still standing there holding the five mimosas.

"Yes, I got engaged!" Chris yells back at me. "I love her. Why wait?"

"She's like nineteen!"

"I'm twenty-one!" Molly shouts.

I take a deep breath. "Okay guys? Just listen. We really do need to get off the street. The fat people in New York have gone rabid and are trying to eat everyone else."

"Just get out of here!" Chantal shouts

at me. "Haven't you been nasty enough already? You're just like you were in high school—a mean, spiteful bitch. Only now you're skinny."

I'm confused by this, since I don't remember ever interacting with Chantal in high school, but I open my mouth to protest—when a crazed yellow cab swerves up Central Park West, dragging an enormous obese man behind it. He's clinging to the bumper by his fingers, leaving a wet trail of blood on the asphalt. The obese man loses his grip and the cab screeches away.

"Oh, God!" the waitress says, setting down the mimosas. She rushes into the street, Chantal behind her, the others following as I shout, "No! Don't get near him!"

The waitress kneels at the obese man's side. Bystanders dig cell phones from purses and pockets. "911's *busy*," someone shouts. The waitress touches the obese man's shoulder.

"Get *away* from him!" I scream, smelling rotting pumpkin.

The waitress emits high, yipping shrieks because the obese man has grabbed a fistful of her hair. He bites into her lower lip and peels it down her chin. Everyone screams. Six or seven more obese now attack the crowd.

"*Run!*" I scream. People flee up the street in a loose, terrified crowd. Chantal grabs Dora and shouts, "My building!"

I run after them. Ferdinand's just behind me. Chris and Molly follow us. Outside her building—a beautiful, architecturally gorgeous pre-War building; French Second Empire style, I think—Chantal hesitates. "Wait… "

"What?" Molly cries.

"Herbie, my doorman. He's, well… "

"Fat," Dora says. "Even fatter than me."

Chantal nods, torn. She looks like a woman who feels guilty for being afraid that a black man will steal her purse.

"Look." Ferdinand points down the block, where nine or ten obese advance north in a loose pack, their mouths dark with gore, their *num num num*s like a retarded sea chanty.

"Inside!" Chris yells, and, disregarding the Herbie threat, Chantal leads us in. The lobby's empty. It's also marble-floored, with gorgeous columns and what I'm pretty sure is an actual Liechtenstein on the wall. Our footsteps echo. Chantal leads us to a white marble staircase that winds upward.

On the stairs, our footsteps echo more; the sound climbs to the top and bounces back down. I touch Chantal's shoulder and she stops.

"What?"

"Thought I heard something up there."

We listen. Nothing. She leads us past the second floor, then the third. Each landing has entrances to two apartments and an elevator. The stairwell smells faintly of rotting pumpkin.

"Wait." I stop. "Did you guys hear it that time? Someone's up there. A few floors up."

We listen again.

A faint sound. Something wet.

Chewing.

"Come on. Quick." We move up to the next landing. Chantal unlocks a door marked 4NW and we enter the most beautiful apartment I've ever seen.

* * *

Apartment is not the right word; this place has nothing in common with dwellings like those in which my friends and I live. We stand on what looks like original marble mosaic tile in the grand gallery entry, and through an overscaled French door I can see the living room; there is a chandelier. The ceilings seem to stretch into darkness. It's like a cathedral.

"Do you have roommates?" I say.

"No," Chantal says.

"Do you live with your parents?"

"No," she says.

"Um, so how do you live here?" I say softly. Everyone ignores me. Her parents must have bought it for her, or it's in the family. Jesus.

A solemn, chocolate-colored dog lopes up to Dora, who kneels fatly and hugs its head as if they're old friends. The dog allows this. "Oh Buster," she says. "Oh my God."

Chantal hurries down the hall. We follow her into a cavernous living room. One wall is dominated by a flat-screen TV the size of a dining room table, which Chantal turns on. She flips to the news. On the crystal coffee table sits a laptop, which Chris opens. He goes to Google News.

On the TV, Anderson Cooper's standing on a midtown street, reporting live, chaos visible in the background.

"*Again, preliminary reports from the public health officials who spoke to us said that the toxin was introduced in the city's drinking water. They believe it can be ingested or absorbed through the skin. Again, DO NOT SHOWER, BATHE, OR DRINK WATER FROM YOUR FAUCET.*"

"Look," Chris says. "Look, look, look. Here it is."

He's got an AP news story up on Google News, hastily written, posted five minutes ago—

Several officials told us off the record, however, they were confident that the epidemic of violence was caused by a biological agent introduced into the drinking water. One official called it "absolutely an act of biological terror." He said he believed that the biological agent is a toxin that accumulates in the body over days until it reaches a level of toxicity, at which point the affected person is overcome with psychosis and driven to acts of homicidal rage and even cannibalism.

Anderson Cooper glances over his shoulder as the obese charge a police barricade. The police open fire. Cooper tries to narrate the action, then just shuts up, letting the camera watch. When it seems the police have held the line, he turns back to the camera.

"*According to most reports, it started happening last night and this morning. Extremely overweight individuals, now being referred to colloquially as 'gobblers,'...*"

When asked why only extremely overweight individuals were affected, the official said, "The toxin is stored in adipose tissue. Only very fat people have enough adipose for a toxic level to accumulate. When enough of the toxin builds up in their system, they go berserk."

"*...stay in your home until the crisis is over. If you can't, for whatever reason, safe areas are being established by the police and National Guard, including the 92nd Street Y and the World Financial Center—we'll be playing a complete list onscreen as soon as we have it—*"

The camera goes wild as Anderson Cooper has no choice but to flee from an obese stampede, disappearing offscreen, and the cameraman-or-woman has to run, too. The cops scatter, overcome in some cases, dragged to the ground, trampled and torn by their enormous attackers. The camera swings back and we can see Anderson Cooper himself on the ground, screaming as the obese grab and claw at him, breaking his neck and beginning to feed on his limbs.

* * *

"One of us is dangerous," I say with no little pleasure. "And I think we all know who."

Chantal folds her arms. "Don't even go there."

I point dramatically at Dora, looking around at the others. "Okay, which one of us looks *just like* the homicidal maniacs we just saw tearing people limb from limb outside? And that glass of water I saw in front of her at brunch? I'm gonna guess that wasn't Perrier. I'm gonna guess that was *tap water*."

"I hardly drank any!" Dora protests. Molly looks nervously at Chris, takes his arm.

"Nina," Ferdinand says warningly.

"It could be working on her brain right now!" I say, my voice high. "The only reason she's not one of them already is she just got into the city two nights ago. She could go berserk at any minute! You want to be trapped in here with her?"

Dora looks cowed, but Chantal's fuming. Trembling with self-righteous anger, she jabs a finger at me. "You leave her alone! You're just a bully at heart. You hate her because she reminds you that *you* were fat in high school."

"*I wasn't fat in high school!*" I shout, starting to feel dizzy again—little black neon-rimmed spots appearing in my vision. "I'm not being mean. I'm

saying we need to get her out of here, or at least lock her in a bedroom, *for our own safety*."

"She's right," Molly says bravely. "You heard the news. What if she changes?"

"I'm fine," Dora insists. "I'm totally fine."

"Look at her," Ferdinand says. "She is completely normal."

"Are you guys *crazy*?" I say. "You want to take the chance? You saw what's happening out there."

Molly's nodding. "It's not safe for us being stuck in an apartment with her," she says. I can't believe Molly and I are on the same side.

"What do you want to do?" Chantal snaps. She and Ferdinand each take a position on one side of Dora—her guardians. "Drag her out there and feed her to those things?"

"If I start to feel anything weird," Dora says, "I'll say something, and you can lock me in a bedroom. It's not like I've drunk gallons of tap water. I've hardly had any!"

"Oh, really?" I feel dizzier, the neon-rimmed black spots in my vision pulsing and gaping. "As soon as you walked into my apartment two nights ago, you drank a big glass of water from the Brita. That's tap water. And then what did you do? You took a long, hot shower. I bet that wasn't the last shower you took, or the only glass of water you drank, in the last thirty-six hours."

Dora turns pale.

"Why don't we just lock her in a bedroom *now*?" Molly suggests.

"We're not keeping her prisoner!" Chantal shouts.

Molly hugs Chris fearfully, whispering, "I don't want to stay in here with her."

Dora begins to cry. Chantal touches her arm. Ferdinand rubs her shoulder, leaning in, whispering in her ear: "Don't worry, sweetheart... you will be just fine... I will not let them do anything to you."

I can't take it.

"What the *fuck* are you talking about, Ferdinand? *You* won't let *us* do anything to her? Last night—you know, after we fucked four times—you told me about how much you *hate fat girls*. Remember that? How you were going to help me punish that 'fat bitch' Dora who broke into my email account and ruined my career? *Remember that?"*

The neon-rimmed black spots in my vision convulse, metastasizing in fast-motion like little cancers as my dizziness surges, and suddenly my knees buckle—

—jump cut to an impossibly luxurious bed, under cream-colored silk sheets, with Chris sitting at my side. My ex-boyfriend is a handsome guy, about five-ten, with sandy hair, serious brown eyes, and slight stubble. He's a derivatives trader. The neon-rimmed black spots still hover in my vision, but small, and only slightly pulsing.

"I passed out."

"Here." He's holding a glass of orange juice for me. So many grams of sugar. But my willpower's gone. I accept it and sip weakly. The most delicious thing I've ever tasted. Raisin-like little cells all through my body expand as they sponge up the nutrient-rich juice. I drain half the glass and feel bloated, sick.

Buster, the chocolate-colored dog, sits patiently beside the bed, looking at me. The dog has the demeanor of a wise old man.

"Is it all real?" I ask.

He's just looking at me, kind of sadly. "What happened to you, Nina? I mean, you were always skinny, but now... "

"Did I dream it? The—"

"No, it's real," he says. "Obese people are killing at random on the streets of New York."

"And you're engaged to her."

"That's real, too."

"How could you?" I sit up, but the dizziness returns, so I lie back. "We were together for two and a half years. You've known her for two months. You said you didn't want to get married before thirty-five."

He gives a serene shrug. "All those things I said were true. But I fell in love with her."

"In *two months*?"

"In two seconds. I just knew. Like that!"

"But you said you broke up."

"Oh, that." He sighs, chagrined. "I got scared because she's so into me. But as soon as I thought we were broken up, I realized I was that into her, too. So last night I bought a ring on my Amex and went to her place and proposed. And she said yes!"

"And you don't think it's a little too... fast?"

"When you know, you know."

"Know *what?*" I say plaintively.

He gets a dreamy expression. "That I love waking up next to her. That I love hearing her sing in the shower in the morning. That I—"

"Okay, okay, *stop it.*"

"You shouldn't resent her," he says gently. "She's a lot like you."

I'm struggling for a devastating response when Molly herself enters.

"You okay, babe?" Chris asks.

"Can I talk to you a second, babe?"

Chris nods and rises, the ex-girlfriend in the bed forgotten. Molly lets him enclose her in an infinitely loving embrace. Then she takes his hand and leads him into the adjacent bathroom—we're in some sort of a master bedroom, its walls lined with bookshelves bearing Philip Roth and Saul Bellow and little African sculptures, and through the bathroom door I can see a huge, glass-walled shower and, beside it, a Jacuzzi bathtub.

They close the door, but I can still hear their voices faintly. Molly going, *"We're not safe here... she could change at any minute,"* and Chris trying to calm her, saying, *"I know... I know, babe, I know... whatever happens, I won't let you get hurt..."*

I want more orange juice. Even after I drain what's in the glass, my body craves it. Buster the dog watches me crawl out of bed. I go down the long, ridiculously beautiful hallway (her parents must be billionaires, literally), looking for the kitchen. But before I find it, I hear something.

Fucking. I hear fucking.

With chills of dread, I approach the bedroom doorway from which the *fucking* sounds emanate. The door is slightly open. (*She* did that. *She* left it open.) I edge up to it and, in spite of myself, peer inside. It's like a jarring photoshop joke: His chiseled perfection embedded into her great shapeless dough-pillow of a body... thrusting, thrusting, pushing into it... her gaspy mooing, his near-orgasmic groans... oh God, I can't *even*—

—I tear myself away and hurry down the hall, gagging a little, thinking how I can never unsee that, thinking how humiliating it is, he probably doesn't have to use Viagra with *her*.

In the kitchen, Chantal wears a nasty little smirk. She can hear them too.

"Don't look so jealous," Chantal says.

"I just hope she doesn't turn into one of those *things* while he's in her. I guess you're willing to ignore that danger."

The flawless bitch gives me a superior look. "Do you even remember me from high school?"

"Not really, no," I say honestly.

"That figures."

"Well, yeah, it does. Because from what little I *do* recall, you literally never spoke, always sat in the very back, and had no friends."

Chantal crosses her slim, smooth arms. "I did sit in the back and never talk, but I watched," she says. "I was very observant. For example, I remember this chubby girl who sat a few rows in front of me and didn't have any friends. She always came into class alone, and she'd sit there and look around her at all the gossipy conversations going on that she wasn't a part of, and she'd get this hopeful look, but no one ever included her. And I thought— *she's* an outsider just like me. *She's* a girl I could be friends with, if I just knew how. Sometimes I'd see her sitting alone at lunch, and I'd be sitting alone too, with my acne and my mouthful of braces, and I wanted to go sit with her, but I never had the nerve.

"Then one day, during gym class, we were out on the soccer field. And I got my period early. Before I even knew it, I had a little stain on my gym shorts. You remember those shorts we wore for gym, right? Those grey, flimsy things. It didn't take much. So I sat down on the grass beside the field and crossed my legs, and I told Coach Hardy I had a stomachache. There was still half an hour left in the class and I didn't know what to do, because by then the stain would be even worse, and I'd have to walk back across the field with the other girls. Just then I saw this girl, the chubby girl from class, coming to the sidelines to get a water bottle, and I thought—I can trust her. So I waved at her, and I explained what had happened and asked her if she could run back to the locker room and grab a sweatshirt or a towel for me to tie around my waist, so I could go in without anyone noticing. And the chubby girl looks at me with these earnest eyes and says sure, she'll be right back. I was so grateful. I watched her run across the field... but she didn't go back to the school. She went to this cluster of popular boys instead. And she whispered to them. And then they all turned to look at me. And they laughed."

Chantal tilts her head, looking at me curiously. "Did you think it would make them like you, Nina? That suddenly they'd start inviting you to parties?"

"I don't—"

"You looked *pathetic* to them." Her face reddens with anger. "Yeah, they laughed. But you looked like a fat little dog trying to get a pat on the head. I've always wanted to tell you that, you bitch."

"Chantal, I don't know what you're talking about." It's true—I don't. At least, I don't think I do. I feel confused. "I mean, *maybe* there was one time when I—"

A scream cuts me off.

*　*　*

One of them has gotten inside the apartment. Herbie, the obese doorman. Chris and Molly were trying to sneak out. But Herbie was lurking in the stairwell, and he got in.

Now we're all huddled in the hallway, holding kitchen knives, listening to him eat the dog in the living room.

"We'll have to trap him in the pantry," Chantal says softly. "It's like a passageway between the kitchen and the little kitchen. Doors on both sides. If someone runs through there with him chasing them, then slams the door on him, and somebody comes from behind and slams the other door, we'll have him trapped."

"Right," I say. "Who's going to be the bait?"

"I'm too slow," Dora says helpfully.

"You, Chantal," I say. "It's your house, you're familiar with the layout."

"Fine," she says, glaring at me. "I'd tell you to get the door behind him, but I don't trust you with anything that requires courage. So Ferdinand?"

Ferdinand nods. "I'll do it."

"Okay," Chantal says. "I'll run past him through the living room and he'll chase me. Ferdinand, you follow behind him and slam the pantry door as soon as he goes in. I'll run out the other side and slam that door."

Gripping knives, we move toward the living room. From deeper in the labyrinthine apartment: soft wet crunching. Chantal and Ferdinand lead us, knives ready. Chris and Molly hang furthest to the rear.

We peer into the living room. Empty. A big bloodstain on the rug. Smell of rotting pumpkin.

"Shit," Chantal says. "Where'd he go?"

We move through the living room. Little sounds, gentle crunching and dripping, reach us. Herbie must have gone into the hallway on the opposite side of the living room. Chantal ventures a peek. She shakes her head, whispers, "I think he's in the kitchen."

We enter the other hallway—this apartment is so fucking huge, I haven't even seen this one yet—and edge toward the kitchen. Through the kitchen door, I see a hulking figure crouched on the tile, his back to us, eating messily.

Chantal looks at Ferdinand. *Ready?*

Ferdinand nods.

Chantal takes a deep breath. It occurs to me that the image of a bloody, obese man hungrily chasing a sexy young model like Chantal would be a good concept for, say, a provocative Terry Richardson shoot. "Okay," Chantal says. "One... two... "

A noise from back in the living room stops her... a tentative, *"Num... num?"*

Chantal looks at Chris. "You did *close* the front door, didn't you?"

A stricken look comes over his face. Before he can utter a word, an obese woman in a gore-soaked garment that can only be described as a denim nightgown charges out of the living room at our back, bellowing, *"Num-num-num-num-num-num-num!"* and collides with Molly like a rhinoceros, slamming her into the wall so hard I'm afraid all her birdlike little bones will shatter to bits inside her. Chris leaps to her aid, stabbing Nightgown Woman.

Herbie lunges out of the kitchen, covered in blood. We're trapped. He slams into me and Chantal, his gigantic arms flailing and clubbing at me. It's like being beaten with ham hocks. Chantal and I hack Herbie's face. Blood gouts, but he's still trying to eat us. I slam my blade into his belly. Ferdinand stabs him in the chest. Gradually... *gradually...* he slows... we've probably stabbed him thirty times.

As Herbie sinks like a big red barge going down, Nightgown Woman opens a meaty flap in Chris's throat. Blood sprays the ceiling. Molly screams.

Herbie starts getting back up. He wasn't dying—just taking a breather.

An obese guy in a bloody business suit appears from the living room. From elsewhere in the apartment, I hear, *"Num num num num—"*

More of them. Coming in through the open front door.

"Run!" Chantal yells.

A mad sprint through the apartment. Out the front door... onto the landing... where we collide with an obese man dressed, inexplicably, as a clown. Chantal pushes him down the stairs and he goes rolling down like a slow, enormous beach ball.

* * *

Back out on the street, Molly is hysterical.

"We can't leave *Chris*," she sobs. "We can't just *leave* him there."

Chantal slaps her. "Molly—he's dead." Down the street, the obese rampage. Sirens scream. "We have to get somewhere safe. If we can get across the park to the 92nd Street Y, the National Guard will protect us."

"NO!" Molly screams, a little girl throwing a tantrum. Her voice attracts the attention of the obese.

Ferdinand and Dora sprint for the park. I go after them. Chantal hesitates, then follows. Molly screams after us furiously: *"COME BACK HERE! DON'T YOU LEAVE CHRIS B—"*

A *whump* and a choked scream as the obese take her down. And then we're in the park. It's a beautiful day. Leafy trees, blue skies. Chantal stops. "Shh. Hear that?"

Rustling. Snuffling. In the foliage near the path.

We notice her at the same time: Half-hidden in the bushes, an obese little girl—nine, ten years old—feasts on the slick, meaty, brown intestines of a vagrant.

Onward we run. More corpses lie up ahead, littering the grass—crooked, gnawed, disemboweled. A short way down the path, a group of the obese crouch around a man they've felled. They've got his ribs split open and they're feasting on the soft belly area, eating out of it like a giant bowl.

Their big moon-faces rise.

"Shit," Chantal says.

They start toward us. Chantal and Ferdinand flee to the left. Dora and I scramble right, up a ridge. I glance back to see our enormous pursuers struggling up the ridge, yammering, "*Num! num! num! num!*"

I descend the other side with Dora behind me. We see an elderly man coming toward us. He cries, "Don't go that way! Fatties!" Then he sees our pursuers crest the ridge and shrieks with fear.

Up ahead, water. The lake. We're at the lakeshore. Fifty yards down the shore an obese maître d' snuffles around in the mud. The obese maître d' sees us, starts lumbering toward us.

"Come on—the boat!"

A little pier juts out from the shore. A rickety wooden rowboat floats at the end.

Dora follows me down the pier and we climb into the boat.

Our pursuers gallop along the shore. I scramble to untie the boat. The pack thunders down the pier. I get the rope loose and push off. The obese get to the end of the pier and don't stop running—like enormous lemmings they plunge into the lake, the first one—the maître d'—so close to the boat that his forehead actually *hits* it, cracks directly down into the rim with such concentrated force that it takes a chunk of wood out, rocking the boat badly. The impact seems to kill him, though, because then he just floats face-down while the others behind him also go straight into the lake, still running. We watch them drown.

Soon seven obese, sodden bodies bob gently near the edge of the pier. Other obese prowl the shore, watching us.

We have no oars.

* * *

A plane etches its perfunctory white scar across the sky. Ducks honk crankishly on the water. From beyond the trees, gunshots and screams, dim, can be heard.

Dora hunches on her end of the boat, glowering.

"You ruined my life," I say.

"You're a horrible person," she says.

"How are you feeling, right now? Does anything feel weird? Do you feel like you might be… changing?"

"I feel fine."

"You know I'm going to have to kill you if you turn into one of them, right?"

"Go fuck yourself, Nina."

I call 911 but it's busy. I call again and an operator answers, but the call is dropped. Fucking iPhone… fucking AT&T. I text Ferdinand that we're trapped in a rowboat with no oars in the middle of the lake. I don't know if he's even alive. I call my mother.

"Hello dear. How are you?"

"Mom! I need you to call someone and get help! I'm trapped in the middle of the lake in Central Park and 911's busy. I'm in a rowboat with no oars!"

I hear the infuriating steel wool of AT&T's shitty network.

"Honey, you're breaking up. You're in Central Park? I hope it's as beautiful there as it is here. Is Dora staying with you? I told her mother you had a couch for her."

"Mom! Haven't you been watching the news?"

"Washed whose what? Listen, I want you to introduce Dora around, all right? Her mother thinks she has social anxiety disorder, but she's just a bit shy because, well, because of her size."

"Mom! I need you to call 911!" I'm *yelling* as she's speaking, and she doesn't slow or acknowledge me. This is not such an unfamiliar experience. "Listen! Mom, turn on the news—you have to call 911 and tell them where we are…"

"Hello? Hello hello? Darling, honey, I have to go, I'm about to have brunch with Sylvia, but call me later. And for God's sake, switch to Verizon already."

And that's it. I try to call back but it goes to her voicemail, then drops the call. My battery's running low. I text her: "Look at the fucking news, mom!! Need help, trapped in lake in C Park. No oars. Pls call 911/ get help!"

Then I send a mass text—"Need help, trapped on lake in Central Park. Boat w no oars. Pls call 911/get help if u can!!!"— to everyone I can think of. Then I go to Facebook and see the news feed, status updates like—

Courtney Wu
omg so sad and horrified is this real??
#obeseriot
12 minutes ago via Twitter ·
Comment · Like

Hugh Clemens
Okay… so… who's up for a game of
Hungry Hungry Hippos??
26 minutes ago · Comment ·
Like

Jillian Keera is single
18 minutes ago

More bulbous corpses drift on the lake now. We've been floating here for about half an hour, and every so often, one of the obese will charge out into the lake, toward us, and drown. A few stay alive in the lake, walking around in water up to their necks. Their heads move across the surface like the heads of crocodiles.

Their pumpkin stench hangs over the water like invisible mist.

At least, I think it's coming from them. It could also be coming from Dora.

"Call Ferdinand," she mutters, her already burly voice now weirdly hoarse. "Call him again."

"Okay," I say, watching her. I call him and, of course, the call is dropped after two rings. Wasting battery. It's almost dead. "The reception is shit here."

"Bullshit," Dora mutters. "It's fine."

"No, it's not, Dora. It's fucking AT&T. It's useless. Try *your* phone."

"I left it in the bedroom." Tossed aside in the heat of passion, no doubt. "You know what Ferdinand said? He said he hates skinny girls. He said when he was fucking you, he was thinking about me."

"He didn't even know you existed then!"

She hugs herself, bending forward a little, the edges of her mouth turned down. Her hair is lank with sweat.

"I'm hungry," she says. "I'm really, really hungry."

"You're changing, aren't you?"

"Do you have anything to eat?"

"Of course not."

"Of course not. Of course *you* don't have anything to eat. How does it work, Nina? Do you just stop being hungry after a while?" She starts rocking back and forth.

Fuck. Should I try and kill her right now, before she goes berserk? What with? At some point, I dropped my knife. Wait, there's hers. Sitting at the bottom of the boat, in two inches of water. I snatch it up. Dora looks at it.

"You're going to kill me now?" she says. "Because I'm fat?"

"Because you're changing into a monster that wants to eat me."

"You're going to stab me to death?"

"Trust me, I won't enjoy it."

"But Nina... you need me," she says slowly. "That water at the bottom of the boat? It wasn't there a few minutes ago."

I look down at the two inches of water. She's right.

"Where's the leak?" I bend down, hands in the water, feeling the bottom of the boat. "I don't feel anything. Fuck, where's the leak?"

"When the one guy hit the boat, when his head hit the side," Dora says, "maybe it loosened the boards lower down."

"Well, it's definitely taking on water," I say.

"If we paddle together," she says, "we might make it to shore."

I glare at her. I put the knife down and we start to paddle. Me and Dora, working together. Dora, slowly changing into a monster. Me, unable to kill her because I need her to paddle.

I keep my eye on the knife.

We're heading for the east side of the lake. There's another pier there, with another boat tethered to it. There's not enough time. We'll have to paddle our boat into the shallows, then bail.

The more waterlogged the boat gets, the slower it goes. We crawl across the lake like a slug. Some ducks paddle by, ignoring us.

Then two *non*-corpulent figures creep out of the trees. Ferdinand and Chantal, alive! They stay low and hurry out onto the pier.

"He came," Dora sighs.

"He got my text."

They clamber down into the other row-boat, untie it from the dock, and start rowing in our direction. We're in bad shape by the time their boat pulls alongside ours.

"Get in." Ferdinand beckons.

"Carefully," Chantal warns. "This boat is not supposed to hold four people."

"Especially if one's obese," I say.

Chantal says incredulously, "Must you be a Mean Girl even *now?*"

"She's changing. She's starting to turn into one of them. Can't you smell her?"

"Oh, shut up. Get in the boat. Dora, you come first."

"I'm *fine*," Dora says churlishly. "Nina's the one who isn't acting right. She was going to kill me!"

Chantal shakes her head in disgust. "You're a real cunt, aren't you, Nina?"

"She's changing! She's getting hungry!"

"Come on. Dora, get in the boat."

* * *

We run like fuck through the park. Heavy artillery fire, stomach-shaking blasts, in the distance. Dora lags, huffing and puffing. She moans. "Ungh... uh-uh...num num... "

"Did you hear that?" I hiss. "She's starting to make the sound."

"She's just breathing hard!" Ferdinand says. But he looks worried, too.

We see packs of obese on the roam. On a playground, eight or ten build a feed pile—dragging their kills together, piling them up, *sharing*.

"They're getting smarter," I say. "They're working together."

Fifth Avenue is mostly empty. A few bodies lie in the street. We're at 79th. Four or five police cars rocket past us, wailing, headed downtown. They don't slow for our screams, our waving arms. They head for a pack which is surging westward from maybe 75th or 76th Street—the biggest pack I've yet seen, at least forty or fifty obese, a *horde*. The police cars disappear into the mob.

"We can make it to the Y," Chantal says, gasping for breath. "Fifteen blocks."

We run north up Fifth. Ahead, fifteen or twenty obese prowl the wreckage of a city bus, scavenging corpses. We're not going to get past them. We're not going to make it to the Y.

To our left looms the Metropolitan Museum of Art. Enormous banners flank the entrance. On the right, the lovely Christy Turlington (who bears a certain resemblance to Chantal) represents the *Models* exhibition; on the left, a screaming and tormented Pope Innocent X represents the *Francis Bacon* show.

But the doors are locked. A corpse lies in pooled blood on the great hall floor.

Then I glimpse movement, shadow, on the stairs beyond. We hammer on the glass, Ferdinand and Chantal and I, screaming our heads off. *HELP* and *LET US IN* and all that, while Dora hunches behind us, rocking back and forth, and the Horde surges up Fifth Avenue toward us, a thousand *num*s filling the air.

A skinny guy with horn-rimmed glasses comes down the stairs, peers out of the shadow.

Chantal, knowing instinctively that our chances of rescue are higher if Horn-Rimmed Glasses sees *her* as the representative of our little group, pushes herself up against the glass to wave frantically.

"Help me!" she shrieks. "Gobblers! Oh my God, please! You, I can see you—please let me in!"

Horn-Rimmed Glasses hesitates, looks back up the stairs, says something to someone. (Perhaps, *She's hot.*) Then he runs down the stairs. Following him is a tall, slim, balding man. Horn-Rimmed Glasses unlocks the doors and we scramble inside.

"Oh thank God, you guys," Chantal gushes, putting her hands on Horn-Rimmed Glasses's shoulder as she catches her breath. "You just saved us. You guys are heroes. Thank you so much."

The two men are fortyish aging hipsters, both pure ectomorphs, the type who have to work out every day so they won't *lose* weight. Horn-Rimmed Glasses is a professor of some kind, I'm guessing, probably the kind who fucks the prettiest undergrad in every seminar. His friend, Seems Gay, must be a writer, or maybe an editor, because he's wearing a faded green t-shirt advertising The Moth storytelling series.

These guys are Pretentious Douchebags. Any other day, I'd hate them immediately.

"Not at all, not at all," Seems Gay says, looking at Chantal. I'm certain he's one of those straight guys who fucks women by seeming gay at first and telling funny anecdotes and touching their arms a lot, then just getting them really drunk. "You girls are lucky we saw you. We've found a lovely little hideout up on the second floor—we blocked off one of the exhibits."

"We just came down to see if we could get a gun off one of the dead guards," says Horn-Rimmed Glasses, also looking at Chantal. "But they dragged the bodies away."

"They're doing that," I say. The Pretentious Douchebags barely glance at me. "Collecting their food. Hunting in packs."

Seems Gay is already backing toward the stairs. "Shit, look out there. And some are still roaming around inside."

A crowd's gathering outside the entrance, watchful and threatening, like crows on a playground.

"Hold on, hold on." Horn-Rimmed Glasses looks at Dora, who's sort of panting behind us. "What's going on here? What's this?"

"She's from out of town." Chantal takes a protective step toward Dora. "She just got here—she didn't drink

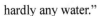

hardly any water."

Horn-Rimmed Glasses takes a step closer. "Uh-uh. No way. Something's wrong with her."

"Nothing's wrong with her! She's a victim, just like us."

Dora begins to shudder slightly, her eyes vacant, sweat trickling down her shiny cheeks.

"She's not staying in here with us!" Seems Gay says.

"He's right." Horn-Rimmed Glasses holds up his hands in a *this is final* gesture. "Either she goes, or you all do."

"Oh really?" Ferdinand steps up menacingly. "You are going to throw us out, the two of you? Maybe *we* are going to throw *you* out."

I glance back at the doors. Twenty or thirty obese out there, watching. More arriving every moment.

"What's wrong with you, man?" Horn-Rimmed Glasses shouts, nodding at Dora. "Do you see her? She's about to go full-on *28 Days Later* on you!"

Ferdinand opens his mouth to retort, but glances back at Dora and falters. She *is* obviously on the verge of full-on rabidity.

"Shame on you!" Chantal shouts at the Pretentious Douchebags. "I mean, how *dare* you? Put her out there at the mercy of those things?" Her eyes shine with furious passion. "It's sad, and I feel sorry for you, that you can't see her for the person, the *individual*, who she really is—but that doesn't mean I'm going to let you take your size bigotry so far that it *costs this girl her very l*—"

Chantal doesn't even have time to scream properly. She does make something like a quick high "*Yeee-yeee-yeee!!*" as Dora tears a tremendous chunk of flesh from her throat. The obese outside start slamming the doors. Blood pulses out of Chantal's carotid artery in cartoonishly

intense jets as everyone starts screaming and we run for the stairs.

* * *

Iconic beauties surround us: Twiggy, Heidi Klum, Kate Moss, Veruschka, Diana Werbowy, Paulina Porizkova, Shalom Harlow.

We're all covered in Chantal's blood. She's back downstairs, most of her on the floor of the great hall, the rest presumably being digested by Dora. Ferdinand and I are upstairs with the Pretentious Douchebags and their dates, holed up in the *Models* exhibition. We've tried to barricade the entrance with heavy display cases. Ferdinand hasn't spoken since watching Dora kill Chantal.

The Pretentious Douchebags' dates are both nerdy/hot late-twenties brunettes with black-framed glasses. Grad student types. Rachel and, I think, Anais.

With my remaining iPhone battery, I call 911 again. Of course, it's still busy. I call my mother.

"Hello, darling! I'm still at Kupferbaum's having brunch with Sylvia, so..." Her voice disappears under a tide of AT&T static.

"Mom!" I scream. "We're trapped in the Metropolitan Museum of Art! We need help—please, keep calling 911 for us. My phone's about to die—"

"Your home's as bad as a sty? Well, clean it up! Do you think we let you use that apartment so you can—"

The static washes her voice out and overcomes the call. With the very last of the battery, I go to Facebook. On Dora's Facebook wall I post a message—

Dora has turned into a gobbler. She just killed Chantal Epstein at the Met and now she's trying

to kill me. Also she hacked into my gmail and emailed Jezebel as me in an effort to sabotage my career.

—just to put that information out in the world. Then my battery dies.

The steady *boom*s of the obese slamming against the front doors echo through the museum. What's scary is that the *boom*s are evenly spaced. It's not just the mob banging haphazardly against the glass. They're slamming the doors en masse at coordinated intervals, using their numbers as a battering ram.

"They're going to get in, aren't they?" nerdy/hot Rachel says.

Horn-Rimmed Glasses bites his lip. "There's already some loose down there. Plus their friend Dora. Hope to God they're not smart enough to open the doors for the ones outside."

"It's been hours since this thing started," says nerdy/hot Anais, who has a tiny nose stud. "Where's the National Guard? Why aren't they out there just shooting gobblers dead?"

"Think about it, babe," Seems Gay says, coming up behind her for a patronizing embrace. "Remember, these were people's parents, children, brothers, sisters. What if the change isn't permanent? What if the toxin wears off in twenty-four hours?"

"Yes." Ferdinand nods, his voice oddly toneless, his face still ashen. "That makes sense. I think that's what will happen."

Anais, being nuzzled from behind by Seems Gay, sticks out her lower lip. "Well if I ran the National Guard, I'd be slaughtering them like cattle."

Ferdinand abruptly turns, strides deeper into the *Models* exhibition. I follow, leaving the others. Out of their sight, he stops under a larger-than-life-sized Lauren Hutton. He

gnaws his knuckles, face screwed up with anguish.

"This isn't real," he says. "None of it's real. I'm having a nightmare. That makes sense."

"Hold it together. We'll get to one of the safe areas, or we'll be rescued by the military. They *are* out there, you know."

"No," he says. "It's a dream. One of my dreams. All the time, I have dreams about fat girls." He looks up at me, eyes moist. "I lied to you, last night."

"I know. You don't hate fat girls. You love them."

"I can't help it!" He begins to cry a little, furiously wiping at the corners of his eyes. "They're so very… comforting. And warm, and so welcoming with the big arms and the bodies, and they like to eat and I, I like to feed them! But after I fuck, then I look at them… and I see them with different eyes. I am *disgusted*."

He's openly weeping now. "I think, why do I want this beast? If anyone can see me now, they will laugh at me. They will think I am sick. And they will be right! Why do I want the hippopotamus girls? Why can't I want skinny girls… like you?"

From downstairs: *Boom… Boom… BOOM…*

"You're not even attracted to me, are you?"

Ferdinand gives me a guilty look, wiping his eyes. "You are just… so skinny, with the pointy little bones jabbing."

"But you fucked me four times last night."

He sighs, sniffling. "Yes, I imagined a fat girl. I'm sorry." He shrugs apologetically. "And I took several Viagra pills. I had to. There is just so little there…."

I don't know what to say to that, so I don't say anything. His face crumples again. "Often I have dreams of many fat girls," he sobs. "Fat girls in a field, hundreds of fat girls, naked and running. Running so quickly, and I am running with them. Happy and naked. But now this… you see, it is just the reverse? So it is okay, it is only my nightmare. I will just wake up soon."

"Ferdinand. It's real."

He buries his face in his hands. "Why?" he weeps. "Why do I have to like them? Why do they have to exist?"

Moved, I reach out to touch his shoulder, but the next *BOOM* from downstairs is accompanied by the musical splash of safety glass hitting a marble floor.

* * *

Anais says breathlessly, "I used to be a tour guide here. We've got a few minutes to make it downstairs and out one of the employee exits."

The six of us dash through *Models*. Iman, Cheryl Tiegs, Naomi Campbell, Marisa Berenson. Pouting down at us, posed and draped. Nadja Auermann, Suzy Parker, Dovima between the elephants. And then we're out of the exhibit, finally, running down a corridor.

"This way!" Anais turns a corner—and runs right into Dora. She's almost unrecognizable under all the blood. Behind her hulk seven or eight other obese. She's got a pack.

"Dora, no!" Ferdinand says.

Dora lunges at Anais and chomps into the poor girl's cheek. Seems Gay doesn't try to save her, he just backs away as Anais screams.

"Shit!" Horn-Rimmed Glasses yells. They charge at him. He shoves Rachel at the nearest one. Then both the Pretentious Douchebags take off running. They head for the stairs as Rachel and Anais are torn apart by the obese.

Ferdinand and I run, too.

We head for *Francis Bacon*. The space has glass doors at the entrance and we close them, but can't figure out how to operate the lock. You need a key. An abbatoir-like painting dominates the room. From Linda Evangelista to screaming popes. Ferdinand yanks his belt loose and loops it through the door handles, buckling it tight. Moments later, the sound of feet clapping marble echoes up the corridor outside. It's the Pretentious Douchebags—guess they couldn't get downstairs.

I start to unbuckle the belt to let them in.

"No, fuck these guys!" Ferdinand yells. "They *killed* those girls."

"Yeah," I say, "you're right. Fuck them!"

I help him hold the doors closed. Horn-Rimmed Glasses and Seems Gay hurl themselves against the glass, panicked, but we're equally strong, and the belt holds.

"Please!" Horn-Rimmed Glasses wails. *"Please!"*

It's too late. Dora's pack catches up. Dora herself leaps on Horn-Rimmed Glasses, bites his scalp while others tear at his torso and legs. He kicks, shrieking. Seems Gay disappears under a ravenous clawing pile. Horn-Rimmed Glasses's abdomen gets ripped open, and the sight of his meat-coated rib cage, when it appears, is a weird echo of the Bacon paintings on the wall.

The obese look through the glass, raising their bloody heads like enormous prairie dogs, watching us. *"Num num num… num num… num num…"* It's like they're all sharing one mind… one thuggish mind that thinks only of food.

A mind that now turns itself to a single challenge: how to get through the glass doors that separate it from two large, frightened pieces of food.

I am astounded at the universe's cruelty. A pack of rabid obese, did it really have to be a pack of rabid obese?

All at once, they rush at the doors. Dora claws her way to the front of the horde. She's one of them, yes, dead-faced and ravenous—but in her eyes I still see *Dora*. She knows it's us trapped in here.

"FUCK YOU, YOU COW."

"Num num num num NUM!"

Ferdinand braces himself against the door with his eyes closed, head down like he's praying. "It's a dream… it's a dream… *it's a dream, it isn't real.*"

They rush the doors a second time. Dora gets one massive hand through. That's all it takes—the obese at her back maintain forward pressure… the doors push inward until the belt snaps… Dora breaks through first, burbling with de-light, and Ferdinand and I stagger back-ward. The obese horde swarms in.

The Bacons glare down with ma-jestic indifference as Ferdinand, like a martyr, steps toward the obese, chant-ing, "*It's a dream, it's a dream…* " and they take him down. I hear his screams. Dora slams into me so hard I see black neon-rimmed spots. I'm still seeing them when her pack takes me down and they start tearing off pieces of my body.

BRIAN ALLEN CARR

LOCATION:
McAllen, Texas

STYLE OF BIZARRO:
Western Peculiar

BOOKS BY CARR:
The Shape of Every Monster
    Yet to Come
The Last Horror Novel in the
    History of the World
Motherfucking Sharks
Edie & the Low-Hung Hands
Vampire Conditions
Short Bus

DESCRIPTION: My work is part western, part neo-absurdist, part whatever else I'm into at the time. I like merging/blending aesthetics, I guess.

INTERESTS: Mostly I just kick it.

INFLUENCES: Sergio Leone, Albert Camus, Charles Portis, Shirley Jackson, Aesop, Hemingway, Faulkner, Cormac McCarthy, Shakespeare, Dickens, Wes Anderson, Ennio Morricone, Tomas Rivera, Elliott Smith. There's 14. Which one you think is the burglar?

WEBSITE:
vampireconditions.com

MOTHERFUCKING
SHARKS

I

The streaked stranger showed a few days ahead of the storm, his body inked with indigenous-mannered images, his haul dragged by a one-eyed mule called Murm. The stranger went by Crick.

He carried a bouquet of roses ahead of him as though the flowers cast light and he traversed dark-stained wilderness, but the sun brightened all things the moment he arrived. Less than a day later, the great-orange orb seemed pulled behind blankets of gangrenous flesh, dead to the world that lay prone to the flood from the rain, but when Crick appeared he had to thin his eyes at the strength of life's shine.

He was a gentleman, Crick, and the flowers were gifts for the women of the town. Kindness was his heart, but the look of him was some awkward grind of tomfoolery and horror. His beast of burden dragged a wagon, the wagon brimming with harpoons and nets, and shambling behind the rickety wooden carriage, on tethers of varying lengths, were the naked jaws of sharks, their multitudes of teeth chipping and chirping along the rocks as Murm the mule dragged them. There was a music to it all, a sort of macabre waltz or a hysterical dirge. All percussion. All noise. Bloodcurdling. Amusing. Daffy. Absurd.

The township reluctantly welcomed him.

"What are you?" asked Mom, her skirt chalk blue and her eyes almost colorless. "You look wacky."

Crick handed her the flowers. "For you," he said. Then, "I'm a salesman." Crick looked back at the mountains he'd just dragged through, over a slow, gnarled path the shape of intestines. "You got trouble coming," he said. "Without what I've got," he continued, "you won't stand a chance."

A stub of a man leaned against the eave post of the porch Crick stood in the shade of, chewed some brown clot and drooled himself. "What kind of trouble we talking?" he asked.

Crick smiled. "Ever been to the ocean?"

Mom motioned to a lass with yellow hair who came skipping up silent and clutched the flowers away to find them water to be plopped away into. "Once," Mom said, "when I was a daughter to a drunk. We drove out there in an automobile and Dad fell asleep in the sun. His skin blistered and he couldn't sit for days. You see," she said, "he was naked and on his stomach when the sleep took him. I had to rub his ass with salve."

Crick nodded. "A sunburn is a mild malady for the ocean to bestow," he said. "You get in the water?" he asked.

"The water?" Mom said.

"And not just a toe."

Mom thought. "I did," she said. "I swam in it. The waves dragged over me, and I paddled along with them and was tossed in the currents." She smiled. "I got a sunburn too, but I'd the good sense to keep clothes on."

"You can't get in the water no more," Crick said. "It's infested with them."

The stubby man moved the clot from one cheek to the next with his tongue, the slurp sound of its moving the color of oysters. "Them what?" he asked.

Crick licked his lips. "When I was a

boy I premonitioned it. My mom would take me to the gulf waters and have me play in the brown waves capped with white, the solution the consistency of a soup you'd never choose served to you, and the nightmares of the knowing what lurked in the murk of that non-translucent fluid filled me with terrors of violence to come upon me. Sharks," said Crick, "motherfucking sharks. Their eyes the shape of murderers' intentions and their mouths filled with these," Crick walked to the back of his wagon, and dragged a tether from hand to hand until he'd pulled a shark jaw into his grip, and he held it aloft for Mom to see. "Teeth," he said, "teeth as," he stuttered, "teeth as sharp as razor blades."

Mom eyed the jaw. "I don't follow," she said.

Crick clenched his free fist tight. "Motherfucking sharks," he said.

Again the man repositioned his mouthed clot, a lurching noise like a horse hoof in mud. "Strange a man who gives flowers then speaks that word," he dabbed brown drool from his chin, "in front of a lady."

"Bad words seem sweet compared to what I've seen," said Crick, "compared to what's headed your way."

Mom then stared at Crick as though his mind was awash with hallucinations. "I still," she said, "don't understand what threat you mean." She shook her head. "You've talked about oceans and you've talked about sharks, but we are days from the water, and I don't believe any of us had it in mind to travel that direction anyhow."

"Don't matter," said Crick. A satchel strap lay across his chest and he tugged it so the bag rested at his waist in front of him. He reached inside, and, as he did, the drool-stained man put his hand on the butt of his revolver, but he relaxed once Crick fished out the first skull. "This," said Crick, "was my mother." He fished another, "This my Pa." And another, "This my dear wife." Another still, "This my son." He had the four skulls rested in the crook of his left arm, cradling them against his belly so they stared out toward Mom.

She looked at them. "I'm sorry for your loss," she said, "but I'm still only confused."

"Ha," said Crick, "let me enlighten you," and in saying this, he shuffled two of the skulls into his right grip, and chucked one aloft, and then the next, and his left arm did the same, which surprised Mom, you could see in her face, and the man dabbed his drool again, and his eyes went wide, and in the background the noises of doors opening and closing and steps in the street as the several dozen townsfolk amassed to watch the wicked-featured stranger, streaked with lines, juggling skulls at the center of their town and screaming his hysterical tale of death and doom and dismemberment and catastrophe.

"I am not from the coast myself," said Crick, "I am from a valley. And it started with rain as it always does. It comes on winds that smell of blood, the storm that sweeps the motherfucking sharks from man-dwelling village to man-dwelling village, where they fall as . . . fall as rain, as spores in the drops, to land on the land, and emerge from the wetness," his speech stuttering every time the juggling became labored.

"These dastardly creatures are made to kill and fit with some magic that enables their swimming through the same air, the same air we now breathe." As he spoke, the skulls clapped Crick's hands in the juggling, the sound of bare feet dancing on tile to despicable tunes. "They've an unquenchable thirst for the, unquenchable thirst for the blood of man, and had I not been in a cage when they came for us, I'd not stand in front of you now.

"I was a magician before this, practicing a, practicing an escape. My wife had locked me inside a containment to be dropped into a pond. We'd been indoors for days waiting for torrential rains to abate, but the sun had, the sun had broke the storm and warmed the day for us to emerge in.

"My family watched on, anticipating my triumph at the new trick, and my son was just about to push the cage from the platform and into the waters below when the first shark sprang from the grubby puddles, its rage audible in its thrashing the atmosphere, and its wickedness like a hiss that filled your veins with fear.

"You've never known horror until you've watched your son's arms bitten from his body by a creature you felt certain could only exist in imagination, and felt the warmth of his red blood spray your skin as you rattled inside a cage incapable of coming to his aid."

Crick's juggling ceased, as he caught his son's skull in his right hand, held it aloft for the onlookers to ogle, and he cradled the other three skulls in his left arm.

"He screamed, 'Daddy!' his eyes wide, his upper half limbless, his skin paling as his life flooded from where his arms had once been." The juggling resumed. "And I forgot. Forgot all my tricks. Inside that cage, even at the bottom of the pond, I knew to take the ferreted key from my waistband and calmly unlock the containment, but faced that way with the, faced that way

with the murder of my loves, I merely clenched my fists around those black-iron bars and pulled wildly, watching as my wife," again the juggling ceased, the wife's skull now on display above Crick, "had her tummy severed in one great chomp, her guts spilling from her like confetti that she tried to pack back into the place they'd once been, but of course that was useless." Again he juggled. "She heaped about in the gore as a multitude of mako sharks descended upon her, hiding their ravenous feeding from my eyes with their fins, bodies and tails.

"But my mother," the juggling stopped as the mother's skull was displayed, "was a quick bite for a great white," Crick juggled, "and I watched the whole of her disappear feet first into that giant monster, her face drawn into a blood-colored scream as he chomped down, and she screamed for my father," the father's skull was now showed its reverence as the juggling ceased, "who himself was taken by four hammerheads, each beast grabbing their own limb," the skulls were sent around, "and going in their own, going in their own direction, and he burst as a water-filled balloon may, the goop that filled him heaving from force in all directions as I cowered in my cage, closing my eyes as tight as I could to those horrors and plugging my ears with my fingers."

Crick stopped altogether and put the skulls back in his satchel. "Seemed to take an eternity for those sharks to give up on eating me. They rammed their heads into my cage and snarled their snarls until the sun dried them up again as vapor, and the storm that housed them moved along." Crick looked at the crowd of shocked faces. Then he pointed at the mountains in the distance. "That same storm is just on the other side of those peaks. Those same motherfucking sharks are coming for you," he said, and he pointed his right index finger at each individual in his presence.

The man who chewed the clot pulled it from his mouth and flung it to the ground, and it dragged like a comet through the dirt road, leaving a trail of brown yuck in its wake. He looked about from man to man in the crowd, each of their eyes laboring knowingly toward his own.

He nodded gently.

He gave the signal.

They descended upon Crick, driving him to the earth and pulling his arms behind his back, and he could only fight feebly as they cuffed him.

They stood him up.

"Sorry for this," Mom said to him. "But here, we lock the crazies away."

The men of the town dragged Crick toward the jailhouse, his legs kicking as his body scuffed over the street, the dirt dusting his pant legs which drew forward against their will.

"You'll regret," he screamed as they arrested him, "you'll regret what," he screamed, "you'll regret what you've done."

The man packed a fresh chew and chewed it into place. He looked at Mom. "The mule?" he said.

Mom looked at Murm, at his single eye and ragged body. "Doesn't look like a working mule," she said. "I suppose," she continued, "we should down him."

The man eyed the mule as well, and he nodded thoughtfully, showing approval. "Fair enough," said the man. Then he gave another signal.

Two odd-looking brothers came to take the mule away.

II

This is the shark: a blood-hungry thing, utterly addicted—a machine made to hunt the thing it desires.

You aren't much different.

If a human is a molar, the shark is a fang, but both creatures are just instruments the mouth of the world uses to chew its prey. The shark hunts in bursts and bites, the human hunts in endless stroll. Forward, the shark screams. Forward, mutters the human.

Most likely, this is for several reasons:

1. Sharks must swim to breathe; humans can sleep and snore.

2. Humans can hold what they desire in their hands and contemplate it; a shark must hold everything in its mouth, out of sight.

3. Sharks do not blink, their eyes stay open. To them, everything is either there or gone. Humans can hold something in their hands, behind their back while their eyes are closed, and know where it is. Because of this, humans have the luxury of being less absolute—their perception of existence working in increments—so their addiction seems less constant.

It is a trick of perception.

The shark labors only in the physical world, while the human schemes in the universe of its mind. The shark is a murderer, but it's an honest one. It is killing you, or you are alive. The human can kill you a million times in its imagination while pouring you a glass of water. If you don't believe me, get a job waiting tables. Contemplate how many murders you plot while hurrying to gather customers their food.

Here is the future and the plight of that world: Crick is in a jail cell, and Murm is being led away by executioners.

The next town over is beset by motherfucking sharks.

Two identical twins have holed up in a barn, the sole survivors of the town. Her name is Tilly; his name is Tim. They've cotton-colored skin and eyes the shade of sorghum fields when gazed at from a distance. His hands, tight as sun-dried clay. Her hands, smooth as sunflower petals. Fear holds them both in its sinister grip, their hearts haphazardly pumping in their chests in sporadic fashion, metaphorical loose stones down a mortality-shaped hillside.

They can hear the gray-bodied sharks bouncing against the broad, red walls of the barn they've sought refuge in. They hunker in the loose hay, trying to quell their possessed breathing, the stale stench of the feed and straw sits thick in their throats, and their ears flitter with the music of splintering wood and nails and screws singing loose from their sockets.

"What do we do?" Tilly asks.

"We'll die here," says Tim, a resigned sheet of panic making milky his eyes. "Just you and me."

Outside the sun dries the wet of the world back toward the medicinal blue of heaven's expanse, begging the land away from its state of recent flooding, and shivers of sharks swim rampant through the trees and streets gone red with the spilled human blood. Crimson drops bloom oddly through the murky rain puddles the color of caramel. Skeletons sit ramshackle in queer repose, spare bits of sinew cling to the bones being picked over by courageous carrion birds that the sharks seem only remotely interested in. It is an odd jury indeed that has descended upon the town to cast its un-uttered but obvious verdict. It's a simple sentencing really: Pure, imperfect death.

On the day their town came under siege, the citizens had flocked to the square to witness Tim's hanging. He'd been found guilty of horse thievery, and had been ordered hanged the day the rains came, his execution postponed by the inclement weather. Tim didn't mind. He sat in his cell drawing nude breasts on butcher paper with a charcoal pencil.

"You've a sick mind," the sheriff's deputy had told him as he ogled Tim's artwork through the bars of his confinement, "but," he said clicking his tongue, widening his eyes, "a damn steady hand."

Tim touched the side of his head, "All from in here," he said, "pure imagination."

The sheriff's deputy tilted his head in thought. "Whatcha mean, boy?"

Tim, who'd been busy shading out breasts, lowered his pencil to the page. "I ain't never been with no woman," he said.

"Never?" said the sheriff's deputy.

"Not a once," Tim said.

Outside the rain sheeted heavy against the roof, spilling through the gutters in belches and slurps. Thunder crashed righteously, and the skies strobed with lightning.

"Hell," said the sheriff's deputy, "if it weren't raining like this," he moved to a window and drew a curtain away with the back of a hand, "I'd score a whore for you myself."

"Maybe when it stops?" said Tim,

and he jumped to his feet and clenched the cell bars in his grip. "Just quick like?"

The sheriff's deputy looked at him sadly. "We'll see," he said, and of course, nothing came of it.

The morning the sun broke through on the storm, the sheriff's deputy stood on the gallows with a mask over his face, and the sheriff fetched Tim from the cell himself, on account of all the commotion.

"Some people," said the sheriff, "don't wanna see you hanged, but I'm not one of them."

"Yessir," Tim said.

"You're young," said the sheriff, "but you are guilty."

After they dropped the noose around his neck, the sheriff asked Tim if he had anything to say.

He nodded, his body trembling, his skin paled by fear, eyes red at the edges.

"I took a horse," he said. "A nag," he continued, "to eat on. Y'all knew my pa, how he disappeared in a manner mysterious, and how my sister and I've struggled in his absence. Look at me," he said, looking down at his thin frame, "I'm near bones from hunger."

"Thief," cried someone from the crowd, then another hollered, "Hang 'em."

"Fine," yelled Tim. "Hang me till I'm dead. You're gonna do it, I know. I don't appeal for your change of heart. I don't appeal to your sympathies in that regard, to look back at your histories with my family and find in those friendships evidence to implore you to turn the other cheek, to take the noose from my neck and allow me to walk free," Tim looked down at the platform he stood on. "But there's one thing I do ask," he said, "and I ask it in earnest.

"I'm a young man," he continued. "And, aside from horse theft, I've lived a pure life."

The crowd was silent. If you knew what to listen for, you could have heard it—the sharks rising slowly from the puddles that glimmered in the sunlight. As it was, the crowd was oblivious, their attentions solely on the last words of Tim.

"On account of my pureness," said Tim. "I have never known a woman."

An odd shock took the crowd.

"I've never even seen one's form fully disrobed."

Whispers from the crowd at the oddity of Tim's statements came bundling up.

"I'm just asking for a glimpse," said Tim and he looked down from woman to woman, "just show me your body," he said, "you don't gotta let me feel nothing, just lemme look."

"Boy's a pervert," someone in the crowd yelled, and laughter filled the square, and the sheriff dropped a black bag over Tim's head, and Tim started screaming.

"Just lemme see," he hollered, his voice muted by the bag, "just a glimpse," he yelled again. "Just some titties," he pleaded, "not even everything."

A scream came from the edge of the crowd. A shriek the color of death. A thing jagged to the ears, so coarse that the whole town turned to see the commotion, the shape of which was so impractical that it didn't initially register in their eyes. Gray figures thrashed violently and drops of blood flung from the shrieking body of the screamer much as water scatters from a wet, shagging dog.

"Jail break," hollered the sheriff, who assumed what was being witnessed was some posse amassed to try and rescue the condemned, and he signaled his deputy to drop the hatch on the prisoner, which he did.

The trapdoor opened, and Tim tugged toward the earth, but, just as he fell, a shoal of tiger sharks descended like fists upon the platform, shattering the gallows that the rope was tied around, splintering wood in every conceivable direction, and Tim dropped to the soft earth and landed face first in a puddle with his hands tied behind him. In the dark, he did not see, but he could hear the screaming and it confused him.

What did he build then in his mind? The mind of such pristine imagination? The mind that made nude breasts emerge from the clothes they'd always hid behind? We'll never know. But it is inconceivable that he envisioned what truly transpired.

Allow yourself to see this slowly.

A town of dirt roads, all roads leading to a square.

At the center of the square, a gallows.

Surrounding the gallows, standing on swollen grass made magically green by the recent rains, dressed in clothes of bandaged fabric, thread thin from near constant wear and colors faded from hand-washing, sun drying, a scant hundred citizens, their faces lustful with the anticipation of witnessing a thief's death by hanging, loitering unaware of the miserable fate about to befall them.

This town—the buildings constructed from rescued and forgotten timber, patched together with twice-used nails and painted with colors stumbled upon in discovered paint buckets, seemingly erected by wayward carnival folks who'd grown wearisome of entertaining and had decided to root themselves where the fatigue toward their occupation became unbearable—is ill-equipped for any attack, let alone an impossible one.

Imagine one hundred sharks springing from the edges of puddles the way mushrooms blossom from dung heaps when watched at high speed.

If witnessed in actuality, you wouldn't believe it.

Some things go so against the line of logic we've branded hot on our brains, that their impressions on our minds echo with madness and are rejected, spat away, and even if you look twice you still don't believe it.

Many members in that crowd actually walked toward the sharks that had emerged with their hands out in front of them in hopes of touching away the apparitions that had gathered, because when the world appears insane to us, we trust touch more than sight.

For this reason, several from the crowd quickly lost limbs, and, "My arm, my arm," was the first curse hollered in English—not just the noises of death that erupted from the throats of those screaming.

Let us watch from high above the choreography of the sharks as they circle the hanging's crowd pushing the would-be onlookers further inward toward a clump of struggling men, women and children ferocious with fear and dizzy with their thwarted attempts at fleeing.

Any soul who moves toward the perimeter of the square is met with myriad sharks circling in opposite directions, and, in this way, the sharks are able to corral the entirety of the crowd in mere moments.

Great whites and makos and tigers and bonnets and lemons and nurses and threshers and blacknose and black-tips and spinners and bull sharks and duskys and finetooths and smalltails and silkies and dogfish and hammerheads, sharpnose, and browns. All circling, circling, circling their death-patterned courses, pushing the mass of horror-stricken humans deeper into their clump of false-security safety-in-numbers, huddling together with their backs to the murderous fish that had somehow stripped away order from the universe and learned to navigate against the laws of the physical world.

Have you ever seen a thing the first time and known its name?

These were the motherfucking sharks.

And the name of them came cackling up from the mass of terror-stricken crowd members who, though moments before stood with eyes glistening toward the gallows, mouths watering for the thief to be dropped and dangled by the noose until dead, recognized now in the eyes of their encroachers the same glistening premonition of a death to be witnessed and swelled with apprehension, their spastic bodies floundering toward the nucleus of their pile, the weight of those out toward the crust of the lump of them crushing and suffocating those trapped in the core.

Once contained, paralyzed by the quagmire birthed by their instinct of flight, the sharks began to plunge against those at the edges, tearing bodies in swift jabs, their felony-sharp teeth exposed in their draped-open mouths, and the sharks merely had to swim their death orifices against their victims, plucking away mouthfuls from the clump of them at random.

But what of the hooded Tim?

Last seen, he lay bound and blinded from the slaughter transpiring, a limp noose around his neck.

Indeed, a frail rescue attempt was worked out for him.

His sister, his twin, had set to it even before her brother's guilty verdict had been announced, because she'd lived long enough in that town to know that those who dwelled there would always disappoint her, and she'd prayed thanks to God when the rains came, because without them, her fragmentary draft toward his rescue could only be dreamed over.

Sadly, her plan was only a first step. It involved tunneling.

From the ramshackle red barn that housed the community dry storage, Tilly dug each night a portion of passage from the dirt floor of that building to the shadow of the gallows.

The night before Tim's original execution date, Tilly wept in the tunnel as she worked her shovel, well aware that her efforts would fall short, and, come break of day, there'd exist still several feet of dirt between the subterranean channel she'd slaved over and the spot in the earth where she'd hoped the tunnel would emerge.

Tilly labored alone.

She trusted that several of her friends and family members would lend assistance if asked; however, she did not trust that any one of them would be able to keep the endeavor secret until the thing's completion.

She had to rescue Tim in private, unassisted, and she struggled herself delirious in the solitary scramble of the chore. During the last several feet of the undertaking she heard phantom voices casting whispers through her imagination and saw invented, colorful explosions smearing through the hovel's dark quarters. She broke ground mere seconds after her brother dropped to the earth—the sharks' attack being infinitely fortuitous in this regard, because without it, she would have merely managed to emerge from the dirt in time to see her brother's death. As it was, in the hysteria of the odd attack transpiring, Tilly was given the perfect diversion under which to operate. The only flaw to the sharks' presence was, for several moments, Tilly assumed she'd ground herself into utter insanity, and that what she saw—the phantasmagorical sharks hunting human prey—was mere illusion.

Either way, she was able to extract her hooded twin from the scene of it, tugging his ankles until he tumbled into her tunnel where she unhooded and unbound him.

Tim did not understand how, but he was safe, and the two twins crawled to the red barn where they barricaded the tunnel as Tilly explained the shark attack to her brother.

"Impossible," he told her.

She shook her head, "It's true."

They found a hole in the barn wall that faced the town square, and they took turns watching as the shark army minced the men, women and children of the town, tossing the bits and pieces of them like wet rags that sprayed hot blood as they flung to and fro, and they did their best to keep quiet in the full-fledged terror of their witnessing it.

"What happens," said Tilly, "when they're done with all them?"

It is a myth that sharks can smell fear, but they can sense panic, and, as the sharks undid the troop of townsfolk—making them first merely dead and then muck and then bones—the twins' hearts heaved and raced, and their breaths hurried.

Let this be now in your mind—Tim and Tilly in the hay. They've cotton-colored skin and eyes the shade of sorghum

fields when gazed at from a distance. His hands, tight as sun-dried clay. Her hands, smooth as sunflower petals. Fear holds them both in its sinister grip, their hearts haphazardly pumping in their chests in sporadic fashion, metaphorical loose stones down a mortality-shaped hillside.

They can hear the gray-bodied sharks bouncing against the broad, red walls of the barn they've sought refuge in. They hunker in the loose hay, trying to quell their possessed breathing, the stale stench of the feed and straw sits thick in their throats, and their ears flitter with the music of splintering wood and nails and screws singing loose from their sockets.

"What do we do?" Tilly asks.

"We'll die here," says Tim, a resigned sheet of panic making milky his eyes. "Just you and me." He drags his hand through his hair. The sharks are splintering through. "I'm gonna say something," Tim says, "you might not want to hear," he continues, "I almost died today," he takes his twin's hands, "a virgin," he says.

Tilly does not like the look in his eyes. She pulls back her hands. The sharks thudding is like thunder.

"Listen," says Tim, "we're our only option."

The world becomes silent to Tilly. "What are you saying?" she asks. Her mind flitters with memories of her growing up alongside Timmy—her identical in every way except in their sex—and all the things they'd done that did not lead them to this. There were times they'd lay in each other's arms on warm summer nights watching the night sky for comets and listening to the music of crickets, the black of the sky's endlessness draped over them like a blanket, but in that there was no echo of anything beyond sibling affection, though in this new language her brother speaks—a disgusting and twisted English that suggests an occurrence repulsive to her—that old memory seems crippled and twisted, and the dross of Timmy's nature cleaves at the pure parts of him that Tilly has kept in her heart. "What are you saying?" she asks.

"I've never thought it before now," Timmy says, "but inside me there's rage toward the idea of dying without knowing." A wall breaks open and light spills through at them, and in that light they can see a murderous shark's myriad teeth striking wildly at the boards of the barn.

Tilly thinks a time when her brother and she shared a slice of watermelon while sitting naked in a bathtub. They were six or seven. The pink juice of the fruit ran down their chins and into the water.

"Maybe boys and girls are different that way," says Tim, "because I can see that you're not thinking the same."

Now the shark has worked his body into the gape in the barn, his head thrashing, eyes locked on Tilly and Tim.

"But," says Timmy, "I'd do anything for you."

Tilly nods. It is true. Half the reason she'd tunneled to his rescue is because of all the good he'd done her. The horse he'd stolen was on her behalf. He could have left her when their father died and stomped off into the world and into a safer life, but he'd stayed to make sure she was cared for, though she cared for him in turn. Hadn't she mended his clothes and cooked him dinner, and placed cool rags on his forehead when he took ill with flu, and read to him from the Bible while he fever dreamed so he wouldn't catch nightmares, and hadn't she brought him to this barn? So, he'd asked for more.

Tilly sees two clear anxieties working inside of Tim. She sees his fear of death, and she sees the sexual anticipation. She looks at his face, identical to her own but with shorter hair. A soft skin. A smooth form.

She places her hands near his throat. She nods. She runs her hands down his shirt unfastening the buttons. The dirtied cotton falls open. Timmy's chest heaves up and down. The sharks make murder noises. The barn cracks further open. Tilly takes to her own shirt. She spreads it open revealing her soft breast, and Tim touches clumsily at her nipples, lifting the softness of her form, and he lowers his face to her and suckles, licking the dark pink areola shiny with his tongue. He drags his mouth down her smooth stomach, licking away the salty slick of her sweat, and he hoists her skirt to her thighs, and his hands dive between her legs, and he feels the wet of her as he spreads her legs open, and he trembles at the warmth. Tilly breathes nervously and unbuttons Timmy's pants, and drapes them from him, her hands running across his buttocks, and his cock springs up at her, and she wraps her legs around him, and grabs him, guiding it into her. Timmy's face goes slack as he pushes himself through her moistness, and they both whimper unknowingly, and the sharks are chomping a bad-murder music and the light builds as the barn breaks further open, and Timmy lunges into her with all the awkwardness of the universe, and they roll back into the hay, and he lifts himself up and stares down at his twin, and both of their faces grimace with sex pains and horror and longing and shame, and they are both lost in that music of each other, in that wild endless energy of the coming finale, as though all of them is a spitting whisper shot through a vacuum and aimed at eternity.

Then the sharks are upon them.

III

Bark and Scraw were tasked with Murm's execution. They led him down the main road toward their workshop where the two brothers served as butchers, barbers, and doctors to the town. They could not heal you. Most of their visitors were so near death, they couldn't fight their being dragged there. Going to see Bark and Scraw was synonymous with the end, but Murm didn't know this. He walked one-eyed, being dragged by the rope around his neck.

Of the two, Scraw was slower—mentally and physically. He walked alongside Murm and watched the mule's face as they progressed.

"Is this a boy mule?" asked Scraw, "or a girl mule?"

Bark, who pulled the rope a few steps ahead of them, looked back, sneered. "There's only boy mules, idiot," he said, and he leaned harder on the rope.

"Huh," said Scraw.

A silence passed—only the sounds of Murm's heavy breathing and hooves against the dirt.

Bark looked back again, watched Scraw smiling at the mule.

Bark stopped. The rope went slack in his hand as Murm took another few steps before halting.

"Why do you ask?" said Bark as he looked now at his brother's goofiness toward the animal.

Scraw pet Murm's mane. "No reason," he said. "Just curious."

Bark seemed to sniff at his brother, trying to discern a veiled intention.

Both brothers had peculiar features, but, of the two, Bark seemed further human. Their lips hung loose and their eyes seemed pulled back on their heads and their skin seemed dirt-stained even after they'd bathed and their hairlines were high. It was as if you had no choice but to contemplate them through a convex and dirty lens, and their heads twitched slightly every time they talked.

"Nah," said Bark, "there's something to it." He grabbed at Scraw's shirt. "Gum it out. What's in your silly head?"

Scraw gazed at the dirt, then up at his brother. "He keeps winking at me," he said.

Bark's mouth gaped open. "If we'd different mothers," Bark said, "I'd call you a dumb sonofabitch," he said, and he grabbed Murm by the jaw and showed Scraw again how Murm was missing an eye. "All this damned beast does is wink," he said, "at everything." He let the mule go. "What's a wink?" he asked.

"Huh?" said Scraw.

"A wink, you dumb sonofabitch," Bark said, "what is it?"

The sun hung low in the west, and Scraw looked away and saw thick clouds the color of ocean gathering above the mountains in the east. The snow-capped peaks appeared incapably white against the deep-dark backdrop.

Scraw closed an eye and raised a thumb and the tallest white peak disappeared behind his fingernail. Then, "Closing one eye," he said.

"That's right," said Bark, "closing an eye," he continued, "so this mule don't blink, it just winks, and you're just standing on his eye side, so it just seems he's winking at you."

Scraw lowered his thumb, opened both eyes and looked at his brother. "Nah," he said. "I think there's more to it."

"More to it?" said Bark. "More to it?" He turned then and walked forward, pulling the rope. "What more could there be?"

Scraw sighed. "Hard telling," he said, "for certain."

They got to the workshop and raised the door on its rails, the door squealing as the runners rode the rusty tracks and the door tucked up against the ceiling. Murm spooked a bit when they brought him in, presumably because he could smell the blood of prior deaths, but Scraw petted his mane gently and cooed him back to calm. "See," said Scraw to Bark, "I've got a way with him," he ran his hand down Murm's back, "he likes me."

Bark looked at his brother and felt sick at his closeness to the mule. "It doesn't matter," said Bark. "The thing will be dead soon."

Scraw nodded. "I guess," he said.

Bark grabbed an axe off the wall. "No," he said. "There's no guessing to it. It's our obligation to make it so. It is in our job description that when we're asked to slaughter we slaughter. It is not in our job description to discern the intention behind the winks of mules or to spot something larger in the fabric of our ability to soothe a mule out of a panic sparked by the stench of old deaths." Bark took the axe to a sharpening stone, worked the edge of the blade against it. "You're soft toward animals," he said, "and while I don't wholly understand it, I'm sympathetic to your condition, because I grew up watching you follow sheep into the field and naming the breakfast eggs before you cracked 'em," he said, "and I feel sorry for you, in some fashion, because you've that heart inside you and this job as your livelihood, but I do believe, in the core of me I swear it, that much of the lamentation you're forced into is because of behaviors you've decided on for yourself, and I further believe, again from my center, that you could just as easily decide from the get go 'this is a mule, a stupid mule, and I'm going to kill it, and that I don't care if it does wink at me, or if I can calm it, because killing the thing is my job.'" Bark finished sharpening the axe blade, and he raised the axe to his brother. Scraw just looked at the wooden handle of it, worn smooth from use and stained away from its original pine shade by bloodshed. "Take it," said Bark. "Don't make me angry at you."

Scraw ran his hand up and down Murm's back. He put his nose close to the animal's mane and breathed deeply the acrid smell of the animal. He looked in his brother's eyes. "I don't know," he said, "I don't believe I'm able."

Those unfamiliar with the siblings might've witnessed this dispute as an indication of each respective brother's role in their collective endeavors as butcher, barbers, and doctors to the town; however, the evidence emerging from the conflict would prove mildly misleading, as the natures of the brothers' services in day to day proceedings were divided along far less virtuous lines. It was not: Bark the butcher and Scraw the healer. It was: Bark the doer and Scraw the porter. That is to say: Bark butchered, slaughtered, attempted to heal, and gave haircuts. Scraw cleaned, cooked, and kept house. He ran errands. He took notes.

If the task was pedestrian, it belonged to Scraw. If the task bared some significance and affected some manner of drastic, perceptible change, it was Bark's.

This was not the first time Bark had attempted to bestow a fraction of his duties onto his brother in an attempt to cure his deep-seated sensitivities; however, this was the first time that Bark had ventured to press Scraw to go so far as kill. Prior experiments in this regard were confined to ridding Scraw of his aversion to cutting hair or fabricating meat—all things, in Bark's opinion, that seemed easy even for the most genteel characters to execute, but Scraw was averse to these actions.

"I get nauseous at the sound of the scissors," he had told Bark, and when Bark would cut Scraw's hair, Scraw would plug his ears with his fingers.

As for parceling beef or venison or bison or birds, Scraw didn't offer up reasons. He merely kept his fists clenched and said, "No," when offered the butchering blade.

"You can cook it," said Bark. "What's the difference?"

But Scraw just shook his head, said, "I can't explain it."

Here, however, was a much further campaign with the aim of mending Scraw's defective character.

"Take the axe, Scraw," Bark said, his whole form clenching with annoyance at his brother's reluctance.

It had been some years since Bark had grown irritated enough at his brother to render harm to his person, but Scraw saw in his current posture some echo of the fury which had preceded the last violence visited to him at Bark's hands, and, with a reluctance unfathomable, an electric hesitation that seemed to skip on his bones, Scraw let his trembling hand extend toward the implement of slaughter, but, as soon as the wooden handle stroked the skin of his fingers, he pulled the hand back and hid his face with it and whimpered, "I can't."

Then, the oddest thing transpired. Scraw looked down into Murm's eye,

and he saw in it, against the black ball in the socket, first himself reflected and then a future. It was opaque, the prospect imaged there, but what the vision lacked in clarity of specifics it made up for in certainty of promise, and Scraw understood everything even before the mule winked again, before the animal let his eyelids fade gently closed then open back imploringly at him, and Scraw knew what he had to do even before Bark yelled at him.

"You're a goddamned. . ."

"Wait," said Scraw, and he reached his hand out for the axe.

This disorganized Bark's operation and he stammered out a bald reaction, stating plainly, "Huh?"

"Give it here," said Scraw. "Give me the axe."

Bizarrely, a sort of defeated look glossed over Bark's eyes, and, when the axe was gone from his grip, he appeared deflated. Perhaps he'd grown so accustomed to his brother's resistance his form had distended with it, and now, with the hindrance removed, the puss of that swelling leaked out in the world, and the action skinnied him. "You certain?" Bark asked. "You can do this?" he said, but Scraw just hefted the axe over his shoulder and turned his back toward Bark.

Scraw looked down then at Murm. He waited. The brown mule raised his face at him. He waited. The brown mule turned his cheek. He waited. It came again. The mule, for certain, bared his one eye full at Scraw, and, with all the intention that any being could have behind any performance pre-meditated, the mule winked.

Scraw swung then.

He packed all his might into a single swing, the axe racing off his shoulder, slashing its path just over the mule's head, and Scraw rolled his shoulders to face his brother's frame.

Bark's eyes went wide as the axe head whipped around, the blade of the tool torpedoing in a direct line for his chest, where the newly sharpened implement thwacked a burial for itself, the axe mashing Bark's heart back to its handle, and Bark stepped back as Scraw let go and watched Bark grab haphazardly at where he was gotten several times before his legs gave from shock or death, and Bark fell to the ground in a bloody heap.

Crick learned the man who chewed and spat, the man who'd sent the signal resulting in his capture, went by Kinky Pete, and at that knowledge Crick laughed and bit his thumb.

"Strangers often find that amusing," Kinky Pete told him, "but it's on account of my spine." Pete unbuttoned his flannel shirt and let the smooth fabric drape off his shoulders, and he turned so Crick could see the gnarled backbone that swerved and twisted down away from his skull. "If it were straight," Pete said buttoning up, "I'd be a half foot taller than I am."

Crick was locked in one of two cells in the miniature jailhouse adjacent the sheriff's offices. "Ifs are just wishes we should keep to ourselves," said Crick.

"Ah," said Kinky Pete, "you're just sore we got you put away," he said, "but remember," he continued, "it's for your own safety."

Crick eyed the black bars of his cage. He gripped two in his hands and pulled back and the cell didn't as much as rattle. He put his hands to his face and sniffed the metallic odor left behind on his palms and went to his bunk, slunk down on its hardness, said calmly, "It's not my safety I'm concerned with."

"Right," said Kinky Pete, "the. . ." Pete scratched his head, "what did you call them?"

"The mother, mother, mother," stuttered Crick, "motherfucking sharks."

"Of course," said Pete. He rolled his eyes and then there was a knock at the door.

Pete went to it and opened it up.

It was Scraw delivering mule stew for the prisoners.

"How many you got?" Scraw asked.

"Just the one," answered Kinky Pete, and he took from Scraw a pie plate of stew covered with a scrap of flour sack and a brown paper bag of cornbread hunks, and he turned with the vittles and walked them to Crick's cell, slid the pie plate beneath the slot in the cage door saying, "mule stew," and dropped the cornbread through the bars saying, "bread."

Crick nodded, asked, "Mule stew?"

Kinky Pete nodded, answered, "Yup, your mule."

Crick stood and walked to the bag, picked it up and looked inside. He took up the pie plate.

"We had the thing slaughtered and cooked up good for you," said Kinky Pete.

Crick folded back a corner of the flour sack and sniffed at the stew. "Hm," said Crick, "that's not mule."

By now Scraw was gone, but Kinky Pete looked at the door and pointed. "Just ask Scraw next time he's around," Pete said, "it's mule. Your mule. Your-mule stew."

Crick packed a spoonful of stew into his drawn-open mouth, chewed slackly, said, "I've had mule," said, "this is not that."

Kinky Pete turned angry, "You calling me liar?" he asked.

"Or merely misinformed," said Crick.

"I'm neither thing," said Pete, "and won't be called such by a crazy man."

Crick took another bite, "And what," he asked, "makes you assume," he chewed, "I'm crazy?"

"To begin with," said Pete, "the look of you." Pete washed his gaze over the captive. "You're inked up and threadbare and ghastly and unbathed."

Crick swallowed. "I'm dirty," he said, "I've tattoos," he continued, "but that's not a sign of insanity."

"Well," said Pete, "the talk you talk, then."

"The talk I talk?"

"Sure. You tell stories unnatural that could only be strained out of the mind of a madman, and the manner in which you travel and present yourself, and how you juggle these," Pete walked to the wall where Crick's satchel hung on a peg, and he reached into it and retrieved a skull, which he held eyes-out toward Crick, "and that is madness."

Crick nodded, "Still," he said taking a hunk of crumbly cornbread and running it through the stew, "this is not mule. And thus, you're a liar. Or, misinformed."

"I'll not have it," said Pete.

"Liar," said Crick.

"I won't take it," said Pete.

And Crick said, "Misinformed."

Pete's face grew truly nasty at the taunting. He raised the skull above his head as though to slam it to the cement ground, shattering it. "Call it mule," he said.

"Can't do it," said Crick.

"Call it mule, or else."

"I was taught to never lie," and he smiled in a grained-toothed manner at Kinky Pete.

"Fine," said Pete, and he rushed the skull-holding hand at the ground with all his might, the strength of the whole endeavor apparent in his wicked-upped eyes, and he drove the gray human cranium into the ground with a smack that sent shards in several directions, and the chipped-up bone chunk jumped in a ricochet and clipped Pete's cheek with such force that the skin struck split open and coughed out a stream of hot-red blood that spilled swift down his face, and Pete covered up the gash with the same hand that had done the throwing, and he barked out some unintelligible language of anguish, and then he looked up at Crick.

Crick stayed calm. "Looks like that smarts," he said, pointing with the spoon.

Pete said nothing. Shock is the surest way to sew shut a proud mouth.

He kept his hand clasped to his face.

He ran out the jail, the whimper of him softly audible over his brisk-thrown steps.

The battered bit of skull that scraped off Pete had rolled against the cage bars, and Crick snagged it up and pulled the broken half of it into his cell. He knew which skull it was when Pete had showed him the eyes. Any of the other skulls would have forced him to say 'mule.' But, among the skulls he carried, this one was false. In theory, it belonged to his son, but, in truth, he had no idea whose it was. It was a stray thing he'd picked out of a shark-destroyed dwelling, and not even the original one at that. The first one he'd used in the stead of his son's had been long since thrown at an annoying woodpecker. The second, he'd given to a whore. He couldn't remember if this was the third or not.

Crick did not like to think deeply on his two days in captivity in the tiny cage the sharks kept him penned in, but every so often an event forced him back there.

The flavor of murder washed his present-moment eyes black, and the colors of that hideous memory pulled him back into the sick sea wherein he witnessed his family's mutilation—the tide of his misery drawing him down toward abyss.

Into the cage and the family and the day warm and the day warm humid and the sound of day like light like dust and into the cage the tight bars cutting soft shade from the dullard sun and the sound of mom and the sound of dad and wife and son and the sound of 'good luck, you can do it' and the sound of 'when I say when' and the sound of 'when I say when push the cage' and the sound of into the cage, the lock, and the sound of the lock clipping locked and the sound of into the cage and the day, and the 'you can do it, got the key?' and the son's face and the eyes the eyes of the son the blue the blue gray bright day sound of the eyes in the day and the sound of the son just about to press his weight on the cage and the thought of the, 'I'm about to fall' and the thought of 'will I pull it off?' and the sound of the remembering in that remembering of how the trick should work and the sound of how the thing would go or not go and the thoughts in that thought of the thought of 'what if?' and that thought of 'what then?' but the thought then of the form in the mind impossible, the thought of the beast appearing and the thought of the 'how could it be so?'

And then blood blood

Blood

And then screams screams

Screams

AND

The sound of the motherfucking sharks and the sound of the motherfucking sharks and the sound of the motherfucking sharks and the sound of THE motherfucking sharks !

Let us hold now in our minds the image of a man and a boy. The man is Crick, but not the Crick of now or then but the Crick of before we've ever seen him. The boy is his child and he is one and a half and he has just said his first word and that first word is 'Daddy.' The shape of this word slipping from the tongue of his son puffed Crick with pride, though he'd never imagined the word being associated with him. As a young man, his proclivity toward wayward schemes left the impression on most of those who chanced upon his presence that Crick would one day die wildly and alone, most likely with dirty clothes on. But Crick's wife—who he met on a riverboat in a romantic entanglement that included drinks with mint as a principal ingredient and porch-colored music played by a blind man with sass—possessed a demeanor that soothed Crick away from debauchery and toward domestication, and since first trading the phrase 'I love you' with her, the path of his activities bent away from the wicked. His son's birth seemed the natural conclusion to anything sordid in his nature, but the boy's first word being 'Daddy' seemed to further cement Crick's utter rehabilitation.

Crick was a decent man, even if he did still practice magic.

Before the wife, before the boy, Crick used his sleight of hand proficiency as an apparatus toward quackery, his magic just a method toward charlatanism and deception.

Simply put, he stole.

He was one of those troubling characters who could glance against you in a crowd and take your watch and wallet, spectacles and keys, but his charm also enabled in him larger, more blatant heists. He might come to your door selling religious texts and make away with the family piano as a donation toward an orphanage that never existed, and he'd sell the instrument to a friend of yours for a fraction of its worth, and you'd see it months later at a dinner party and question its origins, and the line of query would lead to the revelation that you'd been swindled and suckered by a man you'd thought sincere.

Family had taken that from him.

Daddy. The word daddy.

If it's never been aimed at you, you don't know its worth.

Diotima told Socrates, in his quest to understand love, that "the mortal nature is seeking as far as is possible to be everlasting and immortal: and this is only to be attained by generation, because generation always leaves behind a new existence in the place of the old," and so if you're ever called daddy, you become a kind of god, because the attribution of the word to your being is testament to the notion that some shadow of your existence cast by the light of time will stretch into the future and echo toward eternity.

Hold now in your mind two moments:

1. Crick being made immortal by his son calling him daddy.

2. That immortality's bloody revocation when the motherfucking sharks descended upon his son.

And remember both events played out for Crick to witness, and know that the juxtaposition of events in the fold of Crick's mind crashed him toward devastation.

Let us now think of Crick in the cage while his family's devoured. He can do nothing but watch or try not to watch. He can do nothing but listen or try not to listen. The smell of blood and rain puddles thickens the air, and the sun stains Crick's skin as the sharks swim around him.

Sharks ram the cage fruitlessly, their mouths sprawled open to reveal teeth stained by the blood of Crick's loved ones. Their wicked, vacant eyes lock with Crick's. They thrash their bodies as they swim through the air.

Slowly, Crick watches as the sharks' forms pale away. Over the course of his two-day captivity, he sees their skins go transparent so the veins of them are visible, their cartilaginous skeletal systems apparent, and then they can be seen through like wax paper and then they lessen further until they're no more.

Once gone entirely, Crick pulls the cage key from his waistband and unlocks his entrapment, and he weeps his way from skeleton to skeleton, picking up skulls and holding them to his face.

But, a skeleton is gone.

On the ground, beside the cage, he finds the bones of his boy's arms, scattered haphazardly, the fingers of both hands jumbled together, but that is all.

The absence of the skeleton births a quest.

Let us now envision Crick as the wanderer he becomes.

Initially, he is not as our first encounter with him. He is not a streaked stranger inked with indigenous-mannered images. He does not travel with a one-eyed mule. He does not haul harpoons from town to town and profess the coming onslaught of motherfucking sharks. He is less the ancient mariner and more Rapunzel's fallen prince. He bears no warning of things to come, he merely asks the questions as he progresses, "Have you seen an armless boy?"

An armless boy? An armless boy?

Crick crashes his way from town to town eating slop from trash cans and prickly pears foraged from cactus paddles.

An armless boy? An armless boy?

His history plagues him.

An armless boy? An armless boy?

"You look familiar," some say.

Armless boy?

"Didn't you make off with my piano?"

Armless?

"Tell us again about the orphans?"

Boy?

The nature of his twisted experience is made further unbelievable by the fact that his wake is burdened with falsities espoused.

"Sure, sure," most people say, "motherfucking sharks. Armless boy." They shake their heads. "Get to the point," they tell him, "what are you trying to take me for?"

Still, there are whispers. "A carnival. A freak show. A circus act. Some strangers."

Crick gathers shards of stories and crumples them together in his mind. "There was a boy. The boy was armless." And Crick follows any line offered him from place to place through miserable weather and over lands shunned by God.

In some towns, his reputation is so badgered he catches beatings for returning. He sees jail time. In the cells he hears more. From convicts whose pathways chance avenues of ill repute where, as Crick sees it, armless boys may be forced to tarry.

Crick slips down these outlets, himself becoming a wanderer of the underbelly, where he takes odd employments and keeps company with tattoo artists who convince him the drawings now on his skin would render his image unrecognizable from the Crick of the past, and he allows his face and arms to be inked to their now remarkable appearance.

His journeys bring him to dilapidated towns. Broken villages littered with skeletons. Reminders of his family's falling.

But it is not all bad. There are moments of glory as he traipses the earth, as he pauses and sees in distances before him citrus orchards toasting in the bake of sunlight, the perfume of them bright and tangy, soporific and clean. Or further south in his wanderings, into the mountains of Mexico, where ramshackle houses made from cinder blocks and blankets sit in the shadow of Cola de Caballo—Horse Tail Falls—and the sound of the rushing waters fills his ears like white noise as the residents speak their music-shaped language in response to his continuing query, "A boy with no arms?"

And Crick has never found him.

Now there is Crick in the cage with a fragment of skull in his grip, but who the skull belongs to is unknown, and all the armless boys who Crick found in his journeys were the sons of other men. Sad boys with vacant faces straining in dust-flavored dwellings.

That mission, to find his child, was abandoned. Instead, Crick decided to spread word of the terrors of the motherfucking sharks, but so often his labors found him in situations similar to this.

Crick sits on the hard bed in his cell. He stares at the skull. He wonders if he'll ever see his boy again.

The thunder starts.

V

Kinky Pete rushed in bleeding, and Mom watched him absently as he fidgeted a wet washrag from a bucket and began to dab his face.

"What happened to you?" she asked.

"Nothing worth mentioning," he told her.

Mom thought: Nothing with men ever is.

She thought: Look at him with his cut. Damn sad. I've seen him shoot men dead and now he bleeds like a child. I've seen so many silly men. This one. His blood caught in the rag from the water bucket. Was it preordained that I'd be so inundated by puny men? In the pattern of the stars is it organized that my acquaintances with the opposite sex would be bungled? I find them foolish and haphazard, and yet physically I crave them. Perhaps that is the evilest side of my coin. I wish I was as those other women who find breasts and hips mesmerizing, but I can't sway myself in that direction. In my memory my father is feeble, but my mother was absent, and perhaps that's the saddest act of all—to run like a coward from a duty you've gestated. Father was a drunk, but he was there: in the morning light of the kitchen with a sundae bowl of bourbon to 'warm up his bones,' and he never did foul by me sexually, though I'm certain most who smelled his breath figured him a daughter toucher, but in my mind the tragedy of his self-driven destruction was the great undoer of my opinion of him. How can a creature's prime motivation be to poison itself? All he did was drink and hope to drink again. Even when he got ill off it, and had to hide from the sun, deep in whatever shade

he could find with his head wrapped in wet cloth, he would beg me to fetch him whisky to alleviate his malaise and the excruciating moroseness of it, and that always further puzzled me: it was like trying to heal a burn with more fire. And that's what he was: a wound that wanted to be wounded. Here, this Kinky Pete, this face bleeding into a wet rag, here I find it paltry and clumsy, but I get it. Whatever secret situation caused the abrasion matters not. What matters is he's aiming to quell the ache with a sane method. I'd say "Daddy, just wait it out. Sit in the dark. I'll bring you cool water," and he'd laugh and say, "Why wait for what's coming anyhow?" And perhaps there was some logic in that. There never passed a day I didn't see him drinking. Eight in the morning or eight at night: is there much difference?

"He's an odd one."

Mom looked up, confused.

"But he can't hurt no one where we got him," said Pete, and Mom knew he meant the stranger. Pete took the blood-colored rag from his cheek, lowered his face to hers and asked, "Think it needs stitches?"

She surveyed the gash and could see clotted fat hanging limp and yellow at the edges. "Probably," she said, and Pete nodded.

"Figures," he said, and he turned and tossed the bloody rag back into the water bucket, stomped to the front door, threw it open and then banged it shut as he disappeared into the street.

Was there much difference? I don't drink, so maybe I don't know. I have drank, but not like that. I have tasted wine and I have felt it change me, but not like that. He would go from sick to swell in a swallow and a half, and he'd sing those foolish songs with a smile on his face, made up things that he pretended were real, the lyrics all rhyming and he'd pause for me to finish the couplets—

The first thing in gumbo is?
Roux
Which is basically a Cajun?
Stew
And the opposite of false is?
True
And the opposite of old is?
New

And he could go on that way for hours with his sundae bowl that he always drank from, and when I asked him why he'd say, "Because I love ice cream."

Fine. Ice cream. The thing that killed him. His smell changing and his skin turning yellow. A real man. Like all the men. Like the one today. Drawn on like a coloring book. Playing with toys. A real man. Shouting make believe stories on the street corner certain that everyone wanted to listen. Because he is a man.

Then the thunder starts.

Mom goes to the door and opens it. She steps onto the porch. In the distance she can see the white lightning coughing fits behind the jagged-peaked mountains, the sillhouettes of them more dramatic in the dark of the oncoming storm.

She thinks: Storm.

She thinks: Just like children.

She thinks: Ice cream.

Mom goes to the cupboard where Kinky Pete keeps the bourbon and plucks a bottle from the shelf. She goes to her room. At the foot of her bed, a trunk. Inside the trunk, her father's sundae bowl.

She thinks: All the same.

She thinks: Nothing but children.

She thinks: I'll take it to him.

Mom makes her way back on to the porch, down the few steps and into the single, proper street of the town.

She thinks: When I first came here there was one house made from mold-freckled timber.

She thinks: It's not where I want it, but it's getting there.

Mom had come to the town after her father died with an aunt who she met only once before her father's funeral. She was a baldheaded woman who wore a black bandana on her skull and smoked cigarettes and played harmonica. They had driven there by donkey-dragged wagon, and when they reached the house the aunt halted the donkey, said, "There you go," and looked out at nothing.

"There I go what?" asked Mom.

The aunt took one long drag on her cigarette, and Mom could hear the paper and tobacco burning to ash, turning to smoke. The aunt lunged the smoke, her face going tight as she breathed deep the air. She exhaled. She pointed at the house. "Get on up there," she said, "knock on that door," her words stained gray with the escaping smoke, "tell 'em what's brought you here."

Mom thought a moment. "You brought me here," she said.

Her aunt shook her head, "I mean your pa," she said, "dead as they come," she smoked again, "buried in the dirt." She nodded. "Tell 'em that and they'll take you in."

Mom looked at the sad little house. It looked like a good rain would wash it away. "And you?" she asked her aunt without looking at her, because she was old enough to figure the answer.

"Well," said the aunt, "I'll be back from time to time to check."

Mom looked at her. The aunt smiled guiltily. Some people are so worthless, they don't bother hiding their lies.

The aunt helped Mom pull her

trunk from the wagon, but she did not help her drag it to the house. "Go and knock," she said, "they'll help you carry it in."

Mom nodded, walked toward the door. The aunt drove on before she'd even gotten there to knock.

Mom thinks: That house was empty.

She thinks: Was probably always empty.

She thinks: And she probably thought I'd die in it.

She remembered knocking and knocking again. She knocked and knocked again. It was summer and the sun shone so bright the light of the world seemed false, and the shadows of all things were darker than midnight, and young Mom sat sweating on that porch of that busted house trying to shade her face with her hand, and she waited until the sun sank away from noon and into evening, and she watched it half itself with the horizon and watched it slip away like an orange ghost, the sky's blue hue fading into nighttime's navy. She knocked again, then sat on the trunk with her knees pulled to her chin, terrified of the noises and the stars and the moon, and annoyed at the mosquitos who sank their poisonous suckers in her. She swatted herself pink. She itched herself awake, watching the moon trace the sky.

In the morning, the dew made her dress sticky.

She knocked on the door again. She knocked again.

She was tired and angry from being tired, and she decided she would no longer follow the etiquette taught to her. She turned the doorknob and went inside. It was as she feared. The house was entirely empty.

Mom thinks: I was only a child.

She thinks: But that childhood didn't last long.

"Wake up," Mom says.

She stands in front of Crick's cell, holds the bourbon bottle in one hand and the sundae bowl in the other.

Crick pulls his eyes open. His slumber breaks oddly. He shakes his head. "Storms always do it," he says, "I love to sleep through the rain."

Mom nods. "It's coming," she says, "you said it would," she pours the sundae bowl full of bourbon and walks to the bars. "Thirsty?" she says.

Crick nods. He stands and goes to her. He takes the sundae bowl from her and contemplates it. "I'd rather it be ice cream," he says and sips at it gingerly.

Mom smiles. She sets the bottle on the ground. In doing so, she sees the shattered skull bits. "What happened here?" she asks.

Crick sips his bourbon. "Ask that Kinky Pete," he says, and Mom nods because now she knows.

She looks about. She sees Crick's satchel. "You know," she says, "I can juggle too." She takes the skulls from the bag. "But I can only do three," she says. She takes a skull in each hand and lets the third rest on her right wrist. Crick watches her nervously.

Mom jerks her right arm toward the ceiling and the skull lifts from her wrist into the air. It begins to drop and she launches the skull from her left hand, catches the falling skull and tosses up the third. Her form is sloppy, but Crick watches her work the skulls from hand to hand, Mom's face pinched with concentration. She catches them and holds them a moment against her. "Tada," she says.

"Bravo," says Crick.

"I could never do four though," she says.

"Neither can I," he says, "I just do two with each hand."

Mom thinks a moment on this. "Is that how it's done?" she asks.

"It is," he says.

"Forgive me if I don't try," she says.

Crick smiles. "I'd actually rather you didn't."

Mom looks then at the skulls. "That's right," she says, "your family."

"That's right," says Crick.

Mom places the skulls back in the satchel. "And do people believe that?" she asks, "when you tell them?"

"Not usually," Crick says.

"And the sharks?"

"The motherfucking sharks," says Crick.

"Yes," says Mom, "the motherfucking sharks." She laughs. "Do people believe about them?"

"Rarely," says Crick.

"But you tell it anyway?"

Crick nods. He sips his drink. "You ever seen a boy with no arms?" he asks.

Mom looks at him oddly. "Is this a kind of riddle?" she asks.

Crick laughs. "Maybe," he says. "But if it is, I'm living it."

They are silent a moment. Thunder can be heard. But, another noise as well. Hollering. Shouting of some sort. The door flings open.

Scraw walks in with his hands on his head. Kinky Pete walks behind him. His pistol is drawn and his left hand holds a rag against his busted face.

"God damn it," hollers Kinky Pete. He looks at Mom. He looks at Crick. He holsters his pistol and opens Crick's cell with a key. "Well," he says, shoving Scraw in with Crick. "You were right," he says to Crick.

Crick laughs.

Mom looks at all the men. "Right about what?" she asks.

Pete just looks at her. He grits his teeth. He dabs his wound. "That stew," he yells, "it was not mule."

VI

Kinky Pete walked the street repulsed at his anger because his anger made him throw the skull, birthed his need for stitches. There's not a person alive who's not phenomenal at hurting themselves. But Kinky Pete was better than most. He cussed himself as he dragged down the street to see Bark.

"You're a foolish piece of shit wrapped in the disguise of human flesh," he said, "throwing tantrums like a baby."

At Bark and Scraw's, Pete banged the door, the deep thud of his fist against the broad portal humming low in the night. "Bark," he hollered, "I'm cut and need sewing on."

The door did not open, but Scraw answered from inside, "Bark's sleeping." That was the extent of Scraw's offering on the matter. Night's silence came on again.

"Well," said Pete, "wake him up."

Silence.

Pete again banged the door, but no answer came.

"Scraw," he screamed, "I'm bleeding. Wake Bark. Tell him I need stitched up."

Silence.

Pete's patience fizzled out quick. He knelt to lift the door, but it was locked. "Scraw," he yelled, "Scraw, open up."

Scraw hollered back, "I can't."

Pete walked to the side of the building. Yellow light glowed from a window, and Pete perched on his tip toes to peek inside. He couldn't believe what he saw. He went back to the the door, and banged it again.

He screamed, "Scraw," and banged the door. He screamed, "Scraw," again. "I looked in your window," he said. "I saw the damn mule."

Then the thunder starts.

Scraw says in a limp tone, "I can't believe what I've done."

Pete puzzles at this, "Open up," he says, "what are you talking about?"

Pete listens as Scraw keys the lock open from inside. He steps back from the door as it raises to reveal Scraw who stands aside the still-living Murm, petting the mule's mane. "I couln't kill it," Scraw says.

Pete nods. "Fine," he says, "where's Bark?"

Scraw leans his shoulder against the mule. "Bark wanted me to kill the mule, but I couldn't bring myself to do it."

"Fine," says Pete, "but where is he?"

"He was pushing me," says Scraw, "or," Scraw scratches his head, "I sure like this mule."

"Dammit, Scraw, don't make me ask again."

Scraw looks at nothing. "I don't know," he says, "because I'm not sure how it works. My only memory of my mother is her telling me how the sunshine became the flowers, and she said 'every time you pick a flower, it's like holding a ray of sun,' because she said that sun was how flowers made their food. I dropped bowls of Bark to the prisoner and to the poor families, but I don't know if that means they're part Bark or if Bark's part them, and what I didn't drop off is in the pot on the stove." Scraw points to a large steel pot that is streaked with brown stew down its sides. "And the bone part of Bark is out back in the bone pile." Scraw looks at Pete. "Do you want me to bring that part back in here?"

Kinky Pete draws his gun. He says,

"Nope, best to come with me," and he leads Scraw to the cell where Crick is held captive and deposits him there.

On Pete's way home with Mom, it begins to rain.

Rain, Rain, Rain

This is the part where it rains. It will rain so good, you will go get lines from it tattooed on your body and every time it is raining outside you will find strangers in the rain, going to them while holding an umbrella, and you will look them in the eyes and say, "How about this weather?" and they will say, "I know," and then you will show them the tattooed line from this book that made you think anew about rain, and their eyes will smile at you, just the two of you beneath your umbrella, locked in the magic of the words on the subject of rain as inked on your body by a tattoo artist who probably likes girl on girl porn.

Mom is home with her face against the window. Kinky Pete is home on his porch playing with his pistol. Crick and Scraw are in the cell. Murm stands inside the slaughterhouse in front of the door swishing his tail watching the puddles grow.

Armies of drops fall, swelling the streets with impromptu rivers. The roofs cast sheets of rain from their lips like waterfalls. The thunder booms. The lightning strobes. The music of the falling rain hisses.

Rain According To Pete

I don't know how it gets in the sky. I'm serious. The rain. They probably taught me at some point, but I didn't pay attention, because my back always aches so much I don't pay attention to school-type things, but I do know enough to know it starts off as water and gets turned to clouds, and that the clouds get too heavy, you can tell by the look of them, and then it just falls. It's a storm. But it can rain with the sun out. Used to we'd say, when it rained and was sunny, that the devil was beating his wife, but I have no idea where that saying came from. Sayings are always stupid things. I had a Mexican aunt couldn't speak English, and she used to say to me, whenever I hurt myself, "Sana sana colita de rana," which meant, "heal heal little frog tail," and her saying it was supposed to take away the pain, but I'm not certain how, and my uncle used to say, "A monkey in a dress is still a monkey," but he never saw a monkey in his whole life, so I don't know where he came up with that.

Rain, Rain, Rain

Rain, Rain!

Rain According to Scraw

Maybe it's like God crying because I killed Bark. Not every time, but this time. I think God exists. I might be going to Hell. The guy in the cell with me definitely is. I'm thirsty. I'm gonna hold my hand out the window and catch some of God's tears and drink them. If the water I catch is salty, well the rain is God's tears for certain.

_____
_____
_____
_____
_____
_____
_____
_____
_____
_____

Rain in Various Languages

German: Regnen
Spanish: Lluvia
French: Pluie
Italian: Pioggia
Pig Latin: Ainray

Rain According to Crick

Fuck the rain, and fuck this weird guy with his hand out the window.

Rain According to You

_____
_____
_____
_____
_____
_____
_____
_____
_____
_____
_____
_____
_____

Rain According to Mom

Because he liked ice cream. That's why he drank liquor from a sundae bowl. I bet it even made sense to him once upon a time. Or, maybe the first time he said it. The first time he said it, it probably got him a laugh, and after that he just said it all the time, but I never laughed at it. I'd just look at him like, "Why?" What he needed was water. It's what we all need. Not this much. The juggler, he was right about the rain, but I just can't believe he's right about the sharks. He doesn't seem crazy when you talk to him, but he doesn't seem honest either. Maybe he tells people about the motherfucking sharks coming out after the rain for the same reason my father said he drank because he liked ice cream. Maybe. Somehow. Somewhere. It worked for him. The story about his family too. Maybe in some towns, the people go in for the theatrics of it. They like the drama of his past's misery, and they celebrate his act and treat him as a renowned performer.

The Rain Stops

Here is how it starts: with a whisper, a hiss. A shallow spray the scent of fresh. It comes first as pure calm. The tree limbs that fooled in the breeze go serious, fall still, and the world seems paused in anticipation. But in that hallowed still there seems a promise. The nutrition of nature is imminent. The ashy second skin of the world sat dry will be washed gone, and dragged on makeshift currents to conclusions only God can perceive.

In the town, the hush of the coming storm dwindles, eaten by the noise of that which is certain, and with silence's tapering, residents seek refuge in dwellings ill-equipped for flood—the security provided by them more mental than actual—and they hold their breaths and seek their misplaced religion, hiding behind verses their forefathers died clucking in battle so that their descendants might lead softer lives—the byproduct of their easy living ironically the cause of their failing beliefs.

But here in this fear of God's hammer, a re-awakening of those cultural touchstones. Soul-shaped hands seek heaven-shaped promises to hold and hold onto, even as the storm douses the streets until they bulge like blisters—the girth of them puny against the eternity of the flood.

Take a coin from your pocket and pour a gallon on it.

Take a coin from your pocket and drop it into a gallon.

Take a coin.

Here the homes wiggle and sway with wind. Here the roofs leak streams from low holes into buckets that miserably perform.

Children hold their mothers. Wives hold their husbands. Husbands hold their breaths.

This storm is a carbon copy.

A carbon copy of prior storms.

Magically, no one dies in the dread of it. The weather seems aware of the townsfolk's limitations.

The relentlessness of it relents.

Family members cross themselves as the deluge dwindles.

The sun.

The sun can be seen.

Behind smoke-shaped clouds that scrape open like lace.

They're alive.

The storm did not kill them.

VII

The sun plows the clouds to nothing. The blue of sky like a sheet of life the fiery coin of the sun just clings to. It is there, casting rays that warm the puddles which sit stagnant and bored in their sockets, children stomping them and ladies looking into them at their reflections.

Here are the people of the town rejoicing at the storm's quelling. Here they are in the sun of the day. The mud of the street clumps to the soles of their shoes, stains the hems of their slacks and dresses, and babies are set in it to wallow like pigs as their parents bare thrive-stained smiles—beaming at their ability to outlive the disastrous weather that had held them tight in their homes the way envelopes hold letters.

Mom stands on her porch in the fresh morning air, and Pete, so pleased at the jolly figures in the roads, plucks his revolver from its holster and fires bullets at the sky, "Can't kill us," he says to God, and then all the men with guns fire heaven-headed rounds, and someone brings a bourbon bottle into the street, and they open it and pass it around like a conch shell and whoever has it says some flavor-laced toast about Jesus or their mothers and then drinks from the thing until every willing party in the town has espoused their happiness and lipped the mouth of the thing, making themselves silly with liquor.

A free-for-all ensues. Guilty pleasures abound. Men kiss women, kiss men. Babies are held up by their ankles and swung, and their laughter emits like helium-drenched music. Souls prance in the shape of smiles. Kittens are given milk. Murm wanders blinking his one eye at the wildness of it, and girls tie flowers to his tail.

Scraw watches from the jail cell window, "That's my mule," he hollers.

"The mule is his own thing," says Crick. He grins blackly at the affronted joy. He knows it will soon perish.

In the puddles that glimmer with sun, the evil things are hatching.

In sun-glittering puddles the sharks are forming.

In the shiny puddles.

The puddles—like mirrors toward the sky.

Look now close at them. Here are the things to see:

1. You in it, a reflection or refraction depending on the stillness of the water.

2. The murk of the muddy slop or the shape of the road beneath the inches of wet depending on the stillness of the water.

3. The disturbances. Tiny tickles of motion. Like mosquitos at first, beating their wings. But something more. It steadies. Outline of shark. So small you could swallow them with just their skin slicked by the puddles they're pulled from. And what then would occur to you? The motherfucking shark's progress so deep in its operation cannot be stopped by normal means, and the expansion of the organism— formulated by the blackest deceit of physics, organics, and chemistry—would continue, and you'd feel it first as an ache in your belly that would broaden like a

rage or fire and maintain its trajectory of expanse until the shark gained full form, and that growth of it, the swiftest of maturations, would sever your figure beneath the force of it, your body blasting open as gore and sludge, the muck of you draping away from the gray-bodied being that would swim out of you whilst gnashing its teeth and thrashing its fins, breathing the flavor of you through its gills that would glisten with your blood.

It is Mom who spots first the trembling puddles. At first it seems joyous to her. The shiny surfaces giggling with light.

But then she thinks: I'd rather it be ice cream.

That thought, that statement from the wanderer, festers.

Maybe it's not a lie.

And further the puddles are disturbed, as though an earthquake shakes them, but the world is otherwise still.

"Maybe," hollers Mom above the drone of the people celebrating the end of the wicked storm, "we should move this party inside."

But, it is too late.

On the ground, near a puddle, its face the smell of chocolate, a toddler toddles.

See this, friend: eyes green, cheeks alight with joy. Blonde hair only ever so slightly feathered by breeze. A giggle. A tummy laugh. You ever touched a toddler's tummy? It feels like suede-wrapped heaven. It smells like milk and hugs and handshakes from God. You see this little boy? This little white boy? If it hurts you more to see a black boy die, then make him black in your mind, I don't care what it looks like so long as you're uncomfortable. Instead, reader, do this. Picture for me, if you will, the child you love the most. Hold it in your head. Dress it with the form you'd least like to see killed. In this way, we have always been a team. I tell you a thing, but you spin it real in your head. So, I won't tell you everything. Hell, make it a girl. Make it your own. Give me a child. Put it in your mind. Put it by a puddle. Put joy in its heart. I'm going to fuck it up. I'm going to unleash a magical shark on it. I'm going to turn that precious thing into a bucket of death shaped the way that hurts you most. Put that fucking child by that fucking puddle and let me kill the fuck out of it. I will strip its skin from its body, toss chunks of it at you like strips of bacon. Your baby. Make the fucking baby. I want to kill the fucking baby you've made in your mind. Is it there? Is it the baby?

Now, up comes the shark.

Now listen, I'm serious here, I'm willing to sacrifice my spot in Heaven to make you feel bad while reading this. I'll quit drinking forever tomorrow, and I won't jerk off to amateur porn anymore—you know the kind that's been stolen and where the women look embarrassed and the men look eager and the light is yellow and you can nearly smell the sin—but it won't matter anymore, because after I kill this toddler out of your imagination, God will think me reprehensible. I want this to all occur inside of you. We're a team, okay? We're gonna kill this little kid together.

Kill this kid with me.

Put it in your mind and let's kill it.

Just you and me.

Just you and me and our imaginations.

Just two people. Taking a kid and killing it in our hearts.

It's not real.

It's just.

Let's take this kid. This cute little kid. It's by the puddle. And in that puddle is something dark.

The child is innocent. The shark is

heinous. Teeth. Teeth. Teeth.

Look at a baby's hand. It's so soft.

Look at a shark's mouth. All those teeth, so sharp.

Take that soft little hand, with those soft little fingers. Piggies. Piggies.

Sing: this little piggy went to market, this little piggy stayed home.

God, I'm gonna fucking put those cute little fingers in that fucking shark's mouth. God, it will be fucked up. I'm gonna drag them over the teeth. Oh, shit, they will not stand a chance.

Hahaha. Look at the baby's face. It's fucking crying.

There's blood everywhere.

It's trying to suck its thumb.

Hey, dumbass, thumb's gone.

I fed it to a fucking shark.hahahahaha ahahahahahahahahahaahaa.

Oh.

It bites the kid again.

Oh, man.

These motherfucking sharks are crazy.

VIII

Kinky Pete bolts into the sheriff's office and races to the open cell alongside Crick and Scraw's. He gets inside pulling the cage door closed behind him. "What the fuck is happening?" he screams.

"I take it you've met the motherfucking sharks?"

Scraw is screaming, looking out the window at the sharks that are destroying the people of the town. Biting and thrashing, spraying the street with blood.

A nurse shark rams its way into the jail. It slams frantically against the cage bars, trying to bite at Pete. Pete cowers, his hands over his face. Scraw cries hysterically. Crick picks at his teeth.

Pete pulls his pistol and fires four

shots at the shark. The bullets pass straight through it.

"No use," says Crick, "only harpoons kill them."

Pete looks at Crick. "Why?" he asks.

"Because they are magical, flying sharks and that's how they die," he says. "Pierce 'em with a harpoon and they burst into flames and the only thing that remains of them is their jaws that drop to the ground from their burning mouths," says Crick. "I've felled loads of them and have the mementos tied to my wagon just outside."

Pete looks sadly at his pistol. "I don't believe it," he says.

"Like with the stew?" says Crick.

Pete looks deeply now into Crick's eyes.

"Go fetch me a harpoon," says Crick, "and I'll show you."

Pete looks at the nurse shark just outside the cage. It gnashes and thrashes. Pete thinks. "Maybe," he says, "we could send out Scraw."

Scraw screams a crazy-girl-shaped holler.

"Shut up," says Crick, and he kicks Scraw, and Scraw hunches toward the floor and screams even louder.

Crick looks at Pete. "I don't think he has the nerves for it," he says, but the noise of Scraw endures.

Pete nods agreement, shakes his head at the commotion. "He's a killer anyhow," he says. He takes aim at Scraw's skull, pulls the pistol's trigger and a shot erupts and Scraw's head oozes open and he goes quiet, his body limping to the floor where a puddle of blood smears out around him. Pete holsters the gun. "How long does it last?" Pete asks pointing at the nurse shark.

Crick shrugs. "All of today," he says. "Maybe some of tomorrow."

The two men go to their respective bunks. They both sit. They quietly watch the shark.

Pete takes a plug of tobacco from his pocket and mouths a chew of it.

Outside the sharks charge the townsfolk into terrified clumps, the bulk of them like wads of fear, pock-marked with terror-stricken eyes. These cowering clusters breathe screams as a single organism would, low-droning shouts blend with pitch-pointed shrieks, and the music of it bellows as a bagpiper tuning may, only the lunging attacks of sharks plunging into the mess of folks like grey and toothed fists pop off the steadiness of the choir by subtracting voices from its congregation, and the strikes change the musicality or add to it depending—the wayward tones flittered with blood and the ache-noise of someone's dying or dismemberment and the sea salt smell of the shark-shaped mastication.

Pete: That one looks mean.

Crick: They're all mean.

An athletic-looking boy races down the road pursued by a hammerhead with evil-fuck eyes. Make believe you are the camera. The boy races toward you.

Now you are the camera above. The shark is after the boy.

You are beside the shark. Its dorsal fin whistles against the air as the fish races on.

Beside the boy. He huffs and pants, his feet skipping across the gravel, the sound of match sticks against striker pads.

Again above. The shark gains ground.

And in front again. The boy so close

the fear on his face repulses you, the skin around his eyes red as fire, and then the hammerhead thrashes down upon the boy's collar, and the two lift above your line of sight until the last you see of the boy is his sneaker cracking your camera lens.

You are now beside them both, high in the air, the boy's neck gushing blood, vomit tossing from his mouth, tears streaking his face, and the shark is thrashing.

Pete: Know any jokes?
　　Crick: No.

A father and daughter race toward home. She is too slow and he raises her to his hip and makes his legs run faster than they ever have. They burn, his legs, but not like fire. It is as though his muscles are filled with saltwater instead of blood, and aching from the corrosion of trying to manipulate that liquid into fuel.

He loves his daughter.

She is his only living kin.

He didn't know his people, and he just witnessed his wife's annihilation, her body scraped open and emptied of its mess—globules and morsels and smidgens and niggles. Things like red marbles slick with oil and pink balloons deformed by age, just quaking from her walloped-around body.

He can't let his daughter die.

He doesn't look behind him.

He knows they are near, and he begs his legs, his lungs, his heart, through some physical prayer the mind makes to the body, to move faster still, to thwart the smarting back to corners and un-anguish in any way imaginable and give him more.

His daughter faints from fear in his clutch.

He makes it to the porch.

To the door.

Reaches for the knob.

Tries to turn it, but it is locked.

Terrified, he turns.

A great white is upon him and the cast-wide mouth sprawls its shiv-sculpted teeth at him, and in his last act, just a cowardly reflex really, he lifts his daughter at the shark, stuffing her body into its jaws, but the monster is so mighty, it bites them both in two.

Pete: There's an alcoholic in a potato sack race.
　　Crick: Is this the joke?
　　Pete: Yeah.

An aging lady holds a crucifix in front of her.

Her entire frame is trembling, her wrinkly little face like a frightened prune.

A bull shark takes its teeth to her leg. She brings the cross down upon it over and over again. It does nothing.

She hears her flesh tear open—like a bed sheet being ripped at—and she just dies from the shock of it.

Pete: He's hopping down the track in the lead, and he sees a bar.

A blind man stands still with his arms outstretched.

A gray whirr scurries by him.

Now his hands are gone and blood gushes from his wrists and his face looks confused—his impotent eyes as wide open as walnuts.

He thinks, 'I'm so far ahead, I'll just hop in here for a quick one.'

Murm walks the street unfazed.

He whips his tail all casual.

He blinks at the beastly bits left behind by the sharks.

Steps over the bones and severed limbs, setting his hooves instead into puddles of blood and muck, shredded flesh and burst-open bladders. Shit and piss. Puss and ooze. Guts caught in potholes like buckets of chum.

Murm finds an onion cart overturned in the road.

He eats one of the maroon-skinned vegetables.

Chews patiently as sharks whiz around him.

He hops up to the bar and says, 'Shot of whisky, please.'

Mom screams, "Follow me," and leads three girls in an odd, stumbling progression through the dregs of the mudded-up street, now slippery with blood and threads of flung human flesh.

In Mom's mind, a fear tone drones, the smack of shark jaws on human flesh providing a percussion ill-timed. Alongside that, the noise of their steps in the soup of the road, the plunking and slurping of their course illustrating their slow, steady migration away from the assemblages of herded townsfolk— in their ill-fated congregations just delaying for death—and toward a hopeful sanctuary of a storm cellar behind a pale-yellow house.

The smell of warm puddles, warm blood, and salt water. The smell of the mud, the fear, the sun.

The three girls shriek like steam fleeing teapots.

They are a chain of humans, fastened by hands.

They are all so terrified, you cannot tell the true age of them, but they seem to descend in maturity, starting with Mom.

A requiem shark sweeps down from the skies at the weakest link of them, shanking her away from the chain of females fleeing.

And then there were three.

Miraculously, mud-streaked, blood-soaked, the now youngest holding still the detached arm of the one they lost— the arm dangling queerly and flexing with nerves—they make it to the cellar.

"You girls first," says Mom, and she pushes them down the steps.

Bartender just looks at him.

A whitetip is upon Mom. It has gripped her thigh through her denim dress just as Mom was about to descend into the cellar. She fights it, driving her elbows down against the dorsal fin, jabbing fists at the gills.

It was the nose she should have aimed for.

Realizing she can't defeat it, won't shake from its grip, Mom slams shut the cellar door, clamps the pad lock of it shut—all the time screams of the girls below ringing hot in her mind.

Once locked, a lucky strike is landed. Mom puts a fist down into the face of the shark, and the thing lets loose a moment, shakes its head.

Mom takes advantage.

She turns.

Her leg is messed with wound, panging wildly, but she flees.

On bungled limbs she runnels forth, murking her way across the flood-gutted street and beyond the town's perimeter into the adjacent spare-grass lands now swampy with standing wet, dotted green by patches of swaying St. Augustine grass.

'I can't serve you,' the bartender says.

There is no more aggressive a shark than the tiger.

The great white might be king, but the tiger is the assassin.

The young are striped, hence the name.

Their noses blunted, their teeth wildly asymmetrical and serrated, their appetites undiscerning so they'll eat the flesh of anything.

They can live fifty years, growing up to fourteen feet long and weigh on average one-hundred pounds per foot.

They swim in shoals, but will hunt alone.

If they see movement, they attack, and they don't let go.

See now the tiger shark above the town where the hollers of those being attacked has quelled to murmurs, whispers, tones?

You see it, and it sees Mom.

It swims now toward her, and she has stumbled to a stop, falling upon soft earth where she pants for breath.

She rolls onto her back, hoists herself to her elbows to look at her town now waylaid by the vicious, impossible creatures.

She sees it, the tiger.

It howls steadily toward her, but Mom has nothing left. She is leaked out through the wound on her thigh, which is now numbed by shock and no longer feels the squelch of shred but instead feels packed away beneath stacks of weights, and it is this weight that stills her. She is pale fatigue on the back of a wooden spoon. She is slow nothing in a pocket of put-away pants.

She thinks: I bet it is a man, this shark.

She thinks: I'll spread my legs at him.

With legs heaved open, Mom lays her head back, and a wild, electric lust spreads over her.

She thinks: We only die once.

She thinks: I will try to enjoy it.

She feels the force of the tiger's speed upon her like a wind, and then the beast traps her pussy in his jaws, driving her back into the mud, and she gives over the smooth surface of it, her path leaving a slug trail of blood and slick, and the shark shakes viciously, and Mom throws her head back in agony, her vision filled with endlessness of sky, and just before the tiger undoes her she thinks: Who will free them from the cellar?

'You're already half in the bag.'

The screams from the street have faded entirely. The sharks amass around the cells. They swim constantly at the bars. Some of the smaller ones make it through. Crick and Pete grab them by the tails and beat them on the floors until they are barely sharks anymore. Even after their skin has been scraped away, and they are essentially piles of organs and yuk, they live in an undead way, wriggling their battered bodies against the floor violently. Pete spits at them.

Pete: I can see the veins in them.

Crick: They'll be gone soon.

VIII 1/2

Pete wakes to find Crick staring at him. "What is it?" he asks.

"They're gone."

Pete pries himself off his bunk, shaking his body into some capable configuration, and he steps to his feet awkwardly, bumbling around with haphazard movement until he finds his balance. He puts his hands over his head. Yawns. Scratches his back. He looks around. He listens. "You sure?" he asks.

"Positive," says Crick. "Watched 'em vanish while you were sleeping."

Pete thinks. He smiles. He fishes the cell keys from his pants pocket, feeds them through the bars and awkwardly unlocks the cage. He pushes the door and it creaks rustily open. He steps out cautiously. It is ungracefully silent. He heads toward the door.

"Ain't you gonna let me out?" asks Crick.

Pete looks back at him. "Why would I?" he asks, and he walks to the doorway and out into the street.

Once he's gone, Crick produces a metal pick from beneath his tongue. He goes to the cell door and jimmies it open. He follows Pete out into the world.

Pete stands dumbfounded. The sun is high and angry, and the gore of the aftermath shines irrationally like a gem. There's a glimmer to the butchering. The puddles, the slick bones, the flung flesh, the wobbled away eyes.

Black birds are hoisted upon everything like flight-gifted rot, tearing scattered death into smaller bits which they fumble ineptly while seeking solitude from their brethren birds.

The homes and buildings, never entirely well put together, are busted and battered from the ungainly patterns of the sharks' feeding frenzies. Splinters of timber are tossed with the bone bits, the debris of destruction like a gravel of death.

Crick walks to his wagon and plucks a harpoon from the bunch of them. "Ain't a pretty sight is it?" he asks Pete whose back is to him.

Pete turns in awe. "How'd you get out?" he asks.

"Magic," says Crick.

Pete's eyes find the blade of the harpoon leveled at him.

He reaches for his pistol, but as he does, Crick flings the harpoon, and before Pete has unholstered the gun, he is impaled by the weapon, which lifts him from the ground and drives him back, stapling him against the wall of the sheriff's building, where he dangles by the heart upchucking blood down his chest.

Crick goes to him with a knife. "People like you," he says, "they don't ever listen."

IX

Howard and Gall sit in the living room playing checkers. It is a battered world, and family members falter. A woman is a woman if she says she is. A man, if he can prove it. Howard's father has been dead three years. His best friend Gall has been helping with the ranch. They are both fourteen, but markedly different. Gall knows horses, has big strong shoulders. Howard still chews his lip, would rather whittle than work.

Gall moves a piece. "King me," he says.

Howard's mother looks into the room. She sees the game at play. "Who's winning?" she asks. She had Howard when young and is still pristine. Her blonde hair is pulled behind her ears. She's been washing in the kitchen, and her white cotton blouse is tight on her breasts, near see-through where wet.

Howard looks at her. "Gall is," he says.

Gall looks at her. "Like always," he says.

She smiles at him and rubs her hands together. "You let me know when you're tired of that kid's game," she says.

"Why come?" asks Gall.

"Well," she says, "thought you and I might play something else."

It is as though Howard is not there entirely, and it has been this way for weeks. He's been listening to their fucking from his bedroom confusedly, and he has seen this foreplay banter displayed in front of him ad nauseum.

"I'm gonna go check the horses," Howard says, and he stands to leave the house.

"Ah, c'mon," says Gall. "You might still come back. Game's not over."

"We'll pick it up later," says Howard, "just leave the board as it is."

As Howard makes his way out of the house and onto the front porch, he hears his mom tell Gall, "Get your little ass in my bedroom, boy. I got something special for you."

Howard steps into the yard just in time to see the wayward traveler, who leads a one-eyed mule. The mule drags a wagon brimming with harpoons and nets, and shambling behind the rickety wooden carriage, on tethers of varying lengths, are the naked jaws of sharks, their multitudes of teeth chipping and chirping along the dirt. There is a music to it all, a sort of macabre waltz or a hysterical dirge. All percussion. All noise. Bloodcurdling. Amusing. Daffy. Absurd.

The traveler looks up, contemplates Howard. "What are the people here like?" he asks.

Howard thinks a moment. "They're motherfuckers," he says.

The traveler nods. "Then you'll need one of these," he says. He takes a harpoon from his wagon, walks it to Howard and sets it in his hands.

Howard is confused.

"You'll understand when the time comes," says the traveler. He smacks his mule's hindquarters and the mule drags forward.

Just as he's leaving, Howard sees, in the front seat of the wagon, sitting on a pillow, a decapitated head with a cut on its cheek.

SHANE MCKENZIE

LOCATION:
Austin, TX

STYLE OF BIZARRO:
Sticky, Icky, Make You Sicky

BOOKS BY MCKENZIE:
Infinity House
All You Can Eat
Bleed on Me
Drawn & Quartered
Muerte Con Carne
Jacked
Fat Off Sex & Violence
Addicted to the Dead
Pus Junkies
Stork
Escape From Shit Town
Sixty-Five Stirrup Iron Road
Parasite Deep
Blood, Sex, Slime, & Chinese Food
Fairy
Toilet Baby
Leprechaun in the Hood: The Musical:
    A Novel
Jackpot
The Oak
The Bingo Hall
Wet & Screaming
Beautiful Monster

DESCRIPTION: Imagine someone tells you to close your eyes. They hand you a cold drink. "It's Pepsi," they say. "Ah, that sounds nice," you think, and you take a drink, but it's milk instead. For a brief moment, you have no idea what is in your mouth and you freak out, but then realize, "Oh, it's just milk. All is well." Then you take off your blindfold and get punched in the fucking face. Yeah. It's kind of like that.

INTERESTS: Gushing blood, slashers, chainsaws, slashers who use chainsaws to make blood gush, peanut butter flavored anything, lucha libre, animated kids' movies, fairy tales, cooking, fishing, football, basketball, belly button sniffing, hadoukens.

INFLUENCES: Michael Jackson's Thriller, 80s and 90s horror movies, Scary Stories to Tell in the Dark, Tales from the Crypt, R.L. Stine, Dr. Seuss, Tim Burton, Teenage Mutant Ninja Turtles, X-Men, Garbage Pail Kids, John Carpenter, Robert Rodriguez, WWF, WCW, Street Fighter, Mortal Kombat, Disney Animated Movies, Weird Al Yankovic, Joe Bob Briggs, Lloyd Kaufman, Charles Band, Joe R. Lansdale, Clive Barker, Richard Laymon, Brian Keene, Edward Lee, Wrath James White, John Skipp, Bentley Little, Carlton Mellick III, and your grandparents.

WEBSITE:
shanemckenzie.org

THE KAIJU KID

FORTUNE CITY

It was a hot day in Fortune City. The citizens slogged through the streets, tongues hanging from mouths, flesh glistening with sweat. The concrete was like a frying pan, melting the rubber on tires and the bottoms of shoes.

So when they first felt the cool breeze blow in, they were grateful. Ecstatic really.

People stopped in their tracks, eyes closed as they allowed the chilled air to sweep over them. Drivers stepped out of their vehicles to feel the arctic caress of this mystery wind slap against their sweat-soaked skin. There was a smile on every face. A collective sigh of relief.

The sighs became screams when the giant bird cast its titanic shadow over the city, zooming over skyscrapers and highways. Its caw was like a clap of thunder, so deep and loud that glass shattered on buildings and cars alike. The bird's eyes shone a dark violet color, like two giant black light orbs. The talons on its leathery feet were as black as ink, as long as sedans.

"Condoria!" a woman screamed, clutching her child to her chest and pointing toward the sky. "Oh jesus... *Run!*"

Others made similar exclamations, and just as the citizens began to scatter, race in all directions, the massive bird squeezed out an egg. It was orange, the size of a house, shining as bright as the sun. The egg smashed into a building, cracking on impact. A wave of molten lava exploded out of the shell, splashing against the building and melting it

almost instantly. Bright orange magma rained down in the streets, along with liquefied metal and glass.

The woman with the child pressed to her chest shrieked once, loud and shrill, before she and her infant were enveloped in lava. Two red skeletons stood in their place, but only for a moment before the bones collapsed and blended in with the rushing magma. Drivers were fused to their vehicles by molten metal and rock, only having seconds to scream in agony before their flesh sloughed off their bones.

Condoria perched on top of the melting building, spread her bat-like wings. Her wingspan was nearly the size of the building she stood upon, an orange glow reflecting off the black, venous membranes of her wings. She screeched— more glass exploded, car alarms went off. She launched herself from the building, swooped over the street. Her wings cut buildings in half as she flew, burying terrified citizens in rubble. She opened her razor-sharp beak, scooped up a mouthful of humans. They screamed, flailing and fighting each other to get out, to jump to freedom even if it meant death. But she slammed her beak shut at the same time that her talons closed over more human flesh. Severed arms and legs, a few heads fell from her mouth, spraying blood as they dropped back to the broken concrete beneath. The few humans who had survived her clutching claws—and who were still in her grasp—exploded into hysterics, thrashing to free themselves, surrounded by dead men and woman who were impaled by the giant bird's talons.

She flapped her wings, hovered over the street, opened her beak. Entrails and tattered flesh and splintered bone littered her mouth, and she jammed one clawful of humans in, crunching them into a thick red paste. Then the other clawful. Blood and meat splashed to the street beneath her.

The ground began to rumble then. The cool breeze that had only moments before brought a smile to every face in the city became an icy storm that cut flesh like razor blades. The sky turned ashen as a heavy snow began to fall, coming out of nowhere, frosting the buildings and concrete in minutes.

A mighty roar rang out, coming from the direction that most of the citizens were running toward. They stopped, tried to turn tail, but Condoria was there waiting, dropped another egg that cracked in the street, sent a wave of molten lava toward them, incinerating the crowd.

One man driving an 18-wheeler climbed out of the cab, stood on the truck's trailer. The vehicle lowered more and more as the lava melted it down. His skin was red, spewing sweat. But the man wasn't paying attention to that anymore. His eyes were aimed toward the horizon where the strong gusts of freezing wind were coming from, hitting him so hard he was nearly thrown right off his truck.

The lava became a solid river of rock and metal, hissing and sizzling as the sudden winter cooled it almost instantly.

"It's…it's A-Avalanx!" He pointed a shaking finger as the giant stomped toward the city. Towering over their tallest building. The fog caused by the frosty winds and snow was so thick that only the behemoth's silhouette could be seen at first. Each step it took covered miles, shook the very earth. In mere moments, Avalanx appeared, giant icicles falling from his white fur and crashing to the street.

One icicle stabbed straight through an SUV, pinning it to the asphalt. The driver within must have been mid-scream when the frozen lance hit him, entering his mouth and stretching it wide like a snake with its jaw unhinged. The corners of his mouth split all the way down to his neck, spraying blood that froze instantly.

Avalanx roared, smashed a building to rubble with a swing of his massive arm. The stone and metal and glass slammed down on the street, turning fleeing bodies into flattened smears on the blacktop. The colossal beast opened its mouth, its eyes glowing a bright, arctic blue, and unleashed a beam of icy breath that froze the horde of panicked patrons, some falling over and shattering on the ground like ice sculptures. The snow and sleet fell heavier now, the winds became more violent.

Avalanx reached down with his massive hand, grabbed the human popsicles, breaking them into pieces as he clutched his fist, then tossed the frozen mush into his mouth. As he swallowed, he swung his arm again, totaling another building. Then another gust of wintery death breath and another mouthful of human flesh slush.

Condoria flew over the city, dropping eggs, unleashing the liquid hell, gorging on the hysterical humans who had nowhere to run, nowhere to hide.

Avalanx smashed buildings as easily as a child knocking over cardboard cutouts. Turning the once smoldering city into an icy wasteland.

The monsters ate and destroyed until they had their fill. Just like they always did.

By the time the military arrived to defend the city, the Kaiju were gone, leaving the streets covered in lava and ice and human remains.

"Jesus fucking Christ," one soldier said, then turned his head and vomited over a pile of bones. The air was still frosty, the snow still falling. The puke turned solid instantly.

"Avalanx," another soldier said, shaking his head and staring at the aftermath. "And Condoria it looks like."

"What's that?"

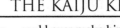

"The most fearsome fucking Kaiju in the world, man. Even if we made it on time, there wouldn't have been a fucking thing we could have done to stop them."

"I…I thought Tyranagon was the most fearsome."

The soldier picked up a frosted skull, ran his thumb over the frozen teeth. "He used to be. But he disappeared. That big fucker hasn't shown himself since the Eternal City incident."

"Eternal City. Those fucking giant fuckwads can't do shit to Eternal City."

"Yeah…well this ain't no fuckin' Eternal City, now is it?"

The soldiers shivered as they began searching for survivors, not expecting to find a single one.

A FUCKING EMBARRASSMENT

"That was sick!" Gigataur said, pumping his clawed fists as Mom soared into their lair. "Did you bring us a taste? Come on… I'm starving."

"Mom, you were awesome," Zapstress said. She grinned wide as blue electric current rode her black, slick flesh. "That city never stood a chance."

Krick sat in the corner of their mountain cave, holding his knees to his chest. He had watched the action along with his brother and sister, but he couldn't find it as exciting as they did. Anytime his parents went out on destruction trips like that, the footage played automatically in the kids' minds, seeing through their parents eyes. Krick wanted to turn it off, but he couldn't. He had to watch as all those poor people were butchered, smashed and melted and frozen and chewed up. It made him sick. Sure, he'd eat the stuff. He had to if he wanted to live. But killing them was different. He wasn't sure if he

could ever make himself do it, no matter how upset it made his parents. Especially his father.

Mom flapped her wings a few times, smiling wide as Gigataur and Zapstress showered her with admiration. Her long, scaly neck quivered as she gagged, then she opened her beak wide and let the pile of meat spill from her throat. Reds and pinks and purples and grays. White bone sticking out here and there. The mush steamed as Dad entered the cave. He patted his belly and picked his teeth.

"Go ahead, kids," Mom said, then stepped aside as Gigataur and Zapstress dug in, stuffing their faces, moaning as they gorged the freshly heaved meal.

She looked over at Krick who stayed in his place in the corner and watched his siblings feast. His stomach rumbled, but he knew better than to try and force his way in. He'd take whatever was left over, just like always. Would probably have to suck the marrow out of the bones again.

"He's a fucking embarrassment," Dad had said just the other night. "He doesn't fit in with the family, Connie. What are we supposed to do with a fucking monster who's too much of a pussy to destroy anything?"

Krick had pretended to be asleep, wiping the slimy tears as they poured from his only eye.

"He's our son, Aval. That's all that matters," Mom had said. "He'll come around. He's just…special. That's all. A late bloomer."

Gigataur slurped up a rope of purple intestine, licked his lips. Each of his four hands was digging into the bloody mound, taking turns stuffing sloppy balls of meat into his mouth, his giant fangs crushing bone with ease. He shot Krick a look, smirked, then belched and snickered.

Zapstress had her back to Krick, ignoring him as usual. She used her electricity to cook the meat before stuffing her face with it. Her eel-like body writhed as she feasted. The electric current crackled as it jumped from her skin and popped in the air.

Krick flinched when a ribbon of current burst just a few feet away from him, memories of his brother holding him down while his sister zapped him again and again flooding his mind.

"Krick, honey," Mom said. She tucked her wings and strolled across the cave. "Aren't you hungry?"

Krick shrugged, pulled his knees in tighter. It was always hard for him to look his mom and dad in the face after they had caused so much death and destruction.

"Let him starve," Dad said, sleet precipitating from his mouth as he spoke. "You want to eat, you need to fight for it. Survival of the fittest...or some shit like that. You hungry, boy? Get your fat ass up and take your share. You don't ask for it, you fucking take it!"

"Yeah, Krick. Come on over. I dare you," Gigataur said, spitting bone shards and blood from his red-painted mouth.

Zapstress just laughed as she whipped her tail, shooting a bolt of electricity at him. It hit him in the arm and he yelped and jumped to his feet.

"That hurt!" Krick said.

Zapstress looked over her shoulder at him, shook her head and smiled. The meat in her hands smoked as she cooked it, then pushed it past her long, pointy teeth.

Mom glared at Dad, hissing, standing tall and stretching her neck. Dad held her stare for a moment, but then snorted and looked away, staring out of their cave and into the distant mountain ranges that surrounded their home.

Mom opened her wings, flapped them hard and fast. Krick's brother and sister were lifted off their feet, thrown into the stone wall across the cave. They grunted, growled, then jumped back on their feet and faced their mother as if they were going to attack her. They quickly lowered their eyes and eventually escaped to their rooms.

"Go ahead, Krick. Eat up," Mom said, then leaned over and kissed him on the forehead, stroked his tiny, flightless wings.

Dad stretched out on the floor, rested his head on a pillow of snow. He yawned, smacked his mouth. Crystalized blood coated his lips, clung to his fur. He watched as Krick tiptoed toward the food, then snorted again and shook his head.

"Goddamn disgrace." Then he turned so his back was to Krick and Mom, and within seconds, was snoring. Each snore released a beam of icy breath that exploded out into the air, hitting mountain tops way off in the distance.

Krick plopped down beside what was left of his parents' kill. He absently grabbed a leg, mostly dissolved by Mom's stomach acids, and popped it into his mouth. The pruned flesh was stripped from the bone as he scraped his teeth across it and pulled it back out of his mouth. A tear escaped his eye, splashed on the cave floor and froze.

Mom sat beside him, wrapped one wing around him. "Don't put too much thought into it, sweetheart. But you know... your dad's right. We're monsters, baby. Monsters destroy. Kill. Without that, we're nothing. You understand that, don't you?"

Krick shrugged, poked at a woman's head with his finger. There was a bite taken out of her cranium, the brains spilling out. Krick scooped them out, sucked them up. Always his favorite.

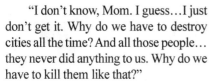

"I don't know, Mom. I guess…I just don't get it. Why do we have to destroy cities all the time? And all those people… they never did anything to us. Why do we have to kill them like that?"

"To survive. Those people? You know what they eat? Smaller animals. Or bigger, stupider animals. That's just the way it is. Everything is food for something else. Except for us."

Krick thought back to all the training sessions he had had with his parents, side by side with Gigataur and Zapstress. His siblings were natural born Kaiju. Destroying was automatic for them. They had discovered their special abilities before they could even walk.

But not Krick. He would always hurt himself somehow, get laughed at by his brother and sister. His father used to beat him, thinking it would toughen him up, accelerate the learning process. But instead, it only made Krick cry, run to his mother for support.

Dad would make giant mock cities with his ice breath and Mom would fly around the mountains, collecting goats to act as fleeing people. Gigataur and Zapstress looked like they were having the time of their lives, smashing ice buildings, devouring handfuls of goats.

Krick, wanting so desperately to fit in and to impress his father, swung as hard as he could, smashing his fist into the nearest building. The ice didn't even budge. Krick's red knuckles split and bled, and he shrieked, fell to the ground bawling. The goats climbed his body and *baaaahed*, seeing him as no threat whatsoever.

"Well maybe I wasn't supposed to be a monster, Mom. Maybe it was a mistake. You know?" Krick scratched one of the black spots that covered his red, spongy body. They always itched,

used to drive him crazy, but he was starting to get used to it.

"Of course you were supposed to be a monster. You're part of the most feared family of Kaiju in the world, don't you realize that? Your father and I…we're legends, baby. Parents tell stories about us to their children. People live in fear at all times, wondering if Condoria or Avalanx will come to their city. And one day, they will say the same about you and your brother and sister. You'll see."

"Yeah, Gigataur and Zapstress, but not me. They'll laugh at me. Their armies would kill me. It wouldn't even be hard. I don't have any special abilities…I'm just a useless pile of blubber." He scooped up the last of the masticated, semi-digested meat and filled his mouth, then wiped another tear from his giant eye.

"Krick," Mom said, holding him tighter, resting her beak on the top of his head. "You'll find your ability. It's in you. All Kaiju have at least one. We just have to search for it. Dig deep."

"I've tried. I've tried so hard…but… but all I can do is this." Krick squeezed his fists, strained so hard that his body shook. One of the black spots on his belly bulged, looked like a zit ready to pop. A tiny version of Krick pushed itself out and floated down to the floor as it flapped its miniature wings. Its skin was a lighter shade of red, paler, diseased. Its eye was dark yellow, covered in pus that leaked down its face and into its mouth. It struggled to walk, dragging its feet, coughing and wheezing. Green phlegm sprayed from its mouth and splashed to the floor. It only made it a few steps before falling over. Dead.

Mom stared at the tiny version of her son, put on an obvious fake smile. "Hey… I've never seen an ability like that. It's… original at least, right?"

Krick rolled his eye, sighed. "Dad was so mad at me when I first did that... I could see how disgusted he was just to look at me. He hates me, doesn't he? Just like Gigataur and Zapstress. They all hate me."

"That's not true. We're family. We might be proud, but we love each other. We stick together."

"You're not ashamed of me, Mom? I can't...do anything." Krick never felt like he truly fit in. There were times he had thought about running away...or just jumping right off the mountain. He didn't think his family would even notice he was gone. Either that or they'd throw a party.

Mom kissed him again, yawned. "Stop talking like that, baby. You've got a big day tomorrow."

"What do you mean...tomorrow? What's happening tomorrow?"

She curled up next to Dad, wiggled her body as she settled in. "Come on, Krick. You know. It's what you and your brother and sister have been training for. It's your first day."

Oh my god...that's tomorrow? I'll be killed!

"Mom...no. I-I can't. You know I can't."

"Shhh. Quiet now, baby. I'm...exhausted. You'll do...just...fine. I know... you will...." And then she was asleep, leaving Krick alone with his thoughts.

Tomorrow. They're going to take the three of us to our first real city tomorrow. And they'll all laugh at me. Even Mom will be embarrassed to have me as a son when she sees me fail.

Krick snuck past his slumbering parents, stood right on the edge of the cliff. Below him was a seemingly endless abyss of ice and snow and rock. Strong winds threatened to push him over, and he contemplated just tipping himself forward, letting the wind take him away.

But his cowardice won, as it always did, and he went back to his corner, curled up, and dreaded being alive.

***

Pelican Bay. Krick thought it was a silly name. Didn't seem very intimidating, actually made him feel a little bit better about the situation.

"This should be a piece of cake," Dad said. "No messing around, though. Sometimes these little cities will surprise you. You remember Cyclopiton?"

Gigataur and Zapstress nodded, licking their lips as they stared at the city in the distance. Krick had never heard that name before.

"It was a city like this that did him in. Hidden missiles. Blew his fat head right off his shoulders."

Pelican Bay suddenly didn't sound so silly anymore.

Dad, Gigataur, and Zapstress waded through the ocean toward the city. Krick sat on Mom's shoulders as she soared over the water. Dad created a curtain of fog to hide them.

"One of you should be able to handle Pelican Bay...so the three of you should take it no problem. I want to see smashed buildings. I want to see people screaming, running in all directions, you got me? I want total destruction. Eat all you can, kids." He pulled Gigataur and Zapstress close, hugged them. "Make me proud."

Krick wanted so bad to be hugged by his father. He sighed from his mother's shoulders, crossed his arms. She turned her long neck so she could look back at him, smiled, rolled her eyes playfully. Then she pecked a kiss on

his forehead before picking up speed and zooming toward the city. She was a great mother. The best mother a monster could ever ask for.

"Here we go, Krick. You can do this, I know you can."

Below them, Gigataur and Zapstress roared as they approached the coast.

It was time to put their training to the test.

PELICAN BAY

It was Fish Fest in Pelican Bay. The biggest festival of the year. Fish Fest was important to the small city because it brought in so many tourists, helped keep the city financially afloat for the rest of the year. The flounder were breeding. Folks could barely step into the water without stomping on one hiding in the sand. The beaches were covered with gig-pole-toting tourists, stabbing their spears into the sand and pulling out massive flounder one after another.

Rachel hated Fish Fest. She thought fish was gross and didn't understand how anyone ate it. Her mom took her to the beach, which she normally loved. Swimming and building castles and pretending like she was the princess who lived inside. But there were too many people during the stupid flounder festival, and she didn't have enough room to do much but dig a hole.

"Can we go home now?" Rachel said, tugging on the bottom of her mother's sun dress.

"Aren't you having fun?" her mother said. She didn't even bother to look up from the novel she was reading. "Look at all these kids, honey. Go make some friends."

"I don't want any friends. I'm a princess. I need my castle!"

"Well that's too bad." Her mother sipped on her margarita, licked the green slush from her lips. "Go entertain yourself. Mommy's busy."

Rachel growled and stomped her foot. She wished all these people would disappear. Just go away so she could play on the beach by herself.

I hate all of these people and I hate flounders and I hate everything!

"What the hell is that?" A male tourist dropped his gig pole and pointed up at the sky. A loud, ear-shattering screech filled the air like Gabriel's trumpet announcing the end of the world.

The fishermen paused, a few with flopping flounder impaled on the end of their spear. Children playing in the sand froze in place. All eyes were on the sky as the giant bird soared overhead.

"Mommy?" Rachel said, now clinging to her mother's leg.

Her mother's book had fallen into the sand. She held her margarita with shaking hands, the straw clinking against the edge of the glass. Her mouth opened and closed, but she was only making a squeaking sound.

"Fuck me! *It's Condoria!*" a man shrieked, then tossed his gig pole into the water and sprinted toward the parking lot.

But the bird never landed. Another monster dropped from its back and slammed down hard on the beach. Sand poofed up into the air, blocking Rachel from seeing the thing too good. The sand cleared and everyone screamed. The monster was on its side, legs kicking, clutching its belly as if the fall had injured it. Its skin was as red as the devil, black spots covering its body like lesions.

As the beachgoers continued to scream and scramble over each other in search of safety, the massive beast flinched, sat up and faced them. It had one giant eye, as orange as pumpkin flesh. Thick arms hung at its sides, the legs short and stubby. The creature was hairless, looked flabby and smooth, almost soft as if it were covered in baby fat. It had tiny bat-like wings on its back that flapped uselessly.

Even as the people shrieked and ran for their lives, the monster just sat there, staring at them, almost as if it were scared of them instead of the other way around. It was such a curious sight that a few of the people stopped running so they could study the beast.

"What's it doing?" one man said.

"Look at it, Mommy," Rachel said as she smiled and pointed up at the monster who was now getting to its feet. "He's not mean. He's cute!"

"Cute? It's…hideous. Let's go home before it gets hungry. I can't believe a Kaiju is right here in Pelican Bay. I never thought they would… Rachel, what are you doing? *Get back here now!*"

Rachel strode toward the monster, now giggling and waving at it. It turned and looked at her, blinked its one eye.

"I like him, Mommy! I want him! Can I keep him? I want him I want him I want him!" Rachel stopped just in front of the monster. She dug her toes in the sand and waved up at him, smiling.

The monster stared at her, then opened his mouth. Rachel gasped, took a step back. She kept her eyes on him as everyone around her screamed for her to run, that the monster was going to eat her. She didn't know why, but she didn't believe that. Not this monster.

"Rachel, get away from that thing!" Her mother grabbed her from behind, tried to pull her away, but Rachel ripped her hand out of her mother's grasp.

The monster still didn't move, still had its mouth open. It looked to be…smiling at her. Though its teeth were sharp, they were small, mostly gums showing.

"What's going on?" another man said. "Why's it just standing there like that? What kind of Kaiju is this thing?"

"Hi," Rachel said.

The monster lifted its giant hand, stared at its palm as if not sure what to do with it, then waved at Rachel.

"See, Mommy? He's nice. He likes me!"

"Well would you look at—"

A ball of bright blue electricity exploded out of nowhere and hit Rachel's mother, enveloping her completely. She shook in place, mouth and eyes opened as wide as they could go. Blood squirted from her tear ducts, from her nose, rushed from her mouth. Her eyes exploded as her skin began to blacken. It wasn't until her body ruptured and sprayed the people around her with boiling hot gore that they took up running again.

"M-Mommy?" Rachel's eyes widened as she stared at the sloppy chunks of meat that used to be her mother lying in the sand. She screamed as she dropped to her knees, grabbing as many pieces as she could carry. *A doctor can fix her. He can put her back together if I get enough pieces.*

The monster whined, stomped its feet. Rachel screamed again when it scooped her up into his huge red arms. She dropped the wet pieces of her mom. The monster held her tight, but not tight enough to harm her. Rachel stopped shrieking as she and the monster faced the water.

Salt water splashed as the sea parted, and a giant form rolled out of the water toward the shore. It spun like a gargantuan bowling ball, covered in spikes twice the size of grown men. It hit the beach and threw sand in all directions, picking up speed. The thing was coming right at them, and the red monster turned his back to it, curled into a protective ball and surrounded Rachel with its soft body.

Rachel couldn't see, but she knew the giant spiked ball hit the red monster when he squealed in pain. There was a hard collision, and then weightlessness. They spun for a few moments, felt like they were floating away, and then a hard slam. Rachel's teeth clicked hard as she bounced around, and there was a sudden pain in her leg. The red monster uncurled itself once they finally settled, and Rachel saw that they were not on the beach anymore, but in the middle of the city. There was a huge chunk missing from the building next to them, pieces of it still falling off. The red monster sat up and groaned, glanced at her with his enormous eye, almost like he was embarrassed.

A few of the black spots on his skin started to pulsate. Rachel screamed when the small monsters crawled out and floated through the air, tiny wings flapping. They made gurgling sounds like they had the flu or something, but before they could land, more pieces of the building detached and crushed the smaller monsters against the street below. Green slime burst from their flattened bodies.

Rachel wept, wiping tears from her eyes and calling for her mother.

The red monster gasped, hopped back to his feet as he grabbed Rachel again and held her close. The spiky ball started rolling again, making the ground shake as it came. The running people screamed as they were rolled over, pressed flat against the sand, ground into the tiny grains, shredding their flesh. Bodies hung from the spikes, blood and organs splattering in all directions as the monster spun forward and the bodies were torn apart.

Another form burst from the ocean, its body long and slick just like an eel's, the mouth full of long, pointy teeth. Blue lightning crackled as it rode this creature's wet hide and shot out of its body. Humans were cooked on contact. The monster ran on four legs, its six snake-like arms scooping up the barbequed remains of its victims and stuffing the black, charred flesh into its mouth. Dark blood and hot grease sprayed from its jaws as it chewed.

The barbed wrecking ball tore a hole right through the city. It broke the highway into pieces and smashed bridges. Countless people and vehicles were flattened and impaled. The monster left a trail of blood-soaked wreckage in its wake as it thundered forward. It finally came to rest in the center of the small cluster of buildings. Tattered bodies hung from its spikes, raining blood and minced entrails over the cracked concrete.

The ball shook, rattling against the concrete, then slowly opened. The monster roared as it burst open. Gore was flung in every direction, slapping against the buildings and slowly sliding down the sides.

Rachel clung to the spongy flesh of the red monster. She chewed on the inside of her cheek to keep from screaming or crying out and alerting the other more fierce monsters. Panicked voices filled the air as the tourists and residents alike scattered. They ran aimlessly; others jumped into their vehicles, all desperately trying to escape from the vicious creatures turning the city into their hellish playground.

The spiked monster stretched its four thick, armored arms, each equipped with long, curved claws. Its massive legs resembled an elephant's, the skin tough-looking and gray. When it roared again, it revealed the rows and rows of teeth, dripping with saliva.

"Don't let them get me," Rachel whispered as tears streamed down her chubby, freckled cheeks.

The red monster whined and turned

its head from left to right. When it took off running, its feet leaving craters in the street, the people scattered and shrieked up at them.

"Get the fuck away from us!" a man screamed as he pulled his family behind him. He reached a brown minivan, and just as he placed his hand to the door handle, a burst of bright current engulfed the vehicle and blackened the metal instantly. The man froze, his body seizing, shaking violently as the voltage entered his flesh, rode into his wife, and then into their two children. They stood in place, hand in hand—cooking. Their flesh smoked and popped as it darkened.

The earth quaked as the electric eel beast charged. It slammed its jaws shut over the family and chewed them all together until they were nothing more than shredded meat and bone shards.

"Nonononono!" Rachel covered her ears and shook her head.

The red monster backed away from the eel, then spun and sprinted in the other direction. It lost its balance, stumbled and slammed its side into a building. Stone and metal rained over the street, but the building held, looked sturdier and stronger than the others. The bits of rubble that had broken free smashed down around the monster's feet, mangling a group of Asian men and women snapping pictures.

The red monster grunted, then dropped to a knee and placed Rachel on the ground. The pavement was sticky with blood. Body parts lay all around her. She shook her head and glared up at the monster, not sure what he was doing.

The monster reached out and nudged her with his knuckle, shoving her toward the double doors of the building. There was already a huge group of people inside, all huddled together and crying, mumbling to one another.

"Take me with you. You can't leave me here!"

The monster rubbed the back of his head and whined some more. The pupil in his massive eye darted around, looked anywhere but at Rachel.

"Please!"

The building started to shake, more glass and rock and metal falling all around them. Rachel screamed and ran to the monster who immediately scooped her into his hand and backed away from the building.

The spiked monster had its four arms wrapped around the building. Its teeth were bared as its claws tore into the structure like it was made from Play Doh. The bigger, scarier monster turned its head and stared right at Rachel, then growled as it peered into the red monster's eye. It roared, ripped the building from the ground with ease. Bodies spilled from the bottom like beans from an open can, splattering against the pavement below. An avalanche of rubble slammed into the congregation of people who had been inside of the building. Blood splashed out, some of it spraying Rachel in the face and stinging her eyes.

"Gghhaaaa!"

The beast shook the building, emptying it of its fleshy morsels, then swung it like a bat at the neighboring building, smashing both to rubble. It reached down, grabbed two handfuls of kicking and screaming human flesh, filled its mouth and swallowed.

The red monster growled, deep and guttural. Rachel realized the sound had come from his stomach just as he bent down and filled his fists with leaking corpses.

"Wh-what are you doing?"

Electricity shot through the air, crackled as it entered flesh and metal all around them. The entire city glowed blue as the eel creature pumped more and more voltage into it. People were cooked, and then consumed in bunches. Dark blood and melted fat coated the streets.

The red monster's pupil rolled until it was aimed at Rachel, then he swung her around and put her behind his back. But she could still hear the sound of him chewing, the bones crunching as he ate. Rachel thrashed and punched at the monster's hand, trying to free herself. She didn't know where she'd go or what she'd do, but she wanted to get away from the monsters. All of them. As far away as she could.

He's not nice. He's just like the others! I want my mommy!

Rachel was able to spin herself around, then wiggle free from the hand. She stood on the thumb, but it was still too high to jump. When she saw that the spiked beast was just in front of her, chewing, she stuffed herself back into the fist, then peered out through the space between fingers.

The creature tilted its head back and swallowed, then opened its jaws and roared. It dropped down to its hands and feet, then curled itself back into a wrecking ball. The spikes aligning its body shot free from its shell, penetrated buildings and pavement and bodies. What remained of the city was turned to ruins as the monster rolled again, its body now almost entirely covered in the blood of thousands upon thousands of humans. When it uncurled, it lowered its face to the streets and gorged on the mutilated remains.

The red monster swung his arm back around so that it could look down at Rachel again. His mouth was dripping with gore. All Rachel could do was cry and pray to God to save her. The monster's eye squinted, and he whined again as he glared at her in his palm.

The two ferocious monsters filled their bellies, satiated their need for destruction, and then retreated back to the ocean where they seemed to disappear behind a white, winter-like fog.

The red monster watched them go, flapped its tiny wings as if expecting to fly away. The giant bird appeared out of the sky, swept down, gripped the red monster with its talons, and then soared into the air.

"No! No, let me go!" Rachel dropped to all fours and bit down hard on the monster's hand. Orange blood filled her mouth just as the fingers opened.

She realized how stupid she was once the wind whipped over her and she began plummeting toward the ground. Her mind was focused on getting away from the monsters, and now as she dropped, faster and faster, she screamed for the red monster to save her.

Its pupil swung toward her and its mouth unhinged as if screaming.

Rachel's body twisted in the air, and the last thing she saw was the blood-stained pavement below speeding toward her.

NO SON OF MINE

Krick and his mother arrived to the cave first, and he immediately ran to his corner, covered his face so he didn't have to look his mother in the eye.

"Krick…" she started, but didn't say another word.

She's embarrassed. Just like I knew she'd be. And I don't blame her.

"Just leave me alone!" He couldn't get that little girl's face out of his head. The way she had smiled at him, trusted him to keep her safe. It was like they had a connection, a friendship—child and monster. A connection he never felt with his own family. And now the little girl is nothing but a splatter of blood, bone, and entrails mixed in with the rest of the massacre they had left behind.

Gigataur and Zapstress entered the cave, cheering and cackling. Their faces and bodies were caked with gore, and they took one look at Krick balled up in his corner, and their laughter grew in intensity.

"What happened, Krick?" Gigataur said, picking bones from between his teeth. "Did all those scary little people frighten you, tough guy?"

Zapstress shook the blood from her face and head. "What the hell were you doing back there, little brother? Carrying that baby human around like she was your girlfriend or something. That it, Krick? You falling in love with the food now?"

"Shut up!" Krick roared, spittle flying from his lips. "Just…just shut up. Please…"

Gigataur puffed up his chest, started toward Krick. "Why don't you make me, blubber boy?"

"Enough," Mom said. "Just leave him be, will you?"

"No," Zapstress said. "I'm sick of him shaming our family. And now the people saw it too? They weren't even scared of him. No…I can't have them thinking our family is weak because of him. I say we kill him. Just end it now. I'll make it quick." Sparks ignited across her body, boiling the blood that still coated her, filling the cave with its meaty scent.

"You won't touch him," Mom said, spreading her wings. "Neither one of you. It was his first time out…give him a break."

"It was our first time out, too," Gigataur said, glaring at Krick over Mom's shoulder. "And we kicked ass. Did you see us? We wrecked that place. You ask me, looked more like he was trying to save the city rather than destroy it. "

"I ate people too!" Krick shouted, returning his brother's stare, but still staying safely behind his mother. "I ate lots of people."

"Yeah," Zapstress said. "I saw you. Picking up the scraps. Those were our kills, not yours. Don't you have any dignity? You're like a goddamn scavenger."

"I am not!"

"Yes you are." Dad stepped into the cave, his expression austere. "You're not a monster. The offspring of Avalanx and Condoria should be feared by every living creature on this planet. Yet a little girl smiles at you…and you carry her around like your own personal pet human? You try and save her? A human child? My own son…*my own fucking flesh and blood!"*

"Aval—"

"Quiet! I've had enough of you protecting him. We are monsters. Kaiju. We aren't supposed to need protection. We're not supposed to hide behind our mothers and shiver."

"Dad…I'm sorry. I tried…I really tried." Krick couldn't hold back his tears, his words coming out sloppy and wet. "Please. Let me try again. I'll do b-better."

Gigataur and Zapstress snickered.

"You've already shown me what you can do. Your special ability seems to be bringing shame to your family. And I'm done with you." Dad's eyes shone blue, and he opened his mouth as if he were ready to blast Krick with his icy breath.

Mom screeched, flapped her wings as hard as she could. Dad didn't budge, but he closed his mouth, bared his teeth. Sleet burst from between his lips with every breath he took and piled up at his feet.

"I don't care what you say. He's my son…*our* son. We don't just discard our children. We might be monsters…but we're not fucking heartless. Aval…please. Think about this."

"I've already thought it over. It's been a long time coming, Connie. And you know it. If you weren't here…I'd eat him myself. I'd rip him to pieces and let his brother and sister strip the meat off his bones."

Mom backed up until her body was pressed up against Krick. Krick could barely see through his tears now, the entire cave blurry. He bawled as his father expressed his hate for him. Not that it was a big surprise, but to hear the words said out loud, to confirm what he had always suspected cut like talons.

Dad snorted, the glow in his eyes diminishing. "He can stay the night here. But this cave is for family. And he's no son of mine. Not anymore. Tomorrow, he's gone." He slammed his fist against the cave wall, shaking it. It felt like it would crumble in on them. Then Dad turned his back to them, just like he always did to Krick, and stared off into the mountains.

"Thank God," Zapstress said. "It's about time."

"Bye bye, dog dick. The next time I see you…I'll bite your face off." Gigataur chuckled as he headed to his room, patting his meat-filled belly.

Mom stayed in front of Krick, shielding him. But she wouldn't look at him. Didn't say another word. She settled in, folded her wings, and laid her head down. Heat radiated off her body, making Krick comfortable and sleepy. He wanted so desperately to hug her, envelope himself in her feathers like he used to. But he didn't dare. He just sat there, rested his head against the wall. Sleep wouldn't come, so he contemplated what was in store for him tomorrow.

Maybe I'll finally do it. I'll just jump off the mountain and let the wind take me away.

HOW TO BE A REAL MONSTER

When Krick opened his eye, the wind whipped his body from all directions. He hadn't even realized that he had fallen asleep.

Dad threw me out of the cave while I was sleeping. I'll be dead any second now.

As the thought flowed through his mind, he wasn't even upset. It was comforting somehow. It was finally over. His family could be happy, didn't have to worry about him bringing shame and embarrassment to them.

But he wasn't alone.

Talons dug into his shoulders, dimpling the spongy flesh to the point of hurting. Mom held him, flapping her wings, soaring high over the mountains.

Krick didn't recognize these mountains, had no idea where they were. The mountains here were black, steam rising from their peaks. The heat was intense, hotter than he had ever experienced in his life. And yet…it was comfortable. Like he belonged here. A nice change from their frozen cave.

"M-mom? What's going on?"

Then it struck him. *She's going to kill me. She brought me here to drop me into one of these fire mountains… maybe to make Dad happy.*

"It's time you learned, Krick. It's now or never."

"Please, Mom. Please don't kill me…I'll do better. I'll even run away. You won't ever have to see me again. None of you will!"

She actually laughed, shook her head. And then finally looked at him.

Krick didn't see animosity in her eyes. No hate. It was the look of a loving mother. The look she had always given him, no matter how many times he failed.

"I'm not going to kill you, sweetheart. I'm rescuing you. Well…kind of."

"Kind of? But…you said… You said it's time for me to learn. Will you please tell me what's going on here?" Another blast of heat hit him in the face. "Where are we? It's hot as hell out here."

"I think it's time you met someone. Someone who I think can help us."

"Who?"

"My dad. Your grandfather. He's been hiding for years…ever since the incident at Eternal City."

"Eternal City? You mean the indestructible city? The place with the giant Hero?"

"Yes. Your grandfather…he—"

"Tyranogon? Is it? Tell me, Mom, is my grandfather Tyranogon?" Even Krick had been impressed with the stories he had heard. Tyranogon was every young monster's hero. Krick had no desire to destroy or kill, but he still couldn't help but look up to him. He was a legend among monsters and humans alike.

His mom chuckled, nodded her head.

And he's my grandfather!

"Mom…why didn't you tell me? Do Gigataur or Zapstress know?"

They continued to fly, his mother now coasting, riding the hellish wind currents.

"No. Your father…he didn't want any of you to know. Pride, that's all. He wanted you all to look up to *him,* not your grandfather."

Krick smiled. "So I'm the only one who knows…"

He took pride in that. There wasn't much for him to be proud of, and he had never had anything that his siblings wanted. He'd always been the jealous one. But if they knew about this…

"He's here? Grandpa has been hiding in these fire mountains all this time?"

"Don't call him Grandpa. He'll kill you." She sort of giggled, rolling her eyes as if reliving some distant memory. Then she went expressionless. "Seriously… he'll kill you. And these are called volcanoes, sweetheart. He's hiding inside one of them…I just can't remember… There!"

She changed directions so sharply that Krick shrieked, reached up and grabbed hold of the feathers on her belly.

They swooped toward the biggest volcano Krick had seen yet, at least twice as big as the mountain where their cave lay. Splashes of lava shot out the top, spraying the neighboring mountains, the glowing orange magma rolling down the volcano's side.

"How can he live inside of there and still be alive? Wouldn't he…I don't know, be melted or something?"

"Honestly, I haven't seen my dad since before you and your brother and sister were born. For all I know, he *could* be dead." She laughed again. "But if I know Tyranogon like I think I do, he's still alive. Way too stubborn to die."

She landed at the top of the volcano just as another small eruption shook the earth. The lava exploded out, sprayed Mom and Krick, but neither was fazed.

"We've got his blood in us. The heat can't hurt us, baby. Don't worry. Dad's a firebreather. The last firebreather as far as anyone knows."

Krick giggled as the lava coated his body, sliding off his red skin like mercury. He leaned over, peered into the volcano's peak.

Two massive black eyes stared right back at him. A growl erupted out along with another splash of lava, and then the mountain began to quake.

Krick jumped back, clutched his mother's belly, buried his face in her breast feathers.

"Daddy? It's Connie. You in there?"

The ground shook so hard and violently that Krick's mother flapped her wings, hovered over it. Another massive eruption blasted into the air, followed by two giant black hands. They gripped the lip of the volcano's peak, crushing rock like it was moist bread.

The head appeared next, bigger than Krick's entire body, covered in dark scales with horns and spikes protruding out in vicious curves. The black eyes landed on Krick and his mother, squinted, then suddenly widened. The jaw unhinged, revealing a mouthful of long, sharp teeth, as yellow as fire. Twin balls of flame shot from the nostrils.

Krick cringed, expected to be eaten whole along with his mother.

It's been too long, he wanted to shout to her. *He doesn't know who you are anymore! And we're going to die!*

But instead of a monstrous roar, the sound that came out of the legendary beast's mouth was more like a squeal.

"Connie!" Tyranogon pulled the rest of his colossal body out of the volcano, hardly able to fit through with his bulbous belly. His wings uncurled, long and black, though there were rips along the membranes. The veins were fat, bulging, and misshapen. Though his grandfather was clearly overweight, it didn't take away from his fearsome presence. His skin shone in the orange glow of the lava, covered in thick black scales like crags of charred rock. A long, purple forked tongue shot out from between his lips every few seconds, covered in thick white mucus. Steam rolled from his mouth constantly.

"Daddy!" Condoria zoomed toward her father, wrapping her wings around his neck, nuzzling him.

Tyranogon wept as he covered her with fiery kisses, rubbing his cheek against hers.

Krick just hung there in his mother's talons, watching as the two winged Kaiju embraced after years and years of being apart. Then one of Tyranogon's black eyes landed on Krick, and a massive, toothy grin spread across his face.

"You brought me something to eat? You shouldn't have, baby." He spit an inferno from between his scaly lips, enveloping Krick completely. When Krick still

hung there, uncooked and unharmed, the old Kaiju squinted at him. "What the hell is that thing? Why doesn't it die?"

Krick's mom laughed, tossed Krick into the air so that he landed on her back. "This is my son, Daddy. Your grandson. Krick."

"My grandson? I...I have a grandson?"

Krick waved. "H-hi...Tyranogon."

"You sure he's yours, Connie? He's not as impressive as I'd always imagined your offspring would be. You still with that giant snow ape?"

"Dad...come on. Be nice."

"Well didn't I tell you all your kids would look like mutant monkeys?" Tyranogon shot fire from his nostrils as he sighed, then looked Krick over again. "Sorry about that. I didn't mean to offend."

Krick just shrugged, put on a fake smile. "Um...it's okay."

The legendary monster wasn't coming off as very legendary to Krick. He had expected for his very life to be in danger in Tyranogon's presence. That the Kaiju would be more out of control, more violent than this. The fat, gargantuan beast in front of him just seemed lonely, sad. Krick could tell by the look on his mother's face that she felt the same way.

Tyranogon clapped his giant hands together, making a sound like thunder. "You guys hungry? There's villages all around these mountains. No cities though. But the people...oh man. The people around here are delicious. Kind of spicy and sweet at the same time. You have to try them."

He stood at the top of the mountain, stretched his wings as far as they'd go. His wingspan was impressive, and Krick could only stare in awe as they began to flap. Then Tyranogon sort of winced, held his side, and folded the wings back down.

"Maybe later, okay? I'm a little stiff

right now." He gasped as if he was out of breath. It looked like the simple act of flapping his wings took it out of him.

Is he out of shape? Krick thought.

Tyranogon didn't look so good, spitting sheets of fire as he panted.

"It's okay, Dad. I can't stay long anyway," Krick's mom said.

"What are you talking about? You just got here! You can't go...why would you even show up if you were going to rush off like that? Connie...please. Stay a while. I miss you." Smoke started to billow from his eyes. "I've been out here all alone for... God I don't even know."

"Well...can't you just leave this place? Come back with the rest of us?" Krick didn't mean to say it out loud. His mom shot him a quick look that told him to shut his mouth, but his grandfather was already glaring at him. "I mean...everyone still talks about you. They're still scared of you. It would be so cool to get to see you in action, that's all."

Tyranogon shook his head. "I wish it was that simple. The giant Hero...he...he beat me. He beat me in front of everyone. I could never evoke fear in the humans again...not after that."

"I love you, Dad. It really is great to see you," Krick's mom said, reaching behind her with her beak and grabbing hold of Krick by the fat on the back of his neck.

"Connie, don't go. I didn't even get a chance to spend time with my grandson."

She placed Krick into the palm of Tyranogon's hand. The giant beast lowered his head and stared at him, his hand shaking, scaly brow furrowed.

"You'll have plenty of time with him now, Dad. I'm leaving him with you."

"What?" Krick and Tyranogon said at the same time, both with their eyes glued to Condoria who was already flapping her wings to make a retreat.

"Mom," Krick said, hands pressed together as if praying. "Don't leave me here. Please."

"You'd rather I take you back to your father? So he can kill you? Eat you?"

"He was upset. He won't—"

"Yes he will. He wouldn't even hesitate, sweetheart. Monsters...especially men," she said and locked eyes with her father, "are very stubborn and proud beasts. They will eat their own young. They will run away from their families and go into hiding at the very idea of being ridiculed or embarrassed."

"Are you punishing me for leaving, Connie? You have to understand... I had to—"

"I know that, Dad. I know. And I don't blame you. No...this is no punishment. I'm trying to save my child's life. That's all. He might be a red little monkey creature, but I love him."

Krick did his best not to get offended by her words. He knew she was only doing what she thought was best for him. One way or another, Krick couldn't help but imagine he was a dead monster.

"Teach him, Dad. Teach him to be a real monster. The kind of monster you used to be."

"Used to be?" Tyranogon clenched his fists, and Krick jumped out of his palm just in time before being smashed to mush. He clung to one of the horns sticking out of his grandfather's forearm.

Tyranogon stood up straighter, flexed his wings again, shot a massive wave of flame from his mouth. "I am Tyranogon! The most...the most feared..." The old Kaiju started panting again, had to sit down, and grabbed his side. His belly jiggled when he sat, and he hung his head.

"Avalanx wants to kill him. Krick... he just hasn't found himself yet."

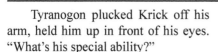

Tyranogon plucked Krick off his arm, held him up in front of his eyes. "What's his special ability?"

Krick wasn't sure if it was the mounting fear boiling inside of him, or just some kind of automatic reaction, but a miniature minion popped free from one of his spots just then, fluttered down, coughing and hacking all the while. By the time it hit the side of the volcano, it was dead, now cooking on the hot rock.

Tyranogon watched it the whole way as it floated down and flapped its tiny wings. Then he shot Condoria another look, shook his head.

"I'll be back soon. We don't have much time. Avalanx will figure it out sooner or later. We need to show him that Krick can destroy and kill just as good as his brother and sister…even better than them. And you're the only one who can show him how, Dad. I love you both."

And then she flapped her wings and was gone.

Krick still dangled from his grandfather's claws, not sure what to say. When Tyranogon's eyes moved from the sky back to Krick, the lonely, tame beast he had been only moments before was gone. He looked ready to bite Krick in half, as if this was all Krick's idea.

"I'm…I'm so sorry. She didn't tell me she was bringing me here."

A ball of flame exploded into Krick's face then, and he stopped talking at once, lowered his eye so as not to meet his grandfather's gaze.

"So you disgraced your family? Father would rather kill you than let you embarrass him?" His voice was like a growl now, lava spilling out from between his teeth. "I don't blame him. Look at you. You're pathetic. Maybe I should just kill you now, make it easy on everyone."

Krick clenched his fists. More of the sick creatures popped out of his spots, fluttered down. "Go ahead. Kill me. Just do it already. I'm sick of everyone talking about it and doing nothing. You want to kill me? *Then fucking kill me!*"

Tyranogon actually flinched, steam billowing from his mouth and nostrils. "Not worth my time." He tossed Krick away like he was nothing more than a booger, sent him crashing into the neighboring volcano, then hurtling down the steep side until slamming into a massive rock. Ash coated his body and he was covered in scrapes and gouges. He peeked around the rock toward his grandfather who was already retreating back into his volcano.

I don't belong anywhere. What is wrong with me?

Krick remained in that spot the rest of the day. Didn't dare move, didn't dare make a sound. He hoped Tyranogon would change his mind, come crawling back out of his volcano to apologize and tell Krick that he would train him, show him how to be a real monster.

But the giant Kaiju never showed. When the day turned to night, Krick lay on his side, still resting up against the rock, and let sleep take him.

***

For the second time, Krick woke up in mid-air. His grandfather flew close to the ground, as if flying any higher was too much of a strain on him. He grunted with every flap of his wings and mumbled something under his breath about being the fiercest Kaiju in the world, but Krick didn't hear all of it over the rushing wind.

"W-where are we going!" Krick shrieked, clutching the scales on Tyranogon's toes.

"Ah, you're…awake. Good."

In the distance, what appeared to be a small village came into view. People began running when they saw the great beast flying toward them, retreating into their huts or their treetop homes. These people didn't wear clothes like the ones Krick had seen, and there weren't any cars or buildings or concrete around.

"Can you please t-tell me what's going on?"

"You're gonna go down there, and you're gonna…you're gonna kill those people. You're gonna kill them and eat them, just like a monster is supposed to." Tyranogon panted, his forked tongue just hanging from his mouth now.

"I-I can't. I can't kill them."

"It's you or them, monkey boy. Because if you don't, you're my…lunch. And I'm getting…hungry."

Then the claws pinching Krick's back released, and he went flying toward the village.

THE VILLAGE OF FIRE

The chief didn't understand why the fire god was punishing them. He and his people had prayed to Him, offered Him sacrifices. The fire god had grown fat on their enemies' flesh, burning their villages to ashes. It was believed that they had pleased Him, that He would reward them.

The fire god roared once and spat fire into the air. It looked like His belly had grown even more since the last time they had seen Him, jiggling as the wind hit it.

He clutched something in His hand. Some kind of red demon, and just as the chief were sure the fire god would wash their village with flame, He dropped the demon and flapped His wings hard, missing their huts by mere feet. It looked difficult for the fire god to lift Himself, barely missing the tops of the trees as He flew away.

The people slowly poked their heads out, exchanged glances with one another and began chattering, each of them wondering what they could have done to anger the fire god. Wondering what this hideous creature could be.

The chief sensed the panic. He threw his hands in the air and called for his tribe to face him, to listen. "May the fire above rain down upon me!"

"May the fire above rain down upon us all!" the men and women chanted back.

The chief—an ancient man, but who still towered over the other men, his shoulders wide and strong—stood on his charred tree stump, slammed the butt of his staff onto the scorched wood. "The fire god burns for us. There is no reason to believe we have angered Him. If that were so, our village would be blazing. Perhaps," the chief said as he spun to face the red demon, "our fire god sent us this creature as an offering. A protector! *Our* protector!"

The great red beast lay on its belly, face buried in the dirt. A deep trench was dug into the ground where the demon had landed and slid across the forest floor. The skin was as red as blood with black spots decorating its hide like a leopard's.

The chief called his men forward, ordered the women and children to stay inside. The men surrounded the chief, and he waved them in closer, spoke in a hushed tone.

"Perhaps this is another test. He is testing our strength. Our fierceness. Be ready."

The men all nodded and grunted their approval, their spears and bows at the ready. The chief stepped forward, wearing a deep scowl as he trudged toward the giant demon.

The demon didn't move. The chief signaled for his people to stand back. As he grew nearer, he could feel the heat emanating off the beast. Sweat began to pour out of his skin.

Some of his men begged him to get away. Begged him to let them check it out first, but the chief insisted. He knew he must remain strong, not just in front of his tribe, but in the presence of the fire god. When he was just beside the demon, he let his palm hover over its red flesh. He prodded the beast in the back with his staff.

When the demon stirred, the men gasped. Even the chief retreated, but only a few steps before puffing out his chest and standing tall again.

A deep groan spilled from the creature's mouth as it sat up, rubbed its face with its massive hands. The demon had one giant eye the color of fire. It slowly rose to its feet, its eye glued to the men. The chief thought he sensed fear there. The demon seemed confused, lost. It could have easily crushed them if it wanted to, but it only stood there, its eye bouncing from man to man.

Then it opened its mouth. The chief thought that maybe the demon was trying to communicate with them, but before it had a chance, one of the men panicked, threw his spear with a shriek.

The spear hit the beast, stuck into one of its legs. Orange blood flowed and the demon roared, fell backward on its rear and yanked the spear out, then rocked back and forth as it pressed its hand to the wound.

The other men wasted no time. They sprinted forward. The chief tried to call them back but none would listen. If this beast was indeed a gift from the fire god,

then they would all burn for their betrayal. Spears and arrows penetrated the monster's flesh, each one making it scream and roar, shaking the trees around them.

As the monster wept, hiding its face from the men, something on its skin began to move. The black spots on its hide began to pulsate, as if each one had its own beating heart. Something began to push against the black flesh from the inside, like a baby kicking from within its mother's womb.

The men gasped, began to back away. The monster continued to hide its face, continued to weep.

Tiny creatures crawled out of the spots. They resembled the giant monster, only they were about the size of the men. They rolled out, plopped to the dirt. Coughing, phlegm rattling at the back of their throats as they tried to breathe. Their skin was a sickly pink color, green mucus coating their eyes, dripping down their faces.

More and more of them kept coming, falling out of the demon's skin. The demon seemed oblivious to this, refusing to look at the men who had just attacked it. As more orange blood pumped from its wounds, more and more of the smaller creatures were birthed from its hide.

And when the smaller creatures saw the men, they moaned, flapped their tiny wings and came for them. The men tried to run, retreat back into their huts or their tree houses where their families waited, where they could guard them from the monsters now swarming their village.

One of the creatures stumbled into the nearest hut, hovering just above the ground. The chief ran toward it, his staff held over his head. He lost his footing and slammed face-first into the dirt, and could only watch as the demon fluttered toward the entrance. The woman and children screamed and hid behind the man of the family, held each other as the creature entered. It coughed, looked ready to fall over and die at any moment.

The man lunged forward, plunged the tip of his spear into the monster's eye, popping it like a ripe plumb. Thick, green jelly exploded from the wound, soaked the man from head to foot.

The monster groaned, clawing at the spear jutting from its face. A stream of hot green bile rocketed from its mouth, splashed across the woman and her two children.

The family shrieked, running around in circles, doing their best to clean the fluid off of each other. It smelled like rotting animal flesh and seemed to burn like acid.

By the time the creature had finally died, the family was no longer panicking. They stumbled out of their hut, all coughing, all wheezing. Most of the other huts and tree houses were already under attack by the creatures, but the hut nearest them was not. As a group, they stumbled inside, vomited over the family within.

The chief rose to his feet and called out to them, begged them to stop, but they ignored him. "Enough! *Enough!*"

The verdant bile sizzled over the family's flesh, soaked in. Within minutes, they were on their feet, stumbling out of the hut and searching for healthy flesh to corrupt.

The creatures that were born from the giant demon's flesh were all dead now. Each one dissolving on the forest floor. But the village was alive with movement. Each of the villagers now shambling around, vomiting and hacking. They all moaned, barely able to walk without falling over. Their skin had become a dark green color, seeping more green fluid as the flesh started to break open and slough off their bones.

They came for the chief, all of them,

reaching for him with slimy fingers. The chief turned to run, now sure that the fire god had turned His back on them, had dropped this hell on them to eradicate the village. Kill them all. But when the chief spun away from the dripping, diseased horde that was his tribe only moments before, he was face to face with the red demon, its fiery eye glaring down at him like the sun.

The monster was no longer weeping. It sat up straight, now ignoring the chief, and sniffed the air. Saliva poured from its mouth. The rumble thundering from its stomach quaked the ground.

The demon stood, licked its lips, and then rushed toward the center of the village, stepping directly over the chief and straight for the tribe.

The sick villagers flocked toward the creature as it devoured them by the handfuls, as if they couldn't wait to be eaten alive. Green slime gushed from the monster's mouth as it stuffed the diseased bodies into it.

The chief hid behind a tree. Watched in horror and disgust as his people, or what used to be his people, willfully gave themselves to the red demon.

Then the wooden trunks nearly bent in half as the wind picked up. The air became so hot, it was hard for the chief to breathe. Sweat spewed from his pores, and he leaned up against the tree, fighting back the tears.

He had done nothing but try and please the fire god. He had taught his people to worship Him, to sacrifice their own children to Him.

The wind continued to grow strength, and then a roar exploded from the sky. The fire god appeared, blocking out the sun with its mass.

A stream of fire exploded from the fire god's mouth as it circled the village, burning the trees, the huts. The chief left his staff behind, ran as fast as his body would allow him into the center of the massacre. He raised both fists into the air and cursed the fire god for betraying him and his people.

A wall of fire swallowed him whole, along with all the trees around him. He only had time to scream once before the fire god's jaws snapped shut over his body and silenced him forever.

A LATE BLOOMER

Krick couldn't stop eating. The smell turned him ravenous—all that succulent, diseased flesh—and he sat cross-legged in the middle of the now-burning village as the sick humans climbed over each other to offer themselves to him. At first, he had wanted to stop his minions from hurting the people, from making them sick. But as soon as that smell hit him, all he could think about was eating. And this meat was…incredible. Nothing like the meat he had force-fed himself before.

If I knew humans could taste like this…I would have been killing them a long time ago.

He thought about what his mother had told him. That humans are food for monsters, just as goats and chickens are food for humans. *There's nothing wrong with eating them,* he told himself as the green and red gore dripped from his mouth. *This is who I am. This is who I was always supposed to be. Besides, they attacked me first.*

Handful after handful, he crammed his mouth, chewed, swallowed, went back for more. The dissolving carcasses of his miniature minions lay all around him. It was like he was in a trance now, gorging himself,

possessed by his voracious appetite.

Something heavy landed behind him, and he knew he should probably face it, but he didn't care. Only filling his belly mattered. He growled, hissed, hoping that whatever was behind him would heed his warning and leave him be.

"What…what did you do?"

The voice sounded familiar, but Krick only growled again, slammed the last of the villagers into his mouth and crushed the contaminated flesh with his teeth, basting his tongue in the spicy juices.

"I've never seen anything like that… why didn't you do that before? If your father—"

"M-my father?" Krick swallowed the masticated meat, stood, curled his hands into fists as hard as boulders. As he pictured his father in his mind, heard his father's voice talking about killing him, disowning him, something in his head started to swell, expand. It felt like an open fire inside of his brain, and he snarled, spun toward the voice behind him. *"My father can burn in hell!"*

An orange and red pillar of fire exploded from Krick's eye, narrowly missing Tyranogon who had to dive out of the way. The fire burned a hole right through the trees behind his grandfather, the entire forest now aflame.

Krick took a deep breath, calmed the pressure in his brain. He wiped the tears from his eye, gasped as Tyranogon struggled to rise back to his feet. Krick ran to him, hands out in front of him.

"I'm so sorry! I didn't-I didn't realize that was you. I kind of…lost myself there. Tyranogon…I'm really really sorry. Please don't—"

"Grandpa. Call me Grandpa." Tyranogon stared at Krick with a wide, toothy grin on his face.

Krick reached up, touched his eye.

Did that fire really come out of me? Was that my special ability?

Krick only wished that his brother and sister could have seen him. They would have shit themselves for sure. And his father. His father might finally be proud of him, might finally accept him into the family.

Krick couldn't help but smile, wanted to jump up and down and shout with joy, but held back, kept cool in front of his grandfather.

"I'll be honest," Tyranogon said. "I thought the villagers were going to kill you. I was kind of counting on it, you know? I was going to tell your mother that there was an accident while I was trying to train you. But clearly…I was wrong about you. Everyone is wrong about you."

Krick was nearly offended that his grandfather was trying to have him killed, but he was still too excited about this special ability to care.

"I thought you didn't like to kill people. You looked pretty pleased if you ask me," Tryanogon said, spitting fire into the air as he laughed and pointed to the burning village.

Krick wiped the mess from his mouth, smacked his lips. "I didn't mean to eat them *all*. But I was hungry…and they smelled so *good!*"

He looked back toward the village, his minions now reduced to bubbling puddles of liquid sizzling in the fire. The village and trees around them crackled as they burned, the air full of black smoke. Krick did feel bad for killing them all, but he couldn't deny that it felt right. Like this is what he was supposed to do.

A late bloomer, that's what Mom said. Maybe she was right. Maybe I finally bloomed!

Tyranogon poked a claw at one of Krick's spots. "Those tiny things that come out of you. What are they?"

Krick shrugged. "Don't know. It just happens sometimes. Whenever I get scared, I think. Any time I feel threatened. There's never been more than a few at a time before, though. I was always embarrassed. My dad said it was a useless, stupid ability. And I believed him…"

Tyranogon just stared at Krick, eyes wide, slightly shaking his head. But it wasn't disappointment in his eyes. Krick was used to seeing that. Tyranogon looked…excited.

Krick put his hands behind his back, rocked back and forth on his feet. "So…what just happened?"

Tyranogon chuckled, flicked his tongue. "What just happened is…I think we may have found the key to destroying Eternal City."

"Wait…what are you—"

Tyranogon stared up at the sky, smiling, the flames dancing around him and casting their orange light over his black scales. "Krick, you just might be the most ferocious monster I've ever seen. Even more so than myself. Now come on!"

Before Krick could say another word, his grandfather's claws seized him by the shoulders and they were flying through the air, back toward the volcanoes.

MONTAGE

His grandfather's words repeated themselves in his mind, again and again. *How can I be the most ferocious monster in the world? That doesn't make any sense.*

Tyranogon had been busy for hours, shaping the molten rock into tall, building-like structures. Krick just sat there, trying to will his minions to pop out of him again. No matter how hard he tried, how hard he concentrated, he could only force out one at a time.

Concentrating on his eye now, he pushed and pushed until he gave himself a headache, but no pillar of fire. Not even a wisp of smoke. He would have thought he had imagined the entire incident if his grandfather hadn't been there to witness it.

"Grandpa?"

"Uh-huh." Tyranogon was making some finishing touches to the cooling rock, stood back and admired his work. It really did look like some kind of stone city.

"How can I destroy Eternal City? I can't even control my abilities. They'll kill me!"

Tyranogon shook his head. "They'll never see you coming, Krick. They're expecting some giant Kaiju. Like myself. They've prepared for it, perfected their defense. Even at my prime, I failed. But you? You're special. You'll get under their skin, destroy them from the inside out."

"But…how?"

Tyranogon opened his wings, stretched them as far as they would go. Lava spilled from his mouth like a waterfall as he stomped toward Krick, eyes now wide with rage. He tilted his head back and roared, so loud that he dwarfed the sound of the volcanic eruptions all around them.

Krick jumped to his feet, searched around them to figure out what it was that had upset his grandfather so suddenly. But they were alone.

Tyranogon shot a massive wall of flame toward Krick, completely surrounding him with fire. The giant Kaiju's hand came crashing down at Krick, barely missing him, crushing the rock where Krick had been sitting.

Krick covered himself, couldn't stop his body from shaking. Whatever semblance of courage he had built up had just been swallowed by Tyranogon's roar.

And then they came. Pushing out of his spots. The minions fluttered toward Tyranogon, but were quickly killed by the heat, uselessly plopping to the ground and melting at once.

And then Tyranogon's roar became raucous laughter, and he slapped his belly as he spat flames into the air with each chuckle. He dropped down to his knees and scooped up a few of the liquefying bodies.

"These minions of yours, Krick. They are the key. This is why you were brought to me, don't you see? It's fate. Together we can take that city down. Show the world that nothing can save them from the monsters."

Krick smiled, picked up one of the minions and studied it in his palm. "Like the people in that village."

"Exactly. This is where all of the others have failed at destroying Eternal City. They concentrate on stopping the weapons. Destroying the buildings. It's the people, Krick. The humans. We get down there with them, destroy them on their level. The rest will follow naturally." The minions in his hand had dissolved to liquid, and he wiped it off, patted Krick on the head. "Your minions will spread the disease, and the people will flock to you, rendering their weapons useless. The buildings…the entire city will be ours for the taking!"

Krick wanted to be excited, but there was still something about Eternal City that couldn't be stopped by tiny disease-spreading minions. "Um…Grandpa? What about the Hero? How am I supposed to—"

"The Hero," Tyranogon said, slamming his fist into the side of the volcano. "That's what this is for." He pointed to the rock structures he had just made. "Now get up, Krick. We need to figure out how to control that fire burning inside of you."

"I can't. I've been trying," Krick said as he stood beside his grandfather.

"It just shot out of me on its own. I can't control it."

"You will. You see these?" Tyranogon said, wrapping his arm around Krick's shoulders. "I want you to imagine these are buildings. The humans have their weapons locked and loaded and pointed right at your face. Destroy or be destroyed. Go!"

Tyranogon shoved Krick in the back with his massive knuckle. The blow sent Krick flying forward, his feet leaving the ground as he spun through the air, finally slamming into one of the stone pillars. Krick landed on his head, his feet hanging over his face. He smiled at his grandfather as stone debris rattled down around him. Tyranogon ran his scaly palm across his face and shook his head.

"We've got some serious work to do," he said. "Now get up. On your feet! Get angry!"

"Angry," Krick said as he rolled back to his feet and dusted himself off. "Okay, yeah. Angry."

"Ready?"

"Ready!" Krick gave a thumbs up, then balled up his fists and faced the mock city. He bared his teeth, tried to picture his brother and sister, tried to picture the little girl he failed to save. A growl rattled from his throat as he bared his teeth, and then he launched himself forward.

Krick lowered his shoulder as he rushed the first pillar. But rather than smash through it, his spongy body bounced off of it, sent him cartwheeling into the next one where he ricocheted off again. His body was like a pinball as it bounced from pillar to pillar, and he grunted with each impact, growing dizzy as he spun and rolled through the air. He hit the final column, breaking the stone in half. He landed in the ash on his back, and could only watch as the top half of the stone building crashed

down on top of him.

Krick groaned as he dug himself out of the rubble, wincing at the sharp pain in his back. He climbed back to his feet, studied the broken pillar for a second, then turned to Tyranogon who still stood in the same spot as before, lava dripping from his jaws.

"How was that?" Krick said.

***

The villagers just stared up at Krick, none of them seeming to know what to make of him.

Krick wanted to roar at them, shake the ground with his stomping feet and make them run in terror, but he didn't know where to start. It felt awkward, unnatural. He looked skyward, hoping to find Tyranogon soaring overhead. If he could just give Krick a head start, get these men and women with white paint spread across their faces to run and panic, Krick thought he could take it from there.

But one glance toward the sky revealed that he was alone.

When he swung his head back down to face the tribe again, they all flinched, some of their spears shaking in their fists.

Hey, look at that. They are scared of me after all. I'll give them something to really be scared of.

Krick squeezed his eye shut, tensed his muscles, and pushed. He concentrated on his spots, tried to visualize his minions squeezing out, birthing from his flesh. And then he felt it. That tingling feeling.

I did it! he thought as his eye burst open.

The villagers had their weapons lowered, some of them tilting their heads as they watched the one minion flutter down from Krick's body toward the forest floor.

"Shit! Shitshitshit!" Krick slammed

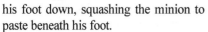

his foot down, squashing the minion to paste beneath his foot.

The tribe flinched again, then charged toward Krick, all screaming and raising their weapons high. Spears whooshed through the air, the pointed tips plunging into Krick's flesh. They stung, but Krick tried to stand his ground, picking the splinters out of his skin and growling at the approaching horde.

But that did nothing to slow them, and they surrounded him, stabbed at him and beat him and cut him. Before long, Krick was balled up again, his usual defensive tactic, crying as the spear tips entered him from every angle.

Tingling. So intense and sudden that it tickled, turned Krick's weeping into giggling. The minions flowed from his spots and descended down on top of the villagers. The men and women fought them at first, but it didn't take long before they were covered in green, juicy disease and running back to their huts where they began to attack each other.

Krick's stomach rumbled and he sniffed the air. Drool flowed past his nubby teeth and splashed over the ground, and he reached out to the newly infected humans and pulled them toward him, ready to fill his belly with spicy sickness. And they obeyed, shoving one another as they came as if fighting for who got to be eaten first.

A strong wind exploded from above, and Tyranogon slammed to the earth. He folded in his wings and held out his massive hands. "Wait, Krick."

"I'm starving. I did good, right? See? Now it's time to eat."

"You control them."

"I can't control them. I tried. They just come out when I'm in trouble, all on their own."

"The humans, Krick. Once the infection is in them, they are yours."

It was true. The minions seemed to have a mind of their own, but once they spread their disease into the humans, Krick could feel them immediately in his mind. Like they became a part of him, an extension of him.

But right now, Krick only wanted to eat. He wanted to eat so bad.

"Tell them to go the other way. There's another village just past those trees there. A sister village, allies to these people. Tell them to infect them, all of them."

Krick growled, could feel the heat building up in his eye. "No. Hungry!"

"Do it!" Tyranogon roared, spitting fire and lava across Krick's body.

The heat in his eye now extinguished, Krick nodded, reached out to the villagers and instructed them just as Tyranogon said.

The tribe halted immediately, green bile dripping from their faces. As a horde, they turned the opposite direction and began trudging through the forest, past their huts, and into the trees.

"Wait for it," Tyranogon said, now grinning. His head was tilted as he listened.

Krick didn't have to hear it to know. He could feel it. The infected had reached the other village and were spreading the sickness. The screams and shouts of the healthy blasted into the air and scared birds from their nests.

"That a boy! You did it, Krick! You did it!" Tyranogon slapped Krick on the back, and though the blow sent tremors of pain down Krick's spine, he managed to smile up at his grandfather.

"Can we eat now?"

"Sure. Just tell them all to march back here, all of them, and you can feast until you've got humans coming out of your ears."

In a few moments, the now larger horde paraded across the forest toward them, splashing slime across the foliage as they gurgled and vomited.

Tyranogon clapped and cackled as he watched them come.

"Fantastic, Krick. Fan fucking tastic. Let's eat."

***

"I can't," Krick said, spitting blood from his mouth. He wiped the sweat from his brow as he climbed back to his feet. His body ached, bruised and battered. He averted his eye, which was swollen almost shut, so he didn't have to look his grandfather in the face. "How can I be the fiercest monster if I can't even destroy a building? I'm not strong enough…"

Tyranogon spat two balls of flame from his nostrils as he scratched his chin. "Destroying buildings isn't important, kid. Any monster can do that. Forget about physical strength. Focus on the inferno burning inside of you. I know you can feel it."

"Grandpa…" Krick fought back the tears. He tried to look deep inside himself, feel the heat, but there was only sadness and disappointment boiling within. "Maybe my dad is right. I'm just a—"

"A failure? An embarrassment to the family?"

Krick nodded.

"You want to talk about an embarrassment…look at me, Krick. When I was younger, I was unstoppable. I crushed cities in my sleep. Adult humans would tell stories to their children about me, teaching them to fear me, filling their heads with nightmares. I was a god. And then…" Small wisps of smoke drifted from the corners of his eyes.

"I didn't know I was related to you until my mother dropped me here. My brother and sister still don't. But we all look up to you. You're like a superhero."

"Monster. Don't say the H word."

"Right, sorry. Supermonster, then. My brother used to pretend to be you when he beat me up. Nobody ever saw you as a failure. Every monster who ever tried to take down Eternal City died. All of them except you."

"Maybe I *should* have died. I still failed. The city still stands. The Hero still lives."

"But you almost destroyed it. You almost defeated the Hero. Nobody sees you as a failure, Grandpa. You are still the most legendary monster ever. I can't believe I'm… related to you." And then he felt it. It started in his gut, bubbling like the magma in the volcanoes. It rose up his body, into his head until he thought he would explode. The heat swelled and filled his eye socket.

Krick's mind raced as the heat intensified. He saw the look of disappointment and shame on his father's face, the sneers and mocking grins of his siblings. He relived all the times his mother had to protect him, all the times his brother and sister made fun of him or beat him up. He heard his father's voice again as he disowned Krick, threatened to kill and eat him.

I'm not a failure. I'm not a disappointment. I'm the fiercest motherfucking monster in the world!

I'm Tyranogon's blood!

"Rrrraaaaaahhhhhhhh!"

A massive beam of fire exploded from his eye, blasting through the stone pillars and turning them to rubble and smoking ash. The inferno rocketed forward, burning its way through a volcano in the distance. Lava sprayed into the air as the mountain was destroyed. Trees burned on the horizon.

When the blast finally ceased, Krick collapsed backward onto his rump. He gasped for breath as he gawked at the destruction he had caused. Flakes of ash and glowing cinders rained down all around him, and he jumped to his feet and cackled, pumping his fists.

"I did it! Did you see? *I did it!*"

Tyranogon was on the ground, using his arms and wings to shield his head. One of his great black eyes poked out and landed on Krick, then he unfolded himself and rose back to his feet.

"You almost blew a hole through me," he said, smoke puffing from his mouth with every word. He turned and faced the devastation his grandson had just caused, stayed that way for long enough that Krick wondered if he had done something wrong.

"I'm sorry, Grandpa. I didn't mean to—"

"Look at that. *Look at that!*" Tyranogon flapped his wings, lifted into the air, then slammed back to the ground just behind Krick. "Again. Do it again."

Krick feared that he wouldn't be able to, that it would be just like before. Like the fire had a mind of its own, just like the minions. But he could still feel it boiling inside of him. He gathered all of his anger and sadness and angst until the pressure built, until his body shook, and then released.

The fiery pillar ripped through the air, obliterating another volcano and sending lava splashing across the scorched earth.

Tyranogon cheered and breathed a massive ball of flame into the clouds. Krick smiled so hard his cheeks hurt, and he turned and beamed up at his grandfather.

"One day," Tyranogon said as he lifted Krick into his arms and flapped his wings until they hovered over the volcanic valley, "they'll tell stories about you, Krick. The monster who destroyed the indestructible city. The descendent of the great and powerful, and motherfucking legendary, *Tyranogon!*"

"Really? You really think so?"

Tyranogon flapped his wings harder, and they soared higher. A mighty roar exploded from his mouth as he shot another celebratory firestorm into the sky.

Krick widened his eye and unleashed another blast that cut through Tyranogon's flame and shot toward the blazing sun.

Tyranogon laughed, stretching his great wings as they soared over the forest. Krick climbed out of his grandfather's hands, gripping the black scales as he crawled up the neck and finally planted himself on top of Tyranogon's head. He wrapped his fingers around the horns there and howled as they cut the sky.

Tyranogon sprayed the trees with more flame, whooping as the foliage blazed. Krick joined him, unable to stop smiling as the optical heat eradicated trees and scurrying animals below. They flew for miles, burning patterns into the earth beneath them, grandfather and grandson.

"You want to see something, Krick?" Tyranogon said as they coasted through the clouds.

"What is it?"

"Hold on. Haven't done this in a long time."

"What are you—"

"Hold tight!"

Tyranogon tucked his wings and spun his body through the air. He shot fire and lava from his mouth, the flame and glowing magma spiraling around them as they drilled through the sky. Krick screamed, digging his claws into Tyranogon's hide, sure he was going to lose his grip and go flying off into oblivion.

And then the sky seemed to open up as if the heat burned a hole right through it. A crackling void filled with the darkest black Krick had ever seen. They sped toward it, Krick now shutting his eye and shrieking.

One second there was fierce wind,

and then nothing. No wind, no sound, no anything. They floated through the nothing in slow motion. And then the nothing opened up, exploded back into reality as wind and color and heat engulfed them once again.

Krick didn't realize he was still screaming until the nothing closed back up behind them and the sound of his shrieking returned.

"Still got it!" Tyranogon said, then flapped his wings again, flying them toward a chain of snow-topped mountains. He perched on top of the tallest peak and folded his wings. "Still with me?"

Krick's fingers ached as he released his death grip on Tyranogon's scales. His chest heaved as he tried to catch his breath, still sitting on top of his grandfather's head. A heavy fog lay across the sky like smoke drifting off smoldering wreckage, but Krick could see shapes on the other side of it, and when he squinted, he could tell it was a city.

"What just happened?" Krick said once he got his breathing back under control. He could still feel the nothing inside of him as if his body had absorbed it as they passed through the void, and his flesh throbbed as if pushing it back out. "Where are we?"

"We teleported. One of my many abilities. To be honest, it's been so goddamn long since I tried that, I wasn't sure I could still do it. Good thing we made it through, too. Don't want to get stuck in the darkness. I know Kaiju who went in and never came back out again."

"You mean...we could have died in the...darkness?"

"Not sure I'd call it dying, but we would cease to exist. But I had confidence. First time in a long time since I could say that. And it's all thanks to you, Krick."

Krick wanted to be upset that Tyranogon had been so careless with their lives, but he couldn't. The only thing he could do was smile.

"You see that there, past the fog?"

"The city?"

"Not just any city."

"Is that...?"

Tyranogon didn't have to answer. He blew a wave of flame into the air and roared. Lava flowed from his mouth and ran down the mountain, melting the ice and causing an avalanche that boomed like thunder as it rolled down.

"We're not going over there, are we?" Krick's bravery began to slip away, rolling down the hill along with the melting ice and snow.

"No. Not yet. Your abilities are powerful. But you still need to get in touch with your inner monster. With the universal Kaiju consciousness."

Krick didn't know what any of that meant, but he trusted Tyranogon. He wanted to make his grandfather proud, wanted to make his whole family proud. He wanted to make other Kaiju look up to him the way they looked up to Tyranogon.

"It's almost time, Krick. Soon, we'll make monster history. Soon, you become a legend."

***

Krick and Tyranogon stood at the top of neighboring volcanoes, the glowing magma spraying from the mountain's blowhole, beading up and sliding off their bodies.

Krick cracked his eye open and peeked at his grandfather who balanced on one leg. His wings were spread out wide, arms posed rigidly in front of him. Wisps of smoke curled out of his nostrils and between his teeth. His scales reflected the bright orange light of the heat.

Waves of acidic euphoria spread through Krick's core as he closed his eye again and refocused. The darkness behind his lid started to swirl and spin. Shapeless blobs of darker black bobbed at the edges of his veiled vision. Sparkles of color began to form, twinkling like stars, and as he tried to focus on them, they would expand and wrap themselves around his being. And they showed him things. It was as if he was looking through the eyes of monsters past, experiencing the destruction of now pulverized cities. He could feel the stone and metal and glass crushing in his fist and beneath his feet; could smell the smoke and blood and cooking flesh; could taste the humans as his teeth ground them up and his tongue was bathed in blood and entrails; could feel the pain and agony as each of these monsters was defeated by the humans' weaponry. As Krick flowed through these visions, the various cities all became one.

Monster after monster fell in Eternal City, some being obliterated by missiles and bullets and fire. But most were slain by the Hero, staring up at his metallic face as the last shred of life drifted away. Krick felt their pain, their shame, their disappointment, and their fear. When Krick opened his eye, now swimming in tears, the only emotion left was anger. Viscous, bubbling anger burning hotter than the lava beneath him. A deep growl crackled from his throat. Minions poured from his skin in a constant flow, each of them dying almost instantly. He bellowed and unleashed an optic heat blast into the air, then dropped to his knees, gasping and weeping. A strong hand grabbed hold of his shoulder and squeezed.

"You felt them."

"All of those monsters. So many…"

"You're ready, Krick. You're ready to avenge them all."

***

Tyranogon sat atop the nearest volcano, doing sit-ups and grunting. He had slimmed down considerably since he began training with Krick, and was starting to look more like his old self.

Krick faced the valley of volcanoes. The inferno rose from his gut to his head, and he held it there, letting it build. He released a small blast that destroyed the closest mountain, then cut it off, turned, and let loose with another controlled shot. He laughed as he destroyed a tall volcano in the distance, his aim perfect, and then wiped the scalding tears from his eye.

I can't wait to see the looks on everyone's faces when they see me now. How about now, Dad? Huh? Am I still a fucking embarrassment?

When the smoke cleared and the throbbing in his head had eased, images of the now deceased monsters spun through his mind, and he cringed from the pain in his skull, clenched his teeth as he imagined blasting a hole through the Hero's chest.

Mom was right. We are monsters. Monsters are supposed to destroy. This is who I really am.

A screech rang out in the distance. *Mom?*

Condoria soared over the volcanoes, flapping her wings excitedly.

Something dangled from her talons. Something huge, weighing her down.

Oh God...Dad?

The giant ice monster held onto Condoria's legs as she flew. The sky thickened with a dense fog as the snow began to fall. Lava became rock instantly, clogging up the volcanoes as Avalanx dropped from the sky and landed just in front of Krick, creating a massive ice-filled crater.

Krick backed away from him, his head thumping again.

Mom landed, and that's when Krick noticed that Gigataur and Zapstress had been riding on her back. They hopped off their mother and faced Krick.

They're here to kill me. I won't let them. His father took a step toward him, hands out as if in surrender. Before he could mutter an icy word, Krick's eye erupted with fire, narrowly missing his father's head.

"Krick! Krick, stop!" His mother's voice.

Krick spun on his heels, faced his mother and siblings. "You betrayed me, Mom. You brought them here...but it's different now. *I won't let them push me around anymore!*"

Another powerful blast exploded from his eye, hitting Gigataur in the middle of his chest and throwing him across the land. He smashed into a volcano, grunted, then fell to the ground, kicking his legs and whimpering.

"Krick...you've got it all wrong!" Mom sped toward him, held him close. "Baby...we're not here to kill you. Your father...your father has something he wants to say."

"W-what?" Krick took long, deep breaths to calm the pounding in his skull. He turned to face Avalanx who had built an ice dome around himself for protection.

Two giant hands burst free from the frozen dome, and the face that emerged was devoid of any rage. It was an expression that Krick had never seen on his father's face. Not toward him at least.

"Krick..." his father started, then shot Condoria a look that said 'Do I have to?'

Condoria squinted at him, nodded, nudged Krick toward him.

"I'm sorry," Avalanx said. "You know...about threatening to kill you and everything. It's just... Look. I was wrong. Dead wrong about you, son." He dropped to his knees, icicles falling from his eyes and shattering on the ground. "We saw you. We saw what you did to those villages. All of us. Right, kids?"

Zapstress nodded, forced a smile when Krick locked his eye with hers. A sheen of electric power flowed over her.

Gigataur brushed himself off, limped toward Krick. The armored plates on his chest and stomach were black, smoking, a couple of them cracked and leaking blood. But when he reached his brother, he put his arm around him. "We saw it, Krick. In our minds. Like when Mom and Dad are destroying. I've...I've never seen anything like that. I'm sorry. I'm sorry for everything."

Tyranogon had still been sitting on his volcano, and he launched himself into the air and hovered over the family, letting lava run from his mouth and splatter all around them. He glared at the Kaiju family as if he were ready to attack.

Krick took one look at him and the smile melted off his face. He pulled Gigataur's arm off his shoulder, faced his father again. "It's not over. There's still something I need to do. For Grandpa. For myself. For monsters everywhere."

"Holy shit…is that Tyranogon?" Gigataur stared up at the great beast with his jaw hanging.

"He's kinda pudgy, isn't he?" Zapstress said. "I always pictured he'd be more menacing and less of a fat ass."

Tyranogon's mouth overflowed with lava as he growled at his other two grandchildren. He unleashed a tidal wave of flame at them, and though they both shrieked, neither was harmed.

"Kids…this is Tyranogon. Your grandfather," Condoria said.

"What?" they both said together.

Avalanx ignored Gigataur and Zapstress as they swooned over their grandfather, firing off question after question, jumping up and down like a couple of excited children. He pulled Krick to the side, put his arm around his son for the first time.

Krick tried to remain strong, to show no emotion. He wanted his father to respect him, and the old Krick, the one who could cry at the drop of a hat, was dead. The new Krick, however, still craved his father's embrace, his acceptance.

"Son…you have no reason to forgive me. I've been a terrible father. But I can admit when I'm wrong. You are my son, my blood. You proved to me that you are a real monster. Please… let's go home. Destroy cities together. As a family."

Krick pushed Avalanx away, puffed out his chest. "There's something I have to do, Dad. A city I have to destroy. Just like you always wanted. Just like you've been telling me since the day I was born."

"Krick, I was—"

"Right. You were right, Dad. I'm a monster. I destroy. I kill. I eat humans. I understand that now."

"Then let's go home. All of us. What city do you need to destroy that's more important than your—"

"Eternal City."

Everyone went quiet then. Avalanx flinched, squinted at his son, then shot a look at Condoria. Her beak hung open, feathers falling from her body and fluttering to the icy, ash-covered ground. Gigataur and Zapstress peeled their attention away from their idol to gawk at their little brother.

Condoria shook her head, hopped into the air and landed beside Krick. She tried to wrap him in her wing, but he pushed her away. "Krick. What… why would you want…?" Then her eyes slowly turned toward Tyranogon. "Dad? Did you put this idea in his head? Fucking Eternal City? Are you insane?"

Tyranogon snorted twin fireballs. "He can win. He can destroy Eternal City. I know he can."

"You son of a bitch!" Avalanx opened his mouth, exhaled an ice beam at the old Kaiju, but Tyranogon countered with his own blast of hellfire. The abilities canceled each other out in midair and filled the sky with steam.

The two Kaiju men roared at each other, the ground shaking and the wind blasting as they closed the distance between them. Even Condoria looked ready to attack Tyranogon, while Gigataur and Zapstress just watched, dumbfounded.

"Enough!" Krick's head pulsed, but he was able to hold back the heat.

His family hushed at once, all eyes on him.

"Dad, just the other day, you said you wanted to kill me. Eat me or let Gigataur and Zapstress do it for you."

"Krick, I—"

"Shut up and let the boy talk, Aval. Goddamnit, you—"

"Mom," Krick said, turning to face her. "You flew me here so my grandfather could teach me to be a real monster. You say it's because you were trying to save me…but I saw the way you couldn't even look at me after Pelican Bay. You were embarrassed too."

Condoria hung her head.

"Gigataur…Zapstress. I think you both know you've done nothing but make my life hell. Always making fun of me, always making me feel worthless. Now what? You see me destroy a couple of villages and you want to be friends now? You don't want to kill me anymore?"

Neither of his siblings had anything to say. Krick couldn't believe he was standing up to his family like this. Part of him believed that he would never survive Eternal City. That this was his last chance to tell them how he really felt before he was killed.

But I have to do this. I can feel it.

"Mom, Grandpa's right. I can do this. He might have put the idea in my head, but it's my decision. I have to go to Eternal City. I have to prove to myself that I can do it. That I'm a real monster. A Kaiju."

Condoria kept her head down, tears splashing to the ground at her feet. Feathers continued to fall away from her body. Gigataur and Zapstress now looked at Krick the way they had looked at Tyranogon—with admiration. Just to see that look in their eyes made Krick feel invincible.

"Let us come with you," Zapstress said. "The three of us. We'll smash that fucking city. Rip that giant hero's balls off and hang them from the tallest building."

"Fuck yeah," Gigataur said, still grimacing and rubbing his injured torso. "Come on, Krick. It'll be fun."

"No. I'm doing this alone. It's the only way." Krick patted Tyranogon on the leg and the giant Kaiju nodded at him. "It's time to show these motherfucking humans who rules this planet."

Gigataur and Zapstress both cheered. Gigataur rolled into a ball, shot spikes into the air. Zapstress put on a light show, turning the sky electric blue.

Avalanx just stood there, precipitating sleet from his mouth with every heavy breath. The entire place was nearly covered in snow now.

Condoria finally lifted her head. "Krick, please don't do this. Monsters have been trying forever to destroy Eternal City. It's indestructible. Your grandfather knows this firsthand. You…you're not ready. You've only just discovered your abilities. How can you possibly hope to win? There's only death waiting for you there."

Tyranogon growled. "Connie. He's got something the city's not ready for. You saw it. He can win. I know he can. He can take that fucking city down for good."

"And what about you? The great and powerful Tyranogon? *You* couldn't destroy that city. How can you send—"

"He's the only chance we got! He's—"

"A child! He's a child who is getting in way over his head. *And it's your fucking fault!*"

Krick patted Tyranogon's leg again. His grandfather swung his head toward Krick, Condoria still screaming and cursing at him.

"Take me there. Now."

Tyranogon nodded, grinned wide as lava poured out from between his teeth. He opened his wings as wide as they would go, flapped them so hard that Krick's family was blown backward. His talons clamped around Krick's arms, lifted him.

Fire and wind and lava and spinning.

Krick could still hear his mother's screams, her pleads as he was smothered with heat.

One moment he was surrounded by volcanoes and ice and his family. And then they plunged into the nothing, the darkness, swam through the deep black until they reached the other side.

Reality washed over them.

"Good luck, Krick," Tyranogon said. They hovered over Eternal City. "Seize your destiny."

The talons released Krick and he plummeted toward Eternal City. The fire inside of him raged as his feet slammed down in the streets.

Within seconds, an alarm sounded. High-pitched and ear-piercing.

Krick grabbed his head, shook it, tilted his head back and roared.

ETERNAL CITY

It had been years since a Kaiju had dared attack Eternal City. The citizens lived in peace, though the streets were becoming too crowded. Everyone flocked to the city, desperately craving to live a life without constant fear. Every time a city was destroyed, the survivors—if there were any—would immediately rush to Eternal City, begging to be let in, pleading for protection.

They let in as many as they could, but the over-population was quickly becoming a problem. Only those who could work were allowed inside. Those who could contribute to keeping Eternal City exactly that—eternal. Free

from the threat of destruction. The only city in the entire world that the monsters feared.

"Another fine day," the general said. He sipped his coffee and watched his men. Expressionless, every one of them. Bored. "Look alive, people."

The men and women of the Eternal Military were becoming restless. Only the best resided in Eternal City, and they craved action. They craved bloodshed. The general felt the same way, but had to keep his craving for violence in check. He had even come up with a plan to fake the giant Hero's death so that Kaiju might be lured into launching some kind of attack. Yes, lives would be lost, but it was for the greater good. The citizens needed to be reminded that they were well-protected. That no creature in the world could defeat their armored city. That they were safer within the iron walls of Eternal City than anywhere else on Earth.

But the only way to remind them was to demonstrate. Lay waste to any Kaiju in plain sight of the people, let them see the power that the city possessed. Remind them why the Eternal Military was an unstoppable force. Undefeatable.

"Sir," one man said. He perked up and stared at his monitor with a wide rictus spread across his face. "Unidentified object hovering above the city."

"Show me." The general finished his coffee and rushed toward his soldier.

"Here, sir. Just appeared out of nowhere. Just like—"

"Tyranogon."

A collective gasp in the room. What had been excitement only moments before warped into fear and uncertainty. The only Kaiju to ever challenge them and nearly win. The Kaiju that was supposed to be dead.

"Ready your stations! Let's remind that son of a bitch why he lost the last time! Let's—"

"Sir, there's something else. It's heading right for the—"

The ground rumbled as the thing slammed down in the center of the city, throwing up a mushroom cloud of dust.

All were quiet. All held their breath and watched. The general squinted at the giant monitor in front of him.

"Get ready!"

The dust cleared. The knot of panic twisting tighter in the general stomach went loose, and he couldn't help but chuckle as he stared at the foolish monster standing dumbfounded in the center of Eternal City.

Thank God for that.

"Look what we got here. You boys and girls ready to play?"

"Yes, sir!" they all said back. Smiles lit faces, some even laughing and joking with each other.

It was a red, spotted, one-eyed beast with tiny bat wings. The thing was almost adorable, not like the ferocious and nightmarish monsters they had defeated in the past. The general damn near felt sorry for the thing.

The citizens, of course, screamed, ran, panicked. But that's what they do. That was their role in this: fear.

The soldiers sat at their stations, ready to blast this monster a new asshole, shower the citizens in its gore.

"Not yet. Let's see what it does first."

The general wanted to take his time. Enjoy this. To kill the monster instantly would feel anticlimactic. No. They needed to prolong this. Let the citizens panic for a little while. Let them wonder if this was the day that they would die. Let them doubt the absolute power of Eternal City and its weaponry. They had to let the monster do a little damage. It brought the people together. Gave them purpose. Fueled their hate for the Kaiju.

The alarm was sounded. Not to warn. But to assist in striking fear into the hearts of the very people they were protecting. And it worked like a charm. If the sight of the monster wasn't enough, that constant siren did the trick. The streets were alive with people and cars, all scattering this way and that. Chaos flooded the city.

Though this was going to be child's play, the general was happy to have it. There hadn't been an actual real threat since Tyranogon nearly ended them all those years ago, but even as gargantuan and deadly as he was, they still won. Since then, Tyranogon had not shown his face again, and for that they were proud. The monster was assumed dead. They even had a holiday on the anniversary of their victory each year, a reminder of their greatest triumph. The general could admit to himself that he was relieved Tyranogon didn't show, but there was a hint of disappointment. He craved a real fight as much as he feared it.

This new monster put its hands to its head, bared its teeth. The siren wailed, obviously irritating the beast.

They waited. Surely, this creature would go into a blind rage, just like the others, and begin breaking buildings, smashing cars. Scooping people out of the street and stuffing them into its mouth. And that's when they would strike.

But this strange Kaiju just stood

there. Clutching its head. It looked down at the screaming people, the cars zooming by and crashing into one another to escape it. And it just stood there.

The soldiers grew restless, impatient. This monster seemed to be waiting for them to make their move. Something they had never experienced before. They couldn't just sit there, doing nothing. The people would wonder what they were waiting for. Might start doubting the competence of their military, the city.

"Fire one missile," the general said. "Just to piss it off. Don't kill it yet."

"Yes, sir."

A hatch opened up on the top of the building closest to the beast. The monster must have noticed it, because it turned, squinted its giant eye at it. The missile launched, hit the monster in the center of its chest.

The soldiers cheered. The general watched.

The monster roared, its eye pinched shut as it stumbled backward right into another building. It clutched its chest, dropped to its knees.

The room went silent as they awaited the monster's counter attack. It would jump to its feet, smash structures, maybe unleash some kind of power. Lasers or fire or ice.

But it never got up off its knees. It curled into a ball...and seemed to be weeping. The first monster Eternal City had seen in years, and it cried when the first missile hit it.

The men didn't know what to do next. Even the people in the streets had stopped running to watch the spectacle.

"Kill the damn thing. This is a waste of time," the general said. *What a fucking disappointment.*

Just as the men were readying their weapons, the general put up a hand.

"Wait...what in the hell?"

Something looked to be growing out of the monster's skin. The black spots covering its red hide pulsated and thrashed. Tiny monsters broke free, floated down into the street.

"What the hell is this? Zoom in!"

The cameras magnified the scene as more and more of the miniature creatures popped out of the larger one, flapped their puny wings and fluttered down. They looked sick, hacking and vomiting. Looked as if they could keel over and die any second.

One of the creatures floated down into the street, right beside a congregation of spectators. The people still just stood there, watching, not sure of how they were supposed to act. The creature wheezed, could barely walk. Then it opened its mouth wide and expelled a stream of green bile that splashed over the faces of the citizens closest to it.

The people shrieked, tried to wipe the sludge off their skin, out of their eyes, spitting it out of their mouths.

The other creatures did the same as the first. They chased down citizens and sprayed them with vomit or coughed into their faces. As each one of them emptied its sickness, they would fall over and die, a lifespan of about a minute and a half.

"Oh Jesus Christ!" The general slammed his fist on his desk.

The soldiers could only stare at their monitors as they watched their citizens turn on one another. Those who had been puked upon were now chasing down the others, dragging them to the ground, spewing green, liquid disease over them. And then those would get up and do the same to others. Again and again and again.

The streets became mayhem once

again as the uninfected scattered. They sprinted and screamed and clambered over one another to escape their friends and family and fellow Eternal City citizens who were now walking plagues. Vomit exploded from mouths and nostrils, splashing over flesh and concrete and iron.

More and more of the tiny creatures broke free from the red Kaiju who was still clutching its chest and weeping, rocking itself, seemingly oblivious to the pandemonium around it.

One woman was pushing a stroller, and she raced away from the creatures and the sick, pushing her baby along as fast as possible. One of the creatures fluttered down on top of the stroller. Before the mother could stop it, the thing unleashed a splash of bile into it. The woman shrieked, knocked the creature away who instantly died when it hit the pavement. In the next moment, an ooze-coated baby leapt onto its mother's face, clutching her hair, vomit gushing out from its toothless mouth and filling hers.

The infected began piling into buildings and businesses. Within minutes, slime and vomit splashed over the windows from the inside. Then the newly infected would stagger out into the streets. There was hardly any room for people to run anymore as more and more bodies added to the crowd.

The infection spread in mere minutes, having an instantaneous effect on its host. Turning them into these vomiting zombies on contact. It seemed there were more infected than healthy now, and the number swelled by the second.

"Kill that fucking thing!" the general roared. "Fire, fire, fire! We're losing control here!"

"Sir...we can't. Our weapons can't reach it."

The missile launchers and giant machine guns had been installed at the top of every building in preparation for the massive Kaiju. But this new creature lay in the street, still curled up. The launchers and guns were not designed to aim down.

"The Hero, sir. We need to call the Hero and end this now!"

"No!" the general said. "We can handle this ourselves. Send the troops."

As the citizens ran away from the monster and the diseased, the troops marched toward it. Armored men and women, each equipped with assault rifles or flame-throwers, a few with rocket launchers resting on their shoulders. Tanks rolled across the pavement and crushed the bodies of the infected. Green ooze splashed over the streets.

As the diseased swarmed them, the soldiers pumped them full of bullets, sprayed them with flame. But it did nothing to slow them. They just kept coming and coming, pulling soldiers to the ground, smothering them with puke.

"Goddammit!" The general grabbed the nearest soldier and punched him in the face. "Get those fucking tanks over there and blow a fucking hole through that giant cocksucker!"

The foot-soldiers were overwhelmed and quickly joined the ranks of the infected. As the tanks rolled on, the infected swarmed them and climbed on. They clawed at the metal to get to the healthy bodies inside.

And then the monster stood.

"Now, now, now! Fire the—"

The door flew open, slamming against the wall. The general spun on his heels, pulled out his pistol. A massive horde of the infected swarmed into the room, most of them his own soldiers. The general fired into the crowd, but his bullets were useless. Not a single rocket was fired before the men were pulled from their stations and marinated in hot, green slime.

Hands clutched at the general, clawed at his skin. A stream of bile shot toward his face, and he ducked it just in time. He threw his pistol, leapt toward the giant red button on his desk. The button that would call the Hero, wake it from its slumber.

The general didn't know what would be left for the Hero to save.

Just as his palm slammed down on the button, he was bathed in boiling plague.

THE HERO

Krick sniffed the air. His belly rumbled. The succulent odor of disease swirled throughout the city, and Krick craved the taste of the infected flesh.

But he could feel them out there. The people he had changed. They chased the rest of the humans, hunting them, ready to spew their virus onto them. Krick wanted to call them over, wanted to eat, but there was no time.

The humans had used some kind of special power on him, hit him in the chest and knocked the wind out of him. He rubbed the spot where they had hit him, winced at its tenderness. It felt like when Gigataur used to hold him down and punch him, not stopping until Krick would start crying.

I hope nobody saw me crying just now. Maybe the old Krick isn't dead after all.

Just as the thought entered his mind, something exploded right beside his head, taking a chunk out of the metal building beside him.

From down the street, a tank rolled toward him, its gun aimed up and directly at his eye. It fired, and Krick leapt out of the way just in time.

Another tank turned a corner, fired, hit him in the shoulder. Orange blood oozed down his arm, dripped from his elbow. More and more of his minions popped out of him, but their vomit did nothing to the metal tanks.

Everywhere Krick tried to run, he was met by another tank. Some of the sick humans climbed onto them, tried to pry them open, but were only shredding their own fingertips.

And then his head began to thump, temples pulsating.

Krick shrieked, swung his head back and roared when another tank blast hit him in the neck. The pain blinded him. Blood gushed from the wound. He fell backward, slammed the back of his head against the iron building behind him. The tanks surrounded him now, their guns aimed at his head, each one covered with infected humans slamming their juicy flesh against the metal, splashing green fluid all over the place.

The fire erupted from his eye, shot straight into the air. The red and orange pillar roared out with more force than before, so strong and violent that Krick could hardly stand.

Another tank fired its gun, but the blast was swallowed whole by Krick's optical hellfire. The tank was reduced to ash and liquefied metal in seconds. Krick opened his mouth and bellowed as he spun in place, taking out every tank, burning a deep trench in the concrete. Water sprayed from the street, but did nothing to put out the fire.

Krick panted, curling and uncurling his fists as he stared at the destruction he had caused. The sweet, delicious destruction. He nearly started cheering. He was almost convinced that he had won. That he had done something no other monster could ever do… that he had made history.

Then he remembered. *Where's the Hero?*

The tallest building in the city began to rumble. Steam billowed from the edges, hissing.

Krick called his people to him, reaching out to them with his mind. He needed his strength, and as they rushed toward him from all directions, stumbling over each other to get to him, he reached down, scooped up handfuls of them, and crammed them into his mouth. Their green, creamy centers ruptured between his teeth, and he moaned as he feasted. His head throbbed and begged him to release the pressure.

The sides of the building began unfolding, opening up like a cardboard box. A translucent goo rushed out, oily and iridescent. It flowed through the streets and splashed against buildings. The massive body inside was curled into a fetal position. Its silver skin dripped with fluid.

Krick wiped his mouth, then touched his neck where his wound continued to bleed profusely. He reached out to his people again, seized them with his mind fingers.

Infect the Hero, he told them.

As the humans sprinted across the city toward the Hero, wading through the sparkling goop that had burst from the building, the Hero uncurled itself, stepped out of its iron womb. Its skin was metallic, sparkled in the light, yet still looked fleshy. Its eyes were dark blue, huge compared to the size of its head. It looked, for the most part, human, besides its size. Its body had humanoid proportions, though long blades stuck out from its elbows. Well-defined, bulging muscles covered its torso and limbs. A cock and balls the size of an apartment building dangled from between its thighs, and just as Krick noticed it, a stream of dark yellow urine flowed out, splashed against the side of a building. The piss blast knocked the infected humans backward as if they were hit with a powerful fire hose.

The Hero stretched, opened his mouth wide and yawned, his voice deep and robotic.

Once he had finished relieving himself, the Hero shook his cock, then stared across the city at Krick. Cracked his knuckles. And smiled.

The plagued humans attempted to climb the Hero, but the goo still coating his body proved too slippery, and they couldn't get any further than his ankle. The Hero studied them, seemed amused, then lifted his foot and stomped down. He didn't seem too concerned that these had once been the very people he had been protecting, didn't show a shred of remorse or compassion. Just kept stomping his feet, turning the horde into a dark green paste smeared across the concrete.

Krick's minions poured out of him, but they were useless against the Hero. Once the Hero became bored with crushing the humans, he glared at Krick again. He struck a martial arts pose and made his eyes light up brighter.

The fire exploded from Krick's eye, sliced buildings in half.

The Hero leapt into the air just in time, kicked off a building and launched himself even higher. He flipped above Krick and let loose with a robotic shriek.

Krick tried to swing his eye upward, but wasn't nearly quick enough.

The Hero's foot slammed into the top of his head and sent him tumbling into the closest building, turning it to rubble underneath him and knocking the wind out of him.

Krick moaned, kicked his legs as he tried to catch his breath. Something jabbed him in the side, and though he couldn't tell what it was, he could feel the blood trickling out. The wound on his neck widened and gushed with more blood.

The Hero grabbed Krick by the head, yanked him out of the rubble.

Krick widened his eye, blasted the Hero in the chest and stomach with a fiery optic blast.

The Hero gasped, dropped to a knee as he clutched at the blackened spot on his torso. He bared his silver teeth, spun and hit Krick with a sweep kick. Krick found himself on his back again, his fire shooting uselessly into the sky. What remained of his diseased humans still attempted to crawl up the Hero's body, but kept failing, splattering across the pavement.

The Hero just stood there, motioning for Krick to stand with a flick of his fingers.

Krick didn't want to. *This was a mistake,* he thought. *He's going to kill me.*

The Hero kicked Krick in the side, then grabbed him by the fat of his chest and hauled him to his feet. Krick wavered, nearly fell right back down.

My family is watching. I can't fail them again!

Krick bared his teeth, roared. He let loose with another pillar of fire, but the Hero dodged it easily. He did a backflip, landed in a handstand at the top of a building, then launched himself into the air. He rocketed down with his razor-edged elbow.

Krick saw the blade speeding toward his face, and he rolled out of the way just in time. The Hero's elbow blade plunged into a skyscraper, slicing its way through countless floors. When the Hero tried to pull it out, it seemed stuck, and he quickly turned his head toward Krick. Panic ignited in his huge, blue eyes.

Krick didn't waste any time. Still on his back, he hit the Hero in the stomach with his most powerful blast yet. The Hero screamed and tugged on his arm to get it free. Krick lowered his gaze, incinerating his enemy's cock and balls, charring the gigantic genitals until they melted off. Strings of black and red gore stretched from the groin down to the pile of meat smoking in the street.

The Hero bared his teeth and groaned. He pressed his foot up against the building and finally ripped his elbow blade free.

Krick tried to aim for his head, but the Hero flipped out of the way, splashing blood across the skyscraper's side. Krick's beam demolished another building instead. The Hero hopped from building to building, black and red fluid spraying from his mauled groin.

Running through the streets to keep up with the Hero, Krick tried to blast him out of the sky, but kept missing. The Hero was too quick, too agile. The horde of diseased humans followed—they changed direction like a school of fish every time Krick did.

Then he lost him.

What the fuck? Krick thought. *Where the hell—*

A whistle from behind him. A playful tune. Krick spun on his heels to face it and was met with a massive chunk of rubble. It hit him in the eye, threw him backward off his feet. He rubbed at the throbbing wound, trying to rid it of the debris that burned and scraped against his pupil. When he was finally able to open his eye again, he saw the Hero flying down at him, elbow out, blood trickling from between his legs.

The blade came down on Krick's arm and severed it at the shoulder. It flopped beside him, spurting blood. Krick screamed, tried to use his remaining arm to clutch at the bleeding stump, but the Hero's foot came down on his wrist and pinned it to the street.

Minions flowed from Krick's body, uselessly fluttering to the street and dying. Krick tried to release another torrent of flame at his foe, but the Hero swung down, punched Krick so hard he nearly lost consciousness. Then he hit him again and again and again. Krick's teeth were knocked loose. His mouth was filled with tooth fragments and blood.

The Hero knelt down, put his mouth right up against Krick's ear. "I will destroy all monsters. None of you can stop me. Eternal City will live forever. Motherfucker."

The Hero's eyes ignited with bright light, particles of energy swirling in front of them, building and building, growing larger and brighter, spinning faster and faster.

Krick closed his eye, turned his head, and waited for his death to come.

I'm sorry, Mom. Dad. Grandpa. I failed.

Something soft drifted onto Krick's face. Something cold. He opened his eye just a crack and couldn't help but smile as the snow fell from the sky.

"Get off my son, you dickless cocksucker!"

An icy beam hit the Hero in the chest, threw him backward. A thick block of ice covered his torso, and he frantically bashed it with his fists, breaking it bit by bit as he got back to his feet.

The ground shook, making the Hero stumble. He grabbed the side of the building to keep his balance, but dropped to his knee when four spikes stabbed into his belly and stuck out the other side. Blood rained down, and he gripped the spikes one at a time to yank them out.

Gigataur came rolling out of nowhere, slammed into the Hero, rolled over him and puckered him with more spike wounds. Blood squirted, then rained back down on the Hero like a fountain.

Before he could even sit back up, blue lightning exploded from the sky, engulfed him in voltage that danced and crackled around his body. He seized and foamed at the mouth. The open wound at his crotch smoked and cooked, the blood bubbling.

Zapstress stood on top of a building, the metal underneath her glowing with energy as her electricity wrapped around it. Gigataur uncurled himself, stretched his arms and roared, then smiled at Krick who was just now rising to his feet, clutching at his bleeding stump.

Avalanx pressed his hand to Krick's stump, froze the wound closed. Krick shrieked, but the cold felt good on his wound, and the bleeding stopped. Then Krick's father turned back to the Hero who had risen back to his feet again, though his body was now spewing blood and smoking. Robotic sounds clicked out of his mouth as he gasped and moaned.

Avalanx widened his mouth, eyes bright with icy blue, and unleashed another frozen beam of energy that slammed the Hero against the building behind him. It froze him to the structure so that only his head could move, the rest encased in an icy prison. The Hero's head rolled as he shrieked, cursing the monsters, promising them he would kill each and every one of them.

Two giant shadows passed over them. Krick smiled up at his mother and grandfather as they flapped their wings, settling into the street in front of the Hero. When the Hero locked eyes with Tyranogon, he stopped screaming, eyes widened. Recognition and fear twisted his expression then, and he fought harder than ever to free himself.

"Krick?" Tyranogon said, keeping his eyes on the Hero. "This is your victory. You defeated Eternal City. But please…let me kill this asshole."

The rest of the monsters laughed.

"Be my g-guest, Grandpa," Krick said.

Tyranogon chuckled, stood tall in front of his foe. Lava flowed from his mouth and his eyes glowed red. Then he opened his jaws wide and spat an inferno into the Hero's face, blasting him until there was nothing left but a black, charcoal nub. Tyranogon reared his head back and roared triumphantly, then swung forward and snapped his jaws over the barbequed head, swallowing it whole.

The family just stood there for a moment, staring at the Hero's decapitated, frozen body. They all gasped, none saying a word. Then they turned toward Krick. And cheered.

"You did it, son," his father said, and picked him up and placed him on his shoulders. "You destroyed Eternal City! You're a goddamn legend!"

The rest of the family danced around Avalanx as he bounced Krick on his shoulders, cackling and sniffling.

Krick forgot about the pain in his arm, the torture pulsating across his body. The rest of the infected humans swarmed the monsters, reaching up to them, begging for them to eat them.

"Let's eat!" Krick said.

The family feasted, complimenting Krick on the zesty flavor of the diseased flesh he had created. Afterward, they patted their bellies, stared at all the buildings still standing in the indestructible city.

"Hey," Krick said. "Let's fuck this place up."

Condoria pecked Krick with kisses, then took to the sky with Tyranogon. She soared over the city, dropping eggs of lava over the streets as Tyranogon cackled and breathed his hellfire down on the standing structures.

Krick, for the first time in his life, joined in on the destruction with his brother, sister, and father. And together, as a family, they reduced Eternal City into a wasteland.

He had never been happier.

VIOLET LeVOIT

LOCATION:
Pittsburgh, PA

STYLE OF BIZARRO:
Transhuman Gothic

BOOKS BY LEVOIT:
I Am Genghis Cum
I'll Fuck Anything That Moves
    And Stephen Hawking

DESCRIPTION: Violet uses perverse grotesqueries, rule-breaking typographic layouts, and genuine literary horsepower to illuminate heartbreaking truths about the hard work of being human.

INTERESTS: Violet is also a film writer and critic for Turner Classic Movies.com, Press Play, Film Threat, Baltimore City Paper, and anthologies like Defining Moments In Movies (Cassell Illustrated). She's earned a BFA in Visual Arts and an MFA in Creative Writing, two talents that combine into a visual/verbal storytelling landscape. She's also a knockout performer of her own work—live readings are not to be missed.

INFLUENCES: David Foster Wallace, William Gibson, Yukio Mishima, Neil Steinberg, Chuck Palahniuk, Jane and Michael Stern, George Saunders, William Vollmann, Nicholson Baker, James Ellroy, Maxine Hong Kingston, George Orwell, Paul Schrader, Greil Marcus, Pauline Kael, Roger Ebert, Chris Claremont, Daniel Clowes, Charles Burns.

I AM GENGHIS CUM

There's 20 sperm banks in California, and by midnight I'll hit them all. The GPS stuck to my birdshitty windshield shows 20 locations, 20 swollen red *here-i-am* darts bobbing placidly over the 16-bit landscape like fat uterine balloons. *Fill me,* they cry, *stretch me out.* I punch the ignition in my crappy hatchback and feel the tingle in my ballsack when I shift gears into fifth.

It's not a sperm bank. It's a *cryobank.* Sounds like cry. Sounds like crank. Sounds like Ted Williams' head. I don't care. It's there, in the phone book, under "Reproductive Services," beneath the listings for abortionists. Let your fingers do the walking. Let your shitty hatchback do the driving. I'm on a rampage.

Get two baseball teams of Chinese guys at random and jerk them off into a cup. Then peer at the spunk under a microscope. Chances are catcher and shortshop will have the same Y chromosome. Exactly the same. 667 million guys in China. And every 13th guy is using the same Y. Why?

Genghis Khan has 16 million descendents today.

I fill out a different form each time. They don't let me lie about height and weight but ethnicity is fair game. I'm Thai, I'm Belgian, I'm Azerbaijani. I'm the mixed race love child of a Jamaican mother and a Scots-Nordic father. No one bats an eye.

A fat matron with an etched scowl takes the form. A juicy blonde escorts me to the room. I smile at her. I know why she's the one leading me to the back room while Mrs. Menopause stays behind the desk. They want you pumped. They want you primed. They want you to sink your eyeballs into the ass cleft of the blonde's big swollen estrus monkey butt cleavage. I just smile. *The vagina's full of acid,* I think. *Your pretty face and your silicone tits hide a secret room full of lemon pulp and battery sludge. I won't waste time on you. This plastic vial in my hand loves me more than your stinking fish cooze ever will.*

Dog-eared porn in the masturbatorium. I don't need it. I close my eyes and think of dynasties, endless flatlands of conquerable steppes. Tents swathed in fur and crying virgins dumped at my feet, their faces all snotty and slick with unstaunchable tears. They're afraid of how I'm going to stick my syphilitic cock into their pink mutton vaginas and they're right. I'm going to soil their silk purse uteri with my sticky baby batter. I can hear the high-pitched scream of infant mews already.

I am Genghis Cum.

I don't wash my hands before I leave. "Have a free pen," the blonde chirps. I smile and make sure I touch each pen in the jar at least once.

Back in the car, Subway sub balanced on my knees. Semen is amino acids, fructose, citrate, zinc, galactose. I have a 32-ounce soda full of high fructose corn syrup. I have a turkey sub, extra meat, extra rubbery white cheese. I pop a calcium-magnesium tablet and a zinc and 2 tabs of vitamin C. An army marches on its stomach.

I learned what cum eats on Wikipedia. There's a picture, an Ivory Liquid splotch on berber carpet. *Here is what semen looks like,* the picture ostensibly says. What it really says is, *you are looking at my cum. I have impregnated your eyes.* The picture's author is Dave. Dave, you sucker. You're just waving the flag while I've planted it on the moon. Go outside and look at the night sky, Dave. There's a little Neil Armstrong on every dot in space, standing next to a Viagra-stiffened flag upright in the windless atmosphere. The next guy who beats you to a parking space could be my son. The next girl to wrinkle her nose in burning-hair, rotting-corpse, maggots-in-your-eye-sockets disdain when you try to impress her at a college mixer (*That cum on Wikipedia? That's mine.*) could be my daughter. My daughter despises you, Dave. She saves my genes for some other prick. I win.

They've got you jerking off into the hollow dust wind cunt of internet porn, Dave. If you want to win dynasties you've got to leave the house.

Genghis Khan died retreating from Egypt. He fell off his horse. My car has a driver's side airbag. I always buckle my seatbelt. I travel more miles in San Francisco rush hour than Khan's hordes rode in a day. They cut a gash in the horse's neck and sucked blood while they galloped. I get In-And-Out.

The next place is a sperm bank for lesbians. *For the special needs of our womyn community*, reads the lavender calligraphy arching over the reception desk. There's another guy in the waiting room. He'll fill out East Asian on the forms, I bet. Skin brown like turds, features high and refined like the British royal family. Blue eyes, shining out from mud skin like Captain Benjamin L. Willard surfacing, whites wide for Colonel Kurtz. See him and it's easy to remember why they're really Indo-Aryans.

I go in and bestow my load.

This time I remember the ones who wanted it. The muddy faced starfuckers of China and India, Afghanistan, Pakistan, Turkmenistan, North Korea, South Korea, big swaths of Russia, Armenia, Turkey, Kazakhstan, the tip of Myanmar and Vietnam and Laos, Iran, Syria, Iraq. The women lining up outside his hut giving each other dirty catty glances, ready to scratch out each other's eyes before the god juice runs out. I smile, the fist around my cock feeling like a thousand mouths. I think about their descendants. Downtown Seoul at rush hour, milling crowds in Tiananmen Square. A little bit of Genghis in every one. Soon that will be me. All the couvade lesbians, all the juicy housewives and their brittle, dried-up husband's testicles, all the brassy single gals who declare over sangria at their book group, *damn you mr. right, I think it's time. I want a baby.* I own a piece of them all. One at a time, ladies. Line forms here.

There's a sperm shortage in Korea, in Canada, in Norway. Because they don't pay donors there. They pay me here, in the United States. Soon I'll have enough money for a plane ticket.

The lesbo hands me the cash. "We have a personal option with donors," she says. "You sit and make a video. Completely private."

I look at my watch. I'm a little ahead of schedule, and I've already eaten lunch. I'm a little tapped out, too. I could use the extra minutes to get my dick in check. I imagine frustrated Hmong and Manchu and Uyghur women slumping against wolf furs, scowling and grinding their teeth in frustration when I leave the tent to confer with my generals.

"Sure," I say.

They lead me to a backdrop, the same gauzy gray clouds as school photos. The bulldagger fumbles with the record button. I fix my face with a pleasant smile and tell her a little about myself. I'm a photojournalist. I want to teach. My granddad's diabetic but still here at age 90. My best birthday was the year me and my sister did a skit for my parents. The dumb cuntmuncher eats it up.

"Why do you want to be an open donor?" she asks.

"Because lineage is the most important thing," I answer. "Lineage propels us into the future."

"We give each donor a private moment," she says, her raisin eyes getting wet at the doughy corners, "to say a few words to the camera. Just you and the mothers of your children will ever see this segment."

"Thank you," I say, and fold my fingers into thoughtful steeples. She gets the hint and steps out.

I wait until she's gone. I turn to the camera.

"I will rape you," I say to the little red light. "I will punch into your womb like a bolt into cattle brains. I infect your womynspace and your herbal tea and your sacred clothcatcher hand-sewn menstrual pads with the force of my seed. I will give you a Trojan horse of a son and I will bring guns and porn and heartless fucking into your safe space for womyn. Your daughter will fuck her way through a dozen baby-daddies, compelled to spread my DNA as far as her treadless tire of a cunt will take it. You will fret and worry and reread your Andrea Dworkin and you will know you were complicit in your own invasion, your own annexation, your own rape. You will carry the genes of a conqueror and like it."

Nothing can dent my good mood as I walk back into the waiting room.

There's another Indian guy there. One of those gas pumpers with a highborn *tennis, anyone?* face like a Chariots of Fire sprinter, but skin one step up from Sambo.

Wait.

I do a double take. It's Indo-Aryan from the last place.

The Indo-Aryan gives me a Bible study group smile. "They call them a brown twin," he says.

"Excuse me?"

"A brown twin." Eyes twinkling like Mr. Rogers. "Women in labor lose control of their bowels. So a fat loaf of shit always comes out, same time as the baby. They wipe it away with gauze pads." He smiles. "If there's time the OB does an enema first. But not always. Brown twin."

"See you later," I say, and back out the door.

I can't get to the next place on my GPS soon enough. That mahogany creep put a cold finger on the back of my neck. I can't shake it. I miss the turn at the next bank before I find the parking lot. I get out of the car. I walk through the door.

He's in the waiting room.

"Brown tw-", he starts. I don't let him finish.

I drive 20 feet before the rage boils up. Fucker followed me. Fucker tailed me. Tatar hoofbeats echo in the distance. This psycho's not going to scare me away. I U-turn and screech into the parking lot again. This is *my* rampage. *My* conquest of Asia. Did Genghis Khan turn pussy because one of his men started talking about women shitting all over themselves? Genghis Khan would have cut that guy's head off. I let this crazy fucker fill up some phantom womb before me? I storm through the lobby, one big hard-on of rage. He's dead. He's dead. *He's dead.*

"You can't go in there," the ugly nurse says but I shove her aside. PRIVATE, the sign says. I kick down the door.

He's just standing there in the jer-katorium. Members Only windbreaker, hands folded above his still-zipped crotch. Waiting, smiling. Like I'm a blind date.

I grab at him. My fingers plunge into him. Into mud, dirt, shit tar from hell. Up to my wrists into his chest, septic tank stench swirling up my nose, curling around my gag reflex like a cat on the radiator. I heave. I gasp. I can't get free, my hands fist deep in the sticky shit of his chest. Tar baby. *Oh, Brer Fox, don't throw me into that briar patch.*

"Brown twin," I gulp.

"Every where you go, I go," he says.

Then he head-butts me, and my face swims in the shit of his face.

As I suffocate I think of Pat Pong, bargirls in hot pants. I'm standing at the bar, drunk, have to pee. "I be toilet," she says, and as I hand over 500 baht she opens her little girl mouth and I put the tip of my dick inside. I'm just drunk enough to let go, to piss in this girl's slurping mouth in front of a bar full of horny soldiers and bored Thai hookers, and as she swallows each drizzle all I can think is *it's not even cum, lady,* and the last thing I think before I inhale the last choking lungful of shit of my brown twin's face is how sad that is.

10
DARLINGS
AND A
HANDBAG

Her stomach was a Martian landscape, the deflated sack of a corpse woman. Bread dough shot through with streptococcus in long pink stretch mark streaks. When she stood up she thought her guts would fall out, right through her navel, right through the bone hole of her pelvis.

"You're so beautiful," her husband said.

The baby woke every four hours. She woke too, and nursed him. Erotic delight died in nipples slammed between his greedy tongue and hard tiny palate. She fell asleep again, fat and milky and sticky. Breasts hard as tumors.

At night she dreamed of labor again. The dawning rollercoaster wave of each contraction, the way it broke like a fever at the high point and snapped itself in two. The setup felt like a switchblade in the cervix. The punchline felt like an internal organ tearing itself in half inside her. Shiv in the cunt, rip in the liver. The baby, sitting fat and placid and heavy and low in the hammock of her belly, punching down with an elbow whenever he felt like it, not doing a goddamn thing to help. Shiv in the cunt, rip in the liver. Shiv in the cunt, rip in the liver. *You're doing so great. I'm so proud of you.* Shiv in the cunt, rip in the liver. Rape and rape and rape. *During the next contraction the midwife will turn the baby's head.*

Night and day came as randomly as a KGB torturer flicking on and off the lights. The days were three hours long now, and they came hard, one after the other. Wake up to the tiny klaxon of a hungry baby, the air raid siren that made her breasts tingle and leak. Suckle, choke, burp. Change diaper, shit sticky like seaweedy tar or sweet like brown yogurt. He sleeps again, blameless and worriless. She sleeps uneasily, midwife's phantom limb fingers creeping into her vagina like black snakes before she dozes. The day starts again. The KGB torturer grins sweetly. The baby didn't even smile yet.

The other mothers' eyes were glassy with joy. They sang about their labor like it was the Battle of Thermopylae, the baby in their arms like the flag on Iwo Jima. They sang about sippy cups and sitting up and she thought about Custer's Last Stand, the Nanking Massacre, Chinese peasants with bayonets buried in their G-spots, the point poking through their navel like a tiny hand. The Battle of Hiroshima. *I looked up and saw a blinding light. Then they picked glass out of my boiled eyes. Kimono flowers burned into my skin.*

One day she bound her monster stomach with a strip torn from a terry cloth towel and strapped the baby to her chest. They walked in the woods, down narrow paths. Knee joints still lax from labor could have turned, twisted, tumbled into the ravine below. She thought about it.

They came to a bridge. The water below. The baby, eyes that noncommittal cornflower blue.

The thought came to her like a fairy godmother.

I can throw you in the water.
And I can make this go away.

She imagined his little body face down on the rocks. So naïve about the world he wouldn't know he was in danger yet.

She thought about her stomach. She thought about the potato sack of ruined bread dough flesh hanging from her. She thought about how nothing would make that go away.

She turned around and went home.

She brought him to the doctor's office.

"We can sell him," said the man in the white coat. "We can sell him for organs and make his skin into a purse. And minus our fee you'll have enough money for all the reconstructive surgery you want."

"I can't do that," she said, aghast. "A child's life is valuable."

"Life is valuable," said the man in the white coat.

"Life is valuable," she repeated, numbly.

"We can put your uterus on the inside of the purse. Velvet lining."

"I have fibroids."

"Doesn't matter. Uterine tissue is tough. You'll never have to buy another purse again."

"He's my son." She held him close. "I'm meant to love him."

He clucked his tongue. "Maternal love will swamp the earth. Everyone wants to keep their baby healthy. Think about what that means for someone else." He pointed to the baby. "Kidneys, two. Liver, heart. That's 4 lives right there. Let's talk quality of life." He pointed to those non-commital blue eyes. "Corneas, two. Lungs, two. Not to mention stem cells. 10 lives, at minimum."

"My son is worth 10 lives," she mused. "10 of someone else's little darling."

"And a handbag." The man smiled. "Don't forget. Women do love their handbags."

She looked at him. "Maternal love will swamp the earth," she said.

They wheeled them in together, his tiny body on the long table, and when he saw her he began to whimper. The impulse to soothe sprung up in her like a jack in the box and her mouth voiced platitudinous lies. "It's all right," she said. "You're safe. You're safe." And then she realized he would be dead in a moment and none of this would matter, none of these thin kitten *save me!* cries were of any worth at all. She let the marionette strings in her face drop. What must have been her blank expression scared him more. The thinner and panicked his cries became, the less she cared. *Where were you when I was raped by labor?* she thought. *You wouldn't lift a finger to save yourself. You made them slice me open rather than compress your precious skull.* With a small thrill she realized she was free now, and the tiny gas mask they put over his struggling face was a mere formality. They placed another mask over her face and the world sunk into a blank and airless gap that picked up again on the other side. Her eyes were squinted closed. *Why?* she thought. *I think I'll open them.*

Pain was starting to surface in her body like tennis balls rising from the bottom of a swimming pool. All over, deep magenta pain, the shriek of tender places kissed by the scalpel. Different than labor. Sharp, synthetic, external. Not the revolt of the body against itself. She opened her eyes. Her body, again, encased in gauze. The handbag by the table. The color of putty, the leather baby soft. She unzipped the opening and reached inside. They'd tanned the uterine hide soft but her fingers still found plasticized lumps of fibroid buried in the smooth leather, like knots in wood.

"Take these," the nurse said, and she let the pill dissolve on her tongue.

The letters came in. *Dear Miss,* they began, penmanship shaky with gratitude. *Our little Mackenzie rode her tricycle for the first time today. Justin blew out the candles on his birthday cake.* Kaylas and Kailas and Mikaylas and Kailees and Bailees and Baileys. Strangers' children, made doubly precious because their tiny bodies housed another mother's darling's organs. Every fall and scrape and mishap was charged now with an extra onus of duty. Parenting their enriched offspring was a babysitting job that never ended. Their children were alive plus one half now, not merely just *alive.* Like a double reduced stock, rich with the bones of many veal. *Thank you, thank you, thank you.*

She returned home and let her husband wait on her, bringing orange juice through a straw, draining shunts, changing bandages, until she was well. Then she left him, for good. She felt every step of her heels work the leather-tight, subtle muscles in her ass—the pubococcygeus muscle was a rolling landscape inside her, every twitch of her heels sending coruscations through her like a Grant Wood landscape. Her body hummed and purred, a cold machine with well-oiled parts. She felt the corset of muscle like a body stocking beneath the skin. *Transverse abdominus, linea alba.* The handbag dangled on her bent elbow and its skin felt almost warm to the touch.

She saw other solo women with the same handbags, sharp-dressed and chic, faces unlined and bellies taut beneath their clothes. They saw her and recognized the bag and ducked their eyes. There were so many of them. She could see that now. They kept her secret and she kept theirs.

WHITE
MAN
RENTAL

Sallie Mae has me and Sallie Mae owns me. Sallie Mae says I need to get a job. I try to tell her I'm trying but she doesn't listen.

"You want to make money in a hurry?" she asks.

She sends me to a storefront at 60th and Kingessing. It's a battleship grey room with a note on the wall.

TERMS OF LEASE

You can't permanently
damage the body

You must give the body food
and rest before returning

"What body?" I say. A piece of paper slides out from under a screen. I sign.

Then something happens.

When they buy my body I know who they are for a split second. I can sense their sense of self. I can tell what they want out of me. Then they're in me, and we're moving around.

Some like to just look at me in the mirror. They like their reflection to be a white guy. Blonde hair, pale skin. They cluck sometimes when they see I have hazel eyes. They wanted blue. (Blue is whiter.) They peek at my dick. They talk about how big or small it is. They poke at the hair on my chest with my fingers. They run my fingers through my hair. They turn me and turn me back and forth in the mirror. They stare. Then they slap me.

They make me do sit-ups and push-ups until I want to spit up blood. They make me run and jump. "Run, white boy," they hiss through my clenched teeth. "Jump around for me." They never feed me like they're supposed to. Then they put me in a suit.

In the suit they walk around the neighborhood. I feel them feel good when they see people cower around me. They think people just acting normal around me is cowering. The women walk around at night in me. They go places they've never been. They sit in parks at 2 am and just sit, just think. I can't hear what they think about but I can feel it, sad and bittersweet and tremendous relief. As if they're just happy to be there, nothing happening. My bladder fills up and they won't go piss in the bushes. They're scared to try. They wait until it hurts me and then they go and they're terrified and then they're relieved and then they're angry. Then they stalk home and when they leave me and I'm just some 25-year-old guy on my couch at home. I think they hate me.

I sleep and wake up at 6 am, more push-ups, more sit-ups, I'm half-asleep when the new one puts me in a suit and walks me out the door to a middle-aged Korean woman who adjusts my tie and walks briskly with me to the bank. She introduces me as her business partner and I parrot out memorized phrases and it hits me, I'm her 7-year-old son, I speak English and she doesn't and today this white boy body is how she's going to get a loan to build an extension on her grocery. And she's all smiles as the papers are signed and she says "Very good, very good." And out on the street he whooshes out of me and I want to limp home to eat breakfast and check my email but suddenly someone is in me again.

And I'm knocking on this door,

knocking hard, yelling, and this black woman answers the door and I yell "Guess who's coming to dinner?" and I'm kissing her. And she's not fighting me but she's a little disgusted, and I say "Check out the merchandise, baby," and for an hour they shove things up my ass and laugh at how flat it is.

I hate when I wear nice clothes. I hate it because they're going to use me to do something terrible. And they mutter under my breath how invisible I am now, a white man in a dark suit. How no one sees me shoplift or double-park. How in a coffee house people ask me to watch their stuff when they go to the bathroom and then I take it. How I jerk off in a park, with kids nearby. How I pistol-whip this one guy and put his body in a dumpster. I hope he was just knocked out. I couldn't stop myself. I pistol-whipped him and put him in a dumpster and walked away and whoosh, I'm still hungry but I can't even care about email.

I don't know why people make such a fuss over me. I'm just average. I'm not powerful. There's so many dudes with more power than me.

They never feed me. They never rest me. They're so thrilled to be me they forget all about it. One afternoon I get empty and I'm frantic, I run into a burger joint and leap over the counter and grab a handful of paper wrapped burgers and run out into the night. Halfway while I'm running down the street, shoving a fried fish sandwich into my mouth I realize no one's following me. The movies are nearby and I try again, I just walk in, and it's true, no one stops me. I can't tell whether I feel good about that or not.

I creep in the theater and hope I can hide here before someone else rents me and while I'm watching *RoboCop*

I think how can I get out of this? and then it hits me: can *I* rent a white man to be inside? A better one? With wider shoulders and a squarer jaw and more money? An alpha dog, who's got this white man thing all sewn up?

I run back to 60th and Kingessing, I want to be a better man, a CEO, a guy who fucks anyone he wants, holds his liquor, makes other men cower. I run all the way there and when I get there Sallie Mae is in the door. "Nuh-uh," she says, wagging what could be her finger, "It's a violation of terms and conditions," and she skins me. My flesh contains her and where she sews me up I can feel my debt sloshing around inside her, stalking off into the night.

NIGHTBOMB

The skyscrapers in THE DISTANT CITY were painted in grey and blue shapes, to confuse the bombers. The newspaper said the actress was still expecting.

"You know what I'd like?" he said. "I'd like to have a family of five kids, all of them cute as a button. And I'd take them to the circus to watch the dancing horses."

She raised the blinds.

"Did you ever see the television program *Nightbomb*?" she said. "It was a soap opera, in the town where I grew up."

She reached for the lapel of his tuxedo. He grabbed her hand. "Don't touch it. It's a rental."

There was a photograph in the newspaper, but it was out of focus. The dark blue sky in THE DISTANT CITY had searchlights crossing in white Xs.

She was wearing her pearls.

"That actress is still expecting," she said. "You know what I'd like? I'd like to have a family of five kids, all of them cute as a button. And I'd dress them in springtime colors for Easter services." She counted on her fingers. "Green, blue, pink, yellow, and lavender."

She lowered the blinds.

"On *Nightbomb* there was a man. He lay on a red velvet couch. A woman nearby was smoking."

"Why are you telling me this?"

She wiped her wet hand on the couch. He made a face. "Don't touch it. It's a rental."

The skyscrapers in THE DISTANT CITY gave off a low hum like dying insects. A bowl of gladiolas on the table. Sometimes the radio played and sometimes there was static.

He tied his tie, then frowned and undid it.

He tied his tie, then frowned and undid it.

He tied his tie, then frowned and undid it.

"I want to be the actress who is still expecting," she sobbed.

He tied his tie. "You know what I'd like?" he said. "I'd like to have a family of five kids, all of them cute as a button. And then I'd kill them with hatchet blows to the skull and neck and we'd all die in a fire together."

She wrung her hands together. "Why won't you tell me?"

He closed the blinds.

"Are the children dressed?" he said.

She shook her head. "On *Nightbomb* there was a *woman*. Who *smoked*," she insisted. "Her lipstick was *smeared*. A man lay on a *couch*."

He shook his head, impatient. "A *man* lay on a couch. He laughed and laughed and laughed."

"Why did you tell me that?"

He put his cigarette out on the skin of her shoulder. She made a face. "Don't touch it. It's a rental." Then she laughed, too.

She fell down. The buildings of THE DISTANT CITY fell down. The radio was static all the time now. The sky was orange and then it was dark blue again. The people who were watching stopped watching.

LIVE NUDE GIRL

Whenever I tell some cunt I've just met that I'm a stripper, they nod and try very hard to not make their eyebrows rise in surprise but I always see their pupils dilate which means I've shocked them. Good. Then they want to confess why *they* could never be a stripper: they took this women's studies class once? They're too shy. They'd start to *haaaate* those guys, *all* guys, ha ha. I just nod and say something consoling like "Oh, I *know*, be*lieve me*, the *job's* not *easy*." They never give the real reason, which is not a secret: I'm hot and they're not. All those girl power anecdotes are just excuses they can live with. One day I'm just going to tell them, "Don't worry, you're too ugly anyway."

I am *not* ugly. I'm not one of those Smile Train kids that scare you when you open the Sunday paper, fuck no. I'm not even a *normal* amount of pretty. You know how when you go shopping, you can never find jeans that fit? It's because they make those jeans to fit *me*. My ass is perfect. My hips are perfect. When I put my knees together my thighs don't touch. I overhear you complaining one dressing room over and it makes me laugh. Your whine sounds like a mosquito: *I need to lose weiiiiiiiight, these pants give me muffin tooooooops, I want to kiiiiiiill myself.* The girls even say those things in the locker room at work, where I get to see everyone's stretch marks and cellulite and C-section scars. Those come in vertical *and* horizontal. Ugh. God, if guests had to watch that sorry batch of cunts dance under florescent cafeteria lights instead of UV and strobe? I'd be the only one left with a job.

No joke, I'd be a ten if I had bigger tits and longer legs, but really, anything above eight is academic. Seven is fuckable. Eight is the girl you still think about years later when you're married to a six who became a big sloppy four after she had a baby. Anything over nine is enough to make money from it. I make bank, baby.

"God, I hate my stomach," I say in the locker room, just copying, and then I take off my bra in front of Melanie who's still upset about her cockeyed boob job. Suck these, bitch. She doesn't look at me. Good. It's so easy to make someone feel small. The easiest way, because it seems like the nicest, is to give them a nickname. That tells them "I like you" and "I own you" at the same time.

"Mel-Mel, Mel-Mel, gonna be a rich lady tonight," I singsong while I step into the tube of my floor dress and buckle my shoes. She smiles. I smile back. I like how all the women here think I'm their friend. Even Tanisha likes me. Something in the spliff she's sucking is making her eyes glassy.

She's probably going to sit here all shift. God, *fire* her ghetto ass. I've got no respect for people without a work ethic. I *earn* what I am.

I'm all smiles striding out to work. I lean over the bar so my tits overspill as much as possible in case anyone is watching. The bartender says "Someone left this for you." She lifts a brown grocery bag onto the ice chest, the top rolled up like how big hands can roll it. I look inside. One of my sweaters, a *Sex and the City* DVD, some keys, a hair clip I didn't even want back. The trapped air inside the bag smells like sunflower seeds and Speed Stick and him.

I usually don't drink Jack but I want one now. I tell the bartender "*Un* Jack, *por favor*," and she gives me a double. Gulp. Burn, baby, burn. It's good I'm drinking this, I tell myself. I'm PMSing and I had too much VIP champagne last night and the strap on my left shoe is cutting into my ankle. Jack tastes like caramel. It goes to my head because I don't eat.

"You want your bag?" she says as I walk away. I just wave my hand, *later, later.*

Some group got a big plate of wings. It's a bachelor party, a mixed bag. Guy friends nursing beers and regretting inviting the girls sitting ramrod tense on the barstools. I measure them up: two sixes, a five, a seven. I still win. Every one of them ordered a big fruity Cosmo and they're being as loud as possible to hide how scared they are. If I don't make them comfortable the whole group's going to leave and that's the end of my tip.

"Mind if I do?" I say, reaching over someone's shoulder close enough to touch them and picking up a wing. The trick to eating around women is to lunge into whatever's being served, devour two or three pieces like it's an orgasm on a plate, and then ignore what's left for the rest of the night. That gets the cunts thrown off balance because they're all desperately trying not to stuff their face and they hate you and fear you because you can step away and they can't.

"God, these wings are *so good*," I moan, sucking the bone. "Thanks for sharing, ladies. The *men* here *never* share their food." This makes them laugh and then they want to tell me their own stories about how men are terrible. I put my face on automatic pilot, nodding and smiling—the gal pal routine. I can do it while thinking about how much I want to eat. The plate of wings throbs in my peripheral vision. I need something in my mouth, now.

"I think a wedding calls for *champagne*," I say, loudly, and at the sound of *champagne* the bartender clinks down flutes and a magnum in a slushy bucket before anyone can come to their senses. Pop, we pour, I clink, I feel the saucy red wings fade from my radar as I gulp bubbly but as soon as my glass is dry I forget my game and feel my hand dart out for another wing. I can tell the bachelor is mad. I'm poaching his kill. So I force myself to drop it, kiss a girl on the cheek, wave goodbye. "I'm on soon," I call back, conspiratorially. "Wish me luck." They do. Now that they know I'm human they'll tip me. It works the opposite way for men.

I get back to the locker room as quickly as I can. I wanted to eat that entire plate, one bone-sucking wing after another, drink the blue cheese dressing like a shake and shove the lettuce garnish down my throat. I have a Monster in my locker. The caffeine will kill my appetite and hopefully sober me up, plus I haven't shit yet today and when you caffeine-shit it all out, your stomach looks flatter. I drink it, I do,

I touch up my lip gloss. The ugly Russian DJ with the Tap-Out shirt is calling me to the stage. He always says "main stage" like "men stej" and "Angelina" like "Onjelina". He stretches that name as I stretch my hamstrings: "Onnnnnn-je-LEEEE-na!"

I'm not too drunk to still enjoy that delicious little moment right as I start. They are looking at *my* titties, at the crack of *my* ass, they are *looking* at *me,* they *see* me. I get a shiver in my clit as I see the glint of eye whites in the dark audience. Then the moment fades. Food comes back with a vengeance. I think about bacon cheeseburgers, wrapping my lips around the dripping succulent strips of green and red and yellow and brown crowded under a sesame seed bun. Have I waited enough to slide my thong down? One more chorus should do it. I think about chewing and swallowing. Do you like that? I stick my ass in this guy's face. I think about the crunch of calamari, how I swipe it through thick garlicky mayonnaise, the way the resistant meat of a hundred legs tangles around my tongue as the shattering crust crumbles. I should go dance for the bachelor party. But I might eat all their wings. I make eye contact with another man instead and when I squat down in front of him and stroke the tips of my fake nails up and down the insides of my thighs and open my cunt like a butterfly I stare into his smug little eyes and don't see him. I'm looking at an endless smorgasbord groaning with food, a church bazaar buffet stretching to the vanishing point and I'm the only one there. No one can see me dive my hands into a chocolate cream pie and gouge out great handfuls of pudding and cream and graham cracker crust. I can grab a roast chicken by the drumsticks and pull it to me, consume great mouthfuls of fat-crisped skin. I tear off whisper-thin filets of smoked salmon with my finger-nails, stuff my mouth with pink flesh. I move away from the man and crawl on the stage floor. It's all scarred with black heel marks. I stare face down into the snarl of black scars but in my dreams I'm crawling through cherry pie, my knuckles dragging through warm sticky aluminum pans of mac and cheese, of Thanksgiving green bean casserole, of seven layer taco dip and eggplant parmesan and pecan-studded cinnamon rolls. I never get full and I never get fat and I can eat and eat and eat. I crawl so low my nipples touch the ground. My outsides aren't me. I'm only my insides, fat and crammed and happy. I'm starving. Tip me now. They stuff dollars in my thong and I mouth "thank you" as cutely as I can.

When I get off stage I wriggle back into my floor dress. Some yuppie wants to buy me a drink. He asks what I want and I say "shot of Jack." Stupid. I drink it, too. Stupid. He's yammering away about junk bonds and some IPO and I justify to myself that I said Jack instead of the house champagne I'm supposed to ask for because my intuition said he wants a dirty Jack girl, not a champagne princess. Fuck me for wanting caramel. Now I'm drunk. The bachelor party got gravy fries, too. That's why they're fat and ugly, I keep telling myself. They're fat fat fat ugly ugly *ugly*. I want to shove my face in their plate.

"Hello," Junk Bond says, snapping his fingers in front of my face. "You still home?"

"Caught me," I say sweetly. I forgot I'm at work. Toss my hair. Lean in close. Touch his neck with my nails. Make eye contact, fierce and locked and doglike so he thinks *I* think he's God. Take his hand and feel for the callous on the palm that shows there's usually a ring on his finger. If he's married I'll pretend to be the girl he couldn't fuck in high school. If he's not I'll pretend to be porn.

"So why'd you stick with small breasts?" he asks.

"Suck my dick," I say, because it's my stock reply to anything that gets to me. It sounds tough. It puts *dick* and *suck* together for them.

"I'm just curious." He slides another Jack to me.

I down it. "You have a complaint?"

"Let me see them again."

I tease the edge of my top with my finger and scold "Nuh-uh-*uuh*." Doing that's enough to sell a dance.

When I'm grinding on him in the back room I think how "grinding" sounds like grinders. I think of toasted rolls and drizzles of olive oil and the peppery tang of salami and the fragrant herby crunch of a dusting of oregano. I'm getting dizzy thrashing on his lap. I want to eat so much. I want to get off this guy so I can get in my car, drive to a Burger King, say I want one of everything, then push the fat ugly cashier out of the way and run amok in the back. I yank onion rings off the little metal racks and swallow them whole, like a snake. I stick my open mouth under the soft serve machine and let chocolate and vanilla cream all over me. I eat, so full and so stuffed that nothing inside me is missing anymore. I'll fall asleep like a baby that has everything she wants. He's so ugly. His chest hair is like pubic hair. He offers a line of coke. If I do that maybe I'll stop thinking about food. I know the deal is blow for blow and I don't care. I have to make the hunger go away. The line fills my face like mint and

I think of mint chocolate chip milkshakes just before the devil jitter hits my heart. I can't feel the jab jab jab in the back of my throat. He fucks my face like a monster. I wish it was a Creamsicle. I fucking want to bite it off I hate him so much.

God, that fucking asshole DJ calls me up to the fucking stage and now you guessed it, my turn! And that fucking light is so bright and I smile and is this what you want? My titties? My fucking pathetic barely B cup tits, you want to see them so bad? What are you smiling at, Fantasia excuse me Melanie, with your pathetic crooked boob job, you think you're so great? I hope you break your ankles in those ugly ass heels. I want to see you crack your fucked-up monkey nose on the stage in a big smashed splurt of black blood. I want to kill everyone here. I feel my teeth sticky against each other and I want to rip them out of my mouth with pliers. I look out at the customers, the zoo patrons. I'm going to kill everyone here. I slide my ass against the pole while I think about how I'm going to kill all these fuckers: fire, guns, sharp edges. This song is TAKING TOO LONG. Tip me NOW. There's an entire frat here, they're all fat and ugly and can't dress. I go over to them, smile, cup my fucking pathetic little stunted tits in my hands. There's one guy with red hair. I'm going to kill him first. I'm going to kick him in the nuts and while he's doubled over I'm going to gouge out his eyes with my thumbs. The buzz is going away. The frat boys are still hooting and hollering. *We came to see girl parts, hyuk hyuk* but the room is cold. I shudder through the rest of my dance. They tip me. Who cares? I want a drink. My nose hurts. The back of my throat hurts. Where did

Blow Job go again? Does he have more coke? He's talking to some other girl in a booth, not someone who works here. She's laughing and laughing, her head thrown back, screaming. They turn on the strobe. It cuts the room into photographs and makes me sick. "Buy me Jack," I slur as I fall in the frat boy's lap.

I got to this room on somebody's shoulders. I ride a whirlygig ride on five laps in the back, dizzy smears of red hair and puckery frat brandings in freckled skin. I drink from their flasks and scream at their jokes as best as I can. Do they have blow? No, they're too young and too cheap and god I want to eat but one smashes up an Adderal for me and before I know what I'm doing someone is inside me. "Holy shit," one keeps saying, not the one behind me. "Holy shit. Holy shit. Holy shit." I won't lose my job because I'm not doing this for money, I'm doing this just because. But when they give me money I take it.

I have to pee. Or something. I run to the back and the toilet is a rocking horse on an ocean wave as I hug myself in the stall. There's no food here or Jack or blow or customers and so I start thinking about him again. I always told him to come visit me. Wipe back to front, too fucked to care. I'd seen other girls' boyfriends come to pick *them* up. They'd nurse a drink and sit cocksure while their girlfriend worked, walked them to the parking lot on the crook of their arm while every man in the place hated them. Pull up the cutting blade of my G-string. The underside of my knees burn from the pole and the fronts of my knees burn from the floor. I start to cry. He came to see me exactly once. He sat and nursed a gin and tonic that he said was too watery and when I came to dance for him he blushed. The other men didn't look at him with hate and envy in their eyes like I wanted. And then I had to dance for *them* because he didn't want me. He downed his drink and went to an empty table in the back and took out his laptop until it was time for me to go. He drove me home only because it was raining.

They're calling me back. I get on the stage. I'm going to puke. I lean on the pole. I'll roll on the stage instead of dancing. I try to collapse well. I think about how I hoped he would come every week. How he drove me home with his hands white knuckled on the wheel and told me "You can't expect me to be happy about this."

And how I said "I just made you king of that room."

And how he only said "When are you coming back to school?"

That was at the old place. I crawl to the locker room. I could go work there again but they really water the drinks. I throw up in the sink. Tanisha is gone but her joint's on the floor. I pick it up. I take a deep hit. It hurts. Good. For a second I taste the smell of photographs. They treated me good, at the old place. I try to remember if I quit or they fired me, before or after he left me. Then I'm in the truck with him again. I can't hear what he says but he hates me and the swish of the wipers tears in my ears like helicopter blades. Suddenly nothing he said is important because I am on fire and

I
AM
GOD
I'm up on the stage again. I'm invincible, five hundred feet tall. I'm a naked girl, the most valuable thing in the world. Some cunt tries to get me off her stage

but I wave her aside like a branch in my path. I can't believe how far she flies. The slits in her armpits where they put in the implants jump out at me like bullseyes. I scan the room, I'm Superman. My X-ray eyes see all the scars.

On-jelina, On-jelina, MOLLY, get off the stage. I ignore him. Show us your cunt. My cunt is this numb magenta thing miles away between my legs. What is it doing there? I pinch it, hard. I don't feel it. I tug. I claw with my fake nails. Meat falls into my hand. I think I hear screaming.

In another life I see myself walk in on his arm. He pulls out a chair for me. I'm wearing a white cotton eyelet dress that I bought at some Buy Local street fair and it fits me perfectly. I'm not a nine anymore. I'm not even a ten. I'm outside that scale, out in the rarefied atmosphere where my smile lights one man's heart and he's happy for it. I've finally won all the things this body is supposed to win me.

Jesus, stop her. I hold it up. Pink strips of flesh quivering in my fingers. I take a bite. The gristle of my clit crunches between my teeth. I swallow. I'm starving. I reach up inside with all four fingers. I feel a shelf of bone. I tug, doesn't move. I reach deeper, get my thumb in. Feel a knob like the tip of my nose. I can grab that. I pull, hard this time. I turn inside out like a sock and then it's on the ground in front of me, pink rubber in blood brighter than a period.

Chairs fly as patrons flee but I can't understand why. I raise it to my mouth but can't stand. I fall down. *I love you,* he says, and pulls out the chair for me. I hold it up high. Girl parts. "Tip me now," I say, the last thing I say. "This is what you all came here to see."

J. DAVID OSBORNE

LOCATION:
Tigard, OR

STYLE OF BIZARRO:
Weird Crime

BOOKS BY OSBORNE:
By the Time We Leave Here,
    We'll Be Friends
Low Down Death Right Easy
Our Blood in its Blind Circuit
God$ Fare No Better
Black Gum
Elkhoury

DESCRIPTION: Using a sparse, minimalist technique and healthy injections of surrealism, JDO aims to subvert common crime-fiction tropes to find something new and fresh.

INTERESTS: Playing with my dog, going to the beach, drawing comics, rapping.

INFLUENCES: James Ellroy, Cormac McCarthy, Takashi Miike, Harmony Korine.

WEBSITE:
jdavidosborne.com

The Thick Fog of the Alabaster Mountains

John Parks jerked his foot from his boot and shook the brown recluse onto the greasy tile of his kitchen floor. He smashed it and scooped the curled corpse into a paper towel and tossed it in the trash. He didn't feel the bite, just the wild thrashing of tiny legs, but sure enough when he inspected his foot he saw the red mark there, right below his big toe. He turned on his shower and ran the bite under slow cool water, applied some antibacterial cream, and popped an ibuprofen and a vitamin C pill. He set out on a fold-out chair on his porch and opened a beer.

The cardboard box containing Louise's makeup, clothes, candles, lotions, books, and playing cards had collected a thin layer of dust from the morning's work, the waterline across the street having busted open and them in the yellow vests and sun hats having to dig it up and fix it and pour concrete over and smooth it out with long cumbersome brooms. Parks nudged a broken piece of wood with his good foot. He'd broken several things the night prior. Took a bat to his couch and kitchen counter and the rocking chair out front.

But there sat that box, untouched for the dust. And there in his pocket went his phone, and there he went ignoring it again for the warm beer in its soft-edged home. The bite was getting a little upset already, the hot red of the center and now this blooming soft pink around the edges. He didn't pick at it though it bothered him.

After the day had worn on and Parks had sufficiently tied one on, Bill Baldwin knocked on the door and opened it, as it was half-open to begin with. The house smelled like a wet dog. Big flag up on the far wall. A poster of a Bud Light. Green couches and cross-stitches laid out on the recliners. John Parks there on the floor, pouring beer into his mouth and spilling it down into the folds of his neck.

Baldwin brushed dog hair from the couch and took a seat. He smelled himself, heavy duffel bag sweat and dirt and gasoline. "You planning on coming to work again?"

Parks burped. "I imagine not."

Baldwin patted his thighs. "We have a lot of jobs yet. You know how it gets in the summer."

"You work on that river birch today?"

"Well, no John. I didn't. Can't do that by myself."

"I'm sorry."

The sun in the process of dipping. Baldwin cracked one of his own. Warm. "I saw the box out front."

"Did you."

"I did."

"You ever been bit by a spider?"

"Of course. Many times."

"Is it a hospital thing?"

Baldwin shook his head. "Nothing they can do. Just kind of have to stay healthy."

Parks tossed his empty at the wall. "Will do."

"What happened with Louise?"

Parks blinked the blur away. "Nothing. She's just not here no more."

"Well. What happened?"

"I figure it's my fault."

"I think we'd all figure that."

"We'd all figure that. I am up to here with fault."

Baldwin stood up and crushed his can.

"Tomorrow. We have work to do."

Parks closed his eyes and passed out on his floor.

* * *

Branson Collins played Pokemon on his Gameboy. He checked his phone and handed Steve Haywood the nine. He drove with his knees.

Jesus take the wheel.

Haywood tied the rag around his face and leaned out over Collins and fired out the window. 618 Fuller: mailbox folded in on itself / windows shattered / dogs started up in the backyard.

Flashes from inside. They heard the bullets connect with the trunk of the car and Collins stomped the gas.

Haywood ejected the clip and pushed the slide back and pulled the pin. Collins parked around the back of the China Wok and they dropped the top half of the pistol in the dumpster. Waved goodbye to the bottom half behind the Circle K.

Parked in Roosevelt neighborhood and wiped the Lumina down and hoofed it to Brooke's place on D Street. Haywood tossed his gloves on the endtable and adjusted to the smell. Collins dropped onto the couch and took a handful of Brooke's ass in his big hand.

Brooke made dolls. Fabric on the floor/ grey feathers floating like dust motes/sewing machine with a coffee stain down the side.

So many fucking cats.

Collins played several games of Pokemon on the television. Haywood sneezed.

After a time, Collins and Brooke retired to the air mattress in the back room and Haywood left the house wiping his eyes. Couldn't quit the shaking in his hands and legs. Tried to walk it out.

He dipped into Hudson's and bought a dark beer and finished it and got another.

Breathed heavy and watched the foam form a divot and roll over the side of the glass.

The jukebox in the corner was quiet and if it started up on some bullshit he promised himself he'd break the glass in front of him.

A fat man in a button down shirt took pictures of himself with his phone. Haywood squinted at the flash. The man leaned over like he had a secret. "I've got ten cameras at home and I haven't taken a single picture. The quality on these phones."

He pouted his lips and held the camera out again. Face glowing bright white for a second. He checked the photo.

Haywood left his money on the bar and went home and went to sleep and when he woke did some yoga in his room and tried to forget about the violence of the previous night. Felt the burn in his legs and lungs. He sat on the edge of the bed and ran through it: the gun is gone, there are no prints, you won't get a visit today.

He clocked in at the garage and got to work. Jacked up a Scion and changed the oil on a Civic and balanced and rotated tires and spoke to his co-workers with nods and glances.

The morning started off cool and over-cast but by midday the sun was all up in his shit. He stepped around the building and lit a cigarette and drank some water and checked his phone and ignored the texts. The world tightening up.

He walked back into the heavy warmth of the garage and saw his boss talking to the owner of a Chevy Lumina. The customer pointed at the bullet holes in the car's ass and Steve's boss nodded and waved him over.

Haywood's stomach was already pissed off at the heat and the cigarette. The woman looked at him and he felt the edges of his vision go white. *Push it down.*

Haywood's boss clapped him on the shoulder. "Take care of her."

Cleared his throat. "Where are the salesmen?"

The boss smiled and leaned in closer. "Take care of her, Steve."

Haywood didn't know what to do with his hands.

The woman said, "Some dickless fuck stole my car."

Haywood nodded and stared at the blurry green cursive tattooed on her neck.

"I need someone to patch these up. I have insurance."

"I'm Steve." Held out his hand.

The customer took it. "Hello, Steve. I'm Louise."

"Are the bullets still in it?"

She shook her head. "Cops pulled them out."

Haywood knelt and grimaced at the damage. "Yeah, I can do this."

He told the customer when she could pick her car up. Louise walked away. Haywood looked up at the sky and asked god if he thought he was funny, then started bonding and sealing the bullet holes in the blue Chevy Lumina.

* * *

Detective Alexander Janairo had been watching the Super Bowl alone in his apartment and was halfway through his box of beer when the halftime show came on and Beyonce began gyrating and growling at the camera. He'd resigned himself to watch the game alone and as usual he received nary a text to jingle in his pocket. He admired the video dancers behind the pop star, how they weaved in and out of the flesh and blood in front of them and the way the singer controlled everyone, the crowd holding up their cell phones below and the millions of people just like him, probably not alone at home, though, probably at a party with chips and salsa and beer and play-by-play pea-nut gallery nonsense. At the moment the creature with a name older than humankind shorted the power in the Mercedes-Benz Superdome, Janairo opened his lonely heart and Sasha Fierce moved through him. He got off his chair and went down to a bar and ordered a beer and chatted up women and men alike. He played darts and sang a song about quails at the top of his lungs and thrusted his crotch to knock wadded up napkins into the trashcans. "Kobe!" he shouted.

The detective awoke the next day without even the faintest hint of a hangover. He sang through the foam and spittle on his toothbrush and dressed to the nines. Standing before the big whiteboard in the office he saw the names in red not as indictments of his own failures, but potential successes, mysteries that were waiting to be solved. His partner, Bob Rangitsch, surfed the web at his cubicle and nursed a Starbucks cup that Janairo could smell from where he was standing.

Normally the men did not speak, both of them content to be alone in their own miseries. But Janairo was full of the spirit: "How are the bird houses coming along?"

Rangitsch burned his tongue on the coffee. "They're bird houses. That's for sure."

Janairo drummed his fingers on his desk. "I'll bet. Lots of hungry birds out there."

Rangitsch sighed and said, "Eat a dick, Alex."

Janairo tossed yesterday's Far Side calendar page into a trashcan. "Kobe," he whispered.

* * *

John Parks woke up and made a pot of coffee and put an ice cube in it and also a finger of bourbon. He checked the bite in his foot. The center of the wound had split open. He fought the urge to scratch it.

He shook out his steel-toed boots and pulled on his polyester shirt and met Baldwin at the river birch on McAllister. Shirt already plastered to his chest. Baldwin waved from high up in the dead tree, where he'd rigged a piece to fall. Parks grabbed the rope and Baldwin set to sawing. The section of trunk toppled and Parks slowed it to a crawl before it hit the brick in the backyard. He thought on that: *Who needs a fucking brick backyard?*

The old impulses welled up inside of him again. Break the window. Take what you can. Move to a different city. Used to be, when he'd run low on cash, he'd be completely fine with his life as it was, long as he had a little beer in his fridge. But once the hunger hit, that all went out the window. People made of leather ready to be opened and emptied.

Focus: dead tree. His boss made another cut and he untied the bowline and sent it back up the trunk.

Throat dry. Figured he'd have sweat the alcohol out by now.

He'd been doing the job for a few months, and Baldwin promised him over and over again that a raise was right around the corner. But there was always something to ensure that it never happened. His boss was a strange man: he was kind and patient with Parks' constant fuck-ups, but he stubbornly refused to give even a little out of the way of his agreed-upon nine dollars an hour. If Parks forgot to bring water, Baldwin would not give him a bottle.

The tree fell and they hauled it to the trailer and drove it to the dump. The sweet smell of the mountain of trash churned Parks' stomach and he tossed the logs in the pile and sat back in the cool A/C of the truck and wondered for the umpteenth time where his life had gone wrong.

He could see where Louise was coming from: the drinking was definitely a problem. He had texted her a few days ago, begging her to come back, and had received several hopeful responses. He'd cleaned up and prepared the house for her return and called his mother and told her that things were clearing up and that Louise would be back the next day. When he'd hung up he saw the text: no, it was final.

Then that box, that big step, then the beer.

He took a shower and tried to ignore the burning in his foot. He realized that he'd forgotten to throw away Louise's effects from the rim of the tub: soaps and lotions and scrubs. He opened a coconut scented shampoo and held his head and cried.

His foot screamed. Peeking through the tears and the hot water violent against his face, he looked down and reeled backwards and fell out of the tub and onto the cold linoleum.

A spider wriggling its way through the bite in his foot. Long black legs tickling against his toes, then the fat black body. It scurried over the top of his foot and into the corner. And then another emerged. And another. He screamed as the spiders birthed from his wound and soldiered across his person and into the nearest dark corners they could find.

* * *

Branson Collins argued with some kid about Pokemon cards. They had them spread out over the table. Empty cans of Coors along either side.

Collins stabbed a meaty finger into the cards. "I evolved that bitch."

The kid shook his head. Skin and bones and hatchet man tats. "You already attacked, son. You can't do that shit after you attack."

"I got these speciality cards."

The kid sneered. "The fuck does that even mean."

Haywood stepped up to the table and

cracked his beer. "Guys, guys." Pointed at a card in the middle of the melee. "See this one?"

Collins shrugged. "Yeah."

"This one right here. It shows that you're both fucking queer."

Collins laughed hard. The kid just stared.

Haywood leaned on the table. "We need to talk."

Collins folded his cards. "All right." To the kid: "Time to go, buddy."

The kid threw his hands up. "The fuck."

"I know."

"We just got started."

"Yeah, but it's time to go."

Hatchet Tats pushed away from the fold-out table violently. Gathered his cards and stuffed them in his backpack. "I'm taking my beer." He picked up what was left of the 30-pack. Collins gave him a look. The kid set it down. Fished out a cold one. "I'm taking a beer."

Slammed the door.

Collins collected his cards in a neat stack. "He's a good kid."

"Fucking spaz."

"He is that. Didn't wear his clown makeup today, though. Baby steps."

Haywood told him about the woman. The car.

Collins leaned back and stretched out. "That's unfortunate."

"Yeah."

Lit a cigarette. "But, I mean…so?"

"I don't know. It's just a trip."

"It's a small town."

"Too small."

Collins got up and grabbed a beer. "Not here for much longer."

"I know."

"The city."

"The city."

"What about Dallas?"

"What about Houston?"

"Houston, I could do for sure."

"Once we sell to the Gutierrez crew, we'll be good to go."

Three months ago, Haywood had picked up a book from a local coffee shop about starting a small business. He'd paged through a chapter on franchising, the idea catching his attention: build something up, show that it's profitable, and sell it to those with deep pockets. Collins took to the idea immediately. Formerly content to sell their cheap imports to red-faced meth addicts, they'd begun cornering markets: cocaine, weed, heroin. The big dealers from the big cities had no interest in taking a risk on a small town, but once they saw that a market was gift wrapped, they could take the monopoly and put their connections and their money behind it. No bodies on them. A healthy chunk of change in Collins' and Haywood's pockets.

Only a few loose ends, now.

Collins grabbed his laptop from his room and set it on the fold-out table. They smoked a little and watched videos online. Shots/lean/more shots. His phone kept ringing.

Finally they stopped ignoring the calls and opened the safe and loaded the car and made their deliveries and counted their cash. Back at the house Haywood opened the safe in the cubby he'd hollowed out in the floor and dropped the crumpled stacks onto the pile. He removed a large bag of 4fa and a bottle of Niacin capsules and twisted the pills and dumped the Niacin in a trash can and filled the caps with white powder.

Dropped the pills in with the money and shut the safe and locked it and replaced the wood panel and folded the carpet down.

Collins hopped online and made another order.

They left and locked the door and

drove to Burger King and ordered their food and nodded at Wesley Hammond on the frier. He pushed his headset down and held up a finger like "one second."

Old man pushing a mop/brats in the ball pit/a woman pumping ketchup into little paper cups and singing gospel to herself.

Hammond stood over them for a second and Collins held his hand out and the boy took a seat next to Haywood.

Collins dipped his fries in ranch. "You spit in this?"

Hammond cackled high pitched. "Of course not."

"We spoke to Jerry."

Hammond cracked his knuckles. "Yeah."

"Y'all take that money and quit it."

"Jerry's thinking."

Jerry Isassi spent three years in prison for holding Israel Cole's eyes open while his brothers raped Cole's sister. Always waved his beer around and laughed when he told the story. Haywood didn't know Cole well but after he shot himself even mention of Isassi's name set him on edge.

Collins shrugged. "Tell him to think quicker, or it's your ass."

"Jerry-"

"I'm not talking about Jerry, now."

Hammond went pale and adjusted his glasses. Took his hat off and ran his hand through his thick hair. "It's the internet."

"I know it."

"It's not like its a scarcity thing."

"It's a business and you two are fucking me right up the ass. I offered y'all a big sum. Take it and quit it."

Hammond put his hat back on. "I've gotta get back to work."

Collins frowned at his burger and lifted the bread. He lunged across the table. Quick for his size. Grabbed Hammond's collar and yanked his jaw open and hocked a big one in the boy's mouth.

Hammond puked on the floor. A manager shouted half-heartedly that she was calling the cops.

Collins knelt next to the boy. Careful to avoid the puke. "I don't like doing shit like this. But Jerry needs to listen. I can only talk so much."

Watching the kid cough and dry heave, the specks of vomit on his blue uniform, Haywood felt a little bad.

He dropped it and pushed out the door behind his friend into the hot night.

When they got home Collins watched a movie with Brooke. He looked up from the couch and waved and told him to sit down. He jumped up on the couch and pulled his pants down. Brooke sighed and started sucking his dick.

Haywood couldn't figure why he liked it when he watched. But Collins was his friend and he liked to help.

"Get closer," Branson Collins said. Haywood stepped forward. "Really look at it. Look at how good she is."

She closed her eyes and moaned and reached out and grabbed Haywood's crotch. Collins smacked her hand away and pulled her down on him until she gagged.

When Brooke jerked away and gasped for breath Haywood looked at her and she winked at him, and he felt like he needed every beer in the fridge.

He felt disgusting. Collins tilted his head back and came.

* * *

Detective Jon Janairo opted to stand. The couch dipped heavy in the middle and the grey stains mottling the chartreuse smelled sweet. Hagar Simpson sat on an overturned crate in the corner. His girlfriend, Jackie, cowered against a wall. TV broken / lightbulb hanging from a wire / stuffed cow crucified against the wall. Janairo hated visiting the homes on streets with letter names. Rangitsch tossed the baseball bat into the far room.

"What was the bat for, Hagar?"

The tweaker scratched at the robots tattooed over his arms. "I broke the TV with it."

Jackie hollered: "He makes me dance with it. He smacks the ground and yells at me to dance."

Janairo observed the smashed tiles. Nodded. "You need to respect yourself."

Rangitsch knelt beside Hagar. "This kind of shit makes me very upset."

"Y'all DHS now?"

"We're drug police."

Janairo patted his partner on the back. "That was a joke, Range." He dropped the baggie of meth in front of the small man. "This isn't, though."

"Don't you guys have, like, black kids to bust? They love pot."

Janairo shrugged. "Normally, yes. But my bosses get upset when this shit starts to turn violent. There was a house shot up a couple days back. Couple of guys selling stuff like this."

"Did you talk to the people in the house?"

"Sure did. Mr. Jerry Isassi. He wasn't very cooperative."

The tweaker shook his head. "I don't know anything."

The cops looked at each other. "So how well do you know Jerry Isassi?"

Head shaking: *no.*

"Where does he get it? Where does he keep it?"

No.

"Who'd want to shoot at him? Who's moving in?"

No.

Rangitsch moved toward the door. "Another great lead, Alex."

"Fuck yourself, Bob." The door shut. Turning back to the tweakers. "Ignore him."

"No, you're right. This is a waste of your time. Take me to jail and I'll do the time. I don't know anything."

Jackie moved away from the corner, "Baby, just tell them what they want to know."

Hagar flipped the crate over and put a finger in her face. "You shut the fuck up. You shut. The. Fuck. Up. I'm tired of hearing bitch shit from your cunt mouth."

The spirit in Janairo stirred and curled around his soul and growled. "You sit your ass down for just one second." Hagar felt the power and sat. Tendrils of the beast reached out from Alexander Janairo's eyes and salted Jackie's tongue.

Janairo said, "Why do you let him speak to you that way?"

Jackie shrugged. "I love him."

The detective ignored the filthiness of the couch. "Girl, come sit down."

She sat next to him.

He laced his fingers and propped his arms on his knees. "When you were a little girl, what did you want to be."

The corner of Jackie's mouth twitched. "I don't know."

"Sure you do. Everybody wants to be something. Did you want to be a princess? An astronaut?"

Hagar rolled his eyes.

Jackie thought about it. "Well. I always wanted to be a firefighter."

Hagar laughed.

Janairo nodded. "A firefighter. That's good."

"It's whatever."

"What happened?"

"I was in maybe middle school?" She motioned at the bag.

"And suddenly you liked that more

than being a firefighter?"

"It's complicated. It was a process."

"I'll bet."

Hagar yawned.

Janairo took a deep breath. "Here's a story. When I was a kid, I really wanted to be a baseball player. Like, more than anything. I didn't really know shit about baseball, and I never really played it. But I had these cards. My dad was a military man and my mother was depressed and I kind of sucked at everything as a child. But there was something about these cards that I just couldn't get over. Anyhow, I grew up and realized that I was shit for the sport, whatever. Being Batman was also out of the question."

Jackie nodded.

"I walked around with a lot of anger after that. I wanted to be on a baseball card so badly. Got to the point where I would actually set a camera on a timer and pose in a uniform, with a bat, and everything. And kind of chop it up and make it into my own card."

"That's kind of sad."

"It's very sad. But you know what? I took all that pent up rage, and I became a police officer. And I'm now allowed to hurt anyone that I like, as long as I'm careful about it. You wanted to be a firefighter, and there's a good chance it's a bit late for that, now." He walked to the back room and retrieved the bat. "But you can still make others hurt. You can still respect yourself for who you are. As unathletic a person as that might be."

Jackie took the bat. "So you're saying…"

"I'm saying you can beat the everloving fuck out of Hagar here, and I won't tell a soul."

Her eyes lit up. "I can really get him?"

"If you can't live the dream, make sure everybody's in check."

She stood up and tested the bat's weight. Hagar chuckled nervously and stood up. "Now hold on—"

She took his legs out. Bone snapped. He fell to the rank floor and screamed.

Janairo whispered, "Tell him to send you a picture of him crying, weekly. Or we'll be back."

She screamed, "Take a picture of yourself crying and text it to me." Smacked him again. Ribs caved in.

"Now wait a second, girl, I have a question to ask him—"

"You never respected me," she yelled as she brought the bat down on Hagar's skull. Bone fragments and brain matter flung up to the ceiling and over Jackie and Janairo. A chunk of brain dove into an overflowing trash can. "Kobe," the detective muttered, then, "Well, I'd better be going. I'm a man of my word. Just leave this here and find you a new home."

She dropped the bat and cried.

Janairo whispered, "Respect yourself," and took one last look at the caved-in skull of Hagar Simpson and shut the door behind him.

* * *

The spiders covered his person and the memories flooded into John Parks' reality and he experienced them over again from the meager square-footage of his living room. There they were, him and Louise, in Target, and they're buying underwear, and he tries it on in the dressing room and models it for her and she laughs.

Sitting on the couch, night after night, making their way through science fiction television shows, him sweaty and quiet after a day of manual labor, her chatty and drinking cheap beer and tickling him whenever he threatened to fall asleep.

Sea World: they made the trip during an uncharacteristically wealthy summer. They pointed at the dust devils on the side of the road and commented on the frequency and price of the tolls and they ate the best pizza he'd ever had. They wandered into the park and rode the rides and they came upon a crowd pressing against a giant blue pool. A dolphin swam and jumped through the clear water and the ticket holders stretched out their arms to grab a piece of it, just a touch. Louise joined them, she reached her arm out, somehow convinced the ticket price wouldn't be worth it if she didn't feel the slick skin of the mammal's hide on her fingers. John Parks hung back and eventually stood next to his girl and told her that it was time to go, to see other parts of the park, and just like that the dolphin crested the surface, and he was staring right at it. The crowd hushed. He looked into its eyes and it tapped its beak on his nose. He gave it a quick pat and the beast disappeared back into the pool. The crowd looked at him like they might string him up. Louise jumped up and down and told him he was the dolphin whisperer and they hugged and he remembered the smell of hotel blankets fondly.

His room smelled like urine and booze. Bill Baldwin did his routine, he opened the halfway-open door and said "Goddammit John," but before he could finish the prone man's rage was upon him, and the spiders swarmed up his legs and covered him in bites and fell down his throat and crawled into his eye sockets.

When they dispersed Baldwin was a puffy, bloated corpse and Parks was full of an intense urge to run. He got in his truck, spiders still pouring from the green gaping wound in his foot, and he headed for the mountains, away from the scene of the crime, away from anyone else he might destroy with his loneliness and anger.

* * *

Steve Haywood put on his Dickies and shirt. The "Steve" on the sleeve about ready to peel off.

Branson Collins fried eggs in the kitchen. Coffee machine like a cat choking on far-off fireworks. Collins stared at the pan. "You good?"

"Yeah."

"We good?"

Haywood grabbed a fork and stabbed at the eggs. Collins slapped at his hand. Haywood shoveled the eggs into his mouth and said, "We good," and walked out the door.

At work, he finished up the bullet holes in the Lumina and grabbed the key and pulled it around the back of the garage. He checked over his shoulder. He dug through the glove compartment and under the seats. Double checking. He knew they were meticulous that night but couldn't shake the feeling that he'd left something there, couldn't get it out of his head that Louise might be vacuuming one day and find his ID card or a receipt from the burgers he ate that night or something.

Of course that receipt is in a dump, somewhere.

Of course his ID was in his wallet.

He returned the key to the salesman up front and shuffled into the waiting room to get a cup of coffee. A talk show on the TV: thirteen year old girls who want to be hookers. No sound. An older man with a car magazine open on his lap watched the screen and shook his head and talked to himself quietly.

Louise stood behind him and tapped him on the shoulder. "Everything okay?"

The coffee singed Haywood's throat.

"Yeah, it's good. Patched her up."

She folded her arms and grimaced. "They told me this place was bad."

He poured another coffee. Stomach did flips. He calculated how far he was from the bathroom, how much time he'd need if an emergency arose. "The police on it?"

Louise threw her hand up and sucked her teeth. Haywood couldn't stop staring at her face. Couldn't peg it as cute or nice or sexy but he just kept staring. She said, "They don't know shit. They went to the house that they shot up, that shot my shit up. Talked to everyone there. Apparently the place was empty and the dudes there gave some bullshit name. He pissed someone off, someone looking. I don't know. This whole place is fucked."

"Where are you from?"

"The city."

Steve Haywood motioned to the orange plastic chairs. They sat. "Why on earth would you come here?"

"My man. Well, ex-man."

"Damn." Was it her smell? He leaned closer. She smelled normal.

"Yeah. So, here I am."

Haywood wanted to turn her over and press her face into the floor and fuck her stupid. "So what do you do?"

She rummaged through her purse. "I was a vet. I just got here, so, you know. I'm looking."

He motioned towards the shop. "Fuck it, come work here. Change some tires. Get sweaty."

She laughed and put on some lip liner. "Yeah, I could see that."

"You'd look good with a layer of grease."

Louise closed her purse and stood up and walked towards the door. "Well, it was nice seeing you again."

He nodded. "You too."

Before she got to the door she turned and gave him a look. Thinking. She scribbled her number on the back of a receipt and handed it to him and said, "Text me."

Louise left. Haywood crumpled up his paper cup of coffee and stuffed the number in his pocket and felt the previous night's work swirl around his guts.

They texted back and forth through the morning. She got too drunk the night before/her man was acting out/he pushed her/she doesn't know what to do. He zipped lug nuts into wheels and texted and sweated and realized that she was someone he could stand to be around.

Coworkers yelled at each other and wiped black streaks across their foreheads.

Louise wrote that she loved her dog.

That she was hungry.

That she wanted a drink tonight.

Haywood thought about Collins spitting in that boy's mouth and decided then that he'd take her out.

Home: shower/dress/mouthwash Later they sat at the bar and he listened to her talk.

She ordered another drink.

She talked about friends who talked about her behind her back and her problems with addiction in the past and movie stars who she'd like to meet. Haywood recognized it all as that surface level bullshit one comes to expect when there's nothing between two people but a strong drink. But there was something below the surface: a reluctance, an intelligence. He tried to figure a way to talk to her, to really talk to her, but he couldn't think for the poison in his brain.

Louise talked at length about the ex, about their engagement. She seemed to actually be upset, the way she talked about it. There was a distinct change in her demeanor: her shoulders slumped and her voice lowered and her eyes stayed trained on the drink. Normally this would make Haywood lose interest, this clear affection for someone maybe not yet out the door. But tonight he felt himself nodding with her, tuning the music out as best he could, trying his best to give advice, to help her.

After a few hours Haywood's cell phone rang. He picked it up and put a finger to his other ear. Collins said, "They came at us."

"What?"

"They came at us. At Hagar."

"Hagar?"

"Big customer, Steve."

"Okay."

"Someone caved his fucking skull in with a bat."

"I'm assuming this guy maybe didn't have the greatest friends?"

"Don't talk back to me. Get your ass to the Burger King."

"Maybe we should—"

"We're not talking about this. Get over here, now."

Haywood hung up and paid the bill and told her that he had a good time. The disappointment on her face made his dick scream from behind its denim.

Louise ordered another drink. She put her hand over his. "I had a really nice time."

Haywood wanted to grab her by her hair and drag her someplace dark.

The bar lights reflected in her pupils and he wanted to touch her hair.

He patted her hand and left the bar and walked home. A homeless man yelled at his bike and lifted it in the air and threw it in the street. He ran out to it and cradled it and cried. Folks barbecued in their backyards. The night dark blue and sick orange.

The Burger King parking lot was mostly empty. One van in the drive-thru. Haywood and Collins linked up in the bushes and saw Hammond push through the door, take his hat off, and turn to go. They followed him until he rounded the corner to his home. Collins grabbed him by

the back of the neck and pushed him down a small gravel road bent out and potholed from years of neglect. He kicked Hammond's legs out from under him and pushed him against a fence, big piles of brush sticking out on either side of him. Collins reached in his pocket and when his fist came out it was ringed in brass knuckles.

Hammond said, "Wait," and Collins smacked him in the mouth. The boy spit blood and teeth and crumpled over.

Haywood pulled his friend back.

Jesus fucking Christ.

Collins pushed him off and straddled the limp body. The sharp clanking of metal on bone.

Wesley Hammond's face folded in on itself. His eye socket cracked open and the wet orb spilled out, a tangle of nerves leading back to his skull.

Collins wrenched his fist from the black mess.

Haywood stepped back and kept his insides inside.

Collins wiped the blood off his face and stood up and handed Haywood a ten dollar bill.

"Go get Brooke some fries."

Haywood held the bill at his side. "Seriously."

Branson Collins towered over him. Grinding his jaw. The moonlight on his teeth. "I am the provider."

* * *

Rangitsch set a Coke in front of Jerry Isassi. The interrogation room was stark but for the inspirational posters hung on each wall. The south wall featured a cat hanging from a tree. The north wall had a gorilla holding a deer. The west wall had a tiger with a bunch of cubs. The east, penguins. The captain had odd ideas about interrogation. "Bring them back to grade school," he'd said.

Isassi shifted in the cold metal chair. "This shit is mad uncomfortable."

Janairo looked up from the perp's rap sheet. "What? The diaper?"

"Yeah. I don't really understand it."

"Well, we know about your problem. Your mother told us all about it."

Isassi turned red. He flexed. Tattoos on his neck shifting under big purple veins. "This is bullshit."

Rangitsch pointed at his face. "Quiet down, young man, or we're taking away your soda."

The criminal sipped his Coke and hushed.

Janairo cleared his throat. "Well it seems here, young man, that you've been very naughty."

"The fuck."

Rangitsch flung his chair back and came around the table. He tilted Isassi onto the table and smacked him on the butt. "You watch your mouth, mister."

"Oh my god. What's going on?"

"What's going on, is that you've been fighting with other boys on the playground."

Isassi threw his hands up. "I came here to give you guys a tip."

The cops glanced at each other. Janairo: "Wait, you came here voluntarily?"

"Yes. Branson Collins killed my friend. Kid was like my little brother."

Janairo closed the file. "Oh."

"Can I take the diaper off?"

"Of course. Just, you know. Finish your story first."

"They're trying to clear out all the competition. Myself included."

"Are you admitting that you're a drug dealer?"

"I'm not."

"But you said—"

"Listen. He killed Hammond, and I told him I was done. But what he's doing, is he's making this whole town his, so he can sell it to a national drug chain."

Rangitsch raised an eyebrow. "A chain?"

"Yeah. And once those guys get here, that's it for you. You'll be bought off or killed. They don't play."

"Where can we find Collins?"

"He's gonna meet up with the Gutierrez crew tomorrow at five o'clock over in the Alabaster Mountains."

Janairo checked his watch. "Shit."

"Make sure you catch Collins with the shit before he gets to his meet up. If he gets there, those dudes are gonna have firepower. And they're a lot bigger than any of this."

Janairo and Rangitsch left the interrogation room and high-fived. Isassi sipped his Coke and adjusted his diaper and stared at the picture of the penguins and suddenly felt inconsolably guilty.

* * *

John Parks watched the sun go down through the pine and oak trees in the woods below the Alabaster Mountains. He drove along the winding road and ate a bag of Doritos and an orange he'd stolen from the Natural Grocer after the entire store cleared out at the site of a man covered in tittering black spiders. He parked at the base of the mountain and looked out at the prairie dogs poking their heads from their burrows. From beneath the ground he heard a scream rise and the prairie dogs shot from their holes like daredevils from cannons, beating at their heads and bodies and anywhere else the swarm of arachnids found purchase. He sank to his knees, a fountain of poisonous bodies, and looked out at the hundreds of bloated dead rodents.

Hiking up the trail, he was careful to control the beasts as best he could. His foot was now in full bloom, the petals of his flesh peeled back and dragging in the red dirt, a new spider birthed every ten seconds.

He heard voices in the dusk and prayed that he wouldn't see them, wouldn't accidentally fall upon someone, set the horde on them. Heart sank when he saw it through the clearing: a group of teenagers in facepaint, dancing around a newborn fire pit. The teens talked about the moon and the trees and a girl held up a lunchbox and opened it and streamers and toy cars fell into the fire pit. The kids laughed and did handstands and mooned each other.

John Parks remembered the first time they'd gone camping, him and Louise. They'd parked out by a rope swing near his uncle's house and spent the day in inflatable inner tubes catching fish and swimming in the green water. He'd swung out on a rope and nearly landed on a turtle and Louise had been so scared of the helgramites and their big wings and big beaks. They'd slept in a stuffy trailer and they talked about nothing until she'd mentioned that her first date with her first boyfriend had ended similar to this and John Parks could not wrap his head around how a first date might have ended this way. It had made him mad, he'd gone out to the black water and thought about it but when he dipped his feet into the warm river he'd realized that he missed her more than he resented her remark. He'd went back to the trailer and she had fallen asleep and he was content to close his eyes and commit her smell to memory.

He smelled it again as the young people summoned the moon and he didn't want to but he couldn't help it, the spiders set after them, and the tiny mouths ate the paint from the boy's smooth faces and turned blonde hair dark and crawled up inside of their screaming bodies and poisoned them until they swelled pink and drooling around a fire now raging against the dried oak.

A whistle in the dark and John Parks turned and saw a man standing there amongst the trees, a blonde man in blue jeans and a denim jacket and white as snow. The man smiled all sharp teeth and red eyes and when he approached Parks waved him off, shouting about the danger, about the spiders crawling all over him. The man put a finger to his lips and reached into his pockets. He pulled out crushed sage and stuffed them around the spiders and into Parks' ears, and the man took out a bag of rocks and shook it and blue sparks shot from the top, shot out to every crawling thing on his skin, and they all died, a flood of eight-legged carcasses rolling down the dirt path, and the denim man told him: "Get to the top and cleanse yourself."

John Parks stomped the hard carcasses of his former captors and set up the hill, looking for the summit, doing his best not to scratch the open wound in his foot.

* * *

Louise threw on a t-shirt and jeans. She grabbed her purse from the end table and waved goodbye to her new roommates and her dog and stepped out into the heavy heat. She met Haywood at the miniature golf park. She quieted down when she stepped to the green, tongue poking slightly from the side of her mouth, and hit a par. Haywood hit the ball hard and it clanked off the edge and bounced into the grass and they laughed.

She liked him all right. She wanted to get out of town as soon as possible, wasn't interested in starting anything serious, but she got lonely in her apartment. She got tired of painting and rewatching television shows and thinking about John, about how he was certainly setting about destroying himself over her decision. She liked the easy talk, the casual laughter, how it took her mind off of things.

John had put her belongings in a box in the lawn and she was determined not to go to them, even though she knew there were things in there she'd miss. She had to prove a point.

Haywood seemed oddly distant today, and his unease made her stomach twist up. He seemed nervous and jittery, moving around the miniature golf course like he was ready to have it over with.

They went out for drinks and after that he took her home. They undressed in his room and she put him in her mouth and wondered exactly how she should suck his dick: she had been with John so long that she knew what got to him, but wasn't sure if that meant it was any good. She tried different techniques. He tossed her on the bed and put a condom on and when he pushed himself inside of her there was that brief blast of color, the creation of something new that soon faded into a kind of repetitious pumping. She didn't care for the condom or how he fucked her fast. She focused on his body, on his sounds, but never on herself. Neither of them finished but they both lay there, spent.

She stared up at the ceiling and wondered if this is what her life would come to, miniature golf dates and awkward sex. She curled up and fell asleep and when she woke up early the next morning Haywood was dressed and ready to go. He handed her a plate of eggs and his roommate peeked in at her and said, "She's gotta go. It's time."

Haywood sat on the edge of the bed and started shaking. She didn't feel particularly close to him, but she held him all the same. When the tears started dripping on her forearms, she decided this would be the last time she saw the mechanic. She dressed and turned her car on and went to Starbucks and ordered a coffee. She went home and hugged her dog and opened the paper and

looked for jobs, anything to save up a little money to move away, maybe move back with her mother, but anywhere that wasn't here, this awful town and its sad people.

* * *

Alexander Janairo forgot his sunglasses at the office. He turned the radio up and squinted. Rangitsch leaned his head against the window and watched the buffalo eat as they drove further into the refuge.

They pulled down the long smooth driveway into the visitor's center and parked and walked quick to get out of the heat. The air conditioner hit them and they both sighed quietly. The building was quiet. The counter had fliers in plastic holders detailing the beasts and fauna of the Alabaster Mountains. Janairo picked one out, glanced at it, then balled it up and tossed it at the wastebasket by the glass door. It bounced off the edge. "Kobe," he pouted.

The desk behind the counter: a computer next to a half-full cup of coffee. The police detectives crept around the counter, calling out "hello" and "is anybody here?"

After a few moments they found the sole employee struggling to dig himself out of a vicious k-hole that at that moment had him spread eagle on the floor of the janitor's closet. The man had his long hair tied into a bun that acted as a pillow. He tried to mouth words but the cops could make nothing of it. They walked out of the closet and back through the waist high swinging door and sat down in the hard plastic chairs and waited for the horse tranquilizer to loosen its grip.

Janairo checked espn.com while Rangitsch read the Wikipedia article on ketamine.

After about an hour, they heard a groan. They pushed themselves out of the ass-punishing bucket seats and walked to the body's side. He worked his dry lips and rasped, "I'm in a k-hole."

Janairo nodded. "We know." Then Sasha Fierce took over. "You need to respect yourself."

Rangitsch stood up and walked to the door and stared out at the brown grass and the blue sky. "Let's just forget it," he said.

Sasha stood up. "Fuck you, Bob."

Rangitsch sighed. "Yeah."

"I'm not gonna let a dissociated hater keep me from closing this case. I don't have time for this."

The employee got himself into a sitting position. "I am starting to feel my hands."

Janairo knelt next to him. "Have you seen any suspicious activity in this area this morning?"

The employee thought about it for a long time. "I did see a bunch of Mexican dudes pull down the Scissortail Trail a bit ago."

Sasha Fierce nodded. "Point me in that direction."

* * *

John Parks ascended the small mountain. He dug his fingers into the small hairs of a cactus and tore it open and frowned at the small brown droplets of water already evaporating from the ground. A rattlesnake shook in the bushes and he knelt down and held his arm out and the thing struck and dangled from his forearm. He pulled it off and tossed it as far as he could and felt his blood thicken and the wound in his foot go from dark green to black.

Climb.

He got near the top. He remembered Louise, how she looked when the moonlight hit her and she turned to him with tears in her eyes and told him that she loved him, but she didn't like him anymore, how he'd stood up from the bed and paced and when she stood up to hold him

he'd pushed her against the wall and knocked over the alarm clock. She'd run out and he'd plugged the clock back in, it blinking twelve AM at him and he thought about buying a gun.

Parks took his shirt off and ran up the slope. The poisons fought for control of his thick blood.

* * *

Haywood and Collins met Gutierrez at the crossroads of Scissortail Trail and Buffalo Hills Trail. The drug lord dressed in a white t-shirt and cargo shorts. He checked his Facebook and dropped the phone in his pocket and turned to one of his guards and slapped the man across the eyes. The guard fell to the ground and held his face and stood up and adjusted his sunglasses and assault rifle.

"Quit tagging me at your barbecues," Gutierrez said. "My Facebook page is private for a reason. If you or your wife or one of your fucking kids takes my picture, that's cool. But don't tag me."

The guard sniffled. "Sorry, boss."

Gutierrez took a deep breath. "I'm sorry I got mad." He lit a cigarette. "So what's the deal, kiddos?"

Collins stepped forward. "We took care of our shit. We're the only ones selling anything in this town, and that's a guarantee."

Gutierrez said, "We have your word on that?"

"Absolutely."

Haywood hung back and looked at his feet. Gutierrez looked around Collins. "You. You willing to bet your life on this?"

Haywood said, "Yes."

Gutierrez shrugged. "Well, lets do it, then." One of the guards opened the door to the Escalade and brought out a heavy bag full of cash. "There's a lot of money there." He checked his phone. "Holy shit, look at this dog riding a motorcycle!" He showed it to his henchmen. They chuckled. "Fucking dog on a motorcycle. Fucking great."

Collins picked the bag up. "I appreciate your business."

Gutierrez waved him off. "It was a really good idea. Hopefully we can do it again, if you ever want to make a little more."

Collins nodded. "Sure."

* * *

Janairo and Rangitsch laid flat on their bellies in the scrub just south of the crossroads. Janairo whispered, "We have to bust them, Range."

His partner looked at him sideways. "Are you fucking kidding me?"

"No."

"They have assault rifles."

"I see that."

"We have no backup."

Janairo frowned. "You sound like a little bitch, right now."

"John, please…"

"Don't you say my name."

"Keep your voice down."

"We're doing this. Now."

Janairo jumped out from behind the scrub and pulled his piece and yelled "POLICE." Rangitsch cursed and followed suit. The guards turned to the two men and casually lifted their rifles. They opened fire. Rangitsch's head exploded and his brains hit the dirt and his body flopped and convulsed. The bullets ripped through Janairo, and as he fell to earth he saw his fingers and pieces of his torso fly up in front of him and he died before he hit the ground.

* * *

The spirit inside of Alexander Janairo curled away from the bullets and evacuated the body through the mouth. It took one last look at the dead body and took off into the sky. It sensed the fear coming from the two unarmed men and it looked into each of their souls. It could not figure which one it desired less: the brutal man with a penchant for destroying and humiliating those around him, or the small man too afraid to do anything about it. Sasha Fierce decided that the murderer was less worthy, and it flew down into Steve Haywood's eyes and his spirit was so paralyzed by fear he didn't have the will to fight any kind of intrusion. Haywood leapt into the bushes as the cartel trained their guns on Branson Collins, he rolled and got up and did not look back to see his friend torn to pieces under the muzzle flashes. A bullet knicked his calf and he tumbled over the dirt and down a slight incline. He grabbed at the wound to stem the blood and the spirit in him made him stand and hobble, anything to survive.

* * *

John Parks reached the summit of the mountain and he looked out at the hawks circling and he heard the gunfire down below. He breathed in the fresh blue air and looked out at the mottled hills and felt all of his problems disappear. The sage in his ears vibrated and he could hear all the spirits around him, and they closed the snakebite and the spiderbite. Childhood: He won the spelling bee in fourth grade. He scored a goal in soccer and he learned how to tie a perfect fly and he learned that he could talk to people and that they might just like him, maybe. He won employee of the month at the restaurant and he picked up the tree business quick and he could do anything he wanted to. The negativity escaped through his anus, a large purple cloud, and it rolled down the mountainside to the bottom, where it pooled like a great fog. Gutierrez and his men ran over to the side of the small hill and trained their weapons on Steve Haywood when the purple fog wafted over them. All the bad moments of John Parks' life seeped into their brainpans: he was humiliated after school by the boys in the aqueduct, they chased him with bats and they shot him with a blowgun. He once drove a girl home and took his dick out and she laughed and ran inside. He couldn't hold down a job and he was getting old and he wasn't sure if he had anything of value to offer the world. The woman he loved, he spent hours talking to her on her couch and with his arm around her he could smell her but he forgot that smell, and he'd never know it again, she would never come to pick up the box outside of his home. All that purple negativity overwhelmed the drug men and the henchman turned their guns on themselves, painting Gutierrez in blood, and the drug lord took out his phone and wrote a suicide note on Facebook, then picked up a rifle from the cold hands of his dead friend and shot himself, too. The spirit inside of Steve Haywood swelled to a blue fierceness, and the negativity rolled around and off of him.

John Parks descended the mountain a new man. He was quenched. Alive. He investigated the bodies at the crossroads and found Steve Haywood pale and shaking in the brush. He picked him up and carried him down the dirt path, away from the carnage, to where he'd parked his truck ages ago.

He set the dying man in the passenger seat and started the truck and sped off down the road.

"Don't worry," he said. "Everything's going to be fine."

John Parks brushed the hard spider corpses from Steve Haywood's face, and he plugged in the address of the hospital into his GPS.

DAVID W. BARBEE

LOCATION:
Macon, GA

STYLE OF BIZARRO:
Deep Fried Freakazoid

BOOKS BY BARBEE:
Carnageland
A Town Called Suckhole
Thunderpussy
The Night's Neon Fangs
Bacon Fried Bastard
The Buddha Gump Shrimp Company
Death's Hot Coffin Pants

DESCRIPTION: Disturbing pulp tales that mix folksy grit with far out futurism, full of rabidly imaginative landscapes populated by a gruesome sideshow of maniacs and monsters.

INTERESTS: Comic books without superheroes, genre-bending, vulgar cartoons, surreal comedy, sexy violence, violent sex, monstrous humanity, the humanity of monsters.

INFLUENCES: Alan Moore, Frank Miller, Garth Ennis, Cormac McCarthy, Daniel Woodrell, Joe R. Lansdale, Mark Twain, Edgar Allan Poe, Flannery O'Connor, Judson Mitcham, Chuck Palahniuk, Quentin Tarantino, Warren Ellis, Neil Gaiman, China Mieville, Mike Mignola, Carlton Mellick III, Jeffrey Thomas, Edgar Rice Burroughs, HG Wells, Douglas Adams, Monty Python, Mel Brooks, Star Wars.

WEBSITE:
davidwbarbee.wordpress.com

NOAH'S ARKOPOLIS

Abashed, God saw the wickedness of mankind and was so grieved as to send a great flood to cleanse the Earth.

Yet He chose one man to carry His creation into the future. That man was Noah, righteous and noble and falling down drunk.

God instructed Noah to build a massive Ark, and to fill it with his family and all the animals of the Earth, male and female alike. Noah built the Ark with hand and hammer, measuring with bleary bloodshot eyes. Noah's neighbors laughed at his effort, but after the rains began, it turned out they weren't so fucking smart.

Land gave way to ocean, and Noah and his menagerie floated in the Ark as the rest of the world drowned. After forty days and nights, Noah ran out of booze and went insane. He fell to his knees and prayed to God. "My lord!" he cried. "I have done your bidding! When may we find land so we may walk the Earth once again?"

The clouds in the sky parted and the lord God looked upon this new world of smooth blue water. And He saw the Ark, floating in the vastness, dry and alone.

"I believe I like it better this way," sayeth the lord, and so He disappeared from Noah's sight, never to be seen again.

Noah screamed and raged and shook his fists at the sky. "I denounce thee, Lord God! I hold dominion over the Ark, home to all the creatures of land and sky! We shall continue! We shall build! I swear I shall erect a city on the water that rivals the Kingdom of Heaven!"

And they did. Noah released all the beasts and birds and reptiles from their pens and cages. And he bid them all to join together and populate the Ark with generations. And he bid his human family to join with the animals. And from them sprang forth the generations, the chimeric children who would go on to strip Noah's Ark of its vast skeleton and rebuild it into a great city floating on the water.

They called it Arkopolis, and it was good.

* * *

"This isn't good."

The President's Cabin was located at the center of the city, perched atop the highest mast with a view for miles. The room swayed over the city. The city swayed on the ocean waves.

The President himself paced, walking back and forth across his manatee-skin floor rug. It was morning, and the leader of Arkopolis had been up all night with the latest reports from his Cabinet. The three of them lurked in the corners as their leader paced. They had each agreed with his assessment of their reports.

It wasn't good.

The President of Arkopolis was a precise blend of bald eagle and lion. He was from strong predatory stock, with a shaggy pelt of fur and feathers. He raked his talons through his lion's mane beard. His tail swished as he padded back and forth. His eagle eyes were clear, staring away in deep thought.

The President stopped pacing and hopped onto his desk, crouching like a gargoyle. He peered at his Cabinet. "How many empty boats does this make?"

"Forty," said the Secretary of City. She was an old tapir lady with a round turtle shell body and long ostrich legs. She perched on a stool in the corner of the cabin, rifling through papyrus sheets with her stubby paws.

"Same story," said the President. "They were lost while hunting big game out over the depths. Send the boats to salvage, have them broken down."

The Secretary of Industry cleared his massive throat. He had a fat toad body with a possum's tail and gnarled vulture claws. He hung upside down from a ceiling joist, his black feathers sagging downward and his wide mouth locked in a frown. "We need more boats, not less," he said. "There's an energy shortage, the economy is sagging, and the bottom line is we need more oil."

The President of Arkopolis fired his eagle eyed glare at the toad man. "We're already killing enough whales to power the city. The shortage is due to the sabotage in our fuel network." He looked to the Secretary of Military. "Any news on said sabotage?"

The Secretary of Military was head of the Municipal Guard. He was tall and muscular, a mixture of alligator, hippo, and orangutan. His long body had dark gray skin with patches of slick orange hair. He leaned back on his thick reptilian tail and said, "The attacks are random, and no one has seen anything. The only thing we know is that it's all happening inside the city."

"Some kind of damn terrorist," the President growled.

"Be that as it may, sir," said the Secretary of City. "The terrorist is just one of many problems. Arkopolis is floating over extremely deep waters. The kind not seen in generations. My opinion is that we should turn back for the shallows."

The President of Arkopolis ground his beak angrily. His citizens were disappearing and a terrorist was sabotaging the oil network, causing an energy crisis that was already triggering blackouts across the city.

"This city will not turn back," the President said. "We don't turn back. We drift across the water, we take from the ocean until there's nothing left to take, then we drift some more. That's how it's written in the Constitution, and by Noah the Father, that is how we shall continue."

* * *

Gren awoke that morning late for work. He swung out of his hammock, which took up a third of his tiny cabin, and one of his antlers bumped against the low ceiling. He stumbled onto his hooves and hurried out the door.

Gren was seven feet tall from hoof to antler. His father had been mostly moose, though Gren had inherited an equal amount of tiger and a little bit of dog. His mother had come from strong reptilian stock, mostly chameleon and iguana, so his face and tail were scaled, and he had his mother's long tongue and love for snacking on the city's flocks of bug-pigeons.

He galloped through the corridors of his apartment boat, hopping over lumpy piles of dung. There were seventy-seven boats and ships that made up Arkopolis, lashed together with ropes and riggings and whale bones, and filled with all manner of creature. Some said the Arkopolan population reached into the millions, but the ocean always supplied them with enough to keep everyone happy.

Still, Gren was just a lowly dockworker. One of thousands. No one special.

He arrived at Delta Bay an hour late. Fishermen from the previous night were steering their boats into the docks, bringing seafood, seaweed, sealumber, and most importantly, dead whales.

The moose man entered the Bay and hurried to his station. His supervisor, a fat sheep/camel/woodpecker man, scolded him for being late. Gren hurried past him without a word and took his place with the other workers as a long skiff slid in from the open ocean.

The skiff sat heavy in the water, piled with dozens of nets full of slippery tuna. Three rooster/beaver men steered into place and hopped onto the dock as the workers tied the boat in.

Gren and the others unloaded the tuna nets as the three fishermen watched. They were known as the Huuk brothers, scurvy sailors as tough as they were obnoxious. They crowed at the dockworkers lugging their catch. "Nice work, city boys!" said the tallest. "Somebody's gotta carry the nets! After all, not everyone can sail the open seas like heroes!"

The brothers beat their flat tails against the dock and laughed. Gren ignored them and lifted a heavy load of tuna onto his shoulder. He carried it down the dock to a chute that would take the fish to the city's food processing plant. It went on like that until the end of the day, with Gren silently focused on his work.

When the whistle blew at the end of the day, Gren followed the other workers to the dock manager's office. All of them gathered around the little wooden building, trickling through a door in one side and emerging on the other with their stipend for the day.

Gren got his turn after much pushing and shoving. He walked up to a desk with a feathery man with a gopher face and hoof hands sitting behind it. The man pulled a lever in the wall next to him and a single white pearl the size of a rabbit turd rolled down a chute. The man picked up the pearl and dropped it into Gren's open palm. Gren nodded and hurried out the room, happy to be paid.

If Gren got fired for being late to the dock, the tiny pearl in his paw would be his last scrap of money. But he hadn't eaten in several days, so Gren hurried to the nearest marketplace.

He arrived to see vendors selling seaweed wraps, salmon, swordfish, and various flavors of sea slug. Gren wandered along. The market was full of people milling about and eating scallops-on-a-stick. He was just beginning to wonder what he should eat when an explosion ripped through the street.

There was a deafening blast, and a wall of smoke and dust and tumbling people rushed at Gren. He honked in surprise and fell to the floor. The blast was deafening, and even after the noise died down he could only hear the screams of his fellow Arkopolans. He pushed an obese woman who was a cross between a llama and a sloth off of his chest and stood. Dead bodies were scattered around, their flesh torn and shredded. Blood was everywhere. Gren squinted through the smoke and flames all around him.

Then he saw it.

It was a shape, dancing around in the smoky gloom, pumping fists into the air. It stopped and turned to face Gren, like it was looking at him. Something about the figure's size and shape unnerved Gren. He couldn't tell what sort of animal it was. It was a little too slender, the head a little too ovular.

It seemed like the shape of a human, but that couldn't be. There were no purebred humans anymore. No purebred *anything*, actually.

The shape disappeared into the smoke as the city's fire wagons rushed to the scene. A large contraption on wheels, powered by refined whale oil, sped past Gren. It was piled high with rubber hoses and city volunteers, who climbed off the wagon as it pulled to a stop before the flames. They hooked their hoses to water pumps lining the boat's hull and sprayed seawater into the angry fire.

Gren turned and stumbled away from the scene. He wasn't sure what had just happened, but he knew he wanted to go home. He wasn't hungry anymore.

He looked down at his hands.

No pearl.

He'd dropped it.

Gren continued on. He walked through the neighborhood as word spread about the explosion. He couldn't hear the talk, as there was an insistent ringing in his ears. As he trudged home, one voice pierced through the din.

"You have a piece of nose on you."

He turned to see her, an alluring mixture of swan and python, with smooth curves of spotted scales and downy feathers. Her face was defined by round reptilian eyes and a delicate beak. Her feet were webbed and her hands had spindly snakelike fingers. Sprouting from her posterior was a bushy striped tail that indicated a latent strain of raccoon or lemur in her bloodline, but that could be ignored. She was undeniably beautiful, no matter your genus preference.

She was staring at him, and Gren found himself unable to move.

"I said you have a piece of nose on you."

The female reached up and plucked a wet bit of flesh from his furry shoulder. Sure enough it was someone's nose, possibly a dog's. She looked him over with her large cobra eyes. He was a clumsy lummox, but she liked the way his parts came together. She flicked the nose away and wiped her snaky fingers on Gren's chest, leaving gooey blood behind.

"I'm Asa," she said. Gren still said nothing, and she gave him a stern look that said he'd better start paying attention.

"Oh, hi, my name is Gren," he managed to say. "I'm a dockworker."

"Well, Gren the dockworker," said Asa. "What are you doing with a piece of nose on you?"

"Uh, there was a fire. An explosion. A lot of people got hurt."

"Interesting," she said. "Listen, Gren. I'm on my way home this evening, and I shouldn't walk the decks alone at such an hour. How would you like to escort me to my cabin?"

Gren's eyes widened and he smiled. Asa smirked at him again. He was a real dorkfish.

And so Gren walked Asa to her cabin, which was on the north side of town, far away from his place. She sashayed beside him, as if it were the most natural thing in the world, a graceful thing like her walking in tandem with a loutish dockworker. She didn't talk much, so Gren had to make use of his terribly poor conversational skills.

"So," he said. "What do you do?"

"I work for the city," Asa said. "But that's not important. You said there was an explosion earlier?"

"Yes," he said. "It was crazy. It came from up the street, at the market."

"Well, that's interesting," Asa said.

Gren looked down at her. "Why's that interesting?" He wondered if she was making fun of him.

"Haven't you heard?" she asked. "There have been explosions all over the city. Oil spigots rupturing and then catching fire. The official word from the President is that there are some bugs in the pipes. But the explosions so far have only happened to the biggest spigots in the city, and the rumor is that there's a terrorist behind it all. This is me."

Gren looked up and saw the entrance to Asa's high end apartment boat. She thanked him for walking her home and then walked away. He should have said something polite, but could only stand there and watch her. Holy Ark, she was beautiful. He was sure he'd never get to see her again. Their meeting was a chance encounter, one that he wouldn't hope to repeat, no matter how much he wanted to.

After long moments he pulled himself away from staring at her and started for home.

* * *

Gren crossed rope bridges and catwalks connecting the ships and boats of Arkopolis. He passed giant pumping machines that sucked brine from the ocean and boiled it into drinkable water. He passed squads of city janitors swabbing the decks.

When he made it to his cabin, Gren climbed into his hammock, stomach rumbling with hunger. He dreamed of sitting at a feast fit for the President. Gren ate lobsters and clams and succulent fillets until he looked down and realized what he was eating.

It was a leg.

A long swan's leg.

Gren retched and ran away from the table. Eating anything other than fish was barbaric, and that swan's leg looked like a perfect fit for Asa. His stomach turned at the thought. As he ran the floor collapsed and he fell. He fell through fire and smoke and splashed into a great pool of water. He kicked and flailed. He couldn't swim. Then he realized he wasn't alone.

There were things in the water.

Big things.

"Wake up!"

Gren awoke with a honking scream and fell out of his hammock. He thrashed around in the dark, his limbs still trying desperately to swim away from danger.

"Calm down!" said a voice in the cabin with him.

Gren instantly went still. "Who's there?" he asked in a cautious voice. There was no answer for a few moments, and Gren became sure that he'd imagined the voice in his room. But of course the voice came back again.

"You saw it, didn't you? The whales?"

"What whales?" Gren asked.

"The whales, you moron!" said the voice. "The whales out in the ocean! Arkopolis hunts them all day and all night, living off their meat and oil, but they're the ones who rule the world! You saw them in your dreams just now, didn't you?"

"How do you know about my dream?"

"God told me," said the voice.

"There's no such thing as God," said Gren. "Every Arkopolan knows that. Noah the Father said so himself. It's written in the Constitution of Arkopolis."

"Ugh," said the voice. "Don't start with all that talk. It makes my head hurt. Look, no matter how you feel about it, the whales are coming. In the pit of your stomach you know it to be true. The whales have evolved over the centuries, just like the Arkopolans did. They've grown smart and their minds have psychic powers! They can make every Arkopolan do what they want, and they want you to die. They've declared war on the city for all these years of massacre. They're going to come here, rip the city apart, and let her sink into the water."

"Really?" Gren whispered.

"Yes, really," said the voice. "And you and I are the only ones who can stop it. God has sent me here to do just that, and He has decreed that you are to help me on this holy quest."

"So who are you?" Gren asked again.

There was a snapping sound, and a spark jumped into the tiny lantern hanging from the ceiling. Gren's cabin was illuminated, allowing him to see his visitor.

He couldn't tell what species he was,

being so short and human shaped. His little head was bald, and long hair sprouted from the bottom of his wrinkled face. He wore ragged robes, and all of him seemed to be blue and translucent, like he was made of mist.

Gren realized what he was seeing and he screamed, backing away until he tripped over the hammock and fell on his ass. Again.

The misty man stepped toward him. "I'm Noah," he said. "I built this city and now I'm here to save it."

Gren stared at the man-shaped vapor standing in his apartment with him. His green tiger eyes widened as he got to his hooves and stood. "I'm imagining this," he decided, and walked through Noah's misty form and opened the door. Gren left the cabin and closed the door behind him, intent on getting some fresh air to clear his head.

He walked down a promenade that was empty of pedestrians, and made it a few blocks before the ghost caught up with him. "You're lucky nobody else can see me but you. That's the way God wanted it. Always gets what He wants, that one."

"You're not real," Gren whispered.

"Look," said Noah. "You think I wanted you as my little helper? I tried to get the bigwigs to help but even the President is completely clueless. Those government bastards don't see me, all because God won't allow it. He chose *you*."

"I don't believe in God," said Gren. "We were taught never to speak of God. Noah's word was that we didn't need religion because God was an asshole. It's in the Constitution."

"Fuck the Constitution already!" Noah screamed. "I've been living in Purgatory ever since I died, and this mission is my only chance to end all those centuries of sheer fucking nothingness and get my rightful spot in Heaven! Adam and Abel get into Paradise, but not me? That's bullshit and everybody on the other side knows it!"

"Why would God want to save Arkopolis?" said Gren. "Nobody here believes in Him and you always said He didn't care about us."

"He doesn't! That's the twist! He just wants this done because it's the right thing to do!" Noah made finger quotes and rolled his eyes as he said the last part.

"It's still crazy," said Gren. He began walking a little faster, but the ghost just kept drifting after him. "This is make-believe. I'm having a mental breakdown and if I don't lose my job I'll wind up homeless gnawing on old barnacles." Gren shivered at the idea.

"It figures that we'd have to do this the hard way," said the ghost, and with that Noah's misty form dissipated into a cloud of blue vapor. The cloud swirled around Gren and flowed into his mouth and nose. The moose man stopped in his tracks, trying to cough out the mist as it forced its way into him. He jerked and seized as the ghost took hold of his body and experimented with moving his muscled limbs.

"There," the ghost said through Gren's mouth.

Gren found himself stumbling down the street, clumsily stepping in mounds of dung. His legs jerked forward one at a time, steering him off the promenade and down narrow alleys and gangways.

"What are you doing?" he asked fearfully.

"You're a slow one, aren't you?" said the ghost. "No wonder He chose you. You're a weak-willed fuck. God always picks guys like you. Losers."

"Where are you taking me?" Gren said when the ghost was finished talking.

"Well," said Noah. "To stop the war

with the whales, we have to make Arkop-olis stop hunting them. To do that we have to get this city off its oil addiction, and then there will be peace and my mission will be complete."

"You want the city to stop using whale oil? Oil powers everything! There's no way they'll do that!"

"Not willingly," said the ghost.

"But we need that oil to power the furnaces and purify the water!" said Gren. "We need—wait. The explosions! You're the one who's been sabotaging the oil spigots!"

"Yep," said Noah. "Now come on. There's a spigot up the street I've had my eye on, and you're going to help me blow it."

"So you've been blowing up parts of the city... and killing people... so you can save Arkopolis?"

"Yep," Noah said again.

"You're insane," said Gren with fear.

No response from the ghost. Gren could only watch himself stagger faster and faster through the street. Noah steered him down a corridor of tall whale ribs in a vessel full of office cabins that were hope-fully empty at such a late hour.

"We don't have to do this," Gren plead-ed.

"Oh yes we do," said Noah. "Missions from God are always absolutely necessary. And I understand how you feel. God's been fucking with me all my life. You think I wanted to build a city floating on an ocean as big as the world? You think I wanted every beast and creature from across the globe depending on me to take care of them? No! He put me in that position and then He left me there! He violated me, and for centuries there was nothing I could do about it. Until now."

Noah steered Gren around a corner to a room thick rubber tubes and hoses trail-ing across the floor. Gren watchwith ed as

his hooves stepped over the hoses, lead-ing him towards the oil spigot on the other side of the room.

Gallons of whale oil slushed through a wide pipe embedded in the wall. The pipe coupled into a vast cauldron made of cemented coral, and the center of the cauldron had hundreds of circular ports of various sizes, each with a rubber hose plugged into it. The hoses trailed out of the room, draining oil and piping throughout the ship and into neighboring ships.

"I blow up thirteen of these bastards and they just plug more hoses in," said Noah.

Gren watched as his large tiger paws wrapped around a wide hose plugged into one of the larger ports. He watched him-self unscrew the tight hose coupling and pull it away from the spigot. A deluge of slick oil burst out of the port, sending Gren to the floor.

The ghost exited his body as he fell. Gren flailed about on the floor, which was covered in tangles of hose and drenched by the spraying oil. The ghost of Noah looked down at him and laughed.

"We're doing God's work!" he screamed, and then began snapping his ghostly fingers. Gren knew what that meant. He turned and crawled out of the room, slipping along the oily floor.

Finally he was able to get to his hooves and he ran as fast as he could, Noah's laughter echoing after him. The explosion hit, and the force of it chased after Gren and knocked him to the ground, licking at his fur with tendrils of fire.

* * *

Gren staggered out of an alleyway the next morning. He found himself in a pub-lic garden on a rundown barge, filled with bushes of mutated anemones. A drunken kangaroo with flamingo plumage and the snout of a komodo dragon slept on a nearby clamshell bench. A swarm of bug-pigeons buzzed by, and Gren lashed his tongue out at them for a snack.

He missed terribly.

His belly groaned, his muscles ached, and a creeping chill flowed through his veins. He'd been possessed by a ghost, but that couldn't be. Ghosts weren't real. Neither was God. And the whole thing with Noah and the whales? Preposterous. Gren became certain he'd imagined it all.

But the explosion was real. His singed fur was proof of that, and he could hear the sirens of fire wagons behind him. Gren continued onward, eager to put more distance between himself and the trouble.

He crossed a rope bridge from the garden barge onto a floating pavilion, a huge flat vessel with a wide variety of upscale boutiques and restaurants arranged on its surface. It was the kind of boat Gren usually avoided, but his empty stomach and the aroma of sizzling shrimp drew him in. He wandered toward a café decorated with sashes of green silk, his mouth drooling.

"Gren, isn't it?"

He turned to see Asa standing behind him, blinking her large cobra eyes and wearing a faint smile in her delicate swan's beak. Gren became aware of how disheveled he looked. He combed his claws through his fur, pulling away globs of slimy oil tainted with dust and dander.

Asa giggled at him. "You look terrible," she said.

"Sorry," he muttered.

"Maybe I can help. I was just about to have a light breakfast. Would you like to join me?"

Gren heard himself say 'yes' and then he was following her, watching her bushy tail sway over her plump swan's ass. She

was talking, but he was so petrified he could barely hear her. He couldn't help it. She was so beautiful, and he was so hungry. Hungry and dirty and crazy.

She led him into the café and to a cramped booth in the corner. A waitress with the body of a kiwi, the arms of an armadillo, and a long giraffe neck toddled over, took their order, and then toddled away. She returned with a seaweed wrap for Asa and a great basket of blubber-fried calamari for Gren.

As Gren shoveled the little octopi into his maw, Asa looked him over, her cobra eyes narrowing. "Gren," she said. He instantly froze, locking eyes with her in utter fear, his mouth full of chewed up tentacles. "I can see you're in trouble."

He nodded.

"And if you need help," she said, "I'm here for you."

He unfroze. "That's so nice of you," he said. "I've had the worst day in my life. I lost my stipend, I might lose my job, and then there was last night. First I had a really weird nightmare, and then I saw... a ghost."

"A ghost?" said Asa, interested.

"Yeah! It was the ghost of Noah and he told me all this crazy stuff, but it started making sense, you know? He told me about how Arkopolis is in danger and God wants me to help save it."

"You and the ghost of Noah—the human who founded Arkopolis—are going to save the city... for God?"

"Crazy, right?"

"God's not real," said Asa, pecking a bit of calamari out of the basket.

Gren smiled at her, baring bucked teeth paired with long feline fangs. She was as beautiful as ever and here she was, having breakfast with him in a fine café. And she was so willing to help him. Maybe things were getting better. The ghost was gone, replaced now with the kind and charitable Asa, who was the loveliest creature Gren had ever seen.

"Ugh, I forgot how much I hated this place."

Gren looked on in horror as the misty blue visage of Noah sidled into the booth next to Asa, smirking across the table at him.

Asa saw Gren's eyes widen in shock, his thick moose lips quivering in fear. "Are you all right?"

He said nothing.

"Over the last few centuries you guys got *weird*," said the ghost. "You really humped yourselves into a race of monsters! And I won't even start talking about the piles of shit everywhere. You know, it might be better to let Arkopolis get destroyed by the whales."

Gren whimpered and fidgeted.

"It might be better to just leave an innocent dockworker alone so he can live his pathetic little life in peace. But I'm on a mission from God. And so are you, moose boy."

"Gren, what's wrong?" asked Asa.

"You're not fucking this up for me, boy," said the ghost.

Gren's stomach full of calamari threatened to heave up out of his throat.

"Gren?" she said again.

"If you think you're shirking your responsibilities to God," Noah said. "You're sorely mistaken."

"Gren, are you seeing the ghost?" Asa whispered.

"Go ahead and tell her, Gren," said Noah. "I'll hop into your body and make you kill her with your bare paws. How would you like that?"

"Please don't," Gren whispered. He closed his eyes, his mind threatening to snap every moment he looked upon the girl and ghost sitting across the table from him.

"You *are* talking to a ghost, aren't you?"

Gren sniveled and put his face in his paws. Surely Asa thought he was crazy now. She was probably right.

"No one can help you," said the ghost.

"I can help you," said Asa. "I don't think you're crazy."

"You don't?" Gren whispered, looking up from between his tiger claws.

"I'll kill her, Gren," the ghost said. "In a heartbeat. But I'll make you a deal. You can keep your little pet here as long as you get back to helping me with my mission. And you have to buy me a beer. Now."

"Why do you need a beer?" asked Gren.

"What?" said Asa.

"It's God's plan!" Noah sneered. "Don't ask questions, just do what you're told and put your faith in Him!"

"This makes no sense," Gren said.

"I know," said Asa. "But even if you're crazy, you have a point! With the terrorist attacks and the missing fishermen, Arkopolis *is* in danger and someone has to save it! I want to help you, Gren. You look like you really need it."

Gren couldn't believe his ears.

"I like this girl," said Noah. "Now get me my beer or God will cast her into an eternal pit of fire where she'll be raped into the deepest insanity you can possibly imagine."

"God will do that?" Gren whispered in fear.

"Yep," said the ghost.

"BEER!" Gren yelled at the giraffe-headed waitress. Despite the early hour she hurried away to fetch a beer for the giant moose man. She delivered a bottle made from seabamboo to the booth and retreated.

"I'm so sorry about this," Gren said to Asa. "This has been the worst day of my entire life."

"It's okay, Gren." She wanted to reassure the moose man then, but something distracted her. The bamboo bottle floated up from the tabletop. Asa watched it hover next to her, then tilt to meet an invisible mouth.

The beer spilled out into a thin haze next to her. Asa gaped. The golden mist swirled into a shape sitting in the booth next to her. The gold became green, then gave way to blue, and in seconds she was staring at the human visage of Noah himself.

"Holy Ark," she whispered.

"You can see him?" Gren said in astonishment, suddenly filled with the joy of not being the only crazy person in the booth.

"It's real," she said, and turned to look at Gren. Her big cobra eyes welled with tears. Gren smiled at her and she smiled back. "I knew it," she whispered, and took Gren's huge paw into her delicate snake fingers.

"All part of God's plan!" the ghost cheered.

* * *

The three of them left the café, ready to embark on Noah's holy quest. A gorilla lady with cow udders and python scales sneered at Asa and Gren disapprovingly. She thought the lovely female to be walking exclusively with the unkempt moose man, unable to see the ghost between them.

Asa listened to Noah tell stories, enthralled. She asked questions and laughed at his dirty jokes. "And another thing," Noah said, "is the beer. It's pretty good stuff, but nothing like what we had in the first days of Arkopolis. It was way better than the penguin piss you animals are drinking these days."

"Didn't you drink penguin piss yourself?" asked Asa. "All our beer recipes are based on your own brewing methods."

"Well," said Noah, sounding like a wise old diplomat. "While I appreciate a girl who knows her brew, you have to understand that back in my day, everybody was purebred. And the penguin piss we drank back then was absolutely wondrous. It would put you on your ass for *weeks*."

"By purebred penguin, do you mean the penguin you married?" Asa asked. "Legends say that you left your human wife to marry a beautiful penguin. That penguin was the first lady of Arkopolis, and you loved her enough to cross the species line for her, making it okay for everyone else to do the same in order to build this city. Isn't that true?"

Noah smiled, remembering. "I called her Pengy. Sometimes I think I built Arkopolis just for her, so we could live together and fill it with little mutant penguin kids. We would get... *so drunk* together. Every drop of her piss was worth forsaking God for. I'll be honest with you. I miss her more than anything. But she's gone now. I'm alone and all I have is my mission."

Gren rolled his eyes.

"Things are working out," Noah told her. "God is telling me that you will be an asset to our mission, Asa. You and Gren here are going to help me save the city and restore my eternal legacy."

"And how are we going to do that?" Asa said.

"Well..." Noah paused and there were several moments of uncomfortable silence. "I'll let Gren explain the master stroke."

"The whales are after us because we hunt them," Gren flatly said. "The plan is to sabotage the city's oil supply so we'll stop using oil and stop hunting the whales for it." Asa raised an eyebrow at him. Gren sighed, as he'd figured that a smart girl like her wouldn't buy Noah's plan.

"This could work," she said.

"It could?"

"Of course it could!" said Noah.

"That's not to say that it's perfect," said Asa. "There are a few flaws. Just because you deplete the city's oil supply doesn't reduce the basic economic demand for it. Plus you're destroying large sections of the city and killing the people you're trying to save."

"That's what I said!" Gren cried.

"You think you can do better?" Noah said. "You're questioning the will of God, who is both wise and omnipotent and fucks up those who disobey Him."

"The Constitution of Arkopolis says that God doesn't exist because He's an asshole," said Asa. "Those were your words."

Noah stopped and the two Arkopolans stopped with him. They stood on the eighth deck of a ferry along the center square of the city, and the President's Cabin sat atop the highest mast just to the north. The deck was littered with poop.

The ghost looked to his mortal assistants. "You guys really love that Constitution shit, huh? I was drunk as fuck when I wrote that. Fine. If you're so sure, then come up with a new plan."

"As a matter of fact, I have a few ideas…"

An explosion ripped into the ferry beneath them. The entire vessel rumbled and creaked angrily. They heard screams and the rushing of water. Gren, Asa, and Noah hurried to a railing of whale bones and looked downward. An explosion had ripped through the hull, and the ferry was taking on seawater.

Gren and Asa looked back to Noah. "That wasn't me," he said. They looked downward again and saw something emerge from the fountain of water rushing into the ferry.

A silvery form spiraled up, long and fast as lightning. It swam up the length of the geyser and emerged at its peak. Gren recognized the creature. It was a dolphin, a common sight back in the shallows. Only this dolphin was different. Under its slick rubbery skin were rippling muscles, knotted and pulsing with strength. The dome of its head ballooned out, bulging over a giant brain.

The dolphin gazed out with black eyes that were too far apart, and its snout belted out squeals that sounded like laughter. Its brain rippled and within the minds of everyone on the ferry, there came a voice like thunder.

"MONGREL CREATURES OF THE FALSE LAND!" said the voice. Most of the Arkopolans collapsed and clutched their heads, including Asa. Gren caught her in his arms as she fell. "YOUR DAYS OF HUNTING THE WHALE RACE ARE HEREBY DONE! ALL WHO LIVE ABOVE THE WAVES MUST PERISH! JIHAD, JIHAD, JIHAD!"

Sirens approached. Members of the Municipal Guard were hurrying into the ferry. Most of them fell to the decks in anguish as they entered the boat, but others went on, ready to defend Arkopolis.

"This is terrible!" Gren said, holding Asa's trembling body. "We're too late!"

"No!" said Noah. "That dolphin fucker is just an emissary! The main whale army is traveling in a single pod, like when they migrate. The dolphin just means that they're really close!"

Gren said nothing. Noah looked down and saw Arkopolan soldiers attacking the dolphin. They fought with harpoons and tridents, and threw nets. But the dolphin laughed at their attacks, deflecting them with bursts of water shooting out from the geyser.

"Gren!" Noah said. "You have to get down there and help the soldiers! You can help them kill that fucking dolphin and then there will still be time to stop the rest of the whales!"

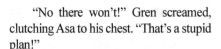

"No there won't!" Gren screamed, clutching Asa to his chest. "That's a stupid plan!"

"No it isn't! You can do it, Gren! I know you can!"

"Why don't you just possess me, then?" he said, scowling up at the ghost. "You had no problem forcing me to do stuff then!"

"That's not the way God wants it!"

"Fuck God!" Gren said.

"You can say that all you want. But this is the way it is. I can't do this for you. It's your time now. You have to save that girl in your arms. You have to be a hero. And in return, Gren, you will be blessed by God and you will live forever in the Kingdom of Heaven."

A tear came to Gren's eye. "Really?"

"Really."

Gren hopped over the railing and off the eighth deck. His let his heavy antlers steer him downward as he fell onto the dolphin. The creature was too busy dodging spears to notice the giant moose flying at him.

Gren's left antler swiped down and scooped into the dolphin's giant head. A sonic squeal erupted from the creature's mouth, and it's thickly muscled body convulsed. The geyser of water stopped as Gren crashed into the deck below. The weakened hull shattered under the impact and Gren went down into the water.

He screamed, tasting salt water, and began sinking. He passed through the kelp patches growing on the city's underside and descended further under the city. He was drowning, just like in his dream.

Then he was being pulled up onto the ferry by a pair of soldiers. They hauled him back into the ferry and helped him to his hooves. Gren stumbled a bit, standing knee deep in water. Other Arkopolans were recovering from the attack and being evacuated from the ferry.

The other soldiers, strong chimeras

of pelican, anaconda, platypus, elephant, buffalo, falcon, and otter, were cheering. A soldier who was half panther, half salamander, and half horse, held a harpoon with the dolphin's corpse on the end of it. He waved the body like a flag as the others roared in approval. The dolphin hung limp and bloody, its ragged head dangling precariously and dripping hunks of mutated brain matter.

Gren looked up and saw Asa and Noah on the upper deck. They were smiling in approval. He'd saved the day.

He puked a gallon of salt water and collapsed.

* * *

The President made a public address from a great crow's nest just underneath his cabin. The nest was made primarily from the skull of an ancient blue whale. He spoke into a funnel that split his voice through a network of rubber pipes, reverberating along until his soft lion's purr rumbled from speakers spread throughout the city.

He spoke of war.

"My fellow Arkopolans. Our city is under siege. I must first tell you that the President's Cabin is currently taking every precaution to protect this city. Our Municipal Guard is in the process of locking down every ship, barge, and ferry. Arkopolis is now under martial law, and all citizens are expected to obey. In times of war our strongest weapon is unity.

"Now, to the threat our city faces. After much deliberation and an examination of the evidence, my Cabinet and I have concluded that there is a new race of beings living beneath the waves. They are a genetic offshoot of the common whale, but with an evolved sense of intelligence and telepathic capabilities that we cannot measure.

"These evolved whales have declared war on Arkopolis, and already they have murdered many of our own. Through their mind control tactics they have sabotaged oil spigots all across the city, causing energy prices to skyrocket. They have attacked our fishermen, our brothers who brave the open waters to feed us. And they have brought their war onto our decks, killing innocent Arkopolans without mercy.

"The days ahead will be perilous. I cannot lie. But since the time of Noah the Father, Arkopolis has forged ahead. We will rebuild. We will mourn our brothers and sisters. We will bring our enemies to justice. We will continue our course and to any who try to stop us, we will meet them head on with the Holy Ark on our side.

"Thank you, fellow citizens."

The speech ended, and somewhere in Arkopolis the ghost of Noah smiled at the President's words. God's plan was going perfectly.

* * *

Gren had nearly drowned. He slept the rest of the day and into the night. He dreamed of swimming in the darkness again. A school of beautiful swans sailed past him in the obsidian depths. He tried to swim after them but they were too fast.

He awoke, coughing and sneezing seawater. Gren looked around. He was in a dark room. It was a dock manager's office in one of the bays.

"Psst!" It was Asa, crouched under the dock manager's desk.

"What's happening?" Gren whispered.

"You've been asleep for almost a day," she said. "I thought you'd drowned, but Noah knew you'd be okay. He just knew it."

"Damn right I did," said the ghost, swaggering into the room.

"Noah!" Asa whispered. "You returned!"

"Of course," he said to her. "I think our new plan is going to work out. There are only two guards patrolling this bay. If we're fast, we can slip by them without a problem."

"Wait," Gren muttered. "What new plan?"

"Well," said Noah. "Asa and I have been hashing out some new ideas to save Arkopolis, and we decided, together, that sabotaging the oil spigots isn't the best route by which to reach our goals. And the new plan stars you, buddy."

Gren sighed. His head started to hurt. "Again?" he grumbled.

"Gren!" Asa hissed at him. "We have to save the city!"

"Those fascists in the President's Cabin locked down the city!" Noah said. "But the whales are still coming and the Arkopolan soldiers are no match for them! The city's a sitting duck and you're *still* the only one that can save it."

They looked at Gren expectantly. He nodded his head.

Asa held something out to him. In her snake tendril hands was a sheet of seaweed papyrus wrapped up into a little round package. "These are bombs," she whispered. "I've made a lot of them. They're mostly whale oil glycerin and sulfuric powder, plus some samples of Noah's peculiar vapor. That part will provide the catalyst. When the whales swallow these bombs, they'll explode when they meet the acid in their stomachs."

"You expect the whales to eat them?"

Noah kneeled down in front of Gren. "The whales are approaching from the west," he said. "We're in a bay on the west side of the city, and there's a barge piled high with dead Arkopolans who've been blown to bits. It all fits together. See, those bodies are going to be buried at sea anyway, so…"

Gren nearly gagged at the thought.

"You're going to sneak onto that barge and head out toward the whales. Then you have to hide the bombs in the meat and drop them down into the water so the whales will eat them and blow up."

"That's stupid!" Gren said.

"No it isn't!" the ghost screamed. "It'll work! They won't be able to resist! God says so!"

Gren wanted to punch Noah in his stupid human face. "I'm not a sailor," he growled. "And I can't swim!"

"Well who else can do it?" said the ghost. "I'm bound to haunt only this city, so I can't leave. Would you rather have Asa head out onto the open water?"

"No," Gren said.

"You're the only one who can save us," Asa said to him. Gren heard a sense of pleading in her voice, and it made his head hurt.

He snuck out of the dock manager's office, stepping softly so his hooves didn't clop. He carried a net full of Asa's bombs over his shoulder, and crept down the line of docks until he found the barge piled high with corpses. Gren hopped aboard, cranked up the oil-powered motor, and steered the chugging vessel out into the open water.

Gren sat on a hill of corpses and steered the barge westward toward the whales. He looked at the bodies around him and imagined all the Arkopolans this meat had once been. Geckos and toucans and polar bears and koalas and geese and hyenas all mixed together, the lifeblood of the world's last city.

Killed and mutilated.

Some had died in the dolphin attack. And maybe that was justified. But it seemed like most of the deaths were thanks to the exploding oil spigots. Despite the damage Noah had caused, Gren hoped that God's divine plan would work. It was the only thing that could save Arkopolis.

Bugpigeons hovered about the barge. They burrowed into the piles of meat, or hopped from corpse to corpse, pecking at the decay happily. Gren snapped his tongue at one of them. The little guy was too fat and content to escape, and the tongue wrapped around him. Gren yanked the snack into his mouth and chewed.

"Hey!"

Gren turned and saw another bugpigeon sitting on another hill of bodies, wisely keeping his distance so Gren couldn't snatch him up with his tongue. "What do you think you're doing?" the bugpigeon yelled. "We're drifting too far from the city!"

"Shut up! I'm on a mission from God!"

"That's stupid!" said the bugpigeon.

"Yeah, I know," Gren muttered. He ignored the bugpigeon and continued onward. His head still hurt. But looking out across the water, the endless peaceful blueness of it, he began to feel calm. He thought of Asa, and how everything seemed to work out when he was near her.

Then the whales began talking to him.

"WHAT ARE YOU DOING?" said the enormous voice. It echoed inside Gren's skull, and to his surprise he remained calm at the sound of it.

"Are you one of the whales?" he said aloud.

"WE ALL ARE," said the voice.

"I'm on a mission from God," said Gren. "I can't let you destroy Arkopolis. I know that they hunt you, but the city can still change. The people aren't perfect, but I can't let you destroy them."

"SO YOU WILL DESTROY US?" said the voice. "YOU ARE BEING USED BY AN IRRATIONAL SUPERSTITION TO COMMIT THE SINS YOU CLAIM TO HATE."

"Hey!" the bugpigeon screamed at Gren. "The whale voice has a point!"

"I've already made up my mind!" Gren said. "I won't talk to you anymore."

He took bombs from the net sitting beside him and stuffed them into the biggest hunks of flesh he could find. Gren fumbled around, putting the bombs into torsos or wrapping them up in guts, then tossing the packages into the water. The whales tried to pry into his thoughts as he worked.

Gren closed his eyes as he worked so the whales wouldn't see through them. They tried to pry into his thoughts, but Gren just concentrated on Asa. He thought only of her, so the whales wouldn't suspect the trap he was laying for them. He thought of Asa's curvy hips, coated in white downy feathers. Her lithe snake tendril hands, squeezing the life out of his paws. He imagined her round cobra eyes and the scales running down her neck and the smooth plane of her chest. He saw those eyes, peeking out from behind the pillowy fuzz of her raccoon's tail, wrapped around her body like a luxurious coat.

Gren promised himself he would marry Asa if he made it back to Arkopolis. If he wasn't arrested and hanged from the Judgment Mast for stealing the barge, or somehow blamed for the havoc Noah had caused while haunting Arkopolis. It occurred to Gren that this promise to himself might be the same thing as praying, but he put that concept out of his mind and focused on Asa.

"THAT GIRL DOESN'T EVEN LIKE YOU!" the whales roared. "IT'S A STUPID CRUSH!" The bugpigeons agreed.

The corpses sank into the water, each one poisoned with explosive ghostly ether. The great pod of whales swam right into it. Orcas, manatees, dolphins, humpbacks, blues, belugas, sea lions, and sperm whales all snatched up pieces and swallowed them whole. Their brains were enormous from centuries of evolution, but they could not resist an early taste of Arkopolan flesh.

Such was their hatred.

When the bombs met the whales' stomachs, they ignited. Dozens of whales exploded, their massive bodies popping like balloons down in the depths. And as they died, their highly evolved minds screamed in telepathic shock, causing the brains of all the surrounding whales to burst.

The whales' rupturing bodies and violent telepathic seizures caused the waters to churn and heave, and massive clouds of dark blood and soggy whale blubber turned the ocean a gory red. The barge was torn apart by the waves. It sank into the water, which was already thick with dead whales. Blood, blubber, and giant chunks of meat floated in all directions.

Gren brayed in fear as the bloody water crept in around him and the corpses drifted out into the soggy gore. He grabbed a long wooden beam that had broken off the barge and hugged it to himself as he fell into the water. Gren kicked his hooves and made slow progress through the stinking soup of meat. Sharks came, but they ignored Gren as he paddled along, instead focusing on the great chunks of whale meat that floated like glaciers in the sea of blood.

The bugpigeons cheered at the stink of it all, and flew out to gorge themselves on fresh whale meat. It was a feast, but they still agreed that Gren was stupid.

* * *

Gren made it back to Arkopolis at sunset, his muscles numb, his fur soggy, and the rest of him completely delirious. He'd done it. He'd accomplished the mission and now God would let him into Heaven just like Noah. Gren climbed out of the water and staggered into the city. There were no guards in sight. The decks were empty, but fresh dung was spread about.

Gren followed messy trails and footprints of shit to the center of town. He saw them gathered in the vessels that made up the central square of Arkopolis, making loud animal calls to the crow's nest up above. Gren looked up to see the President

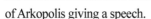

of Arkopolis giving a speech.

"Our troubles have passed!" he said, his voice echoing through speakers spread throughout the square. "Arkopolis has seen rough waters in our past, and today, like all those days behind us, we met our challenges and came through!"

The crowd roared, brayed, squawked, and barked approval.

"With the defeat of the whale army, Arkopolis is once again safe! No longer will we live in fear of sabotage! No longer will our fishermen be stalked and killed while they plumb the depths serving our city! Arkopolis is free!"

More cheers.

"And we owe it all to our founder! He who returned from the dead to help save the city he built! Noah the Father!"

Gren gaped as the President stepped back to reveal the misty blue form of Noah. The ghost stepped forward and stretched his hands over the throng. The people chanted his name, but Gren remained silent. How could they see him now? And why was he with the President?

"Thank you!" Noah shouted down at the Arkopolans. They continued cheering as he spoke. "I built Arkopolis because I believed that all of us deserve a home. The whales didn't believe that. And so they sought to destroy us. But no longer! This city is safe and free from war, just as we all dreamed!"

As Gren stared up at the ghost in disbelief, he saw her. Asa stood just behind Noah. He turned to face her, then took her into his ghostly arms. She opened her beak around his mouth and they kissed for long moments as the Arkopolans below, and even the President himself, clapped in approval.

The kiss went on forever.

Gren turned and trudged away to his apartment boat. He'd lived through three explosions, been possessed, nearly drowned, stolen a barge, and then swam back to Arkopolis through a sea of blood. He felt like dying, but first he needed some sleep. He wanted to fall into his hammock and have something, anything, comfort him.

He was walking down the promenade of a market ship. The shacks and kiosks were closed. Everyone was at the town square celebrating the end of the war. A war none of them were even aware of a day ago. As Gren made his way, he saw a shimmer of blue up ahead. The form of Noah appeared on the promenade, smiling and holding out his arms to embrace Gren.

"Gren!" he said. "We did it!"

The moose man passed by the ghost without a word.

Noah hurried to catch up. "I'm about to ship off to Heavenly Paradise. I just figured I'd say goodbye before I left, but I guess you're not quite in the mood. Maybe that's understandable I guess."

Gren let out a snort. "I take it I'm not hitching a ride up to Heaven with you," he muttered.

"Ah," said Noah carefully. "That's a bit of a complicated matter. You won't get into Heaven right now, but with good behavior God may see to it that you are compensated when you reach the afterlife."

"Good behavior? What about all I did for Him? I completed the mission, not you. You just fucked things up."

"God doesn't see it that way."

"Oh, fuck God!" Gren shouted. "Admit it! You were just making it all up!"

"Oh no," said the ghost. "There's a God and this was all done in His design. You're a bit confused, but that's common with God's plans."

"It was *your* plan," growled the moose man.

"I am merely the agent of His will," said Noah.

"You lied to me, didn't you? I knew

it. You were just using me and I was never going to be a hero. I was just your tool, right?"

"Yep," Noah said. "That's right."

"What about Asa, then? Did you two... you know?"

Noah sheepishly nodded his head.

"And God is okay with this? I did all the work and you fucked the girl I liked! And you didn't even save the city! You just killed them before they could kill us. Arkopolis will keep hunting whales and the other whales will still hate us and it'll just start all over again one day."

"Sure, but there's peace today and that's good enough for Him. Look, it doesn't have to make sense. It's a parable or something. And as for Asa, you and I are *partners*. That means way more than any piece of ass. My heart still belongs to my Pengy, and you shouldn't be holding out for girls like Asa. She doesn't respect you. She told me while we were screwing."

Gren was speechless.

"I kinda warned you about this, Gren. God picks losers like you all the time. He thinks it's cool or something. He screwed me over once upon a time, but now look at me! I'm gonna be kickin' ass in Heaven!"

Noah put a ghostly blue hand on Gren's furry shoulder. The blue was already beginning to fade. "It's gonna be okay. That asshole God works in mysterious ways. Don't think of it in terms of rewards and punishments. Don't think of how unfair it is. Just trust in Him."

Noah's translucent form dissipated into the air. Wisps of him streaked away and vanished. His still-drunken eyes winked at Gren before evaporating into the ether.

Gren went home. When he arrived he found an eviction notice pinned to his cabin door. They'd spelled his name "Gern."

DOUGLAS HACKLE

LOCATION:
Cleveland, Ohio

STYLE OF BIZARRO:
Pre-Eskimocore,
Post-Oarfishcore,
Proto-Applecore
Scribble Scrabble

BOOKS BY HACKLE:
Clown Tear Junkies

DESCRIPTION: In his fiction, Douglas Hackle scrambles the egg of reality, fries it in a talking pan named Pete, and douses it with a generous splash of stupid-silly-moron sauce.

INTERESTS: Polar bears, anvils, clowns, fetal polar bears, fetal an vils, fetal clowns, soup, books, beer, cinema, colorful plastic beads, guitar playing, werewolves (real ones), puppets, poppets, pappets, pippets, peppets (fake ones), and ill-conceived notions.

INFLUENCES: Shell Silverstein, Dr. Seuss, Franz Kafka, Jorge Luis Borges, Gabriel García Márquez, Donald Barthelme, Clive Barker, Stephen King, Bentley Little, Bizarro authors, David Lynch, John Waters, Stanley Kubrick, Quentin Tarantino, Crispin Glover, Tom Green, Tim and Eric, Adult Swim, Troma movies, Gozu, and "Round and Round" by RATT.

WEBSITE:
douglashackle.wordpress.com

The Many Bad Habits of My Main Man, Klin-Klat, a.k.a. the Tap Dance Kid

Klin-Klat had many bad habits, one of which was crashing closed casket funerals in order to climb up onto strangers' caskets and announce, "Back in the day, they used to call me the motherfuckin' Tap Dance Kid!" just before he'd commence tap dancing on the lid.

However, my main man never managed to get very far into his coffin-top dance routines, those pointy tap dancing shoes of his usually executing only a few *tippety-taps* before the angry mourners and funeral parlor staff came charging after him, forcing him to jump down and make a run for it, gleefully yelling his own name in a childlike, singsong voice as he made his escape.

"Klin-Klat! Klin-Klat! Klin-Klat! Klin-Klat . . . !"

Dude also smoked three packs of cigarettes a day.

Another one of Klin-Klat's bad habits was crashing *open* casket funerals for the purpose of climbing inside people's coffins, saying, "Back in the day, they used to call me the motherfuckin' Tap Dance Kid!" and then tap dancing on the faces of the deceased. Like those closed casket funeral incidents, such intrusions invariably ended in chase, my main man always chanting, "Klin-Klat! Klin-Klat! Klin-Klat . . . !" as he booked for the door.

Klin-Klat also liked to pick his nose in both public and private.

Dude ate his own boogers too.

Yet another one of Klin-Klat's bad habits was breaking into hospices in order to jump onto the heads of dying people while shouting, "Back in the day, they used to call me the motherfuckin' Tap Dance Kid!" After he'd deliver his catch-phrase, Klin-Klat would tap dance on the moribund person's face, often hastening that person's already imminent demise. Just like his funeral appearances, these trespasses always ended with my main man getting chased off the premises.

He also chewed his fingernails when he was nervous.

Still another one of Klin-Klat's bad habits was breaking into maternity wards in order to tap dance on infants just after they were pulled from their mothers' birth canals, my main man shouting, "Back in the day, they used to call me the motherfuckin' Tap Dance Kid!" as he did so. Three or four smart taps with those spiffy shoes of his were enough to effectively churn such ill-starred newborns into baby-jam, the poor doctors and nurses never getting a chance to react to my main man's uninvited, unexpected presence.

"Klin-Klat! Klin-Klat! Klin-Klat . . . !" he'd sing as he was chased out of the hospital.

My main man also drank too much booze.

Watched too much TV.

Skipped breakfast every day.

Overate.

Gambled too much.

Dude did way too many drugs, too.

Sure, my main man was not without his flaws. But who isn't? Are you without flaws, bruh? What about you, sis? Are you a perfect person?

No. I didn't think so.

Yes, Klin-Klat was far from a perfect person. But I'll tell you what: While my main man certainly wasn't the most courteous individual in the world, that mofo could tap dance like it was nobody's fuckin' business.

In fact, back in the day, they used to call him the motherfuckin' Tap Dance Kid!!!

TERROR SARDINES IN TERROR SAUCE

"Please don't fuckin' open me up like a can of sardines!" I cried as a can of sardines began to open me up like a can of sardines.

I had just arrived back at my apartment after fleeing TERROR TOWN, where I was to be tortured, executed, and devoured by a variety of unspeakable TERRORs. Having escaped and fled that fabled nightmare necropolis on foot and travelled many miles to get home, I was quite famished. At a cost of 85 cents, that can of sardines was the only thing I could afford when I stopped at the corner store at the end of my street shortly after I stumbled into town. Unfortunately, the can of sardines had turned on me when I tried

to open it back at my digs. Turns out it was no ordinary can of sardines.

It was a can of TERROR SARDINES.

In my rush to get home, I had barely glanced at the label on the can when I'd purchased it, thinking it had read *Sardines in Mustard Sauce—A Product of Spain.*

Now I could see that the label clearly read *TERROR SARDINES in TERROR SAUCE—A Product of TERROR TOWN.*

How had I made such a stupid mistake?

"And you thought you could escape us—we, the TERRORS of TERROR TOWN!" the can of TERROR SARDINES said from its perch on my sternum. "Fool! Now you will learn what pain is. It's TERROR TIME, motherfucker!"

For my part, I lay supine on my kitchen floor, pinned and paralyzed by the thing's unholy TERROR MAGIC, as it reached into the flesh beneath my collar bone with invisible hands and began to pull me open like a can of sardines.

Let me tell ya something: It sucked a big fat, gonorrhea-green dick to be opened up like a can of sardines by a can of TERROR SARDINES. Especially considering I had just narrowly evaded the unpitying persecution of TERROR CLOWN, TERROR MIME, TERROR MAN, and TERROR MARIONETTE, not to mention the infamous and sundry torments of TERROR MOUSE, TERROR THING, TERROR CHILD, TERROR TOT, and TERROR ANVIL.

I watched helplessly as the damned thing rolled back the skin, muscle, and bone that formed the outermost layer of my chest to expose my upper internal organs, wishing I had just stayed in

TERROR TOWN to die. See, to have the likes of TERROR CLOWN devour you, shit you out, and then resurrect you only to repeat that process 17,000 times in a row sounded like a horrible enough fate, sure. But at least there was a certain degree of dignity in going out like that, in knowing that you were being tormented and destroyed by none other than the great TERROR CLOWN himself. Similarly, to have the one and only TERROR MOUSE burrow into your body to devour all your internal pieces and parts save your still functioning, suffering brain, effectively reducing you to a human skin-suit filled with TERROR MOUSE shit, was a death that was not without honor.

But to be opened up like a can of sardines by a can of TERROR SARDINES in TERROR SAUCE? There was no dignity or honor in that. TERROR SARDINES in TERROR SAUCE were one of the least respected TERRORs of TERROR TOWN. Indeed, they were nothing more than a snack food consumed by the town's more illustrious and terrifying denizens when nothing else was available to eat. The only beings below TERROR SARDINES on the rigid social hierarchy of TERROR TOWN were TERROR MAGGOTs and TERROR ALGAE. Hence death by TERROR SARDINES was considered a most ignoble death, even if those TERROR SARDINES were marinated in TERROR SAUCE.

Yet despite my predicament, all hope was not lost. See, luckily I remembered that of all the TERRORs of TERROR TOWN, TERROR SARDINEs were one of the least intelligent, just barely smarter than TERROR MAGGOTs and TERROR ALGAE. Maybe, I thought, I could outsmart this fucking thing.

"Hey, before you finish pulling me open and murdering me," I said, "Would it be okay if I requested a last meal?"

My expanding and contracting lungs and beating heart now visible through the gaping hole in my mortal coil, the can stopped unfurling my chest.

"Last meal?" it said. "Pffft! Whaddaya think is going on here, pal? Do you think the traditions of your prison system apply to this situation? And do you think I'm capable of even one tiny shred of mercy? Okay, buddy, I'll take your request for a last meal. *Haha.* I'll even cook it myself. What would you like? How about filet mignon? Or perhaps lobster? Hey, why not have both? A little surf n' turf, huh? *Haha.* Hey, how about truffles stuffed with fuckin' caviar for an appetizer? *Hahaha.* Hey, I'll tell ya what, buddy. How about I arrange a conjugal visit for you with Scarlet Johansen while you're waiting for me to boil you a fuckin' lobster, huh? *Hahahahaha….*"

"Please. I don't want anything fancy. In fact, you wouldn't even have to go anywhere to give me what I want. See, all I really want for my last meal is to try TERROR SARDINEs in TERROR SAUCE. I've never had them before."

"Whuh?" the can blurted in disbelief. "You've never had TERROR SARDINEs in TERROR SAUCE? Man, you haven't lived until you've had TERROR SARDINES in TERROR SAUCE. There's nothing better on the planet."

"Really? I heard they were just okay."

"Just okay!" the can said, now as indignant as it was incredulous. It began to shake me vigorously with its invisible grip, giving me whiplash and knocking the back of my head against the floor tiles. "Just okay my sweet little tin ass! I'm about to give you the best damn last meal a sorry-ass, almost-dead motherfucker like your-self ever had."

I watched as the old-fashioned key attached to the can's lid began to rotate, and, just as the airtight seal of the lid broke with a metallic pop, my ears captured the beautiful violin music emanating from within. The lid rolled back to the opposite side of the rectangular tin vessel to reveal the tightly packed TERROR SARDINES inside—twelve in all. The things were essentially zombie sardines with Xs for eyes. Some were little more than comb-like skeletons. They were all thickly coated in TERROR SAUCE, which was a sentient, transparent, goopy, ecotoplasmic jelly in which hundreds of beady little eyes swam around like black spermatozoa minus their tails.

A can of TERROR SARDINES always contained at least one normal, non-TERROR sardine—a slave sardine that the others could torment whenever they became bored in the dark confined space that was their home. Not only did these slave sardines take regular beatings from the TERROR SARDINEs, they were also obligated to entertain their masters. As such, the TERROR SARDINES only enslaved sardines that could play musical instruments, juggle, do stand-up comedy, or else provide some other form of entertainment. In the corner of this particular can of TERROR SARDINES was as slave sardine wearing a little red beret. His face was all puffy and cut up, and both his eyes were black and blue as a result of getting his ass beat all the time.

Despite his injuries, the slave sardine was sawing away at a tiny violin. Dude was fuckin' some serious shit up too, playing this real fast classical stuff, like some Paganini or Pagaravioli or Pagapepperoni or some crazy shit like that. Even with the lid now peeled open, the slave sardine continued to play that violin like a goddamn virtuoso.

"Here," the can of TERROR SARDINES said as one of the undead little fish launched out of the container and into my mouth.

It was the worst thing I'd ever tasted. But I chewed it and swallowed it nevertheless. To be more specific, TERROR SARDINEs tasted exactly like dried-out white dog shit boiled in the vomit of a baboon that was in the habit of eating its own feces, while the TERROR SAUCE in which the zombie fish were soaked tasted something like a bad cough syrup mixed with dirty motor oil, wolf piss, and the semen of syphilitic vampire bats.

"Is that not the best thing you ever tasted in your life?" the can asked.

"Hm," I said, feigning an air of indecision as I forced the undead flesh down my gullet. "Now granted, it's pretty good," I lied, "but I don't know that it's the best thing I've ever tasted. I mean, it's hard to say. One TERROR SARDINE is such a small piece of food. It's difficult to make an accurate judgment based on such a small sample, ya know?"

If that can of TERROR SARDINEs had had a set of ears, anger-smoke would have been spewing out of them right about now. The thing trembled with rage before it said, as if through clenched teeth, "Okay then, Mr. Picky-Ass Foodie motherfucker. Here's another one then."

A second TERROR SARDINE shot out of the can to land in my mouth.

"Man, it's still kinda hard to say,"

I said after forcing myself to chew and swallow that second rancid, undead fish and drink more of that disgusting sauce. "They're good—there's no doubt about that—but these portions are just so small that it's really hard for me to tell if they're the best food I've ever tasted in my life. Sorry, but I really need more to go on. And some more of that TERROR SAUCE too, please."

That gullible, shit-for-brains can tossed me yet another TERROR SARDINE, this one dripping with even more TERROR SAUCE. I pressed on with my ruse, telling the can that I was that much closer to being able to make a final decision with each TERROR SARDINE it gave me. I did this until there was only one TERROR SARDINE left in the can.

See, every can of TERROR SARDINES in TERROR SAUCE is always greater than the sum of its parts; its sentience and supernatural powers derive from the collective sentience and supernatural powers of each individual TERROR SARDINE and each molecule of TERROR SAUCE within the can. Thus, each time a TERROR SARDINE or a gob of TERROR SAUCE is removed from the can, the larger organism loses some of its supernatural strength and intelligence.

However, this can of TERROR SARDINEs somehow managed to figure out my scheme just as its cargo was reduced to one TERROR SARDINE and one final dollop of TERROR SAUCE.

"Heeeeyy," it said, all slow and stupid now. "A-duhhh. I seeeee whaaaaat you're up tooooooooooo."

"Hey, how about you toss me that last TERROR SARDINE there, boss. Then I'll know if TERROR SAR-DINES are the most delicious food on the planet."

"Fuuuucck, youuuuuuu, bruhh-hhh! I'm about to open you up liiiike a caaaaan of sardiiiiiiiiiiiiiiiiiiiiiiiiiiines."

But the thing was too weak to pry my chest open any more than it already had. It was barely strong enough to keep me pinned down to the floor.

That beret-wearing, violin-playing, slave sardine was in on my plan now; I'd given him a conspiratorial wink on about the eighth or ninth TER-ROR SARDINE I'd eaten, and he'd winked backed knowingly. Dude was on the fucking level. A second after the can threatened me, the slave sardine stopped playing his music and bashed the last TERROR SARDINE over the head with the violin. The dazed undead fish didn't have as chance to react as the slave sardine then lifted it up in its tiny fins and pitched it out of the can. I caught the slimy little bastard in my left hand and squeezed it to mush.

That last gob of TERROR SAUCE tried to slither away from the slave sardine, its dozens of remaining eyes darting chaotically around inside its jellied mass in a great panic, but it had nowhere to go. My dude the slave sardine used his violin like a ladle to scoop the gunk up and fling it out of the can. At that moment, the spell of the can of TER-ROR SARDINES in TERROR SAUCE broke, and my arms were free to unroll my rolled-up flesh and bone and tuck everything back into place to the best of my ability. However, I was now bleeding all over, the broken spell of the can's TERROR MAGIC no longer staying the flow of my blood as it had done before in order to prolong my agony during the torture.

"You my dog," I said to the sardine. I

gave him a high five—well, a high one—with my pinkie, which he slapped with one of his pectoral fins. "Listen. I need an ambulance fast or I'm gonna die. My cellie is up on the counter over there. I need you to hop up there and dial 911 for me. Can you do that?"

"I got your back, brah," the sardine said. "You saved me from those sick fucks. You freed me from their prison. I'm indebted to you for life."

The sardine did as I asked. He saved my life that day.

His name was Fuckin' Francois. Fuckin' Francois and I became besties. In fact, a week after the events I have described in this narrative up until this point, Fuckin' Francois moved in with me.

***

"Yo, I got your back," Fuckin' Francois said to me one morning five years later. I was sitting at my little kitchen table enjoying a breakfast of Lucky Charms. Fuckin' Francois was standing upright on the opposite side of the table, propped up on his tail fins like feet, red beret in place on his head and diminutive violin slung over his dorsal fin with a strap like a guitar.

"I know you do, man," I said after shoveling a heaping spoonful of soggy Lucky Charms into my Lucky Charms hole. "You don't need to tell me that."

"No. I mean I, like, really got your back."

"I know you do, dude. We've been friends for five years now. During that time, you've gotten me out of more than a few scrapes. Shit, we've traveled the goddamn world together three times over. We've saved each other's lives dozens of times and robbed like over a hundred banks together. We've banged more hot women and hot females sardines than I can count. I got your back too, Fuckin' Francois. We're a team. Bros for life, homie."

"No, you still don't quite understand. See, I *actually* have your back."

"Like I said, Fuckin' Francois, I know you do," I replied, just a hint of annoyance now edging into my voice. "I got yours too!"

"Dude, I'm trying to tell you that I *literally* have your back!"

I chuckled. "Now you're just talkin' silly. You high or something? Hey, if you're holding out on me with some diggity-dank purple or somethin', I'm gonna be reeaaaal pissed."

Fuckin' Francois turned away from me and leaned down towards the chair that was behind him, a chair that I thought was empty. Now I could see a black garbage bag sat on it. I watched curiously as Fuckin' Francois jumped onto the bag, loosened the red drawstring, and reached inside with his little fins to haul something out. (Bear in mind that Fuckin' Francois was strong as hell for a normal non-TERROR sardine.)

My expression of curiosity changed into one of abject horror when Fuckin' Francois freed a long, wide, bloody slab of meat from the bag: a sheet of raw flesh sheathed on one side by a layer of nearly hairless, pale skin dotted here and there with a few familiar-looking moles. He let the unskinned hunk of meat fall onto the tabletop with a sick, wet thud.

"See?" the tiny fish asked.

The awful realization finally setting in, I set my spoon down and slowly brought my hands behind me to feel for my back. Where my probing fingertips should have encountered smooth skin stretched tautly over sculpted muscle, they instead touched the slick, wet bones of my unveiled ribcage. My fingers then traced a path along the slimy ridges of my exposed spinal column before encountering the sickly soft, curved shapes of my kidneys followed by the moist, fibrous texture of the expanding and contracting sacs that were my lungs.

"This morning while you were sleeping," the sardine said matter-of-factly, "I soaked a rag with chloroform and put it over your face to keep you from gaining consciousness while I prepped you. Then I gave you several shots of a strong local anesthetic in your back and administered an epidural block. That's why you're not in any pain right now. However, I didn't do anything to suppress the bleeding. So I'm guessing you have about twenty seconds to live, bruh."

I glanced down at the pool of my lifeblood that was blooming on the floor, suddenly feeling cold and faint.

"Yo, I thought you were . . . my . . . my boy," I croaked. That's when the sardine jumped down to the floor, careful to avoid my blood, and hopped over to the other side of the kitchen, where, to my great surprise, I saw my mom standing in the doorway. She held a suitcase in each hand; one was quite large, while the other was about the size of a 9-volt battery. The little one I knew belonged to Fuckin' Francois.

"Mom? Not . . . not you too?"

"I'm afraid so, Tommy," she said. "Fuckin' Francois and I have been, well, fuckin' for about two months now. He and I are taking all the money you two earned robbing banks and moving to Jamaica. Sorry, honey. Granted, a mother's unconditional love for her child is one of the most powerful things in the universe. But that love just doesn't hold a candle to the exquisite pleasure of having a handsome-ass,

smooth-talkin', beret-wearin', crack pipe-smokin' sardine burrow deep into your ass to play Pagapepperoni on his pointy, but well-lubricated fiddle."

"It's Paganini, not Pagapepperoni, you stupid, whitetrash bitch!" Fuckin' Francois said as he leapt up from the floor and slapped my mom hard across the face, causing her to giggle and blush. "And it's a *violin*, not a fiddle, you ignorant, Jabba the Hutt-lookin', crack-whore!" he said as he sprung up into the air a second time to slap my mom across the other side of her face, making her giggle and blush even more.

"Hey, you keep your dirty hands—I mean fins—off my mom! And don't you talk to her like that! Man, fuck you, Fuckin' Francois! And fuck that cheap hipster beret of yours. I'll . . . fuckin'. . . squash . . . you . . . to . . . ," were my last words. I slipped out of the chair, fell hard onto the blood-slick floor, died, and was reincarnated as a goddamn miserable speck of TERROR ALGAE floating on the slimy surface of a TERROR LAKE, only to be eaten by a TERROR SARDINE four seconds after my reincarnation.

After that second death, I didn't reincarnate into anything else.

That was fuckin' it.

***

Moral of the Story:

Don't trust ANYONE. Ever!

Not even your mom! Because the minute you think someone has your back, you just might find out that they actually have your back!!!!!!!

811

Nearly a year ago, Jason had been the one to initiate his and Jen's first clumsy excursions into the world of BDSM.

Nothing too crazy initially. Handcuffs, blindfolds, ball gags, hot candle-wax—the usual beginner's fare.

But the bees had been Jen's idea.

"You sure about this?" Jason asked, his face a half-scowl of uncertainty. He and Jen were in a broad, sweeping meadow speckled with wildflowers and encircled by lush trees, like a place out of a pastoral poem. They were naked and alone. Jason stood with his rock-hard dick in his left hand, his cell phone in his right. Jen lay spread-eagled on a blanket at his feet, waiting for him to climb aboard.

Waiting for the bees.

A tall, gnarled elm enveloped the couple in its shade. Hanging from the tree's lowest branch was a very large, very active beehive.

"Absolutely," Jen said, already a little breathless in her excitement. "Just call 911 right before you grab the beehive. Tell them we're being attacked by bees. An ambulance will get here before they have a chance to do any real harm. We'll get stung up good, for sure, but that's sort of the whole point. The paramedics will know what to do—they'll have antihistamines, steroids, epinephrine, all that stuff. This is gonna be fuckin' incredible!"

Both Jason and Jen were severely allergic to bee stings. Hence the thrill appeal of combining bees with sex, at least for Jen. Hence Jason's apprehension, as the young man was far less of a risk-taker than his daredevil girlfriend.

"Um...okay," he said, feigning enthusiasm while trying not to let his nerves sap the blood from his unwieldy, purple beast of an erection. Jason took two steps closer to the tree, stopping just beneath the beehive. He looked down timidly, first at his dick and then at his cell phone. Swallowing hard, he dialed the three magic digits and raised the phone to the side of his head.

Jason didn't even bother waiting for the dispatcher's greeting. Instead, he promptly yelled "HELP!!!" just as soon as he thought he heard someone pick up on the other end. "Me and my girlfriend are being attacked by a vicious swarm of bees! Help, help, help! We're being attacked by beeeeeeeeeeees! Fuckin' *bees*! A fuckin' swarm of 'em! Please, send help now!"

Adhering to their plan, Jason then dropped the phone without breaking the connection, reached his hands up, and tore the massive, pendulous beehive from its bough. Thousands of bees instantly evacuated the structure, called to arms by Jason's unexpected assault. Holding the hive aloft, he screamed as he slammed it down upon Jen's bare tits, causing an explosion of beeswax, honeycomb, and really, *really* pissed-off bees. Jason immediately sank to his knees, mounting his audacious little spitfire of a girlfriend, who was already writhing beneath him. By the time he got his meat stick into the (admittedly safer) honey pot between her legs, he'd already been stung thirty-six times—thirty-six times and counting.

Unfortunately for Jason and Jen, Jason had not dialed 911.

He'd dialed 811 by mistake.

Not many people know this, but dialing 811 calls forth a swarm of bees to the location of the caller. If you think about it, this sort of makes sense, considering that the number 8 is kind of shaped like a bee: a bee sans wings. And that's exactly the type of bees that arrive after an 811 call is placed: wingless bees. And these wingless, highly venomous "811 bees" (as they're sometimes called) aren't exactly happy with the fact that they don't have wings. In fact, they're quite sullen about it. Still, their shared congenital handicap doesn't stop them from flying. *Au contraire*, 811 bees are especially adept at flight, spinning their bodies at an incredible hummingbird-like velocity, in effect transforming themselves into miniature helicopter blades. And the only thing that pisses off 811 bees more than the injustice of Mother Nature screwing them out of wings is someone disturbing them by dialing 811.

And these bees don't care if you dialed the wrong number by accident.

So, whereas Jason and Jen had been expecting a little pleasure spiked with pain, followed by a swift rescue, what they got was even more pain with no rescue at all.

Pain spiked with pain spiked with pain spiked with pain...

So yeah, that about sums up what happened to Jason and Jen.

Excuse me?

What's that, now?

Ohhhh, you're one of Jason's boys, you say? You guys go way back? The two of you were in the same fraternity, is that right? Kappa Sigma? No shit. How about that. Well, buddy, I hate to be the one to break the bad news to you, but don't bother calling Jason this Friday to go out drinking or whoring or whatever it is you guys get up to on the weekends.

Because Jason's deader than a dried-out piece of white dog shit.

WHAT EVER HAPPENED TO MONTY MORRIS?

Back when Monty Morris still had eyes with which to see, I took him to see Rob Zombie's remake of *Citizen Kane*. The film starred Will Smith as the eccentric, reclusive media mogul Charles Foster Kane. Will Smith's son Jaden costarred as "Rosebud" the sled. The movie was rated Z, which meant no one under a hundred could be admitted to the theater.

But I'd never let that stop me before.

Monty and I snuck in through the theater's back entrance without incident. I was impressed by his stealth. Of course, this was back when Monty still had legs and feet with which to be stealthy and not the single monster truck tire that functions as his primary means of propulsion today. This was also back before Monty took up the habit of perpetually screaming authentic whale song at a blaring 77.6 decibels.

Sitting front row center, we were the only two people in the theater. About fifteen minutes into the show, Monty tried slipping his arm around my shoulder.

The sly dog.

This was back when Monty still had arms and not the gimpy lobster claws that are attached to his shoulder stumps today.

I shoved his arm away. "I dig chicks, bro. You know that."

"You looked kinda cold is all," he said.

"Quicquid," I replied.

Quicquid is Latin for "whatever." Sometimes it's cool (in an erudite, elitist, douchebag sort of way) to speak or write the Latin, Greek, or Frenchy word when there's absolutely no reason to do so.

The movie was okay. I guess. Scene for scene, it was almost identical to Orson Welles's original 1941 classic, which is another way of saying that the film consisted of three hours of a guffawing Will Smith sledding down a snowy mountainside using his CGI-enhanced, smiling son Jaden as a sled, so I had to wonder what was the point of doing a remake when they hadn't even bothered to mix things up at all.

About an hour into the movie, I was bored outta my face. I lowered my head over Monty's lap, unzipped his jeans, pulled out his cock, and gave him a C+ blowjob. This was back when Monty still had a cock and not the angry, buzzing hornet's nest that's affixed to his crotch today.

"Thought you didn't swing that way, brah," he said as I pulled my head up after I finished.

"I don't," I said, spitting his man-seed onto the grimy floor. "I just got bored, is all. Well? Did you enjoy it?"

Monty shrugged his shoulders, cocked his head dismissively to the side. This was back when Monty still had a head to cock, certainly long before his head ever came to be replaced by that terracotta-potted sunflower plant with Van Damme's face emblazoned upon it, minus the Belgian action-movie star's eyes.

"Meh," Monty said. "I'd give it about a C+."

"I know it was a C+, asshole. That's what I was going for. What, did you think I was gonna give you an A+ blowjob or something? I told you, man, I'm not a queer."

"Relax, slice. No need to get mad." Monty's voice was kind and conciliatory. This was long before Monty's kindness and overall good nature yielded to the sociopathic lack of remorse that characterizes him today, especially when he does things like kidnap the legitimately adopted babies of responsible, Ukrainian, gay male couples just so he can feed them to that bloodthirsty Van Damme sunflower of his.

I was just about to tell him that his dick was a C+ when a voice cried out from behind us.

"Gotcha, ya rapscallions!"

I glanced over my shoulder to see three conical flashlight beams bobbing towards us as a couple of ushers jogged down the center aisle.

"Run!" I hollered as I leapt from my seat, bolting for the red EXIT sign in the dark. Without looking back once, I shouldered my way through the door, hauled ass down the street. I'd assumed that Monty was right behind me the whole time, but when I stopped to catch my breath four blocks and three hopped fences later, I found myself all alone.

***

That was ten years ago. I haven't seen Monty Morris since.

Never did find out what happened to him that night. What little I *do* know about his present physical state—the lobster claws, the Van Damme sunflower face, etc.—I learned from a movie trailer for the biopic *What Ever Happened to Monty Morris?* that hit theaters a few years ago. The trailer doesn't reveal much, certainly nothing about how he became what he is today or the why of it all. It serves merely to dangle the mystery of whatever happened to Monty in front of your face like a big, limp, honey-dipped lumberjack cock.

Directed by Rob Zombie, the film stars Will Smith as Monty and a CGI-enhanced Jaden Smith as the Van Damme sunflower face.

It's rated Z.

Unfortunately for me, the film industry finally started cracking down on underage people sneaking into theaters that screen Z-rated movies. Around the same time that *What Ever Happened to Monty Morris?* was released, they upgraded all the old, faulty exit doors, making them virtually impossible to open from the outside. What's worse, federal law prohibits centenarians from even discussing Z-rated movies with anyone underage. As a result, there is only one way I will ever find out what happened to my friend Monty Morris.

And that is to live to be one hundred years old.

I'm trying. Really, I am. I quit cigs, booze, junk food, whores. I even purchased a membership at a fitness center, and I try to work out at least three times a week. However, I'm having a really tough time of it trying to give up the goddamn clown tear-laced crack.

We'll see what happens, I guess.

Then again, maybe I'll just say fuck Monty Morris and start smoking, boozing, and whoring again. Who knows?

Quicquid.

THE BORED OUIJA BOARD

"My latest problem," the Ouija board said as it eased back into the therapist's couch to get more comfy, "is that I'm bored."

"Bored?" the therapist asked. "Bored of what?"

"Bored of being a Ouija board, I guess. See, Doc, a good deal of my life has been spent rotting on the shelves of thrift stores in podunk towns in flyover states across the country, usually sandwiched between a couple of old, musty board games—Monopoly, Chutes and Ladders, Clue, and the like. And when I'm not rotting on a shelf in a thrift store, I'm usually collecting dust in someone's hallway closet, someone who bought me for a degrading 50 cents or less, where I find myself once again sandwiched between old board games, except now I'm enveloped in complete darkness. On occasion, my owner might take me out during a party, wherein drunken assholes ask me stupid questions and maneuver the planchette themselves in an attempt to scare each other or stir up some laughter by spelling out ridiculous or obscene phrases. Eventually, I'm either sold back to another thrift store or else given away at a garage sale for fucking pennies, the vicious cycle of my so-called life beginning anew.

"Yes, sure, occasionally people buy me who believe in my power, people who use me to communicate with the spirit world. And it used to be that whenever

I fell into the hands of such an owner, I was ecstatic with joy. How I loved when people took me seriously. When these folks used me to contact their dead loved ones, it made me feel important, made me feel like I belonged in the world. After all, that's the purpose for which I was made. But now, even that has lost its charm. See, you can only help so many people connect with their dead spouses or grandmas before it starts getting old. Nowadays, helping people talk to the dead just doesn't give me the sense of fulfillment it used to. I don't want to feel this way; I wish I could get my old verve back. But it's been years since I felt any sort of enthusiasm for my purpose. Like I said, Doc. I'm bored of being a Ouija board."

"Has it ever occurred to you," the therapist said in somewhat condescending, mister-know-it-all sort of tone, "that perhaps your boredom stems from the fact that you might possibly be the biggest fucking asshole ever to walk the face of the planet?"

The Ouija board was taken aback for a moment, its invisible tongue tied. "Um, no, that has not ever occurred to me. I mean, as far as sentient Ouija boards go, I think I'm a pretty nice guy, Doc. What are you trying to insinuate?"

"Oh, I'm not trying to insinuate anything. I was just throwing that out there. Just something to think about, that's all. Let's move on, shall we?"

"Wait. Just something to think about? But why would I want to think about something that isn't in the least bit true. And why would you even say that to me? Why would you—"

"Let's move on now, shall we? So when you called me to set up our appointment, you also mentioned you were having problems with anxiety."

"Um, yeah. Yeah, I am. Like I was saying, I'm usually never in one place for more than a few years, maybe a decade at the most. So I constantly worry that as soon as I start to feel comfortable in, for example, a particularly cozy closet or on an especially nice, well-kept shelf in a junk store, that I'll be sold off and shipped out the next day without any warning. Not only that, but my lost sense of purpose, identity, and self-worth has sent my anxiety levels through the roof too. I also started a new job about a month ago. A real job. It's my first job ever, and—"

"Has it ever occurred to you," the therapist interrupted, "that perhaps—and again I stress the word *perhaps*—your anxiety is actually caused by the fact that you might be a blithering, insufferable, raging asshole of the most epic proportions ever imagined?"

"Hey, I'm *not* an asshole! Who do you keep suggesting that? Why, I oughta leave right—"

"Relax, my friend, relax. I'm just throwing that out there, is all. Just something to think about. Nothing more. Anyways, let's move on, shall we? You also mentioned you're suffering from severe clinical depression. Let's talk a little bit about that."

The flustered Ouija board composed himself before he continued. "Well, yes. The primary cause of my depression, as I told you over the phone, is the recent and tragic loss of my entire family."

"You tell me much about it over the phone, which is perfectly understandable. So why don't you tell me about it now? Remember, I'm your therapist. You can tell me anything, no matter how difficult something is to talk about. Doing so will be therapeutic for you."

"Well, okay. To make a long story short, I met a female Ouija board about two years ago at Foo-Fap's Thrift-World Emporium in Dapperboy, Illinois, where we were both sitting on the same shelf awaiting new buyers. It was love at first sight. At our request, an old sentient cassock that was hanging in the Miscellaneous Clothing section (the kind that the clergy wear) married us right there on our shelf. That first year, my wonderful wife bore me two children. Two little Ouija boards—a boy and a girl—both of them about the size of baseball cards. Our little family then enjoyed a short but happy few months in the thrift store, before a nice, young newlywed couple came in and purchased us. We were thankful beyond words that the couple chose to buy all four of us, when they could have just as easily broken our family apart.

"All was perfect until that horrible, twisted, multiple-vehicle pile-up that happened on the interstate on the way home from the thrift store to the couple's house that day. We . . . we never did get a chance to see our new home. I . . . I was the sole survivor of the car crash." The Ouija board paused before crying out, "And cursed be the day that I was mass produced at a Parker Brothers toy factory in China by malnourished, blinded, hobbled, two-year-old slave laborers!" He lapsed into silence again, overcome by emotion. "That crash," he resumed, "it happened not three months ago. So as you can see, Doc, the root cause of my severe clinical depression is quite obvi—"

"Has the possibility ever occurred to you," the therapist interrupted, "that the *real* reason you're experiencing severe clinical depression is that, of all the self-centered, blithering, raging, drooling, narcissistic, douche-canoeing assholes that have ever stumbled across the face of this goddamn miserable fucking planet, you are without a doubt the most insufferable, inconceivable, unbearable, insupportable, unbelievable, outrageous, and astonishing motherfucking asshole to ever fucking exist *anywhere* in the motherfucking, cock-sucking, shit-eating universe!?!?"

"That's it," the Ouija board said as he hopped down from the couch to the floor. "I don't have to take this kind of abuse from you. I'll find myself another therapist, one who isn't batshit-crazier than me. You're a quack and a disgrace to your profession. And you're not even a human. Shit, you're not even a sentient Ouija board! As a matter of fact, I'm staring at you right now, and I still have no idea what the fuck you are. But you know what, pal? I don't care what you are. Because you, sir, are no longer a part of my life. I gotta go. I'm nearly late for work. So long, asshole."

The Ouija board turned from the therapist and began hopping for the door.

"Do you really want to know what I am?" the therapist called after him.

The Ouija board halted just before the exit and waited for the therapist to continue, though he refused to look back.

"I'll tell you what I am," said the therapist. "Here goes. You know how if Suri Cruise were to put a cheap, plastic Brad Pitt mask on just before using a chainsaw to chop off everyone's head in the world whose name began with the letter "Q," that would not change the fact that, in the video game Frogger, if you land your frog on the back of a diving turtle and sit there for too long, you'll die because the diving turtle will eventually dive back under the water?"

"What? You lost me there."

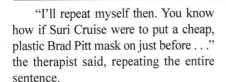

"I'll repeat myself then. You know how if Suri Cruise were to put a cheap, plastic Brad Pitt mask on just before . . ." the therapist said, repeating the entire sentence.

"Um, yeah," the Ouija board said after hearing it a second time. "I guess so. I mean, that's a completely ridiculous, stupid, and pointless thing to say, but I suppose it's true."

"Well, *that* is what I am."

"What? That makes no sense. Are you saying that you're some kind of physical incarnation of that absurd fact?"

"Indeed, that's exactly what I'm saying. Turn around and look at me, and you shall see."

The Ouija board, who was still facing the door, turned to look at the therapist, who was on the other side of the room in front of his desk, hovering just above the carpet: a scrambled blur of shifting images, including a chainsaw-wielding Suri Cruise in a cheap Brad Pitt mask, blood-spattering decapitations, rapidly changing screenshots of the original Frogger video game, and a cyclone of scrolling, wheeling, dancing names, all beginning with the letter "Q"—*Quincy, Quentin, Quimby, Quin, Quill, Qasim, Quetzalxochitl . . .*

After a moment, the Ouija board said, "Wow. I hadn't noticed before. I'm sorry I doubted you. You really are the fact that if Suri Cruise were to put on a cheap, plastic Brad Pitt mask just before using a chainsaw to chop everyone's head off in the world whose name began with the letter "Q," that would not change the fact that, in the video game Frogger, if you land your frog on the back of a diving turtle and sit there for too long, you'll die because the diving turtle will eventually dive under the water."

"You're goddamn right that's what

I am! Now get the fuck out of my office and never come back!"

"I was already on my way out, dick! Fuck you too!"

***

The Ouija board used his short telekinetic reach to open the door and let himself out into the hallway. He had to get to work. Luckily, he didn't have very far to go. In fact, the Ouija worked directly across the hall from his therapist. His place of work was only two hops away.

The Ouija board was a licensed psychologist too.

"Good morning, Shelia," he said to his receptionist as he hopped into the waiting room of his office, letting the door shut behind him.

"Good morning, sir," Shelia said from her desk, not bothering to look up as she finished painting the nail of her left pinky a sassy hot pink. "Your nine o' clock, Eileen Taylor, just called to cancel."

"Oh, swell. Hey, did you get the note I left for you on Friday about buying me a shotgun and normal, non-sentient Ouija board?"

"I picked them both up for you on Saturday. They're on your desk."

"Oh, fantastic. I really don't know what I'd do without you, Shelia."

Sheila blew on the still wet nail polish of her outstretched fingers, looked up, smiled, and winked coyly at her boss.

"Who am I seeing at ten?" he asked.

The receptionist leaned in toward her monitor. "At ten you have a new patient. No name shown here. Just a description."

"Just a description?"

"Yeah. It says here that your ten o'clock

patient is the fact that if Suri Cruise were to put on a cheap, plastic Wesley Snipes mask just before using a chainsaw to chop off everyone's head in the world whose name began with the letter "Q," that would not change the fact that, in the video game Frogger, if you land your frog on the back of a diving turtle and sit there for too long, you'll die because the diving turtle will eventually go back under water."

The Ouija board froze in place just outside the door to his office. "Are you certain it says a Wesley Snipes mask and not a Brad Pitt mask?" he asked.

"Positive," she responded.

"Whew!" the Ouija board said, the interjection surfing on a long sigh of relief. "Well, that's one good thing. Hey, I'm gonna go into my office now, jump on the internet, put on some Ouija board porn, lube up my planchette, and jerk off until the damn thing breaks in half. Then I'm gonna take that shotgun and blow my fucking brains out."

Sheila gasped, raised her fingers to her lips. "But, sir. What about your patients? Should I cancel all of you appointments for today. And should I cancel all of your appointments for . . . *forever?*"

"Oh, no. I have every intention of keeping my appointments. That's why I had you pick up that normal, inanimate Ouija board. When my patients arrive, send them to my office just as you would normally. Only now be sure to inform them that they have to use the Ouija board that's on my desk to contact me beyond the grave so that we can conduct our therapy sessions remotely. Got it?"

"Got it, boss!"

ERIC HENDRIXSON

LOCATION:
Chicago, IL

STYLE OF BIZARRO:
Batcave Gonzo

BOOKS BY HENDRIXSON:
Bucket of Face
Drunk Driving Champion
Precious Blood of the Lamb

DESCRIPTION: Eric Hendrixson writes Bizarro Noir and Batcave Gonzo stories of despair-based humor and romantic absurdism. With a mix of weary cynicism, absolute sincerity, and literary hooliganism, his stories focus on the emotional consequences of decisions made in bizarre circumstances.

INTERESTS: Eastern Bloc weaponry, folly and the human condition, caffeine, folklore and mythology, disc golf, Eastern religion, dealing in absolutes, the outdoors, The Destroyer, radio drama, film noir and serials, independent and low-budget cinema, novelty songs, bad ideas and heroic failures, musical theater and light opera, the art of Albrecht Durer and Mark Cline.

INFLUENCES: Nikolai Gogol, Jim Henson, Italo Calvino, Dorothy Parker, Anthony Burgess, Lloyd Kaufman, Franz Kafka, Rod Serling, William Gibson, Dashiell Hammett, Dr. Demento, Albert Camus, Oscar Wilde, Raymond Chandler, Douglas Adams, Christopher Moore, Flannery O'Connor, Vladimir Nabokov, Alfred Hitchcock, Cormac McCarthy, Hunter S. Thompson, Alexander Pushkin, Albert Murray, Kurt Vonnegut, John Barth, William Faulkner, Lewis Carroll, Bob Burden.

WEBSITE:
erichendrixson.com

GIVING THE FINGER

Chapter One

One morning, while walking to school, Hans Dutch noticed that the dike above the town was leaking. He used his finger to plug up the hole and saved the town from drowning. That was stupid, very stupid.

With his finger in the hole, Hans looked around for help, an adult or some sort of authority figure who could repair the leak. There was no one in sight. "Burbear," Hans said. The dog looked up. He liked to hear his name. "It's up to you now. I want you to go home and get Mom. Bring her back here, and she'll be able to tell someone in charge." He pointed the way they had come. "Now go home and get Mom."

Burbear stared up at Hans with an amiable, open-mouthed expression. English was one language the dog had never quite grasped. When Hans again told Burbear to go home, this time swinging his free hand toward home, Burbear hopped up, spun once, looked around, and sat down again. Hans sighed. He told his dog that a single hole, however small, will lead to a larger breach, the breach to the complete collapse of the dike, and the

dike collapse to a flood that would destroy the entire town. Knowing this, he stood and kept his finger in the hole, even as he heard the school bell ring in the distance. The dog, however, was a slow study, at least where hydraulic engineering was concerned. He didn't budge. It was a few minutes after eight o'clock, and the sun had only been lit a couple hours before. The meringue was still white, and the Cointreau still flickered slightly. "Okay," Hans said. "I'll explain it one more time."

Hours later, the liquor was burning with its full noonday force. Hans was still trying to convince the dog to go for help when Mr. Zylstra, known throughout the town as Mr. Z, walked by. Hans was still facing the wall, but he recognized the slap of Mr. Z's webbed feet on the sidewalk and the smell of stagnant water and root cellars. Hans called out to him.

Mr. Z turned around. It was that Dutch kid, Hands or something. "What are you doing over there?" he asked. "Get away from that dike. You know that dikes and sluice gates are my business, not yours. You have no business with that dike."

"But there's a leak," Hans said. "Look."

Mr. Z looked closely at the wall. He saw a small puddle beside the lunchbox at the boy's feet. Beyond the puddle, there was a small creek of water that crossed the sidewalk and disappeared into the grass. That proved nothing. Just because there was water near the dam didn't mean the water came from the dam. Anyone could have put that water there. Puddles were of no concern to Mr. Z. There was no water coming out of the wall, and that's what was important. Mr. Z shook his head. "There is no leak there that I can see, and I am an expert. Now, get out of here before I find a switch."

"I've stopped the hole with my finger," Hans said.

Mr. Z looked closer. "I see." The boy's finger did seem to stop at the second knuckle and disappear into the wall. He wondered whether this was some sort of optical illusion. "How long is your finger?" he asked.

"It's the normal finger length," Hans said.

"Nonsense. You're just a boy. I am a full-grown man with normal fingers. Are you saying your finger is as long as mine?" He held out his hand and splayed his fingers. "Now, there is a finger of normal size. There are no fingers more normal than mine. I defy you to find any fingers in this town more normal than these."

Hans thought about this. "My finger is normal boy size." After a moment's thought, he corrected himself. "The normal size of a finger for a boy, not a finger the size of a normal boy. I'm a boy myself, and I could never carry a finger as large as I am. If my finger was as large as myself, I would have to be twice large as I am!"

Mr. Z ignored the miscalculation. "You're talking nonsense," he said. "You know the business of dams and dikes is my work, not the work of a boy with his little boy fingers. And if my fingers are bigger, doesn't that just prove that my penis is bigger, and if my penis is bigger, just think how much larger my brain must be. You think you, with your tiny brain and little boy penis know the first thing about dikes?"

"So I can go?" Hans asked.

"I don't care what you do," Mr. Z said. "As long as you do it somewhere else and leave the working of dikes to me."

Hans pulled his finger out of the hole and water started spurting out of the wall. "Now you've gone and broken it!" Mr. Z said.

Hans batted at the spray of water in protest. "It was broken when I got here," he said. "And I was able to fix it by putting my finger in the hole. I've been waiting and waiting for someone to come and fix the hole in this wall, and now that you're here, all you want to talk about is your fingers and your brains. It's after lunchtime, I'm hungry, and I have to go to the bathroom."

"Well, put it back in." Mr. Z guided the boy's finger back into the hole. "You're lucky I came along. Of all the people in this town, I am the one entrusted with repairing the dams."

"I know that."

"Don't sass me, boy. Now, you just stay here and I'll be right back. Don't take your finger out of that hole for any reason."

"Please hurry," Hans said.

Mr. Z's feet slapped downhill, toward the center of town. He walked into the cafe, sat at the counter, and ordered a slice of herring pie and a cup of tea from Doris. Then, after looking left and right to make sure nobody in any position of authority was in the cafe, he ordered a small glass of rapeseed aquavit.

He drank the clear liquor as he waited for his tea. "You know that Dutch boy? His name is Hank or Hands?"

Doris wiped her hands on the front of her tee shirt. "I know the family."

"Well, I was walking past the dike, you know, the one by Water Street?"

"I know the one," Doris said.

"Well, I was walking by there on my way to have lunch, and that Dutch boy had his finger in the dike. It turns out, the wall had sprung a leak, and being the quick-thinking lad he was, he plugged up the wall with his finger. And it's a good thing he did, I can tell you, because you know once a leak starts in a dike, it's not long before the whole thing goes."

"That would be the end of my shop," Doris said.

"It would be the end of this whole downtown district. Why, just last week, it rained up in the mountains. Two days later, I had to open the sluice gate to let out the extra water." He pulled at the suspenders holding up his rubber gaiters, the mark of his profession, and let them go with a snap. "It's an important skill, running a sluice, you know, old family secret. It's an important responsibility. You don't become a sluice man overnight, you know." He couldn't see whether or not Doris was impressed. "So the first thing I will do, after lunch of course, is to go to the hardware store and get mortar to patch up that hole properly. This town is lucky to have me, I'll say."

"Oh, it is," Doris replied, sliding his slice of pie into the oven.

However, when the tea and pie came, Mr. Z was struck with a sense of melancholy. He stirred the minnows in his teacup. They were two small sunfish, with the spots on their sides already visible. "Look at this," he said. "This is unacceptable. These fish are too large to go in a cup of tea. How old are those teabags?" The fish swam in tight circles. "Haven't I been torment-ed enough?"

"I can't really help it, can I?" Doris asked. "I mean, if Boris won't buy new teabags, I can't make those fish any younger. You know how things are these days." She paced in a small circle around a cedar pillar, then walked a sine curve along the counter, wiping it with a damp rag. "Things just get worse and worse."

"Don't tell me about how things are these days," Mr. Z said. He ordered a second aquavit and poured it into his tea. "Things these days are nothing like in the old days, I'll tell you. Back then, children knew how to respect their elders and did not go around sassing their betters and fixing dams that didn't belong to them. People knew their proper place. But now? Who can tolerate it?" He sighed and pushed his fork aimlessly. "Even a herring pie has to be stuffed with so much sawdust and lard, just to fill it out and make it look large enough. If I had the inspecting of pies and not the management of sluices, I can tell you, heads would roll for what people call a pie these days. There's no great profit in the management of water, I'll grant you, but if I had the inspection of the pies, this town would have decent pies, the way pies used to be."

"Shut up about pies, will you? I have to do my job, just like anyone else. I have no more control over the ingredients Boris gives me than you have over how much rain the clouds drop into your canals, do I?" She poured another shot.

"It is a wicked time and a wicked world," Mr. Z said. "The people who light that baked Alaska that passes for a sun these days, I can tell you, they have been skimping on the brandy. The way days keep getting shorter, I would not be surprised at all if their children are stealing little tastes of ice cream. Maybe it's just a bite at a time, but it adds up. We may have no sun at all by December. If only a person could be sure of one honest person as this world goes, that would be something."

As the minnows swam more slowly, the operation of Mr. Z's third aquavit was pushing a solution forth into his brain. It seemed that Doris, this poor woman, living all alone in the cellar below the cafe, might be that one honest person, and perhaps she would be willing to marry him and move into his sluice house. There couldn't be many other men in the town pursuing her, not with that short wooden left leg of hers that left her walking in circles all the time. However, her arms were strong and symmetrical enough to row a boat, and that was what a Mrs. Z would need. Then he thought of the librarian, Wayne. Perhaps Wayne was the rival of his affection. It couldn't be anyone else, since how many single men over the age of thirty were left in this town, anyway?

And who was Doris to think she could pick and choose? With her wooden leg and her second-hand glass eye that was the wrong color and size. It would fall into the soup if she sneezed or looked down. Mr. Z had seen it happen. This skinny, limping cyclops had no right to think she deserved a better man.

Doris gazed into Mr. Z's flat face. He was lost in thought, and she wondered what sort of things he might be contemplating. Of course, a sluice man must be a man of the world, and it was possible that he was contemplating some very learned matter. It was possible that she had poured more into those three glasses of aquavit than she should have. Perhaps there was even more at work here. That extra shot she poured or the extra-large slice of herring pie may have softened his heart and awoken his more gentle feelings on the idea of love. For indeed, Doris did love Mr. Z. She loved him with the sort of certainty that comes from knowing that she was the only unmarried woman over thirty in the village and that he was the only unmarried man over thirty, since Wayne had packed up his library on the backs of a herd of capybaras and ridden off years ago.

And in all fairness, what other woman could possibly love Mr. Z, what with his fat waist and neck, his frog's feet, and the way he always smelled his fingers, as if suspicious of where they had been while he was away. He was rude, disgusting, loud, and pompous. Worst of all, he was a lousy tipper. No other woman could possibly love him, and that made Doris love him all the more.

Mr. Z watched her one eye look straight ahead while the other spun freely in her head. He could see all the duplicity of the female sex in that gaze. The look told him of the nights she had probably spent with Wayne on the piles of burlap in the cellar and what Doris really thought of Mr. Z. It told him how Wayne and Doris would lie on the sacks together, thinking of nothing but ways to disparage Mr. Z, laughing about his infatuation and foolish devotion. Perhaps they had a special pillow, on which Doris had carefully embroidered a satirical caricature of Mr. Z's likeness, which they would stick with pins at Sunday breakfasts or Doris would put under her ass to raise it off the dirt floor during the act. It was probably the same pillow on which Wayne would wipe his penis after intercourse. They would dance with this pillow of mockery between them, singing, "Mr. Z, Mr. Z, what a fool a man can be!" It was a disgusting and insane thought, and he had never thought Doris was capable of it until now.

Now, knowing this, Mr. Z could barely look at Doris, this disgusting traitor, for in betraying him, she had betrayed the romantic soul of all mankind. He tried to think of a crushing phrase he could set upon her to destroy her soul and let her know that he was on to her. He hoped that what he said would somehow wound her so much that the black and rotten part of her heart would die, decompose completely, and fall away. Then, after a time of mourning and correction, it could heal into a heart that was pure and whole again. He couldn't think of anything.

He decided it was better to be a man of few words, condemning her with his silences, which would speak more eloquently and harshly than her ears could bear to hear. He dug through his pocket and counted out some money, which he placed on the counter. He stood up and delivered his closing line to bite and tear at her conscience: "Bye." He knew she would understand the hidden meaning behind the phrase and how it would torture her.

Chapter Two

Back at the dike, Hans was starting to doubt that Mr. Z was coming back. He urged Burbear to go home and get his mother. Burbear tried to understand, but it wasn't like he had a Berlitz phrasebook. Burbear sniffed at the lunchbox at Hans' feet. Burbear was a good dog, and a man can trust a dog's loyalty to the death. For the sake of his master, a dog will endure any hardship but hunger or boredom, and Burbear was acutely aware that it was after lunchtime. This time, when Hans pointed toward home and said, "Please, Burbear, go home and get help," Burbear realized that he must go at once. He rose and sprinted toward home.

Mr. Z crossed the street and entered the hardware store. It was a clean but cluttered place. The front half of the store held stationary, cookware, mason jars, sewing supplies, fishing tackle, toys, lamps, seeds, flower pots, and hobby supplies. The rear of the store carried tools, fasteners, dowels, wires, ropes, pipes, chains, and the bags of powder Mr. Z was looking for. What he wanted was a combination of clay and mortar. The clay would go inside the hole, plugging the leak. The mortar would go in afterward, sealing the breach and holding the clay in place. The decision to take action destroyed an inertia that had been blocking his spirit, and he felt an urge to fix everything. While he was at it, he could use any remaining mortar to patch small cracks in the dike, preventing future leaks. That was, of course, if he could trust that fucking mayor to reimburse him for his receipt.

When he got to the masonry section, Mr. Z. found the mortar and clay he wanted, but the sacks they came in were too large. He went to the clerk. "I'm looking for a five-pound sack of mortar and a five-pound sack of bentonite clay."

The clerk was cleaning out his ears with a hand-powered drill, the old crank-type. He didn't turn his head or stop what he was doing. "That's over there, in the masonry section."

"Well, I looked there, but all you seem to have is twenty-pound sacks."

"Yeah, then we only sell those in twenty-pound sacks," the clerk said.

Mr. Z stepped away from the clerk and slowly counted his money. He shook his head. Store clerks were not helpful at all these days. They were always using hand drills on their ears instead of helping customers. He counted again, silently, moving his lips. If he had skipped lunch, he might then have had almost enough money to buy the stuff, but even if he'd had enough ready money on hand, was he expected to carry forty pounds all the way up the hill? It was nonsense. It was an imposition to expect him to do so much. Sure, he could probably buy the bags and the wheelbarrow on credit, but only if he trusted the town to pay him back. Besides, using credit would require filling out a form, maybe even two forms. It was all too much to bear.

Now, if they would have sold him two five pound bags or even just a couple handfuls of the stuff, he would be fine. Mr. Z knew that even asking would have been ridiculous and pointless. It was clear that Wayne and Doris were behind this. He was helpless in the face of such savage duplicity. They had probably allied the whole town against him. Why should he carry such weight and face such torment for an unappreciative town when it was already clear that the leak in the dam had been fixed by that Hands boy? Indeed, he and the boy were the only innocent people in this matter, and they did not deserve to be the only ones punished. He felt a deep sense of kinship and gratitude toward the boy. Inspired by this feeling, he walked to the front of the store and half-filled a small paper bag with penny candy.

Hans stood fidgeting by the dike, his left hand holding the front of his pants. The only things he had thought of in the hours since Mr. Z left were his bladder and the water pressing against his finger. In the water, he could feel something tickling his finger. It could have been a small fish, maybe an octopus, maybe the whisker of a sea serpent, but it felt like something else. He thought a fish would bite, but this felt like a fingernail lightly scratching the tip of his finger. In his mind, he saw green hair waving under the water like braided kelp.

"Boy," Mr. Z said.

Hans turned his head. He saw that Mr. Z had a small paper bag with him, probably full of dam-mending material.

"Boy, I wanted to thank you for holding back this leak, so I brought you something." Mr. Z offered the bag of candy to Hans' free hand. Hans had not eaten all day, so he pulled his hand away from the dike to reach into the bag. Immediately, a burst of water spurted out of the dike and hit him in the face. Startled, he released his bladder and felt the warm stream flow down his leg, over his shoes, and into the puddle he stood in. Mr. Z grabbed the boy's hand and pushed the finger back into the hole.

Mr. Z's gratitude was replaced with disgust at the boy's incontinence and stupidity. "What are you doing, boy? The leak has gotten worse. You must keep your finger in that hole, don't you understand?"

Hans nodded his head.

"This is very important."

Hans nodded again.

"Good," Mr. Z said. Then, looking at his watch, he handed Hans the bag, tipped his hat, and hurried away.

Now that his finger was even further into the dike, it seemed something had taken hold of it, like a soft, slimy hand holding his finger. It didn't squeeze or bite. It just held on, the way a frightened younger brother or sister might hold your finger in the dark.

Burbear loped in the back door into the kitchen, where Mrs. Dutch was cleaning up from her lunch. On the kitchen table, she had laid out a number of opened envelopes, bills mostly, and a checkbook. "So how's tricks, toots?" he asked in Parisian French.

"Burbear," Mrs. Dutch said. "You're home later than normal. What do you want for lunch?" Her French had an unidentifiable accent, like the haphazard pronunciation of an autodidact.

"Steak," Burbear said. "A rare Delmonico steak with red potatoes and carrots with a beer, something with a nice, floral hop character, but not too bitter."

"Steak it is," Mrs. Dutch scooped a tin cup of dried dog food into a bowl. She carried the bowl to the sink and sprayed a bit of tap water over the food. She put it on the floor.

Burbear sat in front of the bowl. "I think there might be some disconnect here. The steaks that show up in my bowl do not smell anything like the steaks that go up on your table."

"Yes, but the table is much higher than the floor," Mrs. Dutch pointed out. "You have to take altitude into account."

"I guess that makes sense," Burbear said. He started eating. As he ate, he thought there was something he was supposed to mention, but he couldn't work out what it was. He ate quickly, licked his muzzle, and drank some water from a stainless steel bowl. As he drank, the importance of his message shot back into his mind. "I just remembered. There's something very important I have to tell you."

"Hold on a minute," Mrs. Dutch said. She worked out a subtraction problem on the back of an envelope and entered a number into the checkbook. She licked a stamp and attached it to another envelope. While she stuck her tongue out to close the envelope, Burbear felt a distinct tingling between his hind legs. He remembered that it was time to lick himself. That might have been the important thing. He sat down and started licking his scrotum. "Now, Burbear, what did you want to tell me?"

Burbear stopped licking his balls, looked around, shook his head and snorted. "You know, for the life of me, I can't remember." He went back to work.

"Well, it must not have been very important," she said. She took two pairs of alligator clamps and attached them to a squid in a small aquarium. She attached the squid to a monitor and a numeric keypad. After entering a few numbers, she smiled to see that the numbers on the screen matched those in the checkbook. She disconnected the clamps and dropped half a sardine in the tank. "Good boy," she said.

Burbear scurried over to her ankle

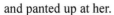

and panted up at her.

"I wasn't talking to you," Mrs. Dutch said.

Hans tried to get the candy into his mouth. His first attempt had been to lift the bag to his mouth, but since he was holding the rolled up top of the bag, that did him no good. He could have chewed through the bag, but that would have spilled most of the candy on the ground. Finally, he turned his palm upward to cup the bag. When he tore through the bottom of the sack with his teeth, he found that the candies were individually wrapped. He shoved them into his mouth anyway and tried to unwrap them with his teeth and tongue.

He heard his sister Greta approaching with her two friends, Marti and Sonja. They were preceded by the sound of their gossip, some of it about how much trouble he would be in for missing school. Since they had already touched on that subject during lunch, they were more interested in discussing what matches could be arranged before the October dance. As the girls approached, Hans tried to face away from them in a way that would hide his stained pants-front from them. At the same time, he wanted to make sure his sister got help from home. With a mouthful of candy, plastic and paper, he cried out, "Greta!" Colored spit and wrappers sprayed from his mouth.

"It's my stupid brother," Greta said to her friends. "Just ignore him. He's always doing something gross." Then looked the other way and talked louder as they passed, pretending he was not there.

A moment later, a group of older, rougher boys Hans usually avoided walked by. As they passed, they took pieces of candy from his outstretched palm and continued without breaking step.

As the last of the liquor burned off, the fiery sun became an amber meringue moon, the entire surface slowly cooling to the temperature of ice cream. As the sun had radiated the heat of its surface, the moon radiated the coldness of its core. Mr. Z pushed his half-eaten supper of turnips and cabbage away. The plate clinked against the previous night's plate of half-eaten cabbage and turnips, scaring a dozen fruit flies into the air. They burst into a frantic cloud for a moment before settling down again. "It's always turnips and turnips," he said. "This is no life for a man." He plugged in his squid and checked his email. He sipped at a pint of distilled turnip juice and considered his inbox. There was nothing from Doris, but he had to expect that. There was a week-old memo from the city council on the budget, and he read it angrily. There was no increase in the sluice allocation or any increase for routine dike maintenance. He yelled at his computer screen, "How do they expect me to carry forty pounds up the hill without a wheelbarrow? I ask you that?" The squid said nothing.

Mr. Z saw that Wayne was behind all of this. He had to show the mayor that this cabal endangered the whole town. He smiled wickedly. If he worded his reply to this email carefully enough, alerting the mayor to the danger of holding back the flood with nothing but schoolboys and showing how Wayne was to blame for it all, perhaps he could increase his budget and have Wayne driven out of town. Cackling to himself, he started typing.

It was cold that night, not freezing cold but chilly in the way the end of summer is always surprising. With his left hand, Hans buttoned his school jacket, which normally hung open. He had dropped the torn and empty paper bag to the ground, keeping only a couple hard candies in the front pocket of his overalls. While his lunch sat in a tin lunchbox at his feet, he was unable to retrieve it without removing his finger from the wall.

As it grew later, he heard a voice, not quite with his ears but inside of his head, like a memory or a wish. The voice was soft and repetitive, a distant echo, and in the dark, staring at the dam, he saw underwater currents, and fanning out in the waves something like grass or seaweed, green hair billowing in different directions. The voice said one thing over and over: "Hello."

He slept occasionally, awakening with a falling sensation. The first couple times, the blow against the wall awoke him, but once he was completely exhausted, Hans was able to sleep leaning against the dike. He dreamed of the girl with green hair, waving one arm under water, as if to say hi.

In a corner between the dam and the street, a little dust devil danced in the darkness. It sang, "Dust devil whirlwind, dust devil whirlwind in the leaves. Dust devil whirlwind, dust devil whirlwind seldom grieves."

"Go away," Hans said, and the whirlwind danced away on the wind. Sleeping outdoors in a village is different from sleeping in a city or in the woods. In the woods, nature is never silent. Nocturnal animals crash through the brush, trees shed branches to crash to the earth, and unexplained feet crash and stomp through the grass and leaves. In the city, the sounds of engines, police officers, and criminals continue all night, and it's not quiet until the hours before dawn. After midnight but before five, when the buses aren't running, the night has an emptiness all its own. In that kind of silent delirium, when dreams are indistinguishable from waking life, Hans heard the voice in his head again. It asked a single question: "Can I have some?"

Hans reached into the pocket of his overalls with his left hand and took out a piece of butterscotch. He tossed it in a high arc and heard it click twice on the stone and plunk into the water. As he drifted off to sleep again, he felt a squeeze on his finger, then the words, "Thank you." He was able to unwrap another piece of candy between his fingers and teeth, but it was coffee flavor. He spat it onto the sidewalk.

Two hours before dawn, Mr. Z read over his masterpiece. He had written it in some very choice bureaucratic language, all the better to highlight the satirical tone of the email. He had outlined Wayne's villainy in the most subtle tones, but a wise man who understood the situation would be able to decode the whole thing and understand. The mayor, he knew, was a shrewd man. He would know that the email was insulting, but it was so carefully crafted that the mayor would not be able to identify any specific insult or offense.

Mr. Z carefully checked the email for any mistakes and lifted the pint of beet brandy to his lips. It was empty. He rose to get another bottle out of the kitchen and felt his feet slapping heavily and his head rolling unsteadily. There was a bottle of beet juice already open in the kitchen. He did not remember opening that one, and it was nearly empty, but nearly empty is still a little bit full, so he carried it back to the table and sat down with a thud. The letter was brilliant, and his stomach warmed with a sense of satisfaction. Still he was a prudent man. "I'd best read this in the morning," he said. "My judgment is clouded right now." The screen was too blurry to do any more writing anyway. Mr. Z closed one eye and squinted at the monitor with the other. He scrolled over to save the email. The screen showed a small box that asked him if he wanted to save all. "Of course I'll want to save the whole thing. The stupid questions computers ask these days," he said. He clicked on okay, disconnected the squid, and fed it a few scraps of boiled bacon left over from his cabbage. Then he staggered to bed, mumbling about how stupid computers can be.

Chapter Three

When the sun caught fire and the smell of burning sugar and orange liquor awoke him, Burbear bolted from his repose at the foot of Hans' bed and ran to his bowl. The bowl was empty. He ran back and looked at the bed. It was empty too. He called out, "Hey, where is the kid? He's supposed to feed me." After a few minutes of waiting, he shook his head. "I left the kid at the dam, didn't I? Well, he can't feed me down there." He ran down the hill to find Hans still leaning against the wall.

Greta walked past her brother, who was still staring at the wall like an idiot, with one hand against the wall. The other was pressed against the seat of his pants. "I really have to go," Hans said. "Help me, please."

"Gross," she said to her friends. "My brother is so disgusting." She dropped his brown lunch bag at his feet. She looked at the crowd of citizens gathered around her brother. "You are in so much trouble when you get home." Then she continued toward school.

Hungry as he was, Hans would not reach down for the food. As it was, he was straining against his sphincter. He would not dare to squat even if he could. He did not turned around to see the gathering crowd, and adding more food to his stomach seemed counterproductive. His forehead was sweating, and his bowels quivered in complaint. Burbear trotted down the hill. "Dude," Burbear said. "What the fuck? Where's my breakfast already?"

Hans looked down at the barking dog. "Burbear, get help," he said.

Burbear looked up at him with a frustrated growl. "Look, asshole, this is supposed to be a bilingual country. If you can't be bothered to learn just a little bit of French, I can't help you. Did you at least bring me my breakfast?" He sniffed around Hans' feet and smelled the food in the bag. He tore into the bag and shook the peanut butter sandwich out of the wax paper wrapper. As he ate the sandwich, he wondered, "Is this what steak tastes like?" Burbear coughed at the gooey mouthful that he could not quite swallow and looked around for something to drink. There was a puddle at the boy's feet, but Burbear would be damned if he would drink that piss. He ran up the hill, gasping and coughing. At the top of the hill, he spat out the sandwich on the grass. Then he worked the sandwich down bit by bit, washing it down with water from the canal.

The crisis did not catch the mayor sleeping. He'd awoken, fortunately, in his wife's bed. She was in the kitchen, making a breakfast of eggs, toast, bacon, beans, and mushrooms. The mayor took a small jar of white powder from the cupboard. He unscrewed the cap and scooped some of the powder with the long fingernail of his little finger. He sniffed at his finger vigorously. He popped three pieces of mint amphetamine chewing gum from a green foil-pack. In the bathroom, he highlighted his eyebrows with a red mascara brush, Brylcreemed his nose hair, and brushed his teeth.

When he came out of the bathroom, his wife was eating her breakfast in front of an Ingmar Bergman sitcom on the television. Some jerk was playing chess badly against a guy in a black robe. She laughed along with the laughtrack, though the mayor knew that she was at best a mediocre chess player and probably didn't get the jokes.

His mistress, however, played chess like no woman he had ever played against. It was what attracted him to her, since she would not have sex or conversations with him. When he did have sex with his wife, he fantasized about meth-fueled chess marathons with his mistress, which would end with him collapsing in her bed alone as she stayed up to work out chess puzzles with her right hand, playing go with her left hand against imaginary opponents until dawn. It was at times like this that the mayor thought that he may be imaginary as well, that and on mornings when he awoke to see his wife eating breakfast.

"Did you make any for me?" the mayor asked.

"There's shredded wheat in the cupboard," she said.

The mayor pocketed a handful of shredded wheat to eat on the way to work. In the garage, he put a bit in the mouth of his mallard duck and trailed the reins back past its tail. The pigeons were harder to find, but once he got them, he slipped one onto each foot. He was about to snap the leather to send the duck forward when the garage was filled with the theme song from the Lady Gaga Superhero Hour cartoon. The mayor answered his phone. "Hello? What? Fuck. Okay. I'll be there. I'm coming all right?" The mayor hung up the phone and fed it a mealworm. He snapped the reins. "Fly!" he commanded. As usual, it didn't work. The pigeons under his feet were not strong enough to carry him. He walked slowly, with a gliding motion, the duck waddling ahead of him. He left a trail of feathers and blood on the ground as he walked.

He glided up to the dike, resplendent in the traditional mayoral lederhosen and cowboy hat, his mayoral robes trailing behind him. Several paces away from the crowd, he halted the duck and stood silently for a moment until he had everyone's attention. "My good citizens," he said, holding his arms out. "Friends, neighbors, voters, constituents—" He realized he didn't have anything to announce. "Who can tell me what has happened here?"

The town crossing guard spoke up. "There was a leak in the dike, but this boy plugged the leak with his finger. It was in the email."

The mayor pulled out his phone and considered plugging it into the jellyfish in his briefcase to check his email, but he figured that would reveal his ignorance. Instead, he decided to ad lib. "It is vital to plug these leaks. As we all know, a small leak can grow rapidly, leading to the collapse of the whole dike, flooding the town. We commend the quick thinking of this young man."

The townsfolk applauded Hans, and the mayor bowed. After several pats on the boy's back and head, handshakes being out of the question, the crowd began to thin out. The mayor saw his audience disappearing and summoned them back for a speech. "But in honor of this boy's bravery, we will construct a statue on this spot, in honor of—" The mayor thought quickly. "In honor of his honor, and on this day every year we will honor the honor of the memory of his memory." He tried to glide forward on his pigeons, but they had been ground to a crunchy paste under his feet. "For indeed, the business of this village is to be such a village as we all know and love. It is the people of the village like this young person who are truly the townspeople of this town."

As the mayor offered his speech, Mr. Z walked behind him, inspecting the dam. "Well, fucking hell," Mr. Z said. He felt along the dike. "This isn't far from collapsing, is it? I'd best go fix this."

"Mr. Z," the mayor said. "I'm trying to make a speech here."

"My apologies, I'm sure," Mr. Z said. He looked over his shoulder and noticed the crowd. "Oh, fucking hell,"

he said. A numbing tingle of cold panic clutched his head and testes. He pulled out his phone and tried to check his sent emails. He saw several dozen replies waiting. He rested his head against the stone wall. "Bloody Christ on my fucking cock." He raised his arms to the crowd, "When I clicked on send all, I didn't know it was fucking all! Don't read that email!"

"Shut up," the mayor whispered. "I've got this." He raised his arms to his constituents again. "And now that the boy has fixed the dike, we can all go back to our homes and places of business and go about the business of our business, for indeed, the business of business is business. Thank you, good night, and God bless."

"But you can't just leave him there," someone shouted from the crowd. "He's unsightly, and he smells bad." There were yells from agreement from the crowd, with phrases like "eyesore," "property values," and "blocks the sidewalk."

The mayor scanned the crowd and saw a man holding a fishing pole. He waddled through the crowd on his dead birds, proclaiming the glories of the little Dutch boy. As he passed the fisherman, he slyly asked, "Could I borrow this?" and slipped a fillet knife out of a sheath on the man's belt. "So in honor of the courageous courage of this young boy, I proclaim today Bobby's Day in honor of this hero, this courageous young youth, Bobby, who saved this town from ruin." As the crowd cheered, he cut into Hans' finger and slid the thin blade into the joint. With a twist of his wrist, he was able to pop the bone out of place, leaving the finger in the dike.

Hans screamed and lost control of his bowels. The mayor tried to hold the kid still as he sawed through the remaining nerves, tendons, and skin. He quickly stepped away from the smell, took the gum from his mouth, and spread it over the severed finger, which poked out of the dike. "Good as new," he said. He considered slapping the boy's butt and sending him home but thought better of it. He patted the kid's head. "Good job, son."

A voice came from the audience, "Oh, come on!"

The mayor recognized the voice and hardened his tone. "Good as new." He glided off behind his duck.

"So just to be sure," Mr. Z asked the crowd. "When I hit reply all, was it really to fucking all?"

Chapter Four

At home, Mrs. Dutch cauterized Hans' finger stump in the kitchen. When he stopped screaming and lay sobbing on the floor, she said, "You know, that's a pretty stupid thing you did."

"But the dike was bursting," Hans moaned. "I had to save the town."

"Save the town," Mrs Dutch mocked. "You can't even save your own shorts." She sent Hans to bed, where he dreamed about a world drowning in green hair and black shit.

Burbear sat by the edge of the canal and watched the water run by. He walked along the top of the dike, to where fish fell over the gate and landed, stunned, in the shallow water below. He crossed the canal at the gate and walked down to the shallows. Some fish recovered from the fall almost immediately. Others were stunned long enough to float

and drift downstream for a couple minutes before recovering their wits and batting their tails. Burbear watched the fish floating in the water and positioned himself to catch a stunned eel as it came close to the stone wall. He dragged it ashore and started chewing. He asked himself, "Is this what steak really tastes like?" A few feet away, a large female dog, a husky or a malamute, watched him. She walked over to him and sat down.

"So what do you have there?" she asked.

"Steak," Burbear said. "You can have some if you want."

She sniffed his butt and learned all she had to know about him. She tore into the eel. "Thanks, Burbear. I've never had steak before."

Burbear sniffed at her backside. "Well, Selma, catching these things is easy. I'm surprised I didn't think of it before."

The next morning, Burbear did not show up for breakfast. It was just as well, since Hans was running late himself. He walked quickly, determined to get to school on time. As he passed the spot in the dike where his finger was, he looked at the wad of chewing gum and the drops of water leaking out from under it, but he didn't stop, not even as he stepped into a puddle on the sidewalk. He was a hero now, and any future leaks were someone else's problem. His mother had taught him about trying to save the world. She'd told Hans' father when he got home, and Hans did not want to take that kind of a beating again. Still, heroism had to have its privileges. He decided to strike immediately. Once in the classroom, he walked straight to Laura, the girl with black hair, and asked her to go to the October dance with him. He was a hero, after all.

Laura looked at his bandaged hand and eager expression. "I'm not dancing with you," she said. "You're a four-finger shittypants." Hans stood frozen on the spot for a moment; then he ran out into the hallway. He hid in the bathroom for an hour, counting his fingers. There were nine of them. Laura was a liar. As many times as he told himself that, it didn't help. When the teacher finally dragged him out, it was time for recess. By then, the whole class had learned a song about the four-fingered shittypants.

They formed a ring and danced around him. "Four-finger shittypants, four finger shittypants," they sang. Hans looked at them dancing, their hands joined. He was a hero. The mayor had said so. He should be able to overcome this with no problem, but no heroic plan came to mind. He sat in the middle of the taunting circle and pressed his hands into the gravel.

The dancing and taunting continued as he dug his hands into the gravel. Below the smaller rocks, he found a larger rock, the size of a small dog's head, maybe the size of an adult fist. "It's nine!" he yelled, but no one listened. He palmed that stone in his right fist and hammered it into the gravel. The blow sent a jolt of pain through his hand, distracting him from his embarrassment. Every time they called him a four-fingered shittypants, he hammered the stone into the ground and shouted "Nine!"

By then, the older students had left the lunchroom. Hans saw his sister approach, flanked by Marti and Sonja.

While the younger students taunted him for being a four-fingered shittypants, his sister and her friends raised another song, "Hans likes Laura. Hans likes Laura." Hans looked up to see his sister leading the taunting song. The two songs were sung in a round. He knew he had to escape. The joined hands could easily be defeated, he realized. All he had to do was run Red Rover like he never had before. He could break out of the circle. Then he had to keep running so the older kids couldn't catch him. He rose from his seated position into a squat.

"He's going to shit again!" Laura said. She had joined with Hans' sister and was taunting along with the others. She had no idea.

Hans burst forward toward Laura and his sister. As he hit the circle of joined hands, he flung his handful of gravel at eye level. The circle broke as the children raised their arms to protect their faces. Hans kept running.

The singing had stopped. There was no sound now but the wind and Hans' own panting as he fled the schoolyard. The jolt of his feet striking the ground sent pain into his right hand, and he ran faster, as if to escape the thing biting and burning his hand.

Soon, there was another sound. Someone was yelling behind him. There were footfalls. Someone was chasing him, an adult. Hans held the rock tightly and ran as fast as he could. Still, within a few yards, arms wrapped around him and lifted him off the ground. He kicked his legs in the air and swung his arms until the stone hit something. The arms let go and Hans fell to the ground. He had lost his stone, but he no longer cared. He picked himself up and ran.

He ran as fast as he could and faster. He ran until his throat and heart hurt. Then he ran until his head felt dizzy. He ran past the school, past the dike, and down the hill into the middle of town. He passed the four blocks of Main Street and crashed into the woods at the foot of the mountain, where Main Street ended. As he ran uphill, toward the sun, he panted deliriously. The hills were hot with fire and smelled of spilled alcohol. He staggered upward, drunk and angry, betrayed and scared. He cut his shoes and hands on the rocks and didn't care. He skidded on gravel and tripped over tree branches. When he got up, he moved more slowly, sometimes crawling on all fours as the mountain got steeper and the woods gave way to rock and loose dirt. Then his head fell onto his arm and Hans' body crumbled into unconsciousness.

At city hall, Councilmember Brecht voiced his opposition to the mayor's proposed monument. "This child does not need a statue. What he needs, what this town needs, is proper governance, for us to do our jobs properly. Heroes only arise when we fail in our duties. This boy does not deserve a statue. He deserves responsible leadership, proper dike maintenance, fiscal responsibility, traditional family values, and the right to be left alone to live his life. What he deserves is ten fingers." He had been pounding on the dais as he spoke. "And the fact that he is missing a finger means that this body has failed in a fundamental way." He paused as if waiting for applause.

Looking up from the dessert cart, Councilmember Kennedy could see that, if she let him, Brecht would go on with another one of his endless speeches. She had arrived early to make sure she got the soup and fish courses, so now that the cheese and tiramisu had already been served, it seemed like a good time to end the meeting. She interrupted. "And how are we supposed to pay for this anyway? It's not like we're drowning in surplus funds."

The mayor was prepared for that objection. "We'll raise a special tax for the monument. This will not affect the general fund. And the fund can even be used to pay for dam maintenance, after we finish funding the monument to Bobby."

"Hans," Member Brecht said.

"Whatever. So it's agreed that we will levy a special tax to create a memorial in honor of the boy who saved our town, whatever his name is." Before Brecht or Kennedy could disagree, he opened the floor to public comment.

Mr. Z walked sheepishly toward the podium. "So when I hit send all, did it really send to everyone in town?"

"Fucking Christ," the mayor said. "We're conducting an official meeting here."

"I mean, I when I was working on the email, what got sent out was just supposed to be the first draft, you know? I swear, I thought it said save all, not send all."

"Why the hell would your Outlook have a save all feature?" The mayor asked. "Who would want to save half a drafted email?"

"That's what I thought," Mr. Z said. "This is so embarrassing."

The mayor struck the dais with his gavel. "Okay, thank you for that. You can sit down now. So we've had public comment. Now for the vote." His secretary called the vote. "So the motion carries 2-2."

Councilmember Brecht objected. "You have two in favor and two in opposition. How is that the motion carrying?"

"The motion carries," the mayor said. "Don't be difficult."

"And the person seconding the motion wasn't even paying attention. She was working out a chess puzzle."

The mayor banged his gavel. "The motion carries, okay? We can only cooperate if we work together. You're just obstructing the process. You're being that guy now, okay? Do you want to be that guy?"

Hans opened his eyes. He was no longer lying on the mountain's quartz teeth. He was under a coarse blanket in a bed of sorts. He saw stacked oak barrels and coiled copper tubing in every direction. He tried to avoid the obvious question, but he had to ask, "Where am I?"

"The sun," said a small voice next to him. Hans looked up and around for the source of the voice. He found he was lying on a mat on the floor of a long, open, wood building. A man in a brown, hooded robe looked at him intently, as if this were a stupid question. Without opening his mouth, he said, "Of course."

"The sun," Hans said. He closed his eyes again. "Of course."

"And for God's sake, shut up already."

Hans didn't hear that sentence so much as feel it inside his head. It was loud and forceful, so disorienting that he slipped back into unconsciousness.

He shivered himself awake on the face of the mountain. By then, the sun had burned out and faded into a toasted meringue moon, cold and amber. Hans got up from the sheer rock and walked lower, to a row of tall yellow grass near the tree line. He wanted the relative shelter of the grass, but a lifetime of warnings kept him from going into the woods after dark. As he settled below a rock outcropping into a small thicket of standing hay, there was a sudden burst of wind.

Hans rolled down the mountain until he hit the trees. He grabbed hold of a trunk and held on. After that, there were two shorter, weaker bursts of wind.

"Would you mind getting out of my mustache?" a deep, stony voice asked. "It makes me sneeze."

Hans looked around for the speaker, but he was alone on the mountain. He rose to his feet.

"Take a left," the voice said. Hans started walking to the left.

"My left, your other left."

Hans changed direction. Then, fearing a trap, he picked up a rock. It was a good rock, rounded on one side and sharp on the other, like a small axe head.

"While you're at it, get off of my face entirely."

Hans dropped his hands and slumped his shoulders, but he held onto the rock. "Well, where do you want me to go then?"

"If you keep going to the left, the proper left, you can sit on my shoulder if you want."

After several yards of walking in the dark, Hans found the shoulder of the mountain and sat down.

"You can stay here until morning, but then you will have to go."

"Why?" Hans asked.

"Because it's my shoulder, not yours," the mountain snapped. Then he calmed down and chucked lightly. "So the monks kicked you out, huh?"

"Why did they throw me out? I'm cold and hungry. I could freeze to death out here."

"They threw you out for talking too much. It's stupid really. They're under a vow of silence."

"Why didn't they tell me they were under a vow of silence?"

The mountain did not answer. He just loosed a gravely laugh.

Hans corrected himself. "I mean that I did not know they were under a vow of silence."

"Well, they're monks, you know. They are born, work, live, eat, sleep, shit, and die in a distillery. It you lived in a distillery, let me tell you, you'd say a lot of stupid things. And there were dozens of them, always drunk, always saying something stupid. Well, one day they were running around, burning the sun and talking about something stupid, and I had just had enough. I yelled, 'For God's sake, shut up already.' Well, right then and there, they all took a vow of silence, one after the other. Of course, I had to listen to the vowing all afternoon, but once the vowing was over, it was worth it. They have been perfectly silent since then."

"Maybe they thought you were God," Hans suggested.

"Maybe they were all just drunk. They cheated anyway. They think I can't hear it, but they have this psychic talking thing down. I can tell you that."

"I remember that," Hans said. "It was like he was talking out of his forehead." The mountain said nothing. Hans sat silent. The gap in the conversation started to grow awkward, as it can when talking to mountains. They have a different sense of time, so awkward silences don't bother them. Hans wanted to talk about food. He had left his lunch in his desk, so he had not eaten since breakfast. He tried smalltalk. "I've never spoken with a mountain before."

"Most people haven't. I assume they just don't have anything intelligent to say. Take those monks, for instance. They take a vow of silence and stop flapping their lips. Then they keep talking with their foreheads, and what they say now is no better then before. The lips were not the problem."

The moon gave the valley an amber glow, and the mountain grew philosophical in the mood lighting. "It's a stupid world you live in, kid." From where Hans sat, he could see the spot where he had stopped the leak in the dam. A wooden box had been built in which to pour the foundation for his statue. "You know the village used to be on the other side of the dam?"

Hans was awed. "Under water?"

"No, not under water," the mountain snapped. "You see what I mean about people always saying stupid things?"

Hans shook his head.

The mountain sighed. "I mean the river used to be on the other side of the dam, where your village is now. Back then, there was a girl who saw a leak in the dam. She stopped the leak and saved the town. She was a big hero."

"What was her name?"

"How the hell would I know? I was all the way up here. I just know it ended badly, and now the river has switched sides. It will again. It always does. Now, that trick you pulled the

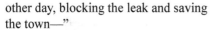

other day, blocking the leak and saving the town—"

"You saw that?"

"Of course I saw that. I see everything."

"Have you seen God?"

"Don't ask stupid questions. Now, that move, saving the town, that made you a hero."

Hans was glad someone remembered. "I told the kids at school I was a hero, but they said I was a four-finger shittypants, even though I have nine fingers."

"The number of digits is beside the point. We're not talking about fingers."

Hans was suddenly aware that the mountain may have had even fewer fingers than he had. While this made him feel superior, it also gave him that uneasy feeling he had for hurt animals or drowning babies, so he resolved to say nothing on the subject of fingers.

"Fingers aside," the mountain said. "You're a hero now. You're very important to this town, and you're going to have to die a horrible death for that."

"If I'm so important, then why do they tease me and chase me?"

"They don't just tease and chase everyone, do they?"

Hans thought about that but could make no sense of it. "Well, I don't want to be teased or chased, and I don't want to die a horrible death. What if I climbed over top of you and went down into the next valley?"

"I've never been over there," the mountain said. "But it's probably not much better."

Hans shivered on the rock. "I'm still hungry," he said. "Do you have any food?"

"Ask the monks," the mountain said. "What are they going to do, say no?" He laughed at his own joke.

"Do you think that will work?"

"Who knows?" the mountain said. "Either way, it will annoy the hell out of those fuckers."

Hans stood up and started walking in the direction of the moon.

"Leave the rock," the mountain said. "It's mine."

Chapter Five

Two hours before dawn, Hans stood at the front door of the monks' distillery. He said, "I want to come in. Let me know if that's not okay." The monk guarding the door said nothing, so Hans walked in. It was warm inside the distillery, and Hans saw a clothesline of brown robes hanging between two wood pillars. He said, "I'd like to borrow one of these robes. Just tell me if it would be too much trouble." Since no one told him not to, he selected the shortest robe he could find and put it on.

Hans was getting a lot of angry glares, and there were psychic objections throughout the distillery, but he pretended he could not hear them and proceeded to the long, wooden breakfast table. When no one objected, he sat in front of a bowl of fermented grains and mashed oranges. As the meal and the alcohol vapors went to Hans' head, he sang a song to fight off his dizziness and drowsiness. "Dust devil whirlwind, dust devil whirlwind—"

When the bouncer monk arrived, he pushed Hans out the door and pointed Hans toward home, which was where he wanted to go anyway. He strolled down the mountain in his robe, singing about whirlwinds and fishing rods.

By the time Hans stepped out of the woods and onto the beginning of Main Street, the sun had already been lit. He wasn't sure who was the first to follow him, but a small procession of townsfolk grew behind him as he marched through town. It started as a whisper then grew to a mutter. From a mutter it became a buzz that traveled through the village. People picked up their phones and started texting and calling each other.

When the phone on the mayor's secretary's desk rang, she knocked on the closed door behind her. The mayor quickly stuffed the brochures from a bird dealership into his desk and admitted her. The secretary said what everyone had been saying for the past hour: "The child has returned."

"Fuck," the mayor said. "What's he doing now?"

As Hans noticed the people following him, he quickened his pace. He wished he had a rock, but he didn't want to slow down to pick one up. He held the hem of his robe as he rushed through the center of town and up the hill toward the dike. When he got to the spot where he had become a hero, he turned to look at the town. To the left, school had already started. Hans was too tired to go to school. Home was to the right, but he knew he would be in trouble when he got there. As he considered which way to go, he noticed that the crowd had stopped on the hillside be-

low him and was waiting to hear what he would say. Hans whistled between his teeth, and within a couple minutes, he saw Burbear running toward him.

"Good to see you, kid." Burbear said. "Let's go home and get some breakfast."

Hans' French had not improved overnight, so he understood none of this. As he knelt to scratch the dog's ears and pluck a few burs from the dog's coat, he scanned the ground for a convenient rock. When Hans rose from his knees, the crowd yelled questions to him, so many that Hans could not make out what anyone was asking him. He spread out his arms in a shrug. He figured they probably wanted to know why he wasn't at school. When the voices died down, he said, "I have been to the mountain."

The crowd seemed awed by this statement, and someone yelled out, "What did you see?"

"Here. I saw this place. That's what you can see from up there, just here. The mountain said a lot of stuff about the river and the town and horrible death."

The crowd let out a collective gasp. Then someone yelled, "What did the mountain say?"

"Just stuff, you know?" He looked down at Burbear. "I'm kind of tired now. I have to go home and feed my dog." He turned and headed toward home.

"First sensible thing you've said all week," Burbear said.

In the crowd, someone asked, "What was that he said about a horrible death?"

The mayor paced behind his desk.

His secretary sat in a straight-backed wooden chair with a pen and a steno pad.

"So after stoning a teacher, he was up there talking to rocks?" he asked.

"That's what they said," The secretary read from her notes. "'Stuff about the river and the town,' 'horrible death,' 'just stuff,' and 'feed the dog.' Then the kid went home. Maybe you should call off the statue thing until you can get this kid checked out. He sounds like a nutcase."

"We can't just call it off. We've already levied a tax for it. Maybe we could have a hero awareness thing. We could call it Hero Crazy Something."

"Post-Heroic Stress Disorder?"

"Disorder, that's good. Write this down. Hero Crazy Disorder. This works because we get the martyr thing in. Everybody would have to forgive him. Now, who do we have lined up to make the statue?"

"We have four finalists. Your daughter has an abstract piece made of coat hangers and mayonnaise jars. Your nephew wants to do a sculpture of the boy, but it kind of looks more like the dog. Then there's a proposed symbolic piece, kind of a melted boomerang Frisbee of peace on top of an empty aquarium." The secretary did not mention the name of this artist, since the mayor already knew it was his tenant/mistress/consultant. The last finalist wanted to do a performance piece. He would ritualistically sacrifice a white elephant on the spot while performing an interpretive dance. However, he was no relation and was not worth mentioning.

"All fine choices," the mayor said. He felt stressed. This was a difficult decision. Each artist would kick back a similar percentage of the commission, enough to upgrade his ride from pigeons to ducks, but the money would be collected through different channels. "I'll think about it. In the meantime, could you get this Hero Crazy Syndrome Awareness Week thing going and—" he paused to build his courage. He whispered, "Make me breakfast?"

"Sir," the secretary warned. "I don't know about this. If your wife found out, if your mistress found out."

"But you're the best at it. They won't find out. I just need this right now."

The secretary sighed, walked behind the desk, and bent over.

"All right!" the mayor said. He stripped off his mayor's robe and hat, climbed on the desk, and unbuttoned his shirt.

The secretary took a half dozen eggs from the fridge under the desk. She cracked an egg against the desk and poured it into the mayor's navel. The second egg went between his pecs. She cracked the third egg on his forehead. She dropped two slices of bacon and a piece of bread on his lap before she walked out of the office. The mayor lay quivering on the desk, too enthralled to even thank her. He was breakfast now.

Hans slept for two days, and no one could wake him up, not even for meals. He arose on the third day feeling restless and groggy, mostly hungry. He walked out to the kitchen, where his mother was talking to some bees in Welsh.

"I'm hungry," Hans said.

"Tell me about it, kid," Burbear said.

His mother turned away from the

bees. "You know who else is hungry? Burbear. He hasn't had breakfast or dinner since you stuck your finger in the dike."

Hans wished he has never seen the damn thing. "You mean you haven't been feeding him?"

"When we got this dog, we agreed that you would feed him twice a day. You can't just pass off your responsibilities because you're off saving the world and holding conversations with hills. Now, let's take a look at that finger."

Hans wanted to protest that he was not talking to hills but to the mountain. It was a completely different thing, but he realized that it is usually pointless to correct people about anything. He gave her his hand.

She examined the stump. The cauterization blisters seemed to be healing and showed no signs of infection. "It looks okay. You can go back to school tomorrow."

"I don't want to go to school. Everyone there teases me."

"They won't tease you tomorrow." She produced a whittled carrot. "Tada! See? Now you'll have ten fingers just like everyone else."

Hans bounced on the balls of his feet, whining vibrato, "But no one else's fingers are made out of carrots."

She handed Hans a black glove and slipped the carrot into the index finger of the glove. "See? Nobody will even notice."

"That won't work," Hans said. "They already know I'm missing a finger."

"It was cut off days ago. Nobody's going to remember that. Tomorrow will be different. I promise."

Hans shook his head and started back toward his room.

"You come right back here and put on this glove this instant," she snapped. "I didn't waste all this time making you a new finger so you could just ignore it."

Hans held out his hand and accepted the glove. He put it on and turned back toward his room.

"What do you say?" his mother asked.

"Thank you," Hans mumbled.

The next morning, Hans fed Burbear and got dressed, remembering to wear the black glove. As he walked past the dike, he noticed that the wall was wet, but he decided to let that issue pass. He'd learned his lesson about heroism. At the entrance to the school, he saw a large, hand-painted banner that said "Happy Crazy Hero Disorder Syndrome Awareness Month." He sighed, sent Burbear home, and walked inside.

Burbear didn't go home. He trotted back to the dike and met Selma near the water. As they chewed on raw eel, a small Yorkshire terrier timidly sidled up to him and asked in provincial French, "Can I hang with you guys?"

Something in the submissive posture of the Yorkie awoke a sense of strength and independence in Burbear. He felt larger, braver, and more dangerous than he had been even a few moments before. With even one follower, he felt himself becoming ten times more important. He remembered a line from Nietzsche he had read in translation, something about getting zeros to follow you. "Sure, kid," he said.

Chapter Six

The mayor called the special meeting of the city council to order at 9:45 a.m. The meeting had been scheduled for 8:30, but there were catering delays. The agenda consisted of two items: an emergency appropriation to upgrade the mayor's transportation system and a special report from Mr. Z on the state of the dikes. The mayor chewed on a carp and nettle kelp wrap as he moved to table discussion of the dikes until the next regular meeting. "The dam issue is resolved," he said. "Our hero took care of that. Now we're taking care of the hero with a public awareness campaign, so the issue has been settled."

Mr. Z rose to comment on the motion. "You can't fix a dike with heroes and chewing gum," he said. "You need mortar, clay, stone, and laborers. And let me tell you, a fucking wheelbarrow would be nice."

The mayor did some math in his head. This sounded expensive. It could wipe out the statue fund completely, and he could not allow that to happen, since he'd already spent the money. "I'm sure the council finds this hypothetical discussion of how to fix a theoretical dam interesting, and your concerns were made well known in your love letter to the cafe waitress." He paused a moment to make sure the councilmembers got the joke. "But as we know, the dam has already been fixed. I fixed it myself, with Bobby's help, of course."

Mr. Z, who had been slouching in shame, stood at his full height. "Mayor, I am sluice man, as my father was before me. I have been looking after the dikes and canals all my life. Even as I was walking here today, I saw wa-

ter leaking out of the side of the dike. Without some major repairs, we'll be lucky if the thing is still standing in a week."

The mayor was encouraged. "Well, we have Mr. Z's assurance that the dam will last another week, so do I have a second on the motion to table the discussion until next week's regular meeting and move on to the next item?"

Councilmember Kennedy returned from the samovar and the buffet line. "What motion was that?"

"A motion to table discussion."

"The discussion we're having right now? I'll second that. And can we do something about the instant coffee they keep putting in the samovar? They're not fooling anyone, you know."

The mayor raised his gavel. "The motion is moved and seconded, can I get a vote?"

"Wait," Councilmember Brecht said. "We should have discussion on the motion before we take a vote."

"Oh, come on," the mayor said. "We can't have a discussion on whether or not to discuss having a discussion." He looked to his secretary for a ruling, but she just shrugged. "Okay, fine." He leaned back in his chair. "Let's make this quick."

Hans sat center-stage in the school auditorium. The school nurse had given a lecture on CHDS in which he had explained that Hans could not be blamed for his actions of the other day, that it was simply the result of a disorder in his brain that kept him from reintegrating with normal society. Ms. Paco, with a bandage around her head, explained that, despite the fact that Hans had attacked her with a rock like some rabid heathen neanderthal, in no way should the little savage be singled out or made to feel different from any of the other students.

Hans estimated that he had been sitting onstage for at least three hours. He had stopped listening to the lectures after the first hour and was now wondering how long he would be sitting there before the next bathroom break.

Hans was not incontinent. He had a good grasp of his bowels and his bladder. However, he knew that everyone in the audience was thinking of him as a four-fingered shittypants. He knew everyone in the audience was wondering how long he could last.

To reassure himself, he quickly tensed the muscle in his urethra. His urethra was strong. Even if he were forced to sit here for two more hours, he would still have no problem waiting to use the restroom. He had gone whole schooldays without using the restroom. However, as he started to relax the muscle he had just tensed, he stopped himself. What if relaxing that muscle was exactly what would cause an accident? What if the only thing that kept him from humiliating himself right there on the stage was the fact that he was holding his urine in by force of will alone? He realized that the idea was ridiculous. He had gone years not pissing himself without even thinking about it. If he really had to hold in his urine manually, how would he ever sleep? Still, the idea stuck with him. He just needed to relax. He started to let out a deep breath, but he then remembered that relaxation was exactly the thing he did just before urinating. This raised the next fear: that tensing the sphincter or even thinking about it would eventually exhaust his ability to

not urinate. It would probably wear out his endurance even faster. He tapped his foot nervously.

The mayor tapped his foot and checked his phone. It was already almost lunchtime, and the discussion showed no sign of ending. For the past two hours, two of the councilmembers had debated from two very different positions. The first approach to the problem was that the hero had absolutely failed in his duties by allowing another leak to appear in the dike. The opposing viewpoint was that the hero had been successful in stopping one leak and could be just as successful in patching future leaks. While one member held that the hero should be punished for his failure, the other member felt that the hero should be required to fix the dam again. Mr. Z had pointed out, once again, that he could fix the dam if they gave him the proper materials, but he was declared out of order. His radical and untried methods could not be risked when it was clear that the boy could stop the leaks. A compromise resolution was moved and seconded that repair of the dam was the boy's responsibility, with a friendly amendment that the construction of the monument be suspended.

When the mayor grudgingly opened discussion, Councilmember Brecht took the floor. He stood and adjusted his suspenders. Then he drew a folded sheaf of paper from his vest pocket. "Mayor, ladies and gentlemen, my fellow councilmembers," he said. "We face a crisis. This is a crisis of morals as much as it is a crisis of hydrodynamics. If I may, I have assembled a chart that should make clear our problem and the necessary course of action." He called for an easel and drew a radio antenna from his briefcase. He extended the antenna and slapped it against the chart dramatically.

"Christ, he has a chart," the mayor whispered to his secretary. "This can take for fucking ever."

Although it was lunchtime, Burbear felt no need to go home. He sat panting in the shade next to Selma, his alpha bitch. All around him, he saw the beginnings of his empire. His pack had grown dramatically in the past few hours, and his followers all conceded his place of privilege. Burbear was an emperor, a Napoleon. He saw respect and submission in the eyes of his followers and admiration in Selma's posture. He felt there was nothing he could not achieve. Spurred by this courage, he rose and walked not toward home but downhill, toward the town. "Follow, my brothers," he said. "We shall eat steak."

When Councilmember Brecht had finished his speech, the mayor's secretary shook him awake. A second friendly amendment had been added that, whereas everyone was sick and tired of Councilmember Brecht's speeches, be it resolved that, while construction on the monument would be suspended, a scaffold would be built on the already-poured foundation for the pedestal and Councilmember Brecht would be hanged from that scaffold by the neck until he was dead. The tax for the monument would remain in place, and the proceeds would be placed in the general fund. Since Brecht was the kind of asshole who would probably be

running against the mayor in a couple years, the mayor called for an immediate vote. The motion carried 3-1, and Councilmember Brecht was placed under arrest.

Chapter Seven

Mr. Z crept toward the cafe and knocked on the cellar door. He looked at his hand and considered throwing the half pint of turnip juice away, but he reconsidered. It might help if she answered. As he was considering, the city council walked by, led by the mayor. The mayor rode on the backs of two geese, led by a swan. The secretary grabbed his arm and led him toward the dike.

"It's time for action," Councilmember Kennedy said. "We all know what has to be done."

"Bring me clay and mortar," Mr. Z said. "I'll take care of it."

"We'll do better than that," the mayor said. When he reached the dike, he turned and led the procession toward the school. Councilmember Brecht was left with the constable near the pedestal while Mr. Z stood by the dike, noting the cracks and loose spots. Next to the aborted pedestal, he noticed a couple bags of Portland cement left over from pouring the foundation.

Burbear found the town empty as he led his army on its raid. They trotted down the middle of the street unimpeded as the townspeople once again walked up the hill toward the dike.

"What are they all doing?" Selma asked.

"Retreating," Burbear said. He looked

at the signs over the various stores, but they were all written in English. None of them said steak. Following his nose, he led his pack into a bakery, where he commanded the dogs to grab the food and run. There was an immediate explosion of fur and teeth as the dogs overturned a basket of bread, seized bags of day-old bagels, and chomped at muffins and cookies. Jelly doughnuts and cinnamon buns were torn apart as dogs tried to balance pie pans in their teeth. Burbear ran to the door with a baguette in his mouth and bounced backward as the ends of the loaf struck the doorway. After trying again, he dropped the loaf and dragged it lengthwise, walking backwards. Then he picked up the bread and ran for the woods, his carbo-loaded pack behind him.

Hans was dropped on the ground in front of the leaking dike. "You said you would fix this," the mayor said. "And look at it. It's leaking worse than before." The mayor stood tall on the backs of his geese, his mayoral robe fluttering behind him in the wind.

"This is not the boy's fault," Councilmember Brecht said. "This is our fault. If we just—"

"Shut up," Member Kennedy said. "Shut up. Shut up. We have no way of knowing that would work. The only thing that we know does work is this boy." She turned to the mayor. "I move that Mr. Brecht not be permitted to speak until the time of his execution." The motion was seconded and carried 3-1.

The mayor glided along the dike on his waterfowl and peered at a few points in the wall where water was clearly seeping through. Where the initial leak had been, he pulled back the wad of chewing gum. A waterlogged and partially eaten finger shot out of the dike, followed by a spray of water. As the water flowed out, rocks flew out of the wall. The hole increased in size until it was as wide around as a beer bottle.

The mayor quickly pushed Hans' hand into the hole. The boy's forearm was not wide enough to stop the leak, but the mayor kept pushing until the boy's arm finally plugged the hole, above his bicep and near the shoulder. The leak stopped, and the townspeople cheered, being delivered from another disaster.

Hans felt the cold water seeping up his shirtsleeve. At first, he was afraid of the things he could not see swimming around his arm. Then he felt another burst of water hitting the side of his face. It was like the leak was a trapped animal that, stopped in one location, found another spot to escape through. This time, it pushed through a circle of a dozen small cracks before a small section of the dike, the size of a pie pan, crumbled and fell onto Hans' shoulder.

The mayor called for help, and the townspeople pushed forward. The mayor now was able to supervise from a distance without the danger of getting his lederhosen wet. It took two men to push Hans' neck into just the right position so that half of his head could be used to plug up the breach while, in the interest of the boy's comfort and welfare, keeping at least one nostril and half of the boy's mouth outside of the dike. Then, as soon as it seemed the leak had disappeared, it sprouted in a new location below the the armhole. The men raised Hans' leg at the knee and pushed it, toes-first, into the dike.

Mr. Z approached with a bucket and a trowel. "This doesn't seem right," he said. "This is the kind of thing Wayne would do."

"Who the hell is Wayne?" the mayor asked. "You mentioned him like fifteen times in your email."

"You know," Mr. Z said. "My rival. The evil librarian."

"We haven't had a library in this town for three years." The mayor shrugged. "Just do your duty to save the town. We will erect a statue to your bravery."

Member Brecht objected, "You said you would erect a statue to this boy, and the only thing we've raised so far is the class of birds you walk on. This boy doesn't need a monument. I've said this before. He needs us to do our jobs and leave him alone. If we managed the town right, we wouldn't need heroes."

"You're out of order," Councilmember Kennedy said. "There was already a vote that you were to keep quiet. Have you forgotten about democracy? Have you given up on order and the rule of law or even common decency? Do you have no shame? I would have no problem sponsoring a resolution to write a letter sanctioning your actions here."

Recognizing his peril, Councilmember Brecht fell silent. Councilmember Kennedy led the constable as he walked Councilmember Brecht up to the scaffold on the unfinished pedestal. She looked down on the citizens and waved her hand toward the boy, who was half-cemented into the wall. She cried out to the crowd, "On this day, it will be made clear that our national heroes cannot be dismissed, abused, and insulted." She turned to the condemned. "Do you have any last words?"

"I do," Brecht said. He raised his voice to address the crowd. He raised both his arms and spread his fingers. "There is something I want to say."

"Oh, fucking hell." Councilmember Kennedy kicked him off the platform. Mr. Brecht's neck snapped with the fall, and he was left hanging over the hero.

Until the cement dried, the townspeople held Hans in place, taking it in shifts. Hans kept half of his mouth closed tightly while he begged with the other half. He said he was hungry. He said he was thirsty. Something in the cement was burning his skin. He wasn't sure, but a catfish might be eating one of his legs. With one eye, he could see his mother standing over him. Mrs. Dutch looked at him, half encased into the wall. "I told you it was stupid," she said.

Under the water, a bone hand held his. "It always goes like this," she said. "I'm sorry, but it always does." Hans opened his eye under the water and saw the bones half-encased in the other side of the seawall. A skeleton in a torn, blue dress with hair made of seagrass held his hand. "Did you know you have a carrot in your glove?" she asked.

Chapter Eight

Hans' fingernails and fingertips went first as he tried to scratch and pull at the cement that compressed and burned his skin. For the first few days, Greta left Hans' lunch next to his foot on her way to school. When it became clear that he was not eating his lunch, that he couldn't even reach it, she improved the situation by leaving his lunch next to his foot after taking the dessert for herself. On the weekend, she didn't come at all. Local boys would come to see him, not to visit him but to dare each other to touch him before running away. The councilmember's eyes were always open, and they stared at Hans day and night.

The days passed as the meringue was lit and burned out, but the liquor burned out earlier and earlier each evening, as if the monks were skimping on the booze. By Monday, Greta was too embarrassed to walk with her friends past her stinking brother. She found another path to school. His arms got thinner, and the whispers from the girl in the water got louder. Birds had started gathering on the scaffold, and even after two crows took the councilmember's eyes, the empty sockets continued to stare at Hans. The boys who came now only dared each other to poke him with sticks, and they ran away when his body shifted.

The October dance came and went, and Hans no longer cared who went or who danced with whom. Fish nibbled at his limbs under water. It tickled at first. Then it grew painful, but as the water got colder and the fish carried away more of his flesh, it no longer hurt. He didn't even try to bat away the birds as they pecked at him here and there. Even as his body and his cares disappeared, melting away onto the sidewalk the same way the councilmember's body had dripped and fallen in chunks, the girl in the water continued to speak to him, telling him stories of when the river ran on the other side

of the valley.

When he opened his underwater eye, he could see a drowned village that the girl with the green hair once lived in and saved before she was walled into the dike. He saw villagers walking the drowned streets, the postman walking from house to house with soggy letters that bled ink like rising black smoke. After a fish ate his eye, he could see even more. He could see inside the houses of both towns, where families prepared meals and slept. On the girl's side, families decorated aquatic plants with tinfoil tinsel and beercan stars from litter the river dropped on their roofs. In his own town, he saw people decorating pines dragged from the mountain's feet. He could see the mountain shrug his shoulders in resignation.

By now, there was snow on the ground and ice on the water. Though Hans had lost his nose and no longer smelled, familiar scents of baking and roasting bounced inside his skull from both sides of the dike. When his ear fell off, he could hear Christmas carols coming from the church and the houses. The girl with green hair squeezed his hand and wished him a merry Christmas. Hans smiled. Now that his lips were gone, he always smiled.

On Christmas Eve, Hans could hear the celebrations and see fireworks in the sky. As his teeth smiled out over the town, he seemed to know things he could not know, like the water was giving him wisdom. He saw Burbear and his pack running through the town, toppling garbage cans in their endless search for steak frites. In their barks and howls, he could understand their cheers, boasts, and quips as if he spoke the language fluently.

In the space between the dike and the street, Hans could see a little dust devil dancing. From the ear that had long-since rotted away, he could hear the thing singing, "Dust devil whirlwind, dust devil whirlwind in the snow. Dust devil whirlwind, dust devil whirlwind, here we go. I am so happy, I am so happy 'cause I'm god. I'm going to kill you. I'm going to kill you. Kill you with a fishing rod."

Even with his brain rotted out and dead worms frozen in his face, Hans knew better than to trust the theology of a passing breeze. He was not afraid of winds or rods. Without lips or a tongue, he called over to the wind the way the monks spoke, through his forehead. "Come here," he said. The whirlwind danced toward him. "Closer," he said.

And the whirlwind danced closer until it blew right through his front teeth, whistling on the wind. As it danced away, Hans' empty eye socket watched the horizon.

As the dust devil disappeared, Hans saw Burbear approach. "Is this steak?" Burbear asked.

Hans' first thought was that this was his blood, his body they were talking about. Then, being dead, he said in perfect French, "Yes, Burbear. This is steak."

Burbear arched his back and howled the word "steak" at the Christmas moon. Soon, a dozen dogs appeared behind Burbear. Again, he said, "Steak," and the dogs ran up the hill, each dog grabbing a bone and ripping it from the wall. More and more dogs appeared, a multitude, each dragging a bone from the dike and running up the hill. As they pulled, water leaked through the dike and down toward the village. As a mastiff yanked out Hans' spine and ran for dry land, the dike burst, sending the flood roaring toward the town.

Doris and Mr Z sneaked away from the celebration, passing a jar of turnip juice back and forth. As the fireworks exploded in the sky, they giggled and stumbled to the cafe's cellar. Mr. Z settled into the burlap bags next to Doris. As he buried his head in her chest and lifted her wooden leg to his shoulder, he heard a roar, like a seashell next to his ear, like the world's first ocean opening before him, like the beginning of the world and the world's end.

ROBERT DEVEREAUX

LOCATION:
Boulder, CO

STYLE OF BIZARRO:
Topsy-turvy, non-literary, fuck-with-your-mind-ism

BOOKS BY DEVEREAUX:
Baby's First Book of Seriously
    Fucked-Up Shit
Slaughterhouse High
Santa Steps Out: A Fairy Tale for
    Grown-Ups
Santa Claus Conquers the
    Homophobes
Santa Claus Saves the World
Deadweight
Walking Wounded
A Flight of Storks and Angels
Caliban and Other Tales

DESCRIPTION: Robert sprawls all across the word-map, seeking out intrigues and oddities and sculpting them into story. There's a vast sprawl of love and rage in his work, erotic juice and heart-healing touch, scorn and sympathy, cloud-lofty optimism entwined with drop-dead despair. Seek and ye shall founder.

INTERESTS: Orgasmic meditation, bereavement, biking, self-righteousness, opera, films with a point and a compelling shape, pacifism, stage acting, singing, wordplay, slow hands, slow sex, slow hearing, acupuncture, lack o' pressure, seeking after his lost senses of taste and smell.

INFLUENCES: Soupy Sales, Dante, Marlon Brando, Robert Coover, Nicholson Baker, Joyce DiDonato, Vladimir Nabokov, Laurence Olivier, Robert Crumb, Ram Dass, Pema Chodron, Jonathan Swift, Henry Fielding, Erich Fromm, Bela Bartok.

WEBSITE:
robertdevereaux.com

LI'L MISS ULTRASOUND

June 30, 2004
Mummy dearest,

It's great to hear from you, though I'm magnitudinously distraught that you can't be here for the contest. Still, I'm not complaining. It's extremely better that you show up for the birth—three weeks after my little munchkin's copped her crown!—and help out afterwards. The contest is a hoot and I want to do you proud, I *will* do you proud, but that can be done from a distance too, don't you think? What with the national coverage and the mega-sponsorship, you'll get to VCR me and the kid many times over. And of course I'll save all the local clippings for you like you asked.

It made my throat hurt, the baby even kicked, when you mentioned Willie in your last letter. It's tough to lose such a wonderful man. Still, he died calmly. I read that gruesome thing a few years ago, that *How We Die* book? It gave me the chills, Mom, how some people thrash and moan, how they don't make a pretty picture at all, many of them. Willie was one of the quiet ones though, thank the Lord. Nary a bark nor whimper out of him, he just drifted off like a thief in the night. Which was funny, because he was so, I don't know, *noisy* isn't the right word, I guess *expressive* maybe, his entire life.

Oh, before I close, I gotta tell you about Kip. Kip's my ultrasound man. I'm in love, I think. Kind face on him. Nice compact little bod. Cute butt too, the kind of buns you can wrap your hands halfway around, no flabby sags to spoil your view or the feel of the thing. Anyway, Kip's been on the periphery of the contest for a few years and likes tinkering with the machinery. He's confided in me. Says he can—and will!—go beyond the superimposition of costumes that's been all the rage in recent years to some other stuff I haven't seen yet and he won't spell out. He worked some for those Light and Magic folks in California, and he claims he's somehow brought all that stuff into the ultrasound arena. Kip's sworn me to secrecy. He tells me we'll win easy. But I'm my momma's daughter. I don't put any stock in eggs that haven't been hatched, and Kip isn't fanatical about it, so it's okay. Also, Mother, he kissed me. Yep! As sweet and tasty as all get-out. I'll reveal more, next missive. Meantime, you can just keep guessing about what we're up to, since you refuse to grace us with your presence at the contest.

Just teasing, Mummy dear. Me and my fetal muffin will make you so proud, your chest will puff out like a Looney Tunes hen! Your staying put—for legit reasons, like you said—is a-okay with me, though I *do* wish you were here to hug, and chat up, and share the joy.

Love, love, love, mumsy mine,
Wendy

Kip brightened when Wendy came in from the waiting room, radiant with smiles.

Today was magic day. The next few sessions would acquaint Wendy with his enhancements to the ultrasound process. He wanted her confident, composed, and fully informed onstage.

"Wendy, hello. Come in." They traded hugs and he hung her jacket on a clothes rack.

"You can kiss me, you know," she teased.

He shook his head. "It doesn't feel right in the office. Well, okay, a little one. Mmmm. Wendy, hon, you're a keeper! Now hoist yourself up and let's put these pillows behind your back. That's the way. Comfy? Can you see the monitor?"

"Yes." Eagerly, she bunched her maternity dress up over her belly. Beautiful blue and red streaks, blood lightning, englobed it. A perfect seven-months' pooch. Her flowered briefs were as strained and displaced as a fat man's belt.

"Okay, now," said Kip. "Get ready for a surprise. This'll be cold." He smeared thick gel on her belly and moved the handheld transducer to bring up baby's image. "There's our little darling."

"Mmmmm, I like that 'our'!"

"She's a beauty *without* any enhancement, isn't she? Now we add the dress." Reaching over, he flipped a switch on his enhancer. Costumes had come in three years before, thanks to the doctor Kip had studied under. They were now expected fare. "Here's the one I showed you last time," he said, pink taffeta with hints of chiffon at the bodice. There slept baby in her party dress, her tiny fists up to her chest.

"It's beautiful," enthused Wendy. "You can almost hear it rustle." What a joy Wendy was, thought Kip. A compact little woman who no doubt would slim down quickly after giving birth.

"Okay. Here goes. Get a load of this." He toggled the first switch. Overlaying the soft fabric, there now sparkled sequins, sharp gleams of red, silver, gold. They winked at random, cutting and captivating—spliced in, by digital magic, from a captured glisten of gems.

"Oh, Kip. It's breathtaking."

It was indeed. Kip laughed at himself for being so proud. But adding sparkle was child's play, and he fully expected other ultrasounders to have come up with it this year. It wouldn't win the contest. It would merely keep them in the running. He told Wendy so.

"Ah but this," he said, "this will put us over the top." He flipped the second switch, keeping his eyes not on the monitor but on his lover, knowing that the proof of his invention would be found in the wideness of her eyes.

Eudora glared at the monitor.

She had won the Li'l Miss Ultrasound contest two years running—the purses her first two brats brought in had done plenty to offset the bother of raising them—and she was determined to make it three.

Then she could retire in triumph.

She had Moe Bannerman, the best ultrasound man money could buy. He gestured to the monitor's image. "She's a beaut. Do you have a name yet?"

"Can the chatter, Moe. I'll worry about that after she wins. Listen, I'm dying for a smoke. Let's cut to the chase."

Moe's face fell.

Big friggin' deal, she thought. Let him cry to his fat wife, then dry his tears on the megabucks Eudora was paying him.

"Here she is, ready for a night on the town." He flipped a switch and her kid was swaddled in a svelte evening gown, a black number with matching accessories (gloves and a clutch-purse) floating beside her in the amniotic sac.

Eudora was impressed. "Clear image."

"Sharpest yet. I pride myself on that. It's the latest in digital radiography, straight from Switzerland. We use intensity isocontours to—"

"It looks good. That's what counts. We win this round. Good. Now what about the swimsuit?"

"Ah. A nice touch. Take a look." Again his hands worked their magic. "See here. A red bikini with white polka dots."

"The sunglasses look ordinary, Moe. Give her better frames, a little glitz, something that catches the eye."

"I'll have some choices for you next time."

She shot a fingertip at him. "To hell with choices. You get the right ones first time, or I'll go to someone else." She'd heard rumor of a new ultrasound man on the horizon, Kip Johnson. He deserved a visit, just to check out the terrain. Handsome fuck, scuttlebutt said.

"Yes, ma'am. But take a look at this. It'll win us this round too. We show them the bikini, a nice tight fit that accentuates your baby girl's charms. I've even lent a hint of hardness to her nipples, which will most likely net you a contract with one of the baby-formula companies. But watch. We flip a switch and . . ."

Eudora had her eyes on the screen, her nicotine need making more vivid the image she saw. It was as if the kid had been suddenly splashed with a bucket of water. No twitch of course. It was all image. But the swimsuit's fabric lost its opacity. See-through. Gleams of moisture on her midriff. Her nipple nubs grew even harder, and her pudendal slit was clearly outlined and high-lighted. Moe, you're a genius, she thought.

"Cute," she said. "What else you got?"

Thus she strung the poor dolt along, though his work delighted her. Dissatis-faction, she found, tended to spur peo-ple to their best. It wouldn't do to have Moe resting on his laurels. People got trounced by surprise that way. Eudora was determined not to be one of them.

When they were done, she left in a hurry, had a quick smoke, and hit the road. The Judge was due for a visit. There were other judges, of course, all of whom she did her best to cultivate. But somehow Benja-min—perversely he preferred the ugly cog-nomen "Benj"—was The Judge, a man born to the role.

Weaving through traffic, she imagined the slither of his hand across her belly.

Benj walks into the house without knocking.

In the kitchen he finds her dull hub-by, feeding last year's winner (Gully or Tully) from a bottle. The beauty queen from two years prior toddles snot-nosed after him, wailing, no longer the tanta-lizing piece of tissue she had once been. Her name escapes him.

But names aren't important. What's important are *in utero* images and the feelings they arouse in him.

"Hello, Chet," says Benj.

Stupid Chet lights up like a bulb about to burn out. "Oh, hi, Benj. Eudo-ra's in the bedroom. Have at her!"

Benj winks. "I will."

He winds his way through the house, noting how many knick-knacks prize money and commercial endorsements can buy. Over-the-hill, post-fetal baby drool is all *he* sees on the tube once the little darlings are born. It never makes him want to buy a thing.

"Why, Benjamin. Hello." She says it in that fake provocative voice, liking him for his power alone of course. As long as he can feel her belly, he doesn't care.

"Touch it?" he asks in a boyish voice. "Touch it now?" He thickens below.

"Of course you can," says Eudora, easing the bedroom door shut and lean-ing against it, her hands on the knob as if her wrists are tied.

Stupid Chet thinks Benj and Eudora do the man-woman thing. Chet wants money from the winnings, so he's okay with it as long as they use rubbers. But they don't *really* do the man-woman thing. Nope. They just tell Chet they do. Benj rubs her belly and feels the object of his lust kick and squirm in there, touching herself, no doubt, with those tiny curled hands, thrashing around breathless in the womb, divinely distracted.

Breathless.

Baby's first breath taints absolutely.

"Touch yourself, Benjamin."

He does. He wears a rubber, rolled on before he left the car. Later, he'll give it to Eudora so she can smear it with her scent and drop it in the bathroom wastebasket. Chet's a rummager, a sniffer. It's safer to provide him evidence of normalcy.

To Benj, normal folks are abnormal. But it takes all kinds to make a world.

His mouth fills with saliva. Usually, he remembers to swallow. Sometimes, a teensy bit drools out.

The baby kicks. Benj's heart leaps up like a frisky lamb. Eudora pretends to get off on this, but Benj knows better. He ignores her, focusing on his arousal, and is consumed with bliss.

July 12, 2004
Mummy dearest,

I'm so excited! Kip is too! The contest cometh tomorrow, so you'll see this letter *after* you've watched me and the munchkin on TV, but what the hey.

I could do without the media hoopla of course, though I suppose it comes with the territory. The contest assigns you these big bruisers, kind of like linebackers. I don't think you had them in your day. They deflect press hounds for you, so you don't go all exhausted from the barrage or get put on the spot by some persistent sensationalist out to sell dirt.

Then there are the protesters.

Ugh! I agree with you, mumsy. They're out of their blessed noggins. Both sorts of protesters. There are the ones who want the contest opened up to second trimester fetuses. The extremists even scream for first trimester. What, I ask you, would be the point of *that*?

Then there are the ones who want to ban pre-birth beauty contests entirely. Life-haters I call them. Hey, I'm as deep as the next gal. But I was never harmed by having a beauty queen for a mother nor by winning the Baby Miss contest when I was three months old. All that helped me, I'm sure—my self-esteem, my comfort with putting my wares on display, which a gal has just got to do to please her fella. I don't mind if Kip likes me for *all* of me, and I sincerely and honestly believe he does. But that includes the packaging. The sashay too, though mine's got *waddle* written all over it these days. Hey, I can work off the belly flab as soon as my baby's born. I know I can. I'll slim down and tighten up you-know-where even if it's under the knife with sutures taking up the slack. That's a woman's duty, as my momma taught me so well!

My point is that I'm *all* of me, the brainy stuff and the sexy stuff too. It's all completely me, it's my soul, and right proud of it am I. Well, listen to me gas on and on, like a regular old inner-lectual. What hath thou raised? Or more proper-like, whom?

Wish us luck, mumsikins!

Your loving and devoted daughter,
Wendy

***

Kip was alone in his office, making final tweaks to his software. Wendy had been by, an hour before, for one last run-through prior to their appearance onstage.

Five more minutes and he would lock up.

His ultrasound workstation, with its twenty-four-inch, ultra-high-resolution, sixteen-million-color monitor, had become standard for MRI and angiography. Moe Bannerman, last year's winning ultrasound man, had copped the prize, thanks to this model. But Kip was sure, given the current plateau in technology, that whatever Moe had up his sleeve this year would involve something other than the size and clarity of the image.

Butterflies flitted in Kip's gut. Somehow, no matter how old you got, exposure to the public limelight jazzed you up.

The outer office door groaned. Maisie coming back for forgotten car keys, thought Kip.

A pregnant woman appeared at the door. Eyes like nail points. Hair as long and shiny as a raven's wing. Where had he seen her? Ah. Moe's client, mother of the last two contest winners.

Wendy's competition.

"Hello there," she said, her voice as full-bellied as she was. "Have you got a minute?" She waddled in without waiting for an answer. "I'm Eudora Kelly."

He opened his mouth to introduce himself.

"You're Kip, if I'm not mistaken. My man will be going up against you tomorrow."

"True. Look, according to the rules, you and I shouldn't be talking."

She approached him. "Rules are made to keep sneaky people in line. We're both above board. At least, I am." Her voice was edged with tease, a quality that turned Kip off, despite the woman's stunning looks. "Besides, even if I were to tell Moe what you and I talked about or what we did—which I won't—it's too late for him to counter it onstage, don't you think?"

"Ms. Kelly, maybe you'd better—"

She touched his arm, her eyes intent on the contours of his shirtsleeve. "I'll tell you what surprises *he's* planning to pull tomorrow. How would that be?"

"No, I don't want to know that." He did, of course, but such knowledge was off limits. She knew that as well as he.

"They say you've got new technologies you're drawing on. A background in the movies. Maybe next year, you and I could pair up."

Kip reviewed his helpers, looking for a blabbermouth.

No one came to mind.

"In fact," she sidled closer, her taut belly pressing against his side, "maybe *right now* we could pair up." Her hand touched his chest and drifted lower.

"All right, that's enough. There's the door. Use it." His firmness surprised him. It was rare to encounter audacity, rarer still therefore to predict how one would respond to it. He took her shoulders and turned her about, giving her a light shove.

She wheeled on him. "You think you're God, you spin some dials and flick a few switches. Well, me and Moe're gonna wipe the floor with your ass tomorrow. Count on it!"

Then she was gone.

The back of Kip's neck was hot and tense. "Jesus," he said, half expecting her to charge in for another try.

Giving the workstation a pat, he prepared to leave, making sure that the locks were in place, the alarms set.

"Fool jackass," Eudora said. "The man must be sexed the wrong way around."

"Some people," observed the judge, his eyes on her beach ball belly, "have a warped sense of right and wrong. They take that Sunday school stuff for gospel, as I once did long ago."

"Not me, Benjamin. I knew it for the

crock it was the moment it burbled out of old Mrs. Pilsner's twisted little mouth. Ummm, that feels divine." It didn't, but what the hell. Benjamin would be pivotal tomorrow. No sense letting the truth spoil her chances.

The judge's moist hand moved upon her, shaky with what was happening elsewhere. Soon he would yank out his tool, a condom the color of rancid custard rolled over it like a liverwurst sheath. "Yeah, I wised up when I saw how the wicked prospered," he said. "How do you *do* it, Eudora? This is the third sexy babe in a row. Your yummy little siren is calling to me."

"She wants it, Benjamin," said Eudora.

Perv city, she thought. It would be a relief to jettison this creep as soon as the crown was hers. Three wins. She would retire in glory and wealth. At the first sign he wanted to visit, she would drop him cold. No bridges left to burn after her triumph. Let the poor bastard drool on someone else's belly.

Benjamin groped about between the parted teeth of his zipper. Eudora said, "That Kip person's going to spring something."

"Who's he?" asked the judge, pulling out his plum.

"You know. The ultrasound guy that Wendy bubblehead is using. Scuttlebutt says he's doing something fancy."

"Ungh," said Benjamin.

Eudora pictured Kip's office receptionist, her hand shaking as she took Eudora's money. She was disgustingly vague and unhelpful, Maisie of the frazzled hair and the troubled conscience. All she gave off were echoes of unease: he has this machine, I don't know what it does, but it's good because he says it is and because they both look so sure of themselves after her visits. Worthless!

"My baby girl's getting off, hon."

"Me too," he gasped.

"You're a sweet man," she said. "Show us your stuff. Give it to us, Benjamin, right where we live. That's it. That's my sweet Benjamin Bunny."

Benj really gets into it. Eudora's bellyskin is so smooth and tight, and as hot as a brick oven. He smells baby oil in his memory.

Eudora has no cause for worry, he thinks. Moe Bannerman's a stellar technician. What Moe's able to do to tease naked babes into vivid life onscreen is nothing short of miraculous.

Benj conjures up the looker inside Eudora's womb by recalling what hangs on his bedroom wall, those stunning images from *Life* last year—better than the real thing though a boner's a boner no matter how you slice it.

He dips into Tupperwared coconut oil, smearing it slick and liberal upon her belly, as he does upon his condomed boytoy. Oil plays havoc with latex, he knows, but Benj isn't about to get near impregnation or STDs.

Benj bets Moe Bannerman will carry his experiments in vividness forward in the coming years. Headphones will caress Benj's head as he judges, the soft gurgle of fetal float-and-twist tantalizing his ears, vague murmurs coaxed by a digital audio sampler into a whispered *fuck-me* or *oh-yeah-baby*.

Or perhaps virtual reality will come of age. He'll put on goggles and gloves, or an over-the-head mask that gooses his senses into believing he's tasting her, the salty tang of preemie quim upon his tongue, the touch of his fingertips all over her white-corn-kernel body.

Benj shuts his eyes.

Eudora starts to speak but Benj says, "Hush," and she does. This time the rhythms are elusive but *there*, within reach if his mind twists the right way. The beauty queen to be is touching him, indeed she is, those tiny strong little fingers wrapped about his pinkie. Her eyelids are closed, the all-knowing face of the not-yet-born, lighting upon uncorrupted thoughts, unaware of and unbothered by the sensual filtering imposed by society on the living.

Her touch is as light as a hush of croissant crust. This, he thinks, is love: the wingbrush of a butterfly upon an eyelash; a sound so faint it throws hearing into doubt; a vision so fleetingly imprinted on the retina, it might be the stray flash of a neuron.

With such slight movements, love coaxes him along the path, capturing, keeping, and cultivating—like a seasoned temptress—the focus of his fascination, so that the path swiftly devolves into a grade, hurrying him downhill and abruptly thrusting him into a chute of pleasure. He whips and rumbles joyously along its oily sides once more, *once more, ONCE MORE*!

July 13, 2004

Mummy mine,

I'm writing from the convention center, just having come offstage from Round One, where our little dolly garnered her first *first*! I had a hunch I'd want to disgorge all these glorious pent-up emotions into my momma's ear. So I brought along my lilac stationery and that purple pen with the ice-blue feather you love so much. Here I sit in the dressing room with the nine other contestants who survived Round One. Ooh, the daggers that are zipping across the room from Eudora Kelly, whose kids won the last two years. Methinks she suspects we've got her skunked!

Baby's jazzed, doing more than her usual poking and prodding. Kip just gave me a peck (would it had been a bushel!!!) and left to check out his equipment for Round Two. If I were a teensy bit naughtier, I'd mention how much *fun* it is to check out Kip's equipment, ha ha ha. But you raised a daughter with that rarest of qualities, modesty. Besides which, it would be unseemly to get too much into that, Willie being so recently deceased and all. But life goes on. Oh boy howdy, does it ever!

I passed through those idiotic protesters with a minimum of upset, thanks to my linebacker types. Joe, he's the beefiest, flirts outrageously, but both of us know it's all in fun. Still, he's a sweetie and you should see the scowl that drops down over his face whenever some "news twerp" (that's what Joe calls them) sticks his neck out where it don't belong, begging Joe to lop it off.

There were twenty of us to start with. 'Taint so crowded here no more! The audience sounds like an ocean, and the orchestra—you heard me, strings and all, scads of them, like Mantovani—set all things bobbing on a sea of joy. Kip gave me a big kiss right here where I sit—no, you slyboots, on my lips!!! Before I knew it, I was standing onstage amidst twenty bobbing bellies, all of us watching our handsome aged wreck of a TV host, that Guy Givens you like so much, his bowtie jiggling up and down as he spoke, and his hand mike held just so. The judges were in view, including the drooly one—you know, the one whose hanky is always all soppy by the end.

First off, oh joy, we got to step up and do those cutesy interviews. Who the heck can remember what I gassed on about? I guess they build suspense at least in the hall. At home, all I remember is that you and me and Dad used that dumb chit-chat as an excuse to grab a sandwich or a soda.

Then Round One was upon us, and we were number 16, not a great number but not all that bad neither. I lifted my dress for Kip—not the *first* time I've done that, I assure you!!!—to bare my belly and of course to show off my dazzling red-sequined panties. For good luck, I sewed, among the new sequins, an even dozen from my Baby Miss swimsuit. The crowd loved my dumpling's first outfit, a ball gown that might have waltzed in from the court of Queen Victoria. It reminded me of a wedding cake, what with all the flounces and frills and those little silver sugar bee-bees you and I love so much. Baby showed it off beautifully, don't you think?

Then Kip played his first card. With a casual gesture, he brought life to her face. Of course, her face *has* life, but it's a pretty placid sort of life at this stage, what with every need being satisfied as soon as it happens. So there's nothing to cry about and no air to cry with if she *could* cry.

Then it blossomed on her face: a flush and blush of tasteful makeup spreading over her cheeks and chin and forehead, a smear of carmine on her lips, turquoise blue eyeshadow and an elongation of her lashes. Huge monitors in the hall gave everyone as clear a picture as the folks at home on their TVs. I could taste the rush of amazement rippling through the hall at each effect.

Then, her darling eyes opened! Just for a second before Kip erased the image. Of course they didn't *really* open, any more than my baby really wore a ball gown. But they weren't just some painted porcelain doll's eyes. Kip's years in Hollywood paid off, because you would have sworn there was angelic intelligence in the deep gaze Kip gave her face—

Oops, we just got the five-minute call, mumsy, so I'll cut off here and pick back up at the next break. Wish us luck! Gotta go!!!

***

Kip followed close behind a stagehand, who wheeled the ultrasound equipment to the tape marks, locked down the rollers, and plugged the cord into an outlet on the stage floor. Wendy had already settled into the stylish recliner.

"Hello, darling," said Kip, taking her hand. Wendy returned his kiss. "How are you two?"

"Fine." Her voice wavered, but Kip judged it near enough to the truth.

The stage manager, clipboard at the ready, breezed by. "Two minutes," he said. Hints of garlic.

Beyond the curtain's muffle, the emcee pumped things up. A drum roll and a cymbal crash rushed the orchestra into an arpeggio swirling up to suggest magic and pixie dust. Kip squeezed Wendy's hand.

When the curtain rose, Guy Givens strode over. "And here's our first round winner, Miss Wendy Sales. Round she certainly is. And ready for another round, I hope. Wendy, how does it feel to be the winner of our evening wear competition?"

"Well, Guy," said Wendy, as he poked the mike at her mouth, "it feels great, but I don't bet on any horse until the race is over's what my momma taught me. All these great gals I've met? Their babies too? They're *all* winners as far as I'm concerned."

"Ladies and gentleman, let's give the little lady's generosity a big hand." The emcee's mike jammed up into his armpit so he could show the audience how to clap with gusto. Then it jumped back into his grip. "Wendy, with that attitude, you'll be a great mom indeed."

"I sincerely hope so."

Ignoring her answer: "And now . . . let's see your adorable little girl *in her bobbysoxer outfit!*" The tuxedoed man backed out of the spotlight, his free hand raised in a flourish.

Deftly fingering a series of switches, Kip hid his amusement at the emcee's tinsel voice, as the orchestra played hush-hush music and Wendy's child came into view.

A tiny pair of saddle shoes graced the baby's feet. Her poodle skirt (its usually trim stitched poodle gravid with a bellyful of pups) gave a slight sway. She wore a collared blouse of kelly green. A matching ribbon set off her tresses, which Kip had thickened and sheened by means of Gaussian and Shadow filters combined with histogram equalization.

When the crowd's applause began to fall off, Kip put highlights back into baby's face, an effect which brought the clapping to new heights.

As if in answer, Kip turned to two dials and began to manipulate them. The baby's eyes widened. She gave a coy turn of the head. Then her eyelids lowered and Kip wiped the image away.

The effect looked easy, but the work that had gone into making it happen was staggering. To judge by the shouts and cheers that washed over the stage, the crowd sensed that. Wendy glowed.

"*Judges?*" screamed Guy Givens into his mike.

One by one, down the row of five, 10s shot into the air. A 9 from a squint-eyed woman who never gave 10s drew the briefest of boos.

Wendy mouthed "I love you" at Kip, and he mouthed it back, as the music swirled up and the curtain mercifully shut out an ear-splitting din of delight.

Eudora watched from the wings as the TV jerkoff with the capped teeth and the crow's feet chatted up her only competition one last time.

The swimsuit round.

Moe's water-splash effect had gained Eudora an exceptional score, but from the look on the ultrasound man's face out there, that insufferable Kip Johnson, she was afraid he was poised to take the Wen-

dy bitch and her unborn brat over the top.

Dump Moe.

Yep, Moe was a goner. Yesterday's meat. Spawn the loser inside her, let her snivel through life, whining for the tit withheld. A dilation and extraction might better suit. Tone up. Four months from now, let Chet poke her a few times. Stick one last bun in the oven.

Then, adrip with apologies, she would pay Kip another visit, playing to his goody-two-shoes side if that got him off. Hell, she'd even befriend his lover. If Wendy had a two-bagger in mind, Eudora would persuade her—strictly as a friend with her best interests at heart—to retire undefeated.

Onstage, that damned tantalizing womb image sprang to life again, this time dressed for the beach. Her swimsuit was a stylish fire-engine-red one-piece that drew the eye to her bosom, as it slashed across the thighs and arrowed into her crotch. Nice, but no great shakes.

Then the kid's face animated again. Eudora knew that this face would bring in millions. For months, it would be splashed across front pages and magazine covers. Then it would sell products like nobody's business.

Would it ever!

Instead of repeating its coy twist of the head, the intrauterine babe fluttered her eyelashes at the audience and winked. Then she puckered her lips and relaxed them. No hand came up to blow that kiss, but Eudora suspected that Kip would make that happen next year.

Her kid would be the one to blow a kiss. *Her* kid would idly brush her fingers past breast and thigh, while tossing flirtatious looks at Benjamin and viewers at home.

Eudora scanned the judges through a deafening wall of elation. There sat the oily little pervert, more radiant than she had ever seen him. Another year would pass, a year of wound-licking capped by her triumph, and Kip's, right here on this stage. *Then* she'd dump the drooler. One more year of slobber, she assured herself, would be bearable.

Eye on the prize, she thought. Keep your eye on the prize.

Benj is in heaven. His drenched handkerchief lies wadded in his right pants pocket. Fortunately, his left contained a forgotten extra, stuck together only slightly with the crust of past noseblows. It dampens and softens now with his voluminous drool.

The curtain sweeps open. Midstage stand the three victors, awaiting their reward.

Wendy's infant has quite eclipsed Eudora's in his mind. The third-place fetus? It scarcely raises a blip. Its mother comes forward to accept a small faux-sapphire tiara, a modest bouquet of mums, and a token check for a piddling sum. An anorexic blonde hurries her off.

Eudora's up next.

Replay pix of her bambina flash across a huge monitor overhead. Beneath her smile, she's steaming. He's in the doghouse for his votes; he knows that. But there's always next year. She needs him. She'll get over it.

A silver crown, an armful of daffodils, a substantial cash settlement, and off Eudora waddles into oblivion, her loser-kid's image erased from the monitor.

Then his glands ooze anew as the house erupts. Like a ba-zillion cap guns, hands clap as Wendy's pride and joy lights up the screen with that killer smile, that wink, oh god those lips.

"*AND HERE'S OUR QUEEN INDEED!*" screams Guy Givens, welcoming Wendy into his arms. Gaggles of bimbos stagger beneath armloads of roses. The main bimbo's burden is lighter, a gold crown bepillowed. Wendy puts a hand to her mouth. Her eyes well.

Then it happens.

Something shifts in the winner's face. She whispers to Givens, who relays whatever she has said to the crown-bearing blonde. Unsure what to do, the blonde beckons offstage, mouthing something, then walks away. Wendy leans against the emcee, who says "Hold on now" into his mike. A puddle forms on the stage where she is standing. "Is there a . . . do we have a . . . of course we do, yes, here he comes, folks."

Benj feels light-headed.

The rest drifts by like a river ripe with sewage. Spontaneous TV, the young doctor, the ultrasound man, a wheeled-in recliner, people with basins of water, with instruments, backup medical personnel. Smells assault him. Sights. Guy Givens gives a hushed blow-by-blow. And then, a wailing *thing* lifts out of the ruins of its mother, its head like a smashed fist covered in blood, wailing, wailing, endlessly wailing. Blanket wrap. The emcee raises his voice in triumph, lowering the tiny gold crown onto the bloody bawler's brow.

It's a travesty. Benj is glad to be sitting down. He rests his head on his palms and cries, mourning the passing of the enwombed beauty who winked and nodded in his direction not five minutes before.

Is there no justice in the world, he wonders. Must all things beautiful end in squalor and filth?

He craves his condo. How blissful it will be to be alone there, standing beneath the punishing blast of a hot shower, then cocooning himself under blankets and nestling into the oblivion of sleep.

July 14, 2004
Mumsicle mine, now GRAN-mumsicle!

Well I guess that'll teach me to finish my letters when I can. I'll just add a little more to the one I never got 'round to wrapping up, and send you the whole kitten-kaboodle [sic, in case you think I don't know!], along with the newsclips I promised.

I'm sitting here in a hospital bed surrounded by flowers. Baby girl No-Name-Yet is dozing beside me, her rosebud lips moving in the air and making me leak like crazy. I do so love mommyhood!

But I never expected to give birth in public. They were all so nice to me at the contest, even that Eudora woman, who seems to have had a change of heart. That creepy drooly judge came up to wish me his best, but Kip rough-armed him away and said something to him before kicking him offstage. I'll have to ask Kip what that was all about.

Oh and Kip proposed! I knew he would, but it's always a thrill when the moment arrives, isn't it? I cried and cried with joy and Kip got all teary too. He'll make a great father, and I'm betting we spawn a few more winners before we're through. We'll give you plenty of warning as to when the wedding will be.

He's deflected the media nuts so far, until my strength is back. They're all so antsy to get at me. But meanwhile Kip's the hero of the hour. There's even talk of a movie of the week, with guess-who doing the special effects of course. But Kip tells me these movie deals usually aren't worth the hot air they're written on, so he and I shrug it off and simply bask bask bask!

I'll sign off now and get some rest, but I wanted to close by thanking you for being such a super mom and role model for me, growing up. You showed me I could really make something of myself in this world if I just persisted and worked my buns off for what I wanted.

I have.

It's paid off.

And I have you to thank for it. I love you, Mom. You're the greatest. Come down as soon as you can and say hello and kootchie-koo-my-little-snookums to the newest addition to the family. You'll adore her. You'll adore Kip too. But hey, hands off, girl, he's mine all mine!!!

Your devoted daughter,
Wendy

RIDI BOBO

At first little things niggled at Bobo's mind: the forced quality of Kiki's mimed chuckle when he went into his daily pratfall getting out of bed; the great care she began to take painting in the teardrop below her left eye; the way she idly fingered a pink puff-ball halfway down her shiny green suit. Then more blatant signals: the creases in her crimson frown, a sign, he knew, of real discontent; the bored arcs her floppy shoes described when she walked the ruff-necked piglets; a wistful shake of the head when he brought out their favorite set of shiny steel rings and invited her, with the artful pleas of his expressive white gloves, to juggle with him.

But Bobo knew it was time to seek professional help when he whipped out his rubber chicken and held it aloft in a stranglehold—its eyes X'd shut in fake death, its pitiful head lolled against the back of his glove—and all Kiki could offer was a soundless yawn, a fatigued cock of her conical nightcap, and the curve of her back, one lazy hand waving bye-bye before collapsing languidly beside her head on the pillow. No honker would be brought forth that evening from her deep hip pocket, though he could discern its outline there beneath the cloth, a coy maddening shape that almost made him hop from toe to toe on his own. But he stopped himself, stared forlornly at the flaccid fowl in his hand, and shoved it back inside his trousers.

He went to check on the twins, their little gloved hands hugging the blankets to their chins, their perfect snowflake-white faces vacant with sleep. People said they looked more like Kiki than him, with their lime-green hair and the markings around their eyes. Beautiful boys, Jojo and Juju. He kissed their warm round red noses and softly closed the door.

In the morning, Bobo, wearing a tangerine apron over his bright blue suit, watched Kiki drive off in their new rattle-trap Weezo, thick puffs of exhaust exploding out its tailpipe. Back in the kitchen, he reached for the Buy-Me Pages. Nervously rubbing his pate with his left palm, he slalomed his right index finger down the Snooper listings. Lots of flashy razz-ma-tazz ads, lots of zingers to catch a poor clown's attention. He needed simple. He needed quick. Ah! His finger thocked the entry short and solid as a raindrop on a roof; he noted the address and slammed the book shut.

Bobo hesitated, his fingers on his apron bow. For a moment the energy drained from him and he saw his beloved Kiki as she'd been when he married her, honker out bold as brass, doing toe hops in tandem with him, the shuff-shuff-shuff of her shiny green pants legs, the ecstatic ripples that passed through his rubber chicken as he moved

it in and out of her honker and she bulbed honks around it. He longed to mimic sobbing, but the inspiration drained from him. His shoulders rose and fell once only; his sweep of orange hair canted to one side like a smart hat.

Then he whipped the apron off in a tangerine flurry, checked that the boys were okay playing with the piglets in the backyard, and was out the front door, floppy shoes flapping toward downtown.

Momo the Dick had droopy eyes, baggy pants, a shuffle to his walk, and an office filled to brimming with towers of blank paper, precariously tilted—like gaunt placarded and stilted clowns come to dine—over his splintered desk. Momo wore a battered old derby and mock-sighed a lot, like a bloodhound waiting to die.

He'd been decades in the business and had the dust to prove it. As soon as Bobo walked in, the tramp-wise clown seated behind the desk glanced once at him, peeled off his derby, twirled it, and very slowly very deliberately moved a stiffened fist in and out of it. Then his hand opened—red nails, white fingers thrust out of burst gloves—as if to say, Am I right?

Bobo just hung his head. His clownish hands drooped like weights at the ends of his arms.

The detective set his hat back on, made sympathetic weepy movements—one hand fisted to his eye—and motioned Bobo over. An unoiled drawer squealed open, and out of it came a puff of moths and a bulging old scrapbook. As Momo turned its pages, Bobo saw lots of illicit toe hops, lots of swollen honkers, lots of rubber chickens poking where they had no business poking. There were a whole series of pictures for each case, starting with a photo of his mopey client, progressing to the flagrante delicto evidence, and ending, almost without exception, in one of two shots: a judge with a shock of pink hair and a huge gavel thrusting a paper reading DIVORCE toward the adulterated couple, the third party handcuffed to a Kop with a tall blue hat and a big silver star on his chest; or two corpses, their floppy shoes pointing up like warped surfboards, the triumphant spouse grinning like weak tea and holding up a big pistol with a BANG! flag out its barrel, and Momo, a hand on the spouse's shoulder, looking sad as always and not a little shocked at having closed another case with such finality.

When Bobo broke down and mock-wept, Momo pulled out one end of a checkered hanky and offered it. Bobo cried long and hard, pretending to dampen yard upon yard of the unending cloth. When he was done, Momo reached into his desk drawer, took out a sheet with the word CONTRACT at the top and two X'd lines for signatures, and dipped a goose-quill pen into a large bottle of ink. Bobo made no move to take it but the old detective just kept holding it out, the picture of patience, and drops of black ink fell to the desktop between them.

Momo tracked his client's wife to a seedy Three-Ring Motel off the beaten path. She hadn't been easy to tail. A sudden rain had come up and the pennies that pinged off his windshield had reduced visibility by half, which made the eager Weezo hard to keep up with. But Momo managed it. Finally, with a sharp right and a screech of tires, she turned into the motel parking lot. Momo slowed to a stop, eying her from behind the brim of his sly bowler. She parked, climbed up out of the tiny car like a soufflé rising, and rapped on the door of Room Five, halfway down from the office.

She jiggled as she waited. It didn't surprise Momo, who'd seen lots of wives jiggle in his time. This one had a pleasingly sexy jiggle to her, as if she were shaking a cocktail with her whole body. He imagined the bulb of her honker slowly expanding, its bell beginning to flare open in anticipation of her little tryst. Momo felt his bird stir in his pants, but a soothing pat or two to his pocket and a few deep sighs put it back to sleep. There was work afoot. No time nor need for the wild flights of his long-departed youth.

After a quick reconnoiter, Momo went back to the van for his equipment. The wooden tripod lay heavy across his shoulder and the black boxy camera swayed like the head of a willing widow as he walked. The rest—unexposed plates, flash powder, squeezebulb—Momo carried in a carpetbag in his free hand. His down-drawn mouth puffed silently from the exertion, and he cursed the manufacturers for refusing to scale down their product, it made it so hard on him in the inevitable chase.

They had the blinds down but the lights up full. It made sense. Illicit lovers liked to watch themselves act naughty, in Momo's experience, their misdoings fascinated them so. He was in luck. One wayward blind, about chest high, strayed leftward, leaving a rectangle big enough for his lens. Miming stealth, he set up the tripod, put in a plate, and sprinkled huge amounts of glittery black powder along his flashbar. He didn't need the flashbar, he knew that, and it caused all manner of problem for him, but he had his pride in the aesthetics of picture-taking, and he was willing to blow his cover for the sake of that pride. When the flash went off, you knew you'd taken a picture; a quick bulb squeeze in the dark was a cheat and not at all in keeping with his code of ethics.

So the flash flared, and the smoke billowed through the loud report it made, and the peppery sting whipped up into Momo's nostrils on the inhale. Then came the hurried slap of shoes on carpet and a big slatted eyelid opened in the blinds, out of which glared a raging clownface. Momo had time to register that this was one hefty punchinello, with muscle-bound eyes and lime-green hair that hung like a writhe of caterpillars about his face. And he saw the woman, Bobo's wife, honker out, looking like the naughty fornicator she was but with an overlay of uh-oh beginning to sheen her eyes.

The old adrenaline kicked in. The usually poky Momo hugged up his tripod and made a mad dash for the van, his carpetbag shoved under one arm, his free hand pushing the derby down on his head. It was touch and go for a while, but Momo had the escape down to a science, and the beefy clown he now clouded over with a blanket of exhaust—big lumbering palooka caught off-guard in the act of chicken stuffing—proved no match for the wily Momo.

Bobo took the envelope and motioned Momo to come in, but Momo declined with a hopeless shake of the head. He tipped his bowler and went his way, sorrow slumped like a mantle about his shoulders. With calm deliberation Bobo closed the door, thinking of Jojo and Juju fast asleep in their beds. Precious boys, flesh of his flesh, energetic pranksters, they deserved better than this.

He unzipped the envelope and pulled out the photo. Some clown suited in scarlet was engaged in hugger-mugger toe hops with Kiki. His rubber chicken, unsanctified by papa church, was stiff-necked as a rubber chicken can get and stuffed deep inside the bell of Kiki's honker. Bobo leaned back against the door, his shoes levering off the rug like slapsticks. He'd never seen Kiki's pink rubber bulb swell up so grandly. He'd never seen her hand close so tightly around it nor squeeze with such ardency. He'd never ever seen the happiness that danced so brightly in her eyes, turning her painted tear to a tear of joy.

He let the photo flutter to the floor. Blessedly it fell facedown. With his right hand he reached deep into his pocket and pulled out his rubber chicken, sad purple-yellow bird, a male's burden in this world. The sight of it brought back memories of their wedding. They'd had it performed by Father Beppo in the center ring of the Church of Saint Canio. It had been a beautiful day, balloons so thick the air felt close under the bigtop. Father Beppo had laid one hand on Bobo's rubber chicken, one on Kiki's honker, inserting hen into honker for the first time as he lifted his long-lashed eyes to the heavens, wrinkle lines appearing on his meringue-white forehead. He'd looked to Kiki, then to Bobo, for their solemn nods toward fidelity.

And now she'd broken that vow, thrown it to the wind, made a mockery of their marriage.

Bobo slid to the floor, put his hands to his face, and wept. Real wet tears this time, and that astonished him, though not enough—no, not nearly enough—to divert his thoughts from Kiki's treachery. His gloves grew soggy with weeping. When the flood subsided, he reached down and turned the photo over once more, scrutinizing the face of his wife's lover. And then the details came together—the ears, the mouth, the chin; oh God no, the hair and the eyes—and he knew Kiki and this bulbous-nosed bastard had been carrying on for a long time, a very long time indeed. Once more he inventoried the photo, frantic with the hope that his fears were playing magic tricks with the truth.

But the bald conclusion held.

At last, mulling things over, growing outwardly calm and composed, Bobo tumbled his eyes down the length of the flamingo-pink carpet, across the spun cotton-candy pattern of the kitchen floor, and up the cabinets to the Jojo-and-Juju-proofed top drawer.

Bobo sat at his wife's vanity, his face close to the mirror. Perfume atomizers jutted up like minarets, thin rubber tubing hanging down from them and ending in pretty pink squeezebulbs Bobo did his best to ignore.

He'd strangled the piglets first, squealing the life out of them, his large hands thrust beneath their ruffs. Patty Petunia had pistoned her trotters against his chest more vigorously and for a longer time than had Pepper, to Bobo's surprise, she'd always seemed so much the frailer of the two. When they lay still, he took up his carving knife and sliced open their bellies, fixed on retrieving the archaic instruments of comedy. Just as his tears had shocked him, so too did the deftness of his hands—guided by instinct he'd long supposed atrophied—as they removed the bladders, cleansed them in the water trough, tied them off, inflated them, secured each one to a long thin bendy dowel. He'd left Kiki's dead pets sprawled in the muck of their pen, flies growing ever more interested in them.

Sixty-watt lights puffed out around the perimeter of the mirror like yellow honker bulbs. Bobo opened Kiki's cosmetics box and took out three squat shallow cylinders of color. The paint seemed like miniature seas, choppy and wet, when he unscrewed and removed the lids.

He'd taken a tin of black paint into the boys' room—that and the carving knife. He sat beside Jojo in a sharp jag of moonlight, listening to the card-in-bike-spoke duet of their snores, watching their fat wide lips flutter like stuck bees. Bobo dolloped one white finger with darkness, leaning in to X a cross over Jojo's right eyelid. If only they'd stayed asleep. But they woke. And Bobo could not help seeing them in new light. They sat up in mock-stun, living outcroppings of Kiki's cruelty, and Bobo could not stop himself from finger-scooping thick gobs of paint and smearing their faces entirely in black. But even that was not enough for his distracted mind, which spiraled upward into bloody revenge, even though it meant carving his way through innocence. By the time he plunged the blade into the sapphire silk of his first victim's suit, jagging open downward a bloody furrow, he no longer knew which child he murdered. The other one led him a merry chase through the house, but Bobo scruffed him under the cellar stairs, his shoes windmilling helplessly as Bobo hoisted him up and sank the knife into him just below the second puffball. He'd tucked them snug beneath their covers, Kiki's brood; then he'd tied their rubber chickens together at the neck and nailed them smackdab in the center of the heartshaped headboard.

Bobo dipped a brush into the cobalt blue, outlined a tear under his left eye, filled it in. It wasn't perfect but it would do.

As horsehair taught paint how to cry, he surveyed in his mind's eye the lay of the living room. Everything was in readiness: the bucket of crimson confetti poised above the front door; the exploding cigar he would light and jam into the gape of her mouth; the tangerine apron he'd throw in her face, the same apron that hung loose now about his neck, its strings snipped off and spilling out of its big frilly kangaroo pouch; the Deluxe Husband-Tamer Slapstick he'd paddle her bottom with, as they did the traditional high-stepping divorce chase around the house; and the twin bladders to buffet her about the ears with, just to show her how serious things were with him. But he knew, nearly for a certainty, that none of these would stanch his blood lust, that it would grow with each antic act, not assuaged by any of them, not peaking until he plunged his hand into the elephant's-foot umbrella stand in the hallway and drew forth the carving knife hidden among the parasols—whose handles shot up like cocktail toothpicks out of a ripple of pink chiffon—drew it out and used it to plumb Kiki's unfathomable depths.

Another tear, a twin of the first, he painted under his right eye. He paused to survey his right cheekbone, planning where precisely to paint the third.

Bobo heard, at the front door, the rattle of Kiki's key in the lock.

Momo watched aghast.

He'd brushed off with a dove-white handkerchief his collapsible stool in the bushes, slumped hopelessly into it, given a mock-sigh, and found the bent slat he needed for a splendid view of the front hallway and much of the living room, given the odd neck swivel. On the off-chance that their spat might end in reconciliation, Momo'd also positioned a tall rickety stepladder beside Bobo's bedroom window. It was perilous to climb and a balancing act and a half not to fall off of, but a more leisurely glimpse of Kiki's lovely honker in action was, he decided, well worth the risk.

What he could see of the confrontation pleased him. These were clowns in their prime, and every swoop, every duck, every tumble, tuck, and turn, was carried out with consummate skill. For all the heartache Momo had to deal with, he liked his work. His clients quite often afforded him a front row seat at the grandest entertainments ever staged: spills, chills, and thrills, high passion and low comedy, inflated bozos pin-punctured and deflated ones puffed up with triumph. Momo took deep delight—though his forlorn face cracked nary a smile—in the confetti, the exploding cigar, what he could see and hear of their slapstick chase. Even the bladder-buffeting Bobo visited upon his wife strained upward at the down-droop of Momo's mouth, he took such fond joy in the old ways, wishing with deep soundless sighs that more clowns these days would re-embrace them.

His first thought when the carving knife flashed in Bobo's hand was that it was rubber, or retractable. But there was no drawn-out scene played, no mock-death here; the blow came swift, the blood could not be mistaken for ketchup or karo syrup, and Momo learned more about clown anatomy than he cared to know—the gizmos, the coils, the springs that kept them ticking; the organs, more piglike than clownlike, that bled and squirted; the obscure voids glimmering within, filled with giggle power and something deeper. And above it all, Bobo's plunging arm and Kiki's crimped eyes and open arch of a mouth, wide with pain and drawn down at the corners by the weight of her dying.

Momo drew back from the window, shaking his head. He vanned the stool, he vanned the ladder. There would be no honker action tonight. None, anyway, he cared to witness. He reached deep into the darkness of the van, losing his balance and bellyflopping so that his legs flew up in the night air and his white shanks were exposed from ankle to knee. Righting himself, he sniffed at the red carnation in his lapel, took the inevitable faceful of water, and shouldered the pushbroom he'd retrieved.

The neighborhood was quiet. Rooftops, curved in high hyperbolas, were silvered in moonlight. So too the paved road and the cobbled walkways that led up to the homes on Bobo's side of the street. As Momo made his way without hurry to the front door, his shadow eased back and forth, covering and uncovering the brightly lit house as if it were the dark wing of the Death Clown flapping casually, silently, overhead. He hoped Bobo would not yank open the door, knife still dripping, and fix him in the red swirl of his crazed eyes. Yet maybe that would be for the best. It occurred to Momo that a world which contained horrors like these might happily be left behind. Indeed, from one rare glimpse at rogue-clown behavior in his youth, as well as from gruesome tales mimed by other dicks, Momo thought it likely that Bobo, by now, had had the same idea and had brought his knife-blade home.

This case had turned dark indeed. He'd have lots of shrugging and moping, much groveling and kowtowing to do, before this was over. But that came, Momo knew, with the territory. Leaning his tired bones into the pushbroom, he swept a swatch of moonlight off the front stoop onto the grass. It was his duty, as a citizen and especially as a practitioner of the law, to call in the Kops. A few more sweeps and the stoop was moonless; the lawn to either side shone with shattered shards of light. He would finish the walkway, then broom away a spill of light from the road in front of Bobo's house, before firing the obligatory flare into the sky.

Time enough then to endure the noises that would tear open the night, the clamorous bell of the mismatch-wheeled pony-drawn firetruck, the screaming whistles in the bright red mouths of the Kops clinging to the Kop Kar as it raced into the neighborhood, hands to their domed blue hats, the bass drums booming as Bobo's friends and neighbors marched out of their houses, spouses and kids, poodles and ponies and piglets highstepping in perfect columns behind.

For now, it was enough to sweep moonlight from Bobo's cobbled walkway, to darken the wayward clown's doorway, to take in the scent of a fall evening and gaze up wistfully at the aching gaping moon.

THE SLOBBERING TONGUE THAT ATE THE FRIGHT-FULLY HUGE WOMAN

Sally Holmes was married to a swell guy. She liked working in the lab. Holding clipboards and making notes for Doctor Baxter while hiding her beauty behind glasses and a tight bun was her idea of fun. She did it well.

And she gave her husband John a nice home. Soon, if they could figure out where children came from, there'd be pattering feet to feed. John was a good man. They'd been childhood sweethearts. Now John was a police lieutenant. She didn't understand his work. Heck, truth be told, she barely understood her own. But all Sally had to do was to poise her fountain pen smartly above her clipboard and act as if she were saying clever things, and Doctor Baxter was more than pleased to keep her around.

The one thing Sally liked about Doctor Baxter, other than her paycheck, was his way with words. He was a blob in pretty much every respect, balding, sags of flesh stuck on his face like sneezed boogers on a mirror. But when he spoke, his labials, his fricatives, his palatals, his urps of intelligence, the way his moist pink tongue oystered in his mouth—all of those oral sorts of things made Sally go all soft and squoozy inside.

For months he'd been working on something top secret, putting in so many hours he might as well have camped out at the institute. He let no one into his inner lab. But the notes he dictated tantalized her. He overworked his staff, but Sally didn't mind (she knew that *John* did). It just meant more toward their nest egg, more smart repartee over the clipboard, and more of that clever tongue.

When Doctor Baxter invited her that evening into his inner lab, just him and her around, Sally had no inkling that anything more than science was on his mind. He held the unsealed door for her, and she stepped in, sniffing a barnyard stench she'd caught wind of before.

John lay there in his pajamas, wanting his wife next to him. It felt so great to hug her, pajamas to pajamas, and give her a pristine little kiss goodnight. And every so often— once every few months if he was lucky— she'd be open to cuddling in the dark, to undoing certain strategic snaps and letting him shoot an icky mess inside her while she lay there so calm and sweet and receptive. He'd give his standard "Sorry" in her ear, then roll off her, shame in him yes, but feeling glad too that she hid her disgust so well.

It proved she loved him.

Still, he sensed there was something missing in their marriage. As Sally flitted about the kitchen or Hoovered the rugs or knelt to dust the baseboards, John felt as if there were a crack in her smile—almost as if, God forbid, a first wrinkle were appearing in that smooth peach-infant face of hers.

His wife needed reassurance.

Oh, heck. He'd drop in at the lab. Yes, yes. He'd dare to be different. Flinging the covers back, he leaped out of bed. Would he put on the clothing he'd tossed into the hamper? No. New ones. He wouldn't sweat too much in them and he could wear them again tomorrow.

Sally'd be thrilled to see him. A sweet surprise.

Baxter anticipated her amazement.

"Oh, my!" she ejaculated, her fetching shoulderblades flexing like coy airplane struts under that white coat she plumped out so well in front.

"You've never seen a ten-foot cock before?" The bird was indeed awesome there in its cage, its magnificent head turned in quirk, one squint-eye wide as a saucer. Too bad he hadn't chosen a hen for his experiments. She would've made one heck of a meal, and there were other interesting avenues (so to speak) that might have been explored. He was tired of cleaning up after Giganto here, and tired of feeding him. Damn rooster was due for death.

"Goodness, Doctor Baxter," Sally exclaimed. "What've you been up to?"

"See that?" he said, pointing to the bell jar on the table, with its throbbing pink crystal. "I concocted that substance. I call it gargantuum. It makes organic matter grow. Don't ever disturb that glass container, or there's no telling what will happen."

"I won't." She shook her pretty little head so that her radiant tresses primped and fluffed like in a shampoo commercial; no, wait, he was imagining that. Her bun held her hair tight, severe, puckered like a clenched rectum.

Baxter stepped in front of her. "But that's not why I invited you into my inner lab."

"It isn't?"

"No." He eased the carving knife from his cavernous coat pocket. "I'd like you to undress for me, Sally—nice and slow, nice and sexy, one button, one snap at a time."

Sally blanched fetchingly. "I can't do that."

He placed the blade against her neck. "You can," he insisted, "and you will. But first, undo that god-awful, fershlugginer bun. Let your Prellity down, sweetcakes."

Tears welled up as she reached to free her hair. Her breasts rose with the motion. Doctor Baxter fixed on them with those ugly eyes of his. He was a loathsome lunk of a man. Except for his tongue. Poor thing seemed shanghai'd into saying awful things, but somehow that didn't diminish its beauty.

The magnitude of her anger startled her.

Sally'd never been angry about anything in her life, not one blessed thing.

But, even as her fingers worked the buttons and tears gathered in her eyes, she was angry about this. Her anger was hot and solid, coming deep from her insides but hiding itself as it grew. He couldn't detect it. But she could surely feel it. And soon, but she feared not soon enough, it would lash out at the scientist Sally had trusted to be good but who was very bad indeed.

"Not fast enough," he said. His free hand shot forth and yanked her lapel to one side, so that her white satin slip showed from her right shoulder strap down to where it cupped in lacy fullness her huge right breast. Where his brutish paw touched her, her flesh ached.

She looked at the knife in his hand, the sharp blade, the brown rippled wood of its handle. She wanted so badly to wrest it away from him, to use it on him.

"Faster!" he said, drool dripping from his lips. You never knew about people. You just never knew.

John adored being a police lieutenant. All the boys in blue, nice decent Christian fellas, loved and respected you. You got to wear stylish suits with papercut creases ironed into the legs. They snugged your badge into a real nice soft-leather case that felt as cozy as suede when you whipped it from your inside coat pocket and held it up for a citizen's eyes.

He maneuvered the Plymouth along the quiet streets, a bouquet of long-stemmed roses lying beside him.

A lanky young man was walking an Airedale. John hit his horn lightly, waved, took the return wave. The dog's no-nonsense yap filled the air with glee. Life was good. Life was very good. Life was very very very good.

But it could be better.

He could assure Sally that he loved her, that there'd never be for him any woman in the world but her. That was what a wife wanted to hear. For John, there'd only always been Sally. No one else. And there never *would* be anyone else. Never never never.

He hummed a sprightly tune.

There was Baxter Enterprises ahead. The guard at the gate grinned at him. He lifted the flowers, said, "For my sweet honey," and the mustachioed geezer in uniform nodded and waved him through. "Say hello to the missus for me," the guard shouted, shrinking in the rear view mirror.

"I will," yelled John. He rolled up the window, the corners of his mouth hurting from his smiles, and pressed on toward the main building.

Baxter had his way with her. Though smart and snappy as always, Miss Holmes was passive like a good dolly ought to be. On the floor, upon the air mattress he forced her into blowing up, he felt all her secret places, he tasted her, he lay his bulky frame on her and forced his manhood inside her. The air was thick with bird smell, tainted by hints of formaldehyde from the embryos jarred on the table above them.

So enthralled did he become and so passive and almost not-there was his victim that he lost track of his carving knife. And suddenly there was a tugging at his hand, and an emptiness there. Then his shoulder caught fire, a jag of outrage sinking thickly inside. His secretary wiggled like a ba-zil-lion panicked eels out from under him as the pain erupted, a swift deep cramp in his upper torso.

He screamed, not continuous but blips—sharp, barked, like a wounded mutt. Her face flared and bloomed. Shrew, he thought. Ter-magant. That's what she had turned into. She gripped the knife handle and yanked it out. He felt somehow as if his lungs followed it, and yet it was a hurt he needed from her. She had repented. She would help him to a hospital, stanch his blood, bandage him, make him all better, hold him, kiss him, dump her dorky boy in blue.

Then she docked him. She fisted his shaft, razored a chill below, pressed it in, cutting through no-resistance, through sponge cake, burrowing and spreading a volcano of agony. Her first thrust had enervated him. He could only make faint shows of protest as she unmanned him. Suddenly he could no longer feel the squeeze, although he saw the purple flesh blanch in her fingers, saw

her pry his member away, felt his groin skin peel up, a gigantic splinter of pain, toward his navel.

His thing thwapped on the floor where she tossed it.

He rocked and screamed, energy draining from between his legs. His attacker—*he'd* been the attacker; now *she* was—bounded up, clattered in his tools above, came back with a bone saw.

And then, oh my god, she severed his hands.

***

Rage drove her on. This monster had touched her in all her secret places. Now she was dismantling him, all his offending parts off and away. That's the way it had to be, Sally's crazed mind told her.

His resistance was all in his voice. The bone saw snagged on the air mattress, which burbled its air away through washes of blood. But the vile hand snapped off, cracking and tearing like an uncooked lobsterclaw. The other, as his stump feebly brushed her back with sticky protest, proved even easier.

Time for his tongue.

She'd brought back a bull castrator—why he had one, she didn't stop to ask. But her bloody hands tore at his jaws and jammed the instrument deep down into his throat, watching the tongue slither in snug where a pizzle would ordinarily go. Then she clamped shut, freshets of blood upshoot-ing, spraying her breasts with hot gore. And out the quivering tantalizing tormenting sucker came.

Though it too had violated her, she didn't toss the tongue to the floor as she'd done with his hands and his manhood. She rose, unlid-ded the first jar she saw, took out the chick embryo, and dropped in the tongue, lifting the jar, hugging its chill to her breasts.

She was aimlessly meandering, slowly, randomly, her face a veil of tears, wounded tears, tears of rage.

Sally's foot struck something. She glanced down at it, Baxter's right hand. The things it had done! Still with the jar hugged to her chest, she bent down, snatched the odious thing up and hurled it away from her.

The bell jar rang from the impact, lifted, tottered, and fell with a decisive clatter to the tabletop, rolling off and shattering on the floor. The pink crystal pulsed and hummed. Its light filled the air. The sound it made rose, higher, higher, like a menacing theremin.

And then the explosion came, pink goop in the air, on her flesh, down her throat. It coated her arms where they hugged the jar, radiating there, pulsing. Sally wanted to scream, but she choked on the stuff, and felt it strangely warm all over her.

***

Just as John killed the Plymouth, he felt a *whumph* in the air. It was a subtle pop but all his antennas of love and protection immediately sprang up and out.

Sally was in danger.

Without remembering how he'd done it, he was suddenly outside the car, his hands on the closed pinging car door. It felt as if it took forever but he raced to the entrance and plowed through, down corridor upon corridor to Sally's lab. "Sally!" he yelled. "Sally! Sally! Sally!"

No one.

But John took in the door to the inner lab, its edge blasted and pulsing pink from lights within. He dashed to it, yanked it open.

His wife was facing away from him, naked and sobbing.

On the floor lay Doctor Baxter, parts of him missing, him nearly dead but not quite so. A gigantic rooster stood in a cage

in the far corner, stinking the place up.

John approached his naked wife. There was yucky pink stuff in her hair, all over her body, on the jar her hands gripped so tight. The residue of some pink substance lay like shards of shattered icicle on a far table.

"Honey?" he said. "Are you okay?"

Her face was slabbed in tears.

She looked down, noticed what she was holding, set it with other jars like it on the table beside her.

She turned to him, held out her hands but then raised them as he approached. "I . . . I'm all goopy."

"Here." He looked around wildly, saw some linen on a shelf. "I'll get you a towel."

He got her a towel.

Doctor Baxter, gurgling, died. "He attacked me," she said. John nodded. His wife was one savage biddy. But, by God, she'd had good reason. There was clean-up needing to be done, here and in their lives. But he vowed, by his love for her, to see things through to the end.

***

Baxter woofed his last breath. His mouth, his groin, his wriststumps felt as if God, frowning from on high, had snapped bear traps on them and salted his wounds, skewering his celestial disapproval in like sharp smoldering stakes that glowed white hot, turning, twisting, searing, never a dull moment in his tormented body.

Then suddenly the pain, pricklike, was cut off.

He was somewhere else. Somewhere cool and moist and cloying. He couldn't see. He couldn't hear. But he felt himself alive and whole, if uprooted. And he could taste, oh yes he could. Yucky tasting stuff; unpalatable, though he had no palate.

But something most succulent lay close by, something he had tasted recently and could still, in sensual memory, recall with wicked delight. He pulsed. He surged. But this new body, if that's what it was—limbless, but mere limb—would take some getting used to, to make it motile, to seek out and taste that recalled succulence once more.

A light shone, warm and pink (now how could he sense, being blind, colors?), a finger's reach from him. It felt like sunlight on seedlings. He sensed arousal, the shift of flexible flesh, an overpowering urge to grow.

In bed that night, after the police procedurals had swept through her, Sally tossed and turned. An extra long bath had helped, steaming there, quite out of it, till the water grew cool. But she still felt Doctor Baxter's vile acts clinging to her—that and the glowing pink goop, the gargantuum the explosion had drenched her with.

At midnight, she woke in a sweat.

John was snoring beside her, big long snuffly snorts that made him less than appealing. His exhalations stank like sodden cigars, like burnt toast threaded with maggoty shreds of pork.

When Sally shifted to turn him on his side, away from her, her pajamas clung tight. The buttons strained at her breasts, alternating left-and-right-facing vees of fabric. Her hips drew the cloth taut as snapped sheets. Breathing was difficult. Had she put on a pair of John's pajamas by mistake? Nope. The monogram, a red SAH, was hers.

John snorted awake.

"You okay?" he mumbled.

"Yes," she said. "Go back to sleep."

She tried to do the same. Funny. Her pajama bottoms used to cover her ankles. Now they'd started to creep up her calves, clinging there like wet wraps of seaweed.

She dismissed it, tried to find sleep. But Baxter's words of warning and the image of a ten-foot cock refused to leave her mind.

John feigned sleep. But it wouldn't come. In the moonlight seeping in their window, he let his glistening eyes open. His wife lay upon her back, dozing fitfully. It was a warm night. The covers slanted at her waist.

My God, he thought, her breasts are mammoth.

Sally was so beautiful. It tore him up inside that she'd endured the nightmare of being violated by Doctor Baxter. The warped deviant deserved to have his . . . but then John remembered. Baxter *had* had his . . . And by Sally's dear hand.

He propped himself slowly on one crooked arm, head in hand, and beheld her. Sweet face. Wanton hair, down now, rioting like rainbows on her pillow. Somehow, there seemed *more* of her tonight. He loved her so. He wished there were some way he could undo her pain.

Undo her buttons.

Her breasts were so huge. Pregnant women, he'd been told, got that way. Maybe they'd have a child after all. But he doubted that. They plumped there under the strain of cotton, huge soft cantaloupe mounds that would one day droop and sag like ugly sacks of pudding, but didn't now. They cantilevered, as magic as flying buttresses in their firmness, their heft, their suspension.

One day, maybe, Sally would let him see them naked.

But that day, he knew, lay far in the future. His wife was no slut. And she'd been through a personal hell that would take time and patience to heal.

The bastard (oops, he amended it to "bad man") ought to have his . . .

Ah yes. Small favors.

Baxter felt in-tight. Jar-shaped. He had to get out before the confinement squeezed him to death. He'd never felt so helpless. Then he realized, with a virtual smack to his nonexistent forehead, that he was all muscle.

He contracted, tensed. Waited until he felt cramped again. Then, abruptly, he flexed.

And suddenly he was free!

Sensing sharpness, he gingerly moved over fragments so as not to cut himself. He tasted wood, fell, thwapped to newly mopped linoleum tile. Licking the ammoniac tang of Mr. Clean, he pulsed and throbbed toward freedom.

A pressure halted him. He smelled the black stink of Cat's Paw shoe polish. Swooping across leather, he found flesh, flesh that shook, jittered. Panicked hands batted at him. But he clung tight, wrapping about an ankle. His spittle turned the flesh soft and absorbable. He took the stuff in, the blood, the bone, lapping up thigh meat as his victim fell, scream-vibes egging him on.

It felt positively erotic to sate himself.

Like lava, he smacked up the body inside the clothes, tasted groin slit, hair, belly, breasts. A female cop, was his guess as he gobbled. And alone, based on the help she didn't get. His tongue-body thinned and imbibed, slapping like a wave, receding, drawing sandflesh, sandbone, after it, trails of bloodbubble foaming behind.

When nothing remained but cop-suit, he ambled on.

Sally, by the dresser, held her glasses confusedly in her hand. The arms had snapped when she tried to put them on. But strangely she could see fine without them.

"Listen," John said to her. "I'll take the day off. I've got time. We'll go to the beach."

"You think that would help?" Nothing would help.

"It's worth a try."

After a time, she relented. Her husband seemed to be standing in a hole, but he was solid and assuring. It was a blessing to be in his care. When she took her one-piece into the bathroom to change, it wouldn't fit.

So they got in the car and went to Macy's.

For some reason a white bikini, one of those new and daring suits, seemed right. When she looked at herself in the dressing room mirror, Anita Ekberg came to mind. Milk bottles. My, my, she thought, I *am* filling out.

She could scarcely pull her clothing over it, the red checked shirt, the slacks. Was it time to diet? No. She wasn't fatter. Just larger. Hmmm.

"Let's go," she said, taking John's arm.

On the drive to the beach, she brooded on gargantuum

Jones Beach was crowded that day. Must be lots of folks on vacation, John thought. They strolled along the shore, his wife's statuesque body—and since when had she become statuesque?—drawing stares. There was no hope of finding seclusion, but between beachfronts, they found a bit more room to spread out the pea-green army blanket.

At a distance, an unchaperoned bunch of teens played jungle music, tinny, from a tiny transistor radio.

Sally tucked her hair into a bathing cap, white with plastic flowers daisied on it. John frolicked with her in the waves, splashing her, being splashed. For the moment, everything seemed normal again.

Back on the blanket, her body glistened with droplets as she lay down. Sleek curvy back. Wondrous front. What a full voluptuous woman his wife was. Odd. In the store, her bikini had fit fine. Now the flesh strained at it and he fancied he could see the cloth tugging, thinning.

"Jeepers, this suit is tight," she said.

John looked over at the teens. They were jiggling to the radio noise. Disgusting. America was in trouble.

He heard Sally prepare a sneeze.

When he turned to her, the sneeze blew into her hand and her suit exploded off her. For a second in the bright sunlight, his wife was bare-ass naked.

She took the Lord's name in vain.

Then she grabbed a towel, two towels, and sat there rocking, crying, lamenting, "What's *happening* to me?"

Baxter tasted dirt, gravel, cinders, dog doo, hawked gobs of spit. He preferred the lady cop. He craved more female flesh, and one dainty dish in particular. When he picked up the tracks of his former secretary, he'd be hot on that cutie's trail, no question.

But in the meantime, he slithered along the edge of downtown North Allville. Somehow his senses of taste and touch were so acute, he could grope along an internal map of the town. He had ghost visions, ghost hearings, faint white whispered things, that corresponded to what was out there.

A malt shop near the railroad tracks.

He sniffed females, lots of them.

The air jittered with passion sounds. He could feel the floor shaking as he slid through the open door. There were seven of them, smelling like high school cheerleader types. With his tip, he eased the door closed, locked it, turned the OPEN sign to CLOSED.

High giggles knifed the air.

Ponytails twirled, hips gyred in long poodle skirts.

Then he attacked, and the giggles turned to screams.

He sucked up girlflesh, swelled, grew. This was the life. Blood, bone, bile, chocolate malts half-digested in smooth taut burst tummies.

Much better than dog doo.

But nowhere near as delectable as sweet Sally Holmes.

Weeks passed. The evidence of Sally's transformation had become so clear that, the day after the beach fiasco, she fled. Nearly seven feet. She was growing and growing fast. As she left, she had to duck through the front door to avoid braining herself.

She kept to the woods during the day, moving at night in a direction that called to her. To clothe herself, she stole sheets off lines, pinning them together with wooden clothespins. She raided gardens, wishing she had money to pay the good people she stole from.

Her mind was expanding too. Her rage. And, God help her, her libido. She'd never been so horny and so angry, and her thoughts had never ranged so widely over being and nothingness, the meaning of life, and the silly putterings of the diminutive creatures she espied from where she hid. Whole passages of Plato and Aristotle she had slid over in school now came back, making sense. She embraced what was right in them, tossed what was wrong.

When she was thirty feet tall, she began not to care who saw her move at night. At forty feet, she bared her breasts, feeling nightbreeze and sunlight tauten the huge nipples. At fifty feet, she started to tease the little people, gripping cars and jiggling them, lifting them by the roofs so swiftly that sometimes—like painfully inept special effects—it seemed she lifted the landscape along with it. She wrecked upright structures. Steeples, radio towers, anything lofty she tore off, feeling enraged and good and sweaty. During the day, she sought out bowllike depressions, cool, lush, comforting, to sleep in.

She had no idea what place instinct drew her toward, but it was good, very good indeed. Of that she was sure.

John fixed upon the US map the sergeant was pointing to. The country was going crazy. His wife, breasts bare as a harlot's, had grown huge and was destroying property left and right. Rumors of a giant tongue circulated, and whole villages' populations disappearing. The only thing left behind? A trail of bloody saliva.

"Mrs. Holmes was spotted here (*thwap*), here (*thwap*), and here (big *thwap*)," the man said. He was square-jawed and steely-eyed. "You men notice where she's headed?"

Everyone grumbled a yes like they were in church with their heads bowed muttering amen.

"That's right," he said. "The Grand Canyon. We can let her be, then zoom in with helicopters, pick her off."

"Hold on," said John. "That's my wife you're talking about."

"Don't be a chump for love," said the sergeant. "We have a public nuisance on our hands. And I aim to wash it off. With steel slugs of civic soap."

"Have you no heart, man?"

"I have a duty to all Americans. That, über alles."

Everyone grumbled yeah, yeah.

John grabbed the pointer. "Listen, men, I know Sally as well as anyone. I can reason with her, persuade her to stop destroying erect edifices."

"She's a monster!"

"She's my *wife*!!!!!"

He put it so strongly, the other cops relented.

The sergeant rested a hand on John's shoulder. John knew he wasn't a bad man. Just a jerk.

"Time to get *you* to the Grand Canyon," he said.

And it was.

Baxter loomed at the edges of the drive-in. The film splashed up there, from his honed sensors, he supposed was some dark and scary thing. Good. Made it easier for him to claim victims. Black night, black screen, black cover.

He liked the juicy females, the ones the crewcut boys liquefied with their fingers, squirming out of clothing as easily as out of their virginity.

In the back row a Dodge rocked. He could tell it was a Dodge because his tip traced the chrome letters. Baxter tasted unwashed car, skimmed through the window crack, and dove for the couple in the back seat. He hated boy-taste, but (just as he'd saved the best for last over dinner as a boy) he absorbed the boyfriend first, while he muffled the screams of the half-dressed dolly. Then he turned his all to savoring dessert.

She was mere appetizer, a speared shrimp.

Sally Holmes' sweetness lay on the wind, and Baxter's drool slathered his pathway toward her. In his future, he sensed a deep wide all-engulfing hole.

***

Sally recognized it of course. She and John on their honeymoon had spent time here, had gone down on donkeys.

The Grand Canyon.

Then it had felt like love.

Now it felt like home.

Oblivious to the gaping miniatures scurrying about at her feet, she unpinned the diaperlike loincloth whose taut clutch vexed her, dropped it, and started her long descent to the bottom where the river was.

One weird-eyed maniac feasted his eyes on her, as she lowered her nude body over the rim. She jiggled her boobs at him, then took a deep breath and blew him, midst debris and rubble, back toward the panicked masses. Lustily, she laughed. Then the rim rose above her skull and she was on her way, night's gravid moon lighting rock and brush along the trail.

The local police tracked her with binoculars and with telescopes, relaying her whereabouts to John at the lowest point of the canyon.

When he came upon her, she was reclining, buck naked, near the river. She was obscene. She was beautiful. His shame, under his pants, grew hard. His wife's hand was on her womanhood, stirring it like she stirred cake batter in her Betty Crocker apron. Her deep throaty moans echoed in the vast rocky gorge.

"Sally," he shouted. She didn't hear him. He yelled her name over and over until he grew hoarse.

Then she noticed him. A look of desire burned in her eyes. "John," she intoned, a deep throbbing need there.

"My dear darling," he mourned, "they say there may be an antidote, they say—"

She grabbed him, not hard, but firm as one might grab a kitten or gerbil. "Fuck antidotes," she said in rumbles of husky thunder. "I *like* being big."

He chided her for her crude language, but she merely laughed, booming, like the genie in *The Thief of Baghdad*.

Then she brought him within whiffing distance of her womanhood. He recognized the morning-after manhood stink (but writ large and overpowering) before his bath.

"Make like a statue," she ordered. "Rigidify."

Before he could ask her why, he found *out* why.

Like a diver just before splitting the silent water, he took a breath. That saved him. Into warm gooshy hugs of pudding he was thrust, splooshing about in smooth dark pulsings that brought cows' udders to mind. It was divine and it was terrifying. Just when he knew his lungs would burst, Sally unencunted him, frotting his forehead against a ruddy nub (what *was* that thing?), above which curled riots of coarse straw abruptly thatched. Then— and by the grace of God he could sense when, so he could gulp a goopy breath— she'd plunge him back inside her, twisting him and turning him like an agitator in a washing machine, like an orange half being brutally juiced.

But abruptly he was out, laid on the ground, chilling in the night air. He blinked his stuck eyelids open. And saw—oh God he wanted to shit—a gigantic tongue throbbing not six feet away, bloated, bloody, spilling icky rivulets of drool down its unclean sides.

Baxter cared not a lick for the jerk. He'd served as—what did whores call it?—a *dildo* for Baxter's bitch.

But now the bitch had Baxter to satisfy her.

And satisfy her he would.

Tasting more sandstone powder as he rolled on, Baxter leaned against her massive thigh, slurped at her perineum, caught her spillage where it dripped, slowly slalomed his tip up the swollen slit of her excitation toward her sweet hillock of delight.

But she seized him, shoved him in.

She embraced him like any animal, and he embraced the opportunity to thrust as deep as he could, elongating, conforming himself to her inner shape, vibrating, throbbing, shuddering, as he moved inward. A tiny bit of him, where she had disembodied him, jazzed at her womanhood. But the rest was inside, not yet releasing his devouring fluid. Time enough, in orgasm, to make her die. He filled her, pulsating against her walls, sweeping beyond the cervix into the uterus itself, filling it like a plum-passioned fetus, poised to wail in ecstasy like a sweaty trumpeter nailing a string of high notes.

She was coming.

And, oh god, she was *squeezing*.

He flexed, but it did no good. She was crushing him. He tried to release the killing fluid. Got some out, felt the beginnings of meld.

But it was too tight. Too fugging tight.

Trapped.

He fluttered.

He died.

Sally tightened in orgasm. Boulders shook loose at her screams. Her husband, with his hands up to his ears, looked like a drooled-upon letter T.

But the golden tongue she'd had to have was releasing venom, was stuck inside, even as she shuddered in ecstasy. It stung her center. She felt the life squeezed off there first, even as her final orgasm played out. The hurt bled outward from her womb, attacking kidneys, pancreas, islets of Lagerhans, on and on.

Lights winked out all over her body.

"I'm dying," she gasped.

"Oh no," said the pipsqueak. "Honey, that can't be."

She tried to expel the inert tongue like unfertilized tissue, tried to yank it out. No go. It stuck there like a wasp's barb, sinking its killing force deeper with every breath.

Her lungs felt the slash of cut glass. Her heart.

"Goodbye, John," she gasped.

"I'll never forget you," he screamed. "Nobody will."

The thing that had killed her pooched out of her like a melting strawberry popsicle, dripping crimson gush along her buttocks and onto the earth. It looked like a wilted poinsettia clasped in a clutching infant's hand.

At the height of the terrible display, she had glowed pink: the same pink as in the lab that fateful day. John had felt a warmth beyond embarrassment along his front but mostly in his manhood.

"Bury me deep." Sally's eyes grew fuzzy.

John did a hasty calculation. "I'll bury you *well*," he said. He was hard. To his astonishment he didn't feel any shame. Not only was he hard. He was thick and long, much longer, much thicker than ever in his life. He felt the blunt bludgeon through his trousers. A fucking spade handle stood there.

Crude language had suddenly become okay. In fact it was a decided turn-on. His bulb-head throbbed.

Thoughts of conjunction soared in his head. Thoughts of people watching him score with lots of chicks, sticking his tool in places it had never dreamt of going before.

"Kiss me, John."

He approached her lips, thinking to peck them. Then she inhaled suddenly and he was a hotdog snug in two soggy bun-halves. But a moment later, her death, huge and final and thick with shadows, flooded out upon a slow exhalation and he fell, body-kissed, cock-kissed, to the earth.

Still erect, he picked himself up.

Sally had left him memories.

He patted his pants.

And she'd left him *this*.

And *this* would guide him henceforth on his solitary way.

KIRSTEN ALENE

LOCATION:
Astoria, OR

STYLE OF BIZARRO:
Machine Gun Fabulism

BOOKS BY ALENE:
Love in the Time of Dinosaurs
Unicorn Battle Squad
Japan Conquers the Galaxy
Rules of Appropriate Conduct
Moon Snake

DESCRIPTION: "Imagine Terry Gilliam directing from a script written by Jack Vance channeling the ghosts of Kafka and Calvino, and you're closing in on the essence of Alene's latest novel. A bold fusion of grounded surrealism, unfettered filth, and wit as dry and dark as a strip of unicorn jerky." — JESSE BULLINGTON, author of *The Sad Tale of the Brothers Grossbart,* on Kirsten Alene's *Unicorn Battle Squad.*

INTERESTS: Bicycles, sock monsters, The Ottoman Empire, vegetarian foods, Romanticism, badgers, dinosaurs, Prog Rock, Moomins, baskets and boxes, fishing, pies, and preparing for the zombie apocalypse.

INFLUENCES: Hayao Miyazaki, Arthur Rimbaud, Ursula K. LeGuin, John Keats, Stanley Crawford, Kimya Dawson, Xinran, Richard Brautigan, Jorge Luis Borges, Aubrey Beardsley, Mervyn Peake, Gabriel Garcia Marquez, Terry Gilliam, Gertrude Stein, L. Ron Hubbard, Angela Lansbury, Kelly Link, Italo Calvino, Trinie Dalton, Woody Allen, Fernando Pessoa, Lady Murasaki, E. M. Forster, Tove Jansson, P.G. Wodehouse, Edward Lear, and Hendrick's Gin.

LOVE IN THE TIME OF DINOSAURS

Prologue
The Myth of the Great Destroyer

At the center of the planet, which is as wide in circumference as one thousand birds flying consecutively from birth to exhaustion, there is a vast, empty cavern, and in that cavern there are forty floating islands which circle each other slowly, propelled by the vibrations of footsteps falling on the surface of the earth.

On each island live an old woman and an old man. Each old woman is unaware of the presence of the old man, and each old man is unaware of the presence of the old woman.

They have been eighty-seven years old since time began. They sleep on the boughs of trees and are wakened each morning by a sun-streak across the sky, like a giant fluorescent light bulb made of the fireflies that orbits each floating island.

At the End of Days—when the islands break free from the cavernous center of the planet and burst into the light of day, the old women and the old men on the islands will find each other and, in ecstasy at the discovery of an-other human, will mate with the fireflies. Their offspring will be the only thing that can stop Jeremy.

Jeremy: the scourge of mankind, the Great Destroyer.

Chapter One
Raptor Reconnaissance

Oomka fidgets beside me. He wipes sweat from his brow, smearing the painted camouflage patches and expos-ing a swatch of pink skin. I'm trying to use this time to catch up on some meditation and steady my hands a bit, but it's hard to meditate beside Oomka. He fidgets too much. Still, it's not like meditating will do me any good. All that comes to me in meditation lately is the story of the Great Destroyer. And Jeremy. Thinking about Jeremy makes me even more anxious. It's understand-able, considering the circumstances.

* * *

In the last twenty-five years, *Jeremy* has taken on a whole new meaning. Before then, a monk in the monastery would have heard the word only once in a while—whenever the community was unlucky enough to be visited by a man-eating tiger, or someone discov-ered a snake in the public bathroom. Someone might scream, "Ah! Jeremy! Back, Jeremy!" as he ran from the toi-let, or "Ah! Look out, a Jer..." before being eaten by a tiger.

Prior to the End of Days, The Myth of the Great Destroyer, the shortest section in the *Book of Meditation*, provided the only knowledge anyone had about Jeremies. Since then, hundreds of books have been written about them, totaling more than one million pages of data, observation, speculation and statistics.

For all that work, all the lives sacrificed in the name of research, and all the slaughter and loss and pain, no one knows where they come from, what they want, or how to defeat them.

What we have gathered is this: Jeremies are dinosaurs, primarily from the Cretaceous period. There are fourteen known varieties, although my dead friend Chip suspected there were more that we've just never seen up close. He had good reason to believe this, and I have no reason to doubt him, as he is currently in the third stomach of some Jeremy cast in plastic about seven miles north of the monastery wall.

In addition to the obvious biological advantage of being dinosaurs, Jeremies are unfairly favored in the fight. Their technology far surpasses ours; their hand-to-hand combat skills are uncanny and they all, without exception, have an insatiable lust for human blood.

The only advantage we seem to possess is our unique connection to and familiarity with our surroundings (mountain forests where the majority of us have spent our entire lives). But guerilla warfare is as taxing as our temple duties and rituals, and coping with our spiritual imprisonment and the constant onslaught of the Jeremy is too much for many of the monks. In the last two years alone, we've lost more than eighty men.

This figure, of course, excludes the countless villagers that have fallen victim to the Jeremy whenever they break through our safe lines.

* * *

Oomka trembles beside me as I struggle to remain in the state of transcendent calm I usually occupy during watch duty. Sure, Jeremies scare the living shit out of me. But what's the use of being a monk if you can't transcend your physical existence when faced with the imminent death of your species?

Of everyone in the monastery, aside from the two elders, I am perhaps the most familiar with the fourteen known varieties of Jeremy. From as early as I can remember, books concerning the Jeremy have fascinated me. Their biology, their technology, their strategy, their tight-knit cooperative communities, their language and intelligent thought are a source of continual amazement and wonder.

I can't help but look at them with reverent, even worshipful eyes. From their perfect rows of bone crushing, razor-sharp teeth to the arched, reptilian spines that allow them to navigate at top speeds through any terrain, every movement, every expression is carefully measured, agile, streamlined and sensual. Especially when compared with the pathetic scrambling movements of the monks and villagers.

To watch them hunt, to see them bring down a human in battle, demands a sort of awful silence of mind. Those who can't find in themselves a cool, observant respect for the creatures don't last long.

* * *

"Look," Oomka whispers in my ear, gesturing with shaking hands through the heavy cover of our tree down to the forest floor. There is a rustle of movement, barely perceivable. Could be anything.

A squirrel.

Or a badger.

Then I hear a high, rapid clicking call.

Raptors.

My body tenses. I aim the ray gun downward and wait for another rustle. Fortunately for us, raptors are shit at climbing, and Oomka and I, as usual, have chosen a tall tree with sparse lower branches, good as a vantage point, but a huge risk as an attack position. I always bank on the sight-advantage giving us ample warning time to descend if an attack comes.

I catch a flash of light from a tree opposite ours, across the ravine. One of the other watch pairs has seen the movement as well. I nudge Oomka and gesture to the mirror signal. Probably more than one raptor, which usually means an attack party. I wait for the undergrowth to shift again. It'd be best to encase these two (or more) Jeremies before descending. Oomka shudders as he aims his gun down at the same spot of undergrowth.

But I plunge my mind into the spongy vat of comfort conjured up from the depths of my being, and my movements become automatic and graceful. I swing the ray gun around, flashing the glass sight so the other team knows what I'm about to do. I wave two fingers at Oomka, and he steadies his gun against his knee.

The raptor nearest us has popped up its head in a clear section of forest floor. It swivels around slowly, face tilted to the side, listening. It has tremendous auditory senses and can probably hear our breaths, our heart beats, the blinking of our eyelids, the creaking of our bones, Oomka's pores squeezing out miniscule drops of perspiration, our sticky hands sliding over the barrels of the guns. It just can't see us.

In the same second, Oomka and I fire our guns. I hit my target, but Oomka misses by a fraction of an inch. My raptor has been encased in hard, flesh-colored plastic, his last scream still echoing through the ravine. The other raptor has wisely put its head down and disappeared into the brush.

Two more shots ricochet off the trees from the other watch team.

As their gun blasts echo, and we sweep the undergrowth for movement, a massive cavern of teeth explodes out of the trees directly behind us. With a moaning exhalation of putrid, meat-smelling breath, the mountainous jaws of a brachiosaurus clamp down on Oomka's lower half.

I yell and swing my ray gun around, but it is too late. The monster has withdrawn into the leaves, taking the bottom half of Oomka with it. The top half of Oomka looks at me, his yellow eyes bulging as fluid and blood pour from the remaining half of his torso. Two exposed ribs dangle below a line of jagged flesh. Organs spill out over the tree limb, coating the branches beneath us in vivid red. He coughs, and a mouthful of blood trickles down his chin, staining the front of his orange robes. He still clutches one of the tree limbs directly above us, but has dropped his gun. It lies half-obscured in the brush below us.

"Oomka?" I say, half-pitying, half-disgusted.

Chapter Two
Pterodactyl High-Jacking

Often I have wished that we were stronger, bigger and more lethal without the aid of our tools, machines and weapons, which barely compensate for our lack of teeth and claws. Born weak and naked into this world, we are helpless. I want to rip into the leathery flesh of the dinosaurs. I want sharp teeth. I want to tear into Jeremies, to disembowel them with my bare hands, to bite them in half and feast on their cold-blooded flesh.

When the dinosaurs first appeared, the elders forbade violence against them. But the number of deaths spiraled out of control. Villagers were devoured, and the constant carnage forced us into action. We had no choice but to defend what was ours—our monastery, our villages, our mountain—from destruction and death.

When the elders decided to act, finally, they armed us with ray guns that did not kill Jeremies instantly, but encased their bodies in hard plastic. Somehow, this was thought to be more humane.

* * *

There's still hope for Oomka. If I can get him back to the monastery, the physicians will be able to fit him with another lower body, and he'll be back on someone else's feet and fighting in no time. The magic kung-fu of the monks, learned from the venerable Elder Zohar—one of the last surviving elders of the monastery—combined with the impressive skills of our physicians, have led to many astounding recoveries that would have been impossible for the monks to achieve twenty years ago. The only things that can destroy us are complete obliteration or ritual self-destruction. But our watch isn't over for another three hours, and it looks like a fight is coming.

"Are you all right?" I ask, shifting my ray gun onto my back so I can climb down to retrieve his gun before more Jeremies show up. Those two raptors were just advance scouts, and one probably made it back to the attack party. The worst is yet to come. And they know our positions.

"Well, yeah," Oomka says matter-of-factly, running a finger around the torn flesh of his lower chest, picking a few leaves off the shredded muscle tissue. "Go get the gun. I can hang here. But when you come back up, I'm gonna ask you to shift me a little. I think I'm resting on my spine, and I can't see very well."

He's acting strangely. It annoys me that he'd let a thing like this get to him, but I can't say anything negative while he's in this state.

"No problem," I say, sliding down onto the next lowest branch, which is slick with Oomka's blood and what looks like some intestine.

By the time I've retrieved the ray gun and clambered back into position, Oomka is still not quite himself. It's a big shock to lose half of your body, of course, but it's not the end of the world. Oomka seems to have taken it pretty hard. I think that if it'd been me, I'd have handled the situation better.

With my half-functional, distracted partner I feel more vulnerable and exposed, so I plunge my mind back into the elastic receptacle of peace I've manifested, isolating each functional part of my body, cooling my blood as it races through my veins, flexing each finger separately, bending each hair toward the sun like blades of grass to absorb the green light filtered through the canopy of leaves above us.

It'll be fine, I reassure myself silently, wondering if Oomka is going to have my back at all. He's still inspecting the ragged flesh of his torso, picking at it.

"Don't do that," I tell him.

"Yeah, I know," he says, but he doesn't stop.

* * *

Oomka and I have only known each other for a few months. Until recently, I'd really disliked him, but we spend a lot of time together on watch duty and patrolling the outer wall, so we've become rather close. We've gotten used to each other, and I've begun to trust him.

It was difficult to take on another partner for watch duty after my previous partner, my best and oldest friend, Chip, was dismembered and eaten by a stegosaurus. Chip was the sort of man who was always present in the moment. I strove to be like him in almost every way. I still do.

When he was dismembered, he sacrificed himself to allow the others and me to get back to the walls of the monastery. If he hadn't dove into that hopeless engagement with the stegosaurus, all seven of us would have died. He had lived for the utility of his every move until his very last second on earth.

But the one aspect of Chip's worldview I never agreed with was his bitter, unbridled loathing of the Jeremy. He hated them to such a degree that he failed to accept or anticipate their ingenuity and intelligence. He was blinded by anger and rage, and no matter how noble his sacrifice had been, it eventually cost him his life.

As the elders taught us, only with respect, careful, minute observation, and unfailing strength of body and mind would we be able to hold out against our enemy. *Hold Out*. For, as I constantly reminded myself, we held no advantage. We had no hope. In the end, we were children.

* * *

Oomka fidgets nervously with the settings on his ray gun now, turning the plastic-thickness knob up and down and gazing through the crosshairs, aiming at trees and shrubs.

This is one of the reasons why I initially disliked Oomka. He fidgets. Chip never fidgeted. He could sit on watch duty like a stone, in one position for the entire five-hour shift. What I wouldn't give to be as centered and calm as Chip had been.

Although I don't twitch and fidget as much as Oomka, I find myself having to change position often, especially straddling this tree limb. My genitals are pinned uncomfortably against the joint of a branch extending from the larger limb we sit on, and no amount of repositioning will make it comfortable. I'm almost envious of Oomka's lack of genitals, but then I figure it's probably just as uncomfortable resting on one of your own exposed ribs.

* * *

Our watch is almost over, and I feel the tension in my muscles releasing. The attack hasn't come. The brachiosaurus had simply been an unfortunate coincidence. Brachiosaurs often attacked at random. Few survive crossing their path.

The raptors weren't armed. But all the same, it makes me anxious to leave our watch so soon after that encasing, especially considering the raptor that got away.

I scan the forest floor below, looking for any sign of movement, any hint of an impending onslaught: a rustle in the ferns, the silence of birds, the sticky smell of raw meat on the breeze. There's nothing out of the ordinary.

But a flash from the adjacent watch makes Oomka and me jump. The movement of our bodies jostles the tree limb. Leaves at the end of the branch shudder, betraying our position to whatever the other watch may have spotted. I place a hand on Oomka's remaining chest to steady him, my body rigid, gun in hand and poised to shoot.

Then a scream rends the air, and we watch as a body plummets from the other watch position, falling into three even chunks in its descent. Blood cascades from the severed pieces, splattering like wet paint over the undergrowth. The mid-torso section bounces as it hits the earth.

Three round steel blades land in a

tree several feet from our own, having crossed the ravine in less time than it took the body of our comrade to fall from its watch position.

Then, in a rush of instantaneous, synchronized movement, a mass of Jeremies clears the crest of the distant hill. Among them, brachiosaurs and tyrannosaurs tower above the heads of the other legions. The tyrannosaurs carry huge, triple-barreled bazookas with badger-sized torpedoes slung across their massive reptilian chests. Enormous jaws roar open and wide for imminent gnashing. Huge tails whip back and forth behind them, spiked with artificial barbs that impale ferns and small animals scurrying from the undergrowth away from the sprinting hordes.

The second watchman across the ravine tumbles through branches and lands broken on the ground below as two stegosaurs with a giant rotating saw held horizontally between them cut down his tree.

The sky explodes with smoke and ash as a torpedo from a nearby tyrannosaurus sends the body flying in fist-sized chunks up into the air.

He would have probably survived the fall. Unfortunately, the Jeremies had caught on to the fact that the monks weren't easy to kill, and desecrating and obliterating corpses had become one of their favorite pastimes.

I look at Oomka. Rivers of sweat streaking his camouflage face paint and mounting panic in his eyes tell me he's thinking what I'm thinking: with-out legs, in a ground battle, he doesn't stand a chance. I can hear Chip in my mind, as if he's yelling from a great distance, as if he's here in the moment with us, but standing far away, "Save yourselves! Back to the wall, go go go!"

And I know Oomka isn't that brave.

And I know I can't leave him to be slaughtered.

Our only chance is escape, to flee now as the blades and bullets fly past our tree, shredding leaves and splintering branches. The smell of raw meat, bleeding vegetation and gunpowder clouds my nostrils, filling my head with pressure. I can't think. We need time. But there is no time. Our present ammunition couldn't get us through this fight, even if every shot made contact (not an impossible feat when aiming at a virtually solid wall of Jeremies, but all the same). Oomka still trembles. Petrified, he stares at me. He isn't about to offer any suggestions. I'll have to come up with something.

My head whirrs around. I search desperately for an escape, willing a solution to come to me. The Jeremy attack force grows nearer, the scent of their filthy, meaty bodies intensifies, clouding my mind even more. I fling my eyes upward. Above the towering heads of the tyrannosaurs: a swarm of pterodactyls.

I duck a huge blade propelled by two large steam engines. It rips into the trunk of the tree behind our heads, cutting the top clean off. Our tree limb whips back. Oomka wedges his body into a more secure position, takes aim and fires at a brachiosaurus. The dinosaur is instantly coated in molten plastic, immobilized mid-stride. Smaller Jeremies leap out of the way of the blast. With sudden clarity, I bend over my ray gun and detach the shoulder strap. I swing the barrels up and aim into the swarm of pterodactyls.

Oomka plasticizes two smaller Jeremies with one shot and takes aim again. My shot has made contact, catching one pterodactyl full in the chest and splattering the wing of another. Both spiral to the forest floor. The Jeremy horde is at the bottom of the ravine, surging up the hill toward us, closing yards every second. The swarm of pterodactyls reacts exactly as I had hoped, rocketing toward us, enraged. They will beat the front lines to our tree, but just barely. Several more beaked bullets zip past us, burrowing their small, razor sharp faces into the flesh of the decapitated tree.

Oomka screams above the roar of the Jeremies: "What are you doing!?"

I gesture for him to shut up and spring onto the raw, severed neck of our tree. "Hold on to me!" I tell Oomka, "Don't let go!" He slings his weapon over his shoulder and grabs my ankle obediently.

"I'm going to swing you up!" I yell, gesturing to illustrate my intention. His eyes widen, but he doesn't argue. The pterodactyls, armed only with close-combat weapons and their own teeth, are nearing our position.

I brace myself on the treetop, hoping that Oomka's upper-half is light enough to fling into the air. He was never very heavy, even when he had legs. It has to work. It's our only chance.

The first pterodactyl dives through the leafy canopy toward us.

In one swift movement, I toss the ray gun strap. It winds around the Jeremy's jaw as I'd hoped, and I hurl Oomka's body, which is even lighter than anticipated, into the air. Oomka lands squarely on the pterodactyl and lowers a hand to pull me up. I yank the Jeremy down by its jaw and clamber up behind Oomka as quickly as possible. The other Jeremies, above and below, are upon us. A bullet rips through the pterodactyl's wing, making it falter and stumble in mid-flight.

"Go! Fly! NOW!" I yell, holding the ray gun against its scaly temple and shoving. My other hand is clenched tight around the strap binding its jaw. It obeys.

In seconds, we're tearing up into the sky, surrounded by other pterodactyls that swoop and dive at us. Their feet clasp long samurai swords that they clumsily slash through the air as they whirl around our injured pterodactyl, clicking and screeching.

Oomka aims the barrel of his ray gun under my arm and shoots a stream of flesh-colored plastic into the air. Pterodactyls avoid the blobs with angry screeches, but one of Oomka's shots makes contact. The plasticized pterodactyl plummets toward the forest below.

The other pterodactyls back away from our desperately flapping prisoner. Several near the back of the swarm turn around to rejoin the battle raging below, probably to dive-bomb some other monks in watch posts in the trees. Overall, there are about forty monks out on watch. They should be able to handle the fight on the ground and retreat on foot to the walls of the monastery.

Once they reach the monastery, the attacking Jeremy horde will break upon the ancient, impenetrable stone walls like water.

But, as I look around, I see we're not anywhere near the monastery. In our haste, and surrounded by other pterodactyls, we must have flown in the wrong direction. The pterodactyl flaps its torn wing lamely. If it goes down now, we'll have to make our way back on foot outside the safe lines, with the attack force of Jeremy not far behind us.

Wet tears stream from the eyes of the pterodactyl. I feel an unwelcome surge of compassion and pity, and draw the ray gun back from its temple. Its body quakes feebly as its torn wing flaps at double speed under the extra weight of Oomka and me.

We still hear distant roaring and the frantic battle cries of monks on the ground. For a moment, I wish, bitterly, that I had stayed behind with them, but it would have meant sacrificing Oomka, a thing I couldn't bring myself to do. He aims the ray gun behind us, under my arm. Together, we sit on the pterodactyl in a sort of awkward, unintentional embrace, but it doesn't bother me.

The other pterodactyls have abandoned our trail, and the skies are clear ahead. Back toward the battle, a huge formation of cumulonimbus clouds amasses over the forest. Mingled with the smoke and steam and explosions tearing through the canopy of trees, the clouds look ominous.

I hope the monks on the ground will be able to subdue a large portion of the Jeremy attack force before they retreat to the walls. That would at least justify losing the monks who would die in today's firefight.

* * *

We are losing altitude fast. Treetops approach at an alarming rate, and nothing looks familiar. I yank up on the gun strap wound around the pterodactyl's beak, but its eyelids flicker. "Don't you dare die, you motherfucker!" I scream into the wind, jabbing the beast's side with my bare foot.

But the wings are folding; the pterodactyl spirals downward. I cling to the strap, but Oomka and I fall away from the pterodactyl. Oomka clutches the front of my robe like a baby possum, the remaining portion of his spinal column flapping beneath us in the roaring wind.

And we fall.

Our bodies shoot through the air toward the treetops. This is the end. The Jeremy is dead, or will be in a few seconds when it hits the ground. I feel a second surge of pity and compassion for the animal and try to shake this strange feeling from my head, not wanting to die mourning the fate of my enemy.

* * *

The green carpet racing up toward us, I close my eyes and dive into the folded fatty tissue of my brain. Swimming through electric impulses, curling around the stalks of neurons, I breaststroke through tissue toward the center. Like the planet, the center of my brain is an empty cavern. Shrill calls rend the air here. I wonder where they are coming from, but don't have time to look around. I have to reach my destination. There are no islands here, only an empty four-dimensional field. Corn grows along the center axis in neat rows. This is what I came for. The corn on the stalks is ripe. I pull the husk off greedily. The kernels are fireflies, buzzing and glowing in an even grid pattern. I take a huge bite, scraping the fireflies from the cob with my front teeth, a smile stretching over my face as I taste their buttery, luminous juices. Suddenly, I realize where the shrill calls are coming from. Hungry pterodactyls race toward me as I drift aimlessly in the center of my brain. I know there's nothing I can do. I want to feed them the corn in my hands, so I lift it up to them, but they bite off my arms, and I scream in pain.

* * *

I am jerked out of my head. Oomka turns himself around so that his back is against my chest, and he rips open his ribcage. His hollow body cavity acts as a parachute, slowing our speed dramatically. We coast toward the trees and drop slowly through the canopy, unharmed. The remains of Oomka cushion my landing, and I roll away from him, sprawling out in the undergrowth. I close my eyes, relief rushing over my body like a tidal wave over a small village, obliterating houses and buildings and streets, and carrying every loose thing out to sea.

Chapter Three
Dinosaur Domicile

I prop myself up on an elbow and look around. I have no idea where we are. Oomka lies a few feet away, his ribcage open like a claw. There's nothing in his body cavity now. He's trying to prop himself up with his arms. I jump up and walk toward him. The pterodactyl is nowhere to be seen; we'll have to find our way back on foot.

Well, on my feet.

* * *

I am cleaning leaves out of my gun when I think I see a flash of movement about fifty yards away, a form darting through the trees several feet off the ground. It's hot and muggy in this part of the forest. Heat waves rise, distorting the shifting shapes. But, for some reason, my hands don't fly to the trigger of my gun. I don't even make a sign to Oomka to shut up. I just stare, waiting. And, in the bare yellow light streaking toward us from the edge of the forest, I think I see a lithe, slender body slip between two trees. I can't understand why my heart has leapt into my throat, or why I am trembling all over. I can't understand why my hands don't grasp my gun instinctively. I could have leveled the barrel, taken aim and fired. I should have fired. I should still fire. Cold sweat breaks out along the back of my neck and drips across my brow.

"What's wrong?" Oomka asks, looking up at my face suspiciously.

"Nothing," I reply quickly.

Several minutes later—Oomka lashed to my back like a weird Siamese twin—we set off in the direction we've agreed must be south. Still preoccupied by my strange vision, I'm not paying attention to where we're going, just treading along through the forest. Without many of his organs, Oomka is very light, but he clicks the power switch of his gun on and off and squirms.

"You're wasting the batteries," I snap, looking over my shoulder. His face falls, and the clicking sounds stop.

We trudge along in relative silence for a while before he starts picking at his teeth. Why someone with two thirds of his body missing would be worrying about his teeth is beyond me. He's slurping and sucking and scraping the enamel with his finger. I bite my tongue and say nothing, although I feel like smashing his open ribcage into a tree.

* * *

It seems like hours have passed, but the sky is still light when the forest begins to thin slightly, and we enter a clearing. I raise my gun, stepping back under the cover of the trees. Distinct signs of the recent passage of a large Jeremy—probably a tyrannosaurus, by the looks of the prints—mark the clearing. A strong smell of meat hangs in the warm, sticky air.

"What's going…" Oomka begins. I elbow his open ribcage sharply. He falls silent, but I feel him straining to peer over my shoulder.

In the center of the clearing is a great mound of earth, easily recognizable as the domicile of a larger Jeremy. During the most recent attack on a Jeremy village, all the buildings and structures were razed to the ground, leveled and burned. Nothing but plastic ruins remain in the war field, so I have never seen a dwelling up close. It looks so humble, so modest, with round, latticed windows, and a small fern garden framing a walkway to the door. It doesn't seem to reflect any of the characteristics of the savage, blood-thirsty beasts that must have constructed it.

Oomka has managed to turn himself enough to see ahead of us. He gasps and whispers, "What the fuck?"

Curiosity overcomes me, despite

the potential danger. I need to explore this home. I need to see inside it. Untying Oomka, I drop him to the ground.

"Stand watch," I say.

"But…" he begins to protest.

I walk away. I hear him grumble and shift at the edge of the clearing as I move across the fern garden.

We have plenty of ammunition, not to mention the element of surprise if the building is occupied. I brace myself outside the entrance, standing between two huge, well-manicured hedges. I seek my familiar state of peace and detachment. I'm not shielding myself from fear or anxious nerves this time, but from a strange, child-like excitement.

Slowing my breathing, I lean my whole body against the massive door, and it swings open.

The majority of the wall space of the domed structure is composed of shelves upon which scores of large books are stacked, pictures in metal and wooden frames, vases, plates and cups. It looks just like a house in the village, only larger, with less furniture. Jeremies, I suppose, don't really need furniture. One glance around tells me the house is empty, although the smell of meat is strong. I walk around the interior. There is just one room with a huge, vaulted ceiling. The architecture is beautiful. From the outside, the home is simple, like a large sandy hill, but inside, crisscrossing beams and tiled floors indicate the Jeremy are just as concerned with the aesthetics of their architecture as the monks.

* * *

Then I see it. In the center, lower than the rest of the floor: a nest. In the nest are eight or nine eggs the size of beach balls. My heart pounding in my ears, I cross the floor and kneel beside the nearest egg. Without thinking, I reach out a shaking hand and place it on the stony brown surface. I yank my hand back. It's warm. I feel like my skin has just brushed the beginning of the universe. I imagine the infant dinosaur, curled up inside the egg, harmless and vulnerable, barely conscious, in need of protection and, in a flash, I know I cannot encase these eggs.

I am about to stand and turn back to the door when a little shuffle of movement a few feet away makes me leap back. In my excitement and wonder upon entering the house, I hadn't even checked for smaller Jeremies hiding in the dark corners. My first thought is that it must be a raptor. I cry out in surprise and swing my gun around in the direction of the movement. But it is a baby. A newly hatched, infant dinosaur. The movement had been the raising of its speckled head. The rest of its body is curled in a tight ball between two other eggs, half-shielded by a fragment of its old shell. It's about the size of a dog, soft and fat, clumsy and wide-eyed.

Oomka will have heard my cry. He's probably dragging himself across the clearing now. Although I know there is no way I can logically defend the nest or persuade him not to destroy it, I kneel down beside the baby dinosaur and reach out a shaking finger.

Its small, scaly nose extends, nostrils quivering curiously. I imagine that when our skins touch I will see a flash of images—all the monks this dinosaur will later kill, all the villagers it will devour, all the children it will dismember, all the men, friends and family members it will gun down and destroy. But when its nose touches my finger, nothing happens, except it nuzzles up against my hand, placing its whole head in my fingers and licking my wrist affectionately with a small, bluish tongue. My heart pounds in my ears.

* * *

I leave the house.

Oomka doesn't ask about the interior, or my yell of surprise as I reattach him to my back. I think he is just glad to get away from the place.

At one point during our return to the monastery, we talk about the possibility of a Jeremy village close to the house. "We should send a party back," he eventually says, in a tone that implies he wonders why I have not said it first.

"It was deserted," I say. "Nothing has been there for months."

Chapter Four
The Monastery

Back at the monastery the next morning, the helicopter-sized gongs in the dormitories awaken me. The gongs create pressure-blasts of sound movement as they ring, vibrating the floors and walls and shaking sleepy-eyed monks from their straw mats. I rise with the overwhelming desire to speak with the elders.

The sun has not yet risen, and the monastery is the purplish color of molding fruit. Monks stumble around like zombies, heavy-footed and battle-weary, some with bones protruding at odd angles, thick bandages shielding the majority of others from the crisp morning air.

Distant pterodactyl cries sound eerie in the mostly silent bustle of the monastery common. I feel a rush of intense rage, then sadness.

Unbalanced and confused, I amble through the overgrown grass toward the makeshift tent of the elders. The second tower had been bombed several weeks ago with huge barrels of explosives made from the deadly combination of starfruit and the dinosaurs' digestive juices, launched over the outer walls by iguanodons. It had been the first attack on monastery soil in twenty-five years.

The second tower was the traditional dwelling place of the monastic elders, and was one of the largest of eight buildings in the compound. Immediate inquiries were launched as to the possibility of a breach of security, or an informant to the outside. How, without direct knowledge of our oligarchic system of government (we had previously been sure that the dinosaurs knew little to nothing about our way of life) and a tip as to where the leaders would be sleeping, would the Jeremies have known to hit the second tower?

Once, the eight buildings of the monastic complex were each assigned a unique and holy purpose. Now, most of them house the remaining villagers. One is dedicated to limb-reassignment surgeries, and the other remaining building, the second tower, had, until recently, housed the temple proper and the quarters of the elders.

Chapter Five
The Oft Retold History of
The Venerable Elder Zohar

In the first days of the Jeremy, one of the elders, Elder Zohar, then just a monk a little older than myself, had been involved in one of the most re-told and recounted battles in the history of the monastery.

Back then, most of the forest still teemed with the Steve. Steves were the product of the union of the meditative energy of the monks and the badgers of the forest. The thoughts produced by the monks were most often inclined to manifest as cloudy, indistinct forest creatures. Usually these meditative cloud-beasts wandered jubilantly into the forest as if conscious and accepting of their temporary state. Once in a while, the strong, negative thoughts of a particularly disgruntled monk would take form and go on a rampage, but, thankfully, the badgers steered clear of these creatures, who typically faded to nothing without ever meeting in union to produce a Steve.

The Steve had once been the most common and abundant creature in the mountain forests. They were shy, but not unsocial, and, when coaxed by kind words, they allowed themselves to be pet and caressed. To those they deemed to be of the most even, transcendent temperaments, the Steve spoke, sometimes at length.

The wisdom of the Steve was said to be the most peaceful and natural of all wisdoms.

They were, after all, the product of an immaculate union: human meditation—absolute purity of thought—and the perfect, innocent, wild nature of the forest's most noble beast: the badger.

Even when Zohar was young, the Steve would converse with him freely. Among his favorite were a small fish-headed cat with huge white wings and soft opalescent eyes, and another with the body of a rhino and the head of a rat. *Fish-cat* and *Rat-head* were the names that Zohar, as a young monk, had given them. There were other Steves that came to speak with Zohar, but Fish-cat and Rat-head were his two oldest and dearest friends.

Those two had taught him remarkable things: secrets of the cognitive world and many interesting facts about outer space, to which both had often traveled. But one of the most useful things the Steve had taught Zohar was a magic kung-fu which only he could practice and teach to no other. Many of Zohar's fellow monks were angry and jealous when they saw him practicing the magic kung-fu, and he refused to teach them the secrets the Steve had given him.

Zohar's loyalty to the Steve caused many other monks to dislike him, and Zohar spent numerous hours wandering alone through the forests meditating, sending cloudy beasts out into the undergrowth to copulate with the badgers.

In his lonely wanderings, Zohar learned much about the mountains and the dense forests that surrounded the monastery. He grew familiar with the villages, often staying with his villager friends late into the night, talking and thinking. He knew every secret pathway and every tree like each were his ancestors.

When the first signs of something amiss manifested in the forest, it was Zohar who noticed them long before any other monk. Zohar went to the elders and told them he suspected something was wrong, but they did nothing. They were too busy and thought Zohar was odd for spending so much time alone and away from all the other monks.

Zohar confided his fears to Fish-cat and Rat-head. "Fish-cat, Rat-head," he said as they sat together one day on a log. "I sense something wrong in the forest. There are no new Steves. The sky is always dark and cloudy. There's a strange smell in the air, like meat, and I've heard no birds singing. I haven't seen a badger in a week."

Fish-cat and Rat-head seemed to look at each other briefly. It was hard to tell because one had the head of a fish, and the other's head was so tiny on its massive body that it could hardly turn its head at all.

Before responding, Fish-cat licked its paws with its fish tongue and blinked its milky eyes. "Soon we will be leaving," it said.

"Zohar, the days of the Steve are ending," Rat-head said in a low, rumbling voice. "The Steve cannot survive what is to come."

Zohar, his worst fears confirmed, could do nothing but stare at his knees. He thought about his two best and only friends leaving him and the forest forever. "Where are you going?" he asked. "Can I come, too?"

"No," said Fish-cat. "We won't be far."

This didn't make Zohar feel any better. He felt betrayed and scared for whatever was coming. And worst of all, he could hardly imagine a world without the Steve.

But that world wasn't far from him. In a matter of weeks, the Steve had disappeared without saying a word or leaving a forwarding address. They hadn't even packed up their houses or sold their possessions. It was as if they had all just stopped what they were doing and walked out of the forest together.

The loneliness of Zohar was great. Then the Jeremy attacked.

The first attacks seemed to be solely for the purpose of feeding. They barged into villages in the early spring—smashing houses and tromping gardens—and snatched up all the people they could reach in their huge, razor-filled jaws. After each attack, they withdrew to some secret hiding place no one could find.

The villagers were being eaten by the handful. Villagers that Zohar knew and loved, and only Zohar seemed to care.

He went to the elders and said, "We must do something! We must find a way to protect these villagers!"

But the elders were still too busy, and they thought Zohar probably had something to do with the disappearance of the Steve. They didn't want to talk to him at all.

Enraged, disappointed, hurt, Zohar said goodbye to the elders, packed up all his worldly possessions and left the monastery. Outside the walls, villagers crowded around the door, pleading to be let in for fear that the dinosaurs would eat them. Women and men shoved their children toward Zohar helplessly.

The tents and makeshift shacks leaning against the wall had multiplied since he had been outside the monastery last, and it worried him. He felt a rush of rage and anger. Rage at the elders for not allowing these villagers to take refuge behind the walls, rage at the mysterious carnivorous dinosaurs with a taste for villagers, but especially rage at the Steve for not telling him how to fight back the monstrous beasts, or even why they were here.

All the time Fish-cat and Rat-head had spent rambling on about magnetic force and gravitational pull and the supernovae-ing of stars, they could have prepared him instead for this fight, or armed him with the knowledge he needed to survive. If they hadn't wanted to teach him, they might have at least convinced the elders he was not mad. They might have at least warned someone who had some power and influence, someone who could mobilize the monks and protect the villagers.

Zohar apologized profusely to the men and women huddled against the red walls. "I'm sorry. So sorry," he said. "I've done everything I can."

An old man stood as Zohar passed the disappointed, forlorn faces of the villagers. "But you're running away!" he said, gesturing to the pack of belongings on Zohar's back.

"I must. I've got to try to find the Steve. They can't be far."

The villagers scoffed and shook their heads. "The Steve left us all, left us to be eaten! We need to stand together," the old man said, and then pointing at the monastery's towers: "You have shelter for the women and children. Well, we have the men, strong men with weapons we saved from the wreckage of our houses. We can fight together. Forget the Steve."

"It's no use telling me," Zohar replied, almost impatiently, but trying not to be rude. "I've already told the elders. They just won't allow it. They don't want the fighting."

The old man's eyes flashed. They were wide and dark. "We must fight," he said.

Zohar rubbed the bridge of his nose. The sack of all his worldly possessions was heavy on his back. It was mostly full of the femurs of his ancestors. A family tradition. All together, he had thirteen femurs. Zohar placed them on the sand in front of his feet, wondering how he might respond to the old man's statement.

He did not think fighting was the answer, and knew there must be a way to defeat the Jeremy without violence, without conflict, through peace and reason, through thought and strength of mind. He just wasn't sure what that way was, exactly. He wanted to tell all of this to the man, to all these people, but couldn't find words to make it sensible. He just knew he had to find the Steve. The Steve knew; they had an answer. They would tell him where the dinosaurs had come from and how to send them back and end the bloodshed.

Three small children were playing in the ferns where the edge of the forest met the monastery wall. All giggled secretively, and Zohar sighed. In the silence of this pause, the somewhat distant sound of heavy falling feet, rustling and breaking branches became audible.

The sound grew nearer very fast, and, in a moment, it seemed just behind the green cloak of the forest. The villagers stopped their quiet babbling; the three children in the ferns looked up at their parents with large, round eyes, but did not move. Then, without warning, a giant crested head swung out of the forest and closed around all three of the children with one deft swoop.

A woman screamed.

The dinosaur swallowed the children without chewing. A greenish tongue flicked out of its massive jaws, and it roared mightily, head thrown back in triumph.

Remembering the magic kung-fu the Steve had taught him, Zohar sprinted toward the massive roaring head and, with a single kick, sent the dinosaur sprawling. But the kick only angered it, and it clambered back to its feet, shaking with rage. It roared again. The villagers cringed and huddled closer to the wall. Fear did not enter Zohar. He breathed deeply and waited for the dinosaur to move.

Villagers screamed and cried. The beast smiled at Zohar and charged.

What came next has been retold and recounted so many times that it has attained legendary status in the monastery.

Zohar crouched low to the ground and sprang right into the open mouth of the charging dinosaur. Rows of dagger-like teeth on the lower jaw severed his legs, but Zohar didn't flinch. He wedged himself between the mandible and the skull of the dinosaur, and, following a mighty explosive yank, tore the dinosaur's head off its body. The villagers were silent and scared.

They thought Zohar was dead. Zohar, too, almost thought this. But then he pulled himself up onto the severed head of the dinosaur. He was soaked in reptilian blood, and his legs were about seven feet away from him. They had been cut off directly below the pelvis.

Zohar reached into the esophagus of the dinosaur and pulled out the bodies of the three children, one after the other. They were dead, but at least they were no longer in an esophagus.

Now, Zohar knew what the old man had said was true. They had to fight. But even after the awe-inspiring kung-fu of Zohar defeated a dinosaur outside the very walls of the monastery, the monks still refused to engage the Jeremy.

Luckily, doctors in the infirmary had two spare hands, severed at the wrist during a game of racquetball. In the first of what was to become a myriad of brilliant reassignment surgeries, they immediately fitted the hands to Zohar's pelvis. Zohar was able to walk on his new hands within days, an unprecedented recovery. But significantly slowed by the movement of ten small fingers instead of two big legs, Zohar was forced to stay in the monastery rather than go out in search of the Steve. He eventually succeeded in convincing the elders to allow the villagers to take refuge inside the walls. Angry and heartbroken by the Steve's desertion, Elder Zohar disobeyed the instructions that Fish-cat and Rat-head had given him regarding the magic kung-fu, and he taught every monk that would listen how to practice it. It wasn't long before he forgot about looking for the Steve altogether and turned the considerable powers of his mind toward fighting the Jeremy.

Chapter Six
Take the Elephant Gun

Elder Zohar is the most respected and revered elder. He is also the oldest, but not because he is very old. Dinosaurs have eaten most of the other elders.

It is Elder Zohar who sits in the makeshift temple-tent when I enter. Well, he may actually be standing. It is hard to tell because, in standing mode, his fingers raise him only about three inches above the ground.

His back is slightly bent. His smooth, shaven head glimmers in the candlelight. I feel bad disturbing his prayer, so I linger at the back of the tent and wait for him to rise. I am only there a moment before a low voice says, "Please, come sit by me."

I tiptoe toward him and kneel at his side. His lower fingers un-flex, and he rests on his palms. He doesn't turn to face me, but stays in this hunched position, bowing slightly toward the rough-hewn gray stone idol with its glimmering golden face. "You seem troubled," he says after several full minutes of silence.

"Yes," I respond, things flickering through my mind like it's fast-forwarding the last three months: Chip's dismemberment, the battle last night, the pterodactyl's tears, Oomka's ribcage catching us as we tore through the sky, the slender body between the trees, the house, the baby dinosaur and the look on Oomka's face when I told him nothing was there.

"I heard news about Oomka," Elder Zohar says, his tone conversational. "They'll be able to give him a leg from the knee down."

I nod, my throat choked by the things I feel compelled to divulge.

After several more minutes of silence, Elder Zohar turns his face toward me. His skin is unlined and youthful, his eyes bright and penetrating. I look at them for only a moment before flicking my eyes back to the idol. "You are feeling uneasy," Elder Zohar says. "Pray, meditate and converse with your spirit."

I nod again, my body close to exploding with words I can't quite form. Another minute goes by. Finally he says, "Take the day, walk in the south fields. Bring an elephant gun and some extra ammunition."

Elder Zohar flexes his thumbs and rises onto the tips of his fingers without another word. I watch him go, wanting desperately to call out. But, in moments, he has scuttled out of the tent, the door flapping lamely in the breeze behind him.

Feeling worse than when I entered the tent, I leave several minutes after Elder Zohar.

The sky is still dark and stormy when I step outside. It seems to reflect my conversation with the elder. I consider my odd behavior, and my body seizes up with sudden embarrassment and anxiety. But I decide it best, after all, to take the elder's advice and go to the armory for an elephant gun.

The elephant gun is fitted with a tall, stainless steel, eyeball-like periscope that extends above my head for a full, elevated, 360-degree view. Extra ammunition is stored in barrels by the doors to the armory. I seize a few elephant gun cartridges. The large plastic capsules are warm in my hands.

In the south fields—once brimming with vegetable gardens, rows of wheat and rice, heads of cattle and flocks of sheep that speckled the hills in the distance—everything is flat and silent. When the Jeremy came, all the crops and livestock had to be moved inside the walls, as the dinosaurs' frequent rampages around the monastery had crushed and destroyed most of the crop. I could not remember the taste of fresh vegetables, although once, in my extreme youth, I must have had an abundance of them—as all young monks did—but in the last twenty-five years, the paltry, shade-stunted vegetables we had been able to produce had to be cooked, softened and blessed before consumption.

Things like vegetables were the easiest to forget. What was more difficult was forgetting the freedom and child-made hugeness of the land outside the monastery, the exquisite peace of wandering through forests unmarred by death and made warm and quiet by the presence of the Steve.

Due to my young age, I had never spoken to a Steve before they disappeared. I had glimpsed them several times on forest walks, but was confused and curious that everyone seemed so sad about their disappearance. I did not feel the coolness, or the subtle changes in the direction of plant leaves. I did not feel the absence of badgers.

In the south fields, I sit in the tall grass with the elephant gun over my knees.

I think about the end of days, the explosion of the center of the planet, the old man and the old woman, and if they will ever meet.

I think about how they must be lonely, about how they never search for each other, about how hopeless and disbelieving they are that a companion lurks just out of sight.

Some infant dinosaurs frolic in the overgrown wheat some distance away. Often, baby dinosaurs play here. We watch them from the walls of the monastery, but don't shoot them because they are just out of range. I wonder if this is why Elder Zohar sent me out here. If he really did know what was troubling me and wanted me to see these infant dinosaurs frolicking in the overgrown wheat, like children, awkward, clumsy and in need of protection.

But he had sent me with an elephant gun and extra ammunition. My stomach lurches uncomfortably.

* * *

I am gazing through the periscope from my low position in the wheat when a flash of movement in the corner of the sight catches my eye. I swivel the periscope around a bit and adjust the lens. Near the baby dinosaurs, a tall, slender form watches from the trees. I recognize this shape immediately. It's the one I saw before we found the dinosaur house, between the trees in the heat-waving forest.

It's certainly a dinosaur. But I don't recognize the species or any of the features. In fact, it's like nothing I've ever seen, in physical aspect or in dress. This dinosaur wears a pinkish robe, similar in shape and proportionate length to our own monk robes. No weapons are slung across its chest, no guns or blades clutched in its claws. I have never seen anything so incongruous.

But strangest of all is the shape of its body. No plates or spines or spikes mark its back, no knobby reptilian skin-warts. Its bluish-gray skin looks smooth and leathery. Its snout is flattened, like a bill, and it has large teal eyes.

A whole new species of dinosaur, just as Chip had said must exist. I'm so amazed I can barely register what I'm looking at. I need to see it closer. I need to know it. I feel so sure I should touch this dinosaur—be close to it and, if possible, speak with it. I'm barely able to disconnect myself from the periscope for fear I might lose sight of it forever.

I drop the gun and scramble, half-crawling, through the wheat. For the first few yards the dinosaur continues to stand still at the edge of the forest, watching the baby dinosaurs play. I know a triceratops or a stegosaurus is somewhere close by, supervising the infants. I veer to the left through an old fence and scurry along the rows of empty stalks.

As I near the dinosaur, she (for I am now sure it is a she) turns casually and begins to walk back into the forest. I want to cry out as fear stabs through me, but I know I would only reveal myself to the babysitter in the trees. So I run faster, tearing through dead plants, my heart pounding, feeling my robes rip and snag on thorns and protruding branches.

When I reach the edge of the forest, she is nowhere to be seen. All that remains to indicate her presence is a faint, fresh-cut tomato scent. I inhale deeply.

This is not the typical smell of a dinosaur, but it can only be her smell; it is so airy and light. I run up the mountain, following the path of the scent on the breeze, praying no other dinosaur will intercept me.

Soon enough, I hear footsteps up ahead. But as I approach somewhat noisily through the undergrowth, the footsteps stop, pause and start again, quicker. She must sense she is being followed.

I run to keep up, catching flashes of bluish-gray limbs and wafts of tomato scent as my feet pound away beneath me. Trees and branches whip my face and bare arms. Suddenly, I lose the trail of the dinosaur.

I continue in the direction I am heading, but find no sign of her. I stumble into a large clearing in the forest, legs aching. I clutch my sides, breathing heavily. Here, the forest floor is awash in tiny yellow flowers floating in a sea of pale green grass. Standing like ghosts all across the field: the jagged remains of long-since exploded plasticized dinosaurs. Spines and skulls lay in random piles or curl like barbed wire from the statues. The yellow flowers lap against flesh-colored plastic like waves. Across the field: a flash of blue.

"Wait!" I call, my first utterance rolling over the somber graveyard field like merry-making, seeming perverse and insensitive.

The dinosaur stops. She looks straight at me. The muscles of my stomach tighten like I'm going to be sick.

"Wait," I say again, not moving for fear of frightening her. "I don't want to hurt you."

She blinks her huge round eyes, the color and the texture of a tropical sea. Little splashes of light play in them like sun on waves. I want to swallow, but the lump in my throat is too big. We stare at each other across the plastic corpse-casts of Jeremies. She looks about to flee, but then I feel my arm reach out toward her.

We are across the field from one another, but this gesture seems to make her pause. She looks around at the plastic exoskeletons, her face seeming pained, although, being unaccustomed to reading the expressions of dinosaurs, it is hard for me to tell.

"We don't want this to happen," I say, not knowing why I'm speaking, or even quite what I'm saying. "*I* don't want this to happen. But I don't understand why…" My words trail into silence.

She blinks again slowly, eyes sparkling, and again I smell the powerful, tomato-y bitterness of her, like fresh growing things, like life.

She folds her claws in front of her chest. Her eyes flicker to the ground. "Neither do I," she says. Her voice is clear and calm. "It's a shame and a waste."

My heart pounds. I can't believe I'm speaking to a dinosaur.

She takes a step forward, and so do I.

"What is your name?" I ask, taking yet another step.

"Petunia," she replies, and I think I see the hint of a smile on her bill-like face.

"Where do you come from?" I ask.

"The top of the mountain." She has taken another step forward now as well. Her steps are much larger than mine.

"Why have I never seen you?" I ask. At the same time, we both seem to realize the strange weight of this statement.

"We don't fight with the other dinosaurs. We are different."

"Oh," I say. "Right."

"I have to go." She looks over her shoulder. "I'm expected. I'll be missed."

"No, wait," I say once again. Taking several more bold steps forward,

I reach out my hand. I expect her to step back, but she doesn't. Instead, she reaches her long clawed arm toward me, and the very tips of our fingers touch. "Meet me here tomorrow," I say.

She squints down at me; her eyes flick to the tips of our fingers.

I pray she doesn't draw back her hand. "Meet me here," I repeat, deliberately, strongly, like an order.

Finally, she nods, pulls away. Our fingers disconnect.

"Meet me tomorrow," I say again.

She whirls around and trots off into the trees, disappearing in a matter of seconds as the steep incline buries her in leaves.

* * *

There are low clouds in the sky, still gray and ominous, as I turn and head back to the south fields.

The chase must have gone on much longer than I had thought, because it seems to already be getting dark. I feel exposed and vulnerable now, walking in the forest without a weapon. I haven't been outside the monastery walls without a gun in my hand since the age of seven. As I walk, the shapes in the trees and the gray sky and the fast-coming darkness all seem menacing. I think of fashioning a spear, or something out of a tree branch, before going on, but I don't want to waste any more daylight.

* * *

As I descend the mountain, a column of smoke becomes visible through a break in the trees, out toward the monastery. I stop. In the absence of my footsteps, I hear distant roars and explosions.

Another attack.

I shiver, cold sweat erupts all over my body, and I sprint as fast as I can through the undergrowth. Several seconds later, my foot catches on an exposed root, and I fly through the air, landing in a crumpled heap in the dirt. Staggering to my feet, I am overpowered by the nauseating smell of meat. Jeremies. Close.

I don't have the elephant gun.

I am scared.

I continue running, each leaping footfall skidding in the soft, mossy dirt. The sky is darker. Suddenly, a flash of red light from near the monastery.

The forest thins. I near the edge of the field. The infant dinosaurs that had been playing there have gone and, with them, their much more threatening babysitter. I should have encountered at least one watch post, but no one has called out to me. They are all fighting. Or dead.

Trying once more to shield my mind from a creeping sensation of panic, I surround my sweating body with stars and galaxies, all spinning around and elongated as if I am seeing them through glass. The stars speak to me: "Don't worry, monk, you are not a physical body. You are only a series of still images conjured into existence by three objective perceivers. They make you. They draw and project you. No Jeremy can hurt you. No dinosaur can eat you. You are not a physical body." But my suspended body is muddy, so I know it exists. "Fuck you!" I yell at the stars and galaxies, and they withdraw.

I still don't have the elephant gun.

What am I going to do when I reach the battle? Can I sneak around to the southern field and pick up the elephant gun? That's ridiculous. It's lying flat in a field of tall wheat stalks. It'll probably take me until morning to find it. And the battery will be dead. And it looks as if it's rained down here, so it'll be wet. I swear aloud a few more times. If Jeremies are sitting on watch, they'll have already heard me stumbling down the mountain for the last fifteen minutes. The smell of meat intensifies.

I hear the sounds of cannons firing and trees splintering in front of and behind me now. Explosive shots light up small areas of conflict under the forest canopy. I see the massive head of a tyrannosaurus roaring, shots being fired from some monks at the knee-level of a stegosaurus with a huge battle-axe. Bits of the forest are illuminated by burning corpses, mostly monks, some villagers. I pass a Jeremy, half-encased in plastic, beside one flaming corpse. He screams in pain as the flames lick his encased bottom half, melting away the plastic.

I have slowed my pace. Individual fights rage throughout the underbrush.

I am almost caught in the crossfire of a close-range shooting battle. I duck to the ground at the last second. Both Jeremies are encased. I run past the cheering monks without stopping or acknowledging their calls.

I think I catch a glimpse of Oomka hopping on his single central foot through the trees, but it could be some other monk. Up ahead, a tree is on fire. The flames shed light over the immediate area. Plastic dinosaurs litter the forest floor. Flesh and bones are spread around too, the obliterated remains of monks.

I don't have the elephant gun. I don't have any gun. I don't even have a knife. There are roars and gunshots and sounds of screaming from every side.

This attack must have been huge, one of the largest in years. I pick up my pace again and sprint toward the monastery walls.

I pass three separate defense lines around the monastery. The first is recovering from a brachiosaurus attack. Farther down, a pile of cleanly severed limbs tells me that pterodactyls have been here with their samurai swords.

The lines grow disordered as I approach the doors. Medics run close to the walls, harvesting useful limbs from piles of monk flesh.

Suddenly, something whizzes past my face, a loose rotating saw blade. It ricochets off the wall and slams into my side. It stops against my spine, but has already severed my arm. A medic runs toward me. I see him pick up my arm. I fall to the ground.

* * *

I am on an island in the center of the planet. Rocks shaped like trees are everywhere, and on the ground, miniscule trees shaped like rocks. I am treading on the soft rock trees with my bare feet.

I think I am alone. I think I am very old. My hands are curled up and wrinkled. I feel content. Fireflies swarm high above me. They make a sound like electric lights or an idling engine. Then I am floating over the island, drifting lazily between the leaves of the tree rocks, dragging my toes through the yellow glowing sun bar of fireflies. They kiss my toes, and I laugh.

I feel a tug on my arm and look down to see Petunia reaching up into the sky. Her hand is wrapped around mine. She is pulling me down. I am in her arms. I feel as if a bluish-gray cloud has encased me.

Petunia is very old as well. She is stooped, her soft leathery skin wrinkled and pockmarked. She smiles warmly at me. Her face is familiar and comforting. I am in her arms, and she walks with me toward a house in the tree rocks. Above us, the fireflies are beginning to descend, one by one, until they fall in a torrent, a deluge of fireflies. They swirl through the air as I push the door open in front of Petunia. We enter our house.

So do the fireflies.

They light on every surface. They

land on high-backed chairs and a little fireplace. They land on a worn-out rug and a big couch with soft cushions. Petunia's arms, wrapped around my body, are covered in fireflies.

We are so old.

We feel very tired all of a sudden, and so we lie down together, on the old worn-out rug, surrounded by dancing fireflies. We fall asleep gazing into one another's eyes.

Chapter Seven
Surprise Attack

It has not been very long. It is still dark. The sky is a dusky orange-ish gray. A shadowy line of treetops flickers with lights from fires in the south fields.

Several firefights still rage in the distance. I hear gunshots and the ping of plastic cartridges discharging.

My temples throb, and my first thought is that the medics have harvested the rest of my limbs and left me for dead on the battlefield. To my relief, I find most of my appendages still intact. I sit up. My right side feels strangely light. Blood trickles in a steady stream from the place where my arm had been, and a large triangular chunk cut out of my side exposes some muscle, ribs and an organ I can't identify.

Columns of smoke continue to rise from the forest north of the monastery. No other monks are in sight; at least not any who could be resurrected by the medics.

It's probably best to get inside. I clamber to my feet, feeling unsteady.

Inside the monastery walls, I'm told by seven separate monks to get to the temple tent. They push me, like they don't think I'm capable of moving myself. I allow my body to be hurried along, still slightly dazed.

Oomka is inside the tent. He looks better than he did the day before yesterday. The medics have attached a leg from the knee down to his sternum. He is a little taller than Elder Zohar now. I look at him curiously, but he doesn't say anything. His eyes are on the ground in front of Elder Zohar, who rests on the knuckles of his hands, looking at a hand-drawn map in front of him.

"You're here," he says. "Finally." He scratches his chin and then points to the map, his small, beady eyes darting up to look at me after a moment. His gaze sweeps over my missing arm, but he doesn't say anything about it.

"You and Oomka are to take an attack party and approach the site from the east. The rocky ground there will hide you until you're practically on top of them."

Oomka still looks deliberately at the map, his brow furrowed.

"Sorry, on top of who?" I ask.

Elder Zohar's eyes narrow, boring uncomfortably into mine. I turn my eyes away just as he opens his mouth to speak. "The Jeremy nest," he says. "Elder Bradley and I agree that we cannot risk the nest being inhabited. It may have appeared deserted, but that is no guarantee the animals are gone for good. Best to destroy it before anything can return."

"Wait," I say without thinking, without knowing what I am going to say afterwards.

Elder Zohar's gaze narrows again, and his eyes dig into my skull, filling my brain cavity with searching, grasping, multi-jointed, tentacle-like fingers. I feel as if he knows what I am thinking. But that's impossible. I see Oomka's eyes flicker up to mine, then back down to the map. I am thinking again about Chip, inside the stomach of a stegosaurus encased in plastic. I am suddenly revolted with myself. "All right," I say, "but I need a gun."

The Elder nods.

* * *

The mountain seems eerily silent after the remnant snatches of battle have faded behind us. No one speaks as we march up the mountain, led by Oomka on his new leg, hopping with a strange determination I have never seen in him. He does not fidget. I watch as familiar portions of forest pass beneath our feet. The hike up the mountain is taking a significantly shorter time than the hike down, despite the fact that we are now laden with plastic ray guns and flame throwers and are traveling up a steep incline.

Before we even catch a glimpse of the clearing in the trees, we hear the sounds of muffled voices.

The house is in sight, its little shuttered windows thrown open to the night air. Smells of cooking and the now-obvious sounds of baby Jeremy squealing and stamping around inside hit the party some twenty feet outside the clearing. The three other monks exchange significant looks. Beads of sweat form on my forehead despite the coolness of the night. I feel a hotness rush through the empty space where my right arm had been, like it is still attached.

At a sign from Oomka, the three other monks rush forward. Oomka vaults himself over the rocky outcrop behind which I still crouch. Using the gun in his hand as a second leg, he hobbles after them quickly.

Flames explode from the guns of the three monks closest to the house, bursting through a window. Screams from inside. The door swings open. The face of a Jeremy appears. Before the Jeremy can register the presence of attackers, Oomka has encased it. Another is close behind. The Jeremy shoves its encased mate through the doorway carelessly, shotgun in hand. Two explosive shots ring out. One monk lets out a scream. A gaping, badger-sized hole through his torso, he falls to his knees, dropping the flamethrower, which ignites the tall grass in the clearing. His body collapses upon itself, and he disappears in the flaming grass.

I leap over the rock, imagining I am leaping into the ocean. Instead of this murderous tyrannosaurus wielding a fourteen-foot shotgun loaded with badger-sized buckshot, blue whales circle slowly around me, singing softly, their music low and soothing, but pervasive, everywhere, filling the water, wrapping itself around me like a cashmere cocoon.

High screeching sounds emanate from the house. A pillar of flames reaches up above the tops of the trees.

Oomka takes aim at the second tyrannosaurus and shoots, but his shot misses by an inch and lands on the roof of the smoldering home. The plastic bubbles and smokes. One of the other monks aims his flamethrower at the Jeremy. Oomka takes another shot, this time making contact. The Jeremy is frozen mid-scream in flesh-colored plastic, jaw stretched wide, the shotgun aimed at Oomka's head.

It is suddenly quiet. The sound of crackling flames is the only sound now. I walk around the home, searching the white and yellow flames and thick black columns of smoke for signs of life. I am on the opposite side of the burning home from Oomka.

There is a rustle in the tall grass. I kneel.

It is a baby Jeremy, crawling soundlessly, clutching at the grass and dirt with its tiny front arms, dragging its legs along behind it. Its eyes are huge in its skull, and beneath the sound of the house burning I hear it breathing short, heavy breaths.

The remaining monks follow me around the house.

I stand and crush its skull with the heel of my foot.

It folds so easily, like a deflating basketball. The body stops moving.

I think of Petunia. My lost arm throbs painfully.

* * *

The next morning, I awake before the other monks. In the hall at breakfast, I listen to them as they mutter to each other. They say that someone is telling the Jeremy how to break through our defenses. The attack last night was the most devastating in years, and so soon after the last one. It doesn't make any sense; something is different, they say. There's a spy. They glare around with suspicious, furrowed eyebrows.

I swallow.

With a pang of sadness, I imagine what Chip would think if he knew where I had been yesterday. Then I think of my heel crushing the soft skull of the baby dinosaur. I feel nauseated. But the Jeremy, as Chip would have said, are not people; they are not monks. They are animals, beasts, dinosaurs.

Petunia.

A red rush of confusion and pain. I feel imaginary blood pulse through the imaginary fingertips of my left arm. I cannot bring myself to say Petunia is not a person, is not a monk, is an animal, a beast, a dinosaur.

I feel I am going insane.

The air in the hall is oppressive and thick.

I wonder where Oomka is, and how he is doing after the attack last night.

I glance around the hall one last time and walk out into the commons. Oomka is probably sitting by himself somewhere, away from the other monks.

Sure enough, I find him on a bench by the rock garden. He is significantly shorter now, his half-leg attached right at the sternum of his remaining ribcage, which has been mostly bandaged shut. He is sort of balancing on the knee with his head bent upward a little.

He doesn't look too bad. The wounds are obviously still healing, but they are much less terrifying than they had been, and not at all the worst this monastery's monks have faced.

Still, he looks up at me somewhat sullenly as I approach. "Where were you yesterday? Are you all right?" he asks, eyeing my missing arm, but not with pity or concern.

"Oh, it's nothing," I say, brushing a hand across the remaining portion of my shoulder. It itches, but it doesn't exist. "How's your leg?"

"It's great," he says with almost-convincing bravado.

"It's just going to take some getting used to," I say, trying to smile kindly while taking a seat on the bench behind him.

"The battle was really something last night," Oomka says. "Probably the most Jeremy we've ever seen at once."

"It looked awful. I got there toward the end, but I'd lost my weapon."

We fall awkwardly silent.

"What were you doing yesterday?" he asks after a moment.

"I was on an assignment from the elder," I lie. Well, it isn't exactly a lie. It *had* been Elder Zohar's suggestion that I visit the south fields.

I think of Petunia, her gray-blue skin and her smooth, soft bill, the electric feeling of her hand touching mine.

Oomka does not respond.

"I've got another assignment, well, for this morning..." I say hesitantly, wondering with a sinking feeling if, after the battle last night, Petunia will still be waiting in the clearing in the south forest.

Oomka nods. "That's fine. I can cover for you on watch. There shouldn't be any trouble today. After last night, you know."

I nod and stand to leave.

"Bye then," Oomka says, his eyes narrowing slightly as if he has something else to say, but he doesn't say anything.

"See you tonight."

"Be careful," he says.

"You too."

I walk out of the monastery, unarmed, for the second time.

Chapter Eight
Fragrant Dinosaur Skin

Petunia stands in the center of the clearing. In a circle around her, a spot of sunlight shines down from the stormy sky. It's as if she's glowing.

I make some noise as I step into the little meadow, so I don't startle her.

She turns around and looks at me with her huge, heart-swallowing eyes. My stomach churns again. I feel suddenly conscious of my body, my missing arm, my bare, leathery feet.

"What happened?" she asks, eyeing my arm-less shoulder with her brow raised in an expression of concern.

"Oh nothing," I respond quickly, brushing the wound as I had done when responding to the same inquiry from Oomka.

She bends low, her face close to mine. My heart is beating so loud it echoes in the space between us, like someone snapping a rubber band.

Her clawed finger brushes the still oozing wound, and it is then I hear her heartbeat, too—the sound between us is the meeting of the two beats, synchronized perfectly.

As before, Petunia and I have the same thought at the same moment. Her face is close to mine, her clawed finger lingering just above my shoulder. Our breaths seem like those of one body. Her eyes are wide, their glassy surfaces sparkling with the reflection of the yellow flower-strewn meadow grass, like multitudes of winking stars in a brightening teal-dawn sky.

Finally, Petunia breaks our silence. "I want to show you something." She bends low to allow me to clamber onto her back where I perch between her massive shoulder blades. I hold tight to her neck, and she races off into the forest.

I have never experienced anything quite like this sensation of movement. Wind rushes past me and around me, lifting my robes and chilling my skin. Leaves and branches whip my legs. I try hard to hold on, but my single arm won't reach all the way around her neck, so I grasp at her leathery hide.

"Am I hurting you?" I ask, speaking loudly in the wind.

She seems to chuckle a little as her wide steps carry us up the mountain. "No," she says, turning her head around a little so I can see one round, teal eye. Her face is crinkled in a smile. "Your hand feels nice."

A rushing wall of green comes into focus as we slow. We're nearing the edge of a steep cliff. When we stop, her heart beats loudly beneath me. I lay my palm, trembling, against the side of her neck and feel blood course through her veins in bursts.

At the edge of the tree line, we look out to where the undergrowth thins and the beginnings of a steep rocky slope become visible.

"You can get off," she says, and I slide reluctantly from her back.

She catches me with an arm and lowers me to the ground. I walk toward the precipice. "I wanted you to see them," she says. She is smiling again. I am sure of that now.

I peer down into the little valley below. The view is beautiful. We are almost all the way up the south face of the mountain. There is no sign of humans, monks, or Jeremy for miles in every direction. A fork of lightening far in the distance lights up the gray horizon.

At first, the valley appears covered in a thin mist, but, as I gaze down at the treetops, I see them quiver and shift— sparkling, thin wisps of smoke shivering in and out of existence like a badly-tuned TV, some twisting around trees and diving up and down jubilantly. They remind me of something I have seen before, but I can't place the memory.

Petunia smiles. "They belong to us, to the trachodon. Other dinosaurs who come to the top of the mountain to live with us send them out, too. They only last a while, but they're beautiful, aren't they?"

I realize these are thoughts—trachodon thoughts—much smaller and less solid than the thoughts of monks. They look like the thoughts of children, but they *are* beautiful, like she said. Questions erupt across my mind, but I am captivated by the wisps of thought flickering like clouds of shifting fireflies.

I smile at Petunia. "They're amazing," I say. I wish I were large enough to carry her, to wrap all the way around her and lift her up into the air with me. I wish I were a huge pterodactyl with a wingspan longer than the entire monastery, so I could take her up in my giant claws and fly away from the forest, over the mountain, across the ocean. As we look at each other, there's no doubt in my mind that she's thinking the same thing. My mind feels calm and soft, like a ripe peach. I feel as if nothing could hurt me, like the whole rest

of the universe is made of soft peaches, too. And what can soft fruit do to soft fruit? I place a hand on Petunia's knee, the highest place I can reach. The place where our skin meets is like a warm pillow. "Let's go," she says after we have stood there for a few minutes. "That storm is coming our way."

Glad to be on Petunia's back again, I clamber up with her help and snuggle into her fragrant dinosaur skin. "Your eyelashes tickle," she giggles. I squeeze her tight with my whole body, and she laughs as we begin the descent.

* * *

After bidding Petunia goodbye and arranging to meet here again tomorrow, I tromp noisily through the forest. The soft peachiness of my mind seems to cushion the sounds, making everything fuzzy and indistinct. I'm lost in the memory of Petunia's body.

It has begun to rain, and I hear the pattering on the canopy above, but only the occasional drop makes it through the roof of trees.

Chapter Nine
Sharing a Dream

Early in the morning, I pace the hallway of the monk's dormitory. Through a window the sky is starless, but not yet gray with pre-dawn light. My eyes feel raw and sore.

I have been awake all night, reading and re-reading all of the major texts on the Jeremy for some hint, some allusion to the trachodons or their thoughts, anything that would explain what Petunia had shown me.

Eventually, I decide to go down to the temple-tent and meditate. No one will be there this early, so I can avoid the company of other monks. Even the calm, rhythmic sounds of their nighttime breathing make me anxious.

The commons are as quiet as the dormitory. I cross the sandy paths, listening for dinosaurs in the distance. On the mountainsides to the south, small lights from campfires flicker through the trees. I can't tell whether they are the fires of the monks or the Jeremy. There are no sounds and no other sign that living things still inhabit the valley. Everything is still.

When I enter the tent, I sense immediately that I am not alone. My heart pounding in my chest, I feel imaginary blood coursing through non-existent fingertips again. The shrine is dark, the only light coming from a single candle lit in one corner. A shadow low to the ground shifts a little, and I search around for something to throw, something to stab, but, before I can locate a weapon, the shadow shifts into the light.

It is Elder Zohar.

I exhale a huge sigh.

His eyes and partially open mouth are three black holes in the light. I am speechless, relieved and a little revolted. He kneels on the knuckles of his lower hands.

"Come closer. You are not interrupting anything," says Elder Zohar in a low, tired voice.

I kneel in front of the shrine beside him once more, feeling anxious and worried. Perhaps coming to the temple-tent had not been a good idea. After a moment, Elder Zohar speaks in his breathy voice. "You have been troubled these past days."

I am silent. I can't think of a response to this statement. Not one I should divulge to an elder, at least.

"Do you have anything you wish to tell me?" he continues.

As before, thoughts rush into my mind, questions that maybe Elder Zohar would be able to answer.

We sit in silence for a moment more. Outside the tent, a bird sings. It is the first living sound of the morning, apart from the sound of Elder Zohar's voice, if that can be said to have been a living sound. Grayness will seep in through the rough canvas of the tent. The giant morning gongs will be struck. Monks will rise. More fighting. More carnage. In only a few minutes.

"Actually," I say, my voice loud in the empty temple tent. "Actually, yes. Well, I have a question."

Elder Zohar inclines his bald head attentively.

"I wanted to ask you if...well... if the Jeremy have thoughts. I mean, do they make thoughts, like the monks used to?" I ask carefully.

Elder Zohar is silent for a few minutes, but I can tell he is contemplating my question. I already feel relieved. Elder Zohar, in his wisdom, will be able to offer a suitable explanation for what I have seen, for what I am feeling, an explanation that neither the books of the library, nor my own meditations could provide.

"The Jeremy are not monks," Elder Zohar says after a few minutes of silence. "They are not people; they are animals, beasts, dinosaurs. They have no thoughts." He turns toward me. His eyes are black holes again, but I see a reflective sparkle at the center of each lightless pit. "You already know this."

My heart pounds again. Petunia's face. The skull of the baby dinosaur. Chip's last screams. Anger and revulsion and pity and sadness and, most of all, confusion shakes me. I make to stand up without response, but the elder places a warm hand on the remaining piece of my shoulder.

"Go where you will today," Elder Zohar says. "Walk in the forest." He sighs deeply and pats my shoulder affectionately, as if he understands my thoughts. "Finish your business there, but remember what I have told you, and remember what you already know."

I am confused by this advice. But I nod and lift the flap. I walk several paces and stop. I hear voices back in the tent. At first, I think Elder Zohar is simply praying aloud, but then there is another voice. I step lightly around to the back of the shrine.

"I want you to follow our friend today, watch where he goes," Elder Zo-har's voice says.

"Do you think he is the spy?" With a stomach–plunging chill, I recognize Oomka's voice.

"I cannot say just yet, but follow him, report only to me, tell no one where you are going."

Rage. Sadness. I rub my arm stump and head toward the armory.

I figure it is less suspicious to be seen sneaking out of the monastery armed than unarmed. I will take the elephant gun.

* * *

The sky is lighter, a dusty pink. The storm clouds that have hung low around the mountaintops have receded. Bare yellow rays of sun shoot up from the horizon now. I swing the elephant gun over my back and start out across the south fields.

If Oomka is following me, he won't be able to hide himself well in the open field, recently ravaged by battle. Bits of ground still smolder gently. I glance quickly over my shoulder and see Oomka hop behind the leg of a plastic tyrannosaur. Oomka may be many things, but stealthy is not one of them. I wonder why the elder would send Oomka, of all the monks, to tail me.

I'll lose him easily in the labyrinthine mountain forest. Only I know where I am headed. I quicken my pace upon entering the trees. Oomka still hops on his lower arm about a hundred yards behind, using his two original arms as crutches.

I cut through the forest diagonally, heading in the opposite direction of my destination. After fifteen minutes of jogging through undergrowth, I am convinced I have lost him. I stand still in the forest, listening to the blood pounding in my ears and the distant sounds of pterodactyls. There is no sign of Oomka.

Satisfied, I head toward the clearing.

I will see Petunia.

I will climb up onto her smooth dinosaur back and hold her closely with all of my remaining limbs.

Rays of sunshine shimmer in the dusty green and yellow air of the forest. My mouth is dry and my hand is hot and sweaty. I feel warm and bright.

* * *

Petunia follows me. I hear her massive crashing dinosaur steps a few yards away. It must be tedious for her to walk this slowly behind me, but I don't know how to explain where we are going.

I turn to face her. She is closer than I expect. My heart leaps in surprise, and the sudden closeness overwhelms me. I want to bury my whole body in the curve of her neck. Instead, I run a hand over her lowered bill. "I wanted to show you this place. It's where my friend Chip is... well, it's where he died." I gesture through the trees, and Petunia looks past me. She straightens up a little. Her head rises out of reach.

We are actually quite close to the monastery, but few people ever come this way. There are no wanderers in the forest anymore.

Towering above us is the plasticized corpse of a stegosaurus. The Jeremy was huge, even for its species. It has not exploded its shell because it was not fully encased. The yellowish bone of its back leg is visible, protruding through the flesh-colored plastic. On its face is a look of rage, I imagine, although its plastic features are hard to read. I glance back at Petunia as I lay a hand on the leg of the stegosaurus.

"He's in there," I say. "He was my best friend."

Hot tears gather in my eyes, but I look up and blink them back. I don't want to cry in front of Petunia.

I can't explain to her what it meant to lose Chip. That it was like losing the most sensible part of myself. That it had been worse than the loss of my arm, worse than being doubted by all the monks.

Petunia seems to scowl. It takes me a moment to realize she isn't scowling in confusion or anger. Instead, she's sad like me.

"I don't understand why this is happening," I say again.

"It won't go on forever," Petunia says. I don't understand this.

"Why don't the trachodons help us? If there are other types of Jeremy," I pause, looking to see if this word has offended her, but she stares unblinkingly into my eyes. "If there are other types of dinosaurs, why don't they help the monks? We could stop all of this. We could fight."

Petunia rubs her chin and sighs, "They're waiting for a sign. That's all I can tell you."

I feel frustrated and angry and can't seem to detach myself here, sitting beside the stegosaurus that ate Chip.

She leans forward and lifts me up in her dinosaur arms. I curl myself around her neck, holding her the best I can in my condition. She sits against the leg of the stegosaurus and rocks me back and forth. Little spots of sunshine drift in and out of the trees, highlighting bits of forest, bits of Petunia, bits of the stegosaurus that ate Chip. I feel light, like I am being carried out to sea.

Petunia's skin is warm and soft. I am inside of it, like Chip is inside the stegosaurus. It is dark because my eyes are closed, but points of light shine through from outside. I realize the light is coming through two windows. I didn't know Petunia's body had windows. I call out to Chip, but he doesn't answer. I knock on one of the window-panes. No answer there, either.

I can't see any way out, but don't feel trapped. I feel enclosed and enveloped, peaceful, like I am wrapped in the skin of a peach, like I am wearing a huge badger-skin coat, like I am swaying in the ocean.

Through the window, I see Petunia and me sleeping together beneath the stegosaurus. Petunia looks beautiful and serene. Her eyes are closed, but on her face is a ghostly smile. I think she is dreaming. I wonder if we are dreaming together. I hope we are.

Then, suddenly, like steam erupting from a teakettle, two wisps of smoke emerge from us. They entwine and merge so quickly I can't tell whether they were ever separate at all. The thoughts swirl around above us, growing increasingly opaque with each turn.

Within seconds, they have become a thick, grayish blob hovering in mid-air. The blob seems to open its mouth, and I hear a shrill cry. I feel myself, the self outside of Petunia, shiver. The blob plunges into my head.

I awake with a start. Petunia curls herself a little tighter around me. I am wrapped in the warm folds of her skin. My head throbs. As I stir, Petunia turns to look at me.

"Were you dreaming?" she asks.

"Yes," I say, rubbing my temples. There is a large lump on my forehead. I prod it with a finger, and stars explode in my eyes. "I have a terrible headache." I rest my throbbing head against Petunia's stomach.

"I wonder what time it is?" she says, looking up at the sky. "I need to get back to the top of the mountain before dark."

I want to tell Petunia that I was inside her; I want to tell her about the grayish blob and the windows, but, before I can speak, there is a rustle in the trees a few yards away. Petunia sits up abruptly. I slip to the ground.

"What was that?" she whispers.

I grab for the elephant gun and aim

it at the rustling. "Maybe a badger, or a squirrel," I say, praying I'm right.

"It seemed larger," she says, standing up.

"Oomka?" I whisper, almost under my breath. A horrible chill settles over the forest.

A one-legged shape bounds out of the trees, back toward the monastery. I can't shoot the elephant gun. I look up at Petunia.

"Who was that," she says. It doesn't seem like a question.

"Not sure. Get back to the trachodons," I say before touching her outstretched dinosaur hand one last time.

She seems to sense the unease in my voice and bounds away without another word.

* * *

My head pounds; the lump swells. It is now roughly the size and shape of an orange. My skin stretches painfully around it.

I don't have time to worry about my head. I must get back to the monastery.

Not far from the watch-line, I catch a whiff of meat. I stop my trudging, stand still and listen. I hear a faint crackle, like a fire burning, but no other sound. I approach the watch-line from the enemy side. I'll spot the monks in just a moment. They should be right ahead, but there is no sound, no call.

They must have noticed already. I continue walking, carefully, aiming the elephant gun in front of me. The first thing I see is a burning bush. Beneath the bush: a half-cooked human arm and a pile of eyeballs.

A few feet away, I find another bit of human, from the same or a separate body, I cannot tell. I hurry west toward the next watch post.

Similar people chunks litter the area.

I break into a sprint.

* * *

At the third watch, I find a whole half of a monk weeping on the ground. I can't stop to help.

At the adjacent post, there is only a discarded gun. I pick it up. The hand of a monk still clutches it. The rest of the monk is missing. I dislodge the hand and tuck the ray gun into my robes.

* * *

The fifth watch site is completely abandoned. A tree nearby has been severed about 20 feet up, the work of tyrannosaurs, no doubt. It seems like five simultaneous attacks. No warning. I can't feel the prickling flood of panic I think I should be feeling. I just know I need to get to the monastery. Now.

Chapter Ten
Mighty Birth

The attack came on so silently and so quickly; no one had any warning or time to prepare.

The south fields swarm with Jeremy. Monks send flocks of pigeons over the walls carrying small plastic bombs. Plastic-encased Jeremy dot the battlefield. The sky is thick with deafening roars and explosions, mixed with the quick pattering of bullets and the squelching sound of guns discharging. I run across the open field, firing into the walls of Jeremy on either side. All around me, dinosaurs freeze in plastic shells. Several small squadrons of monks are in the fray, cutting lines through the massive attack force. This is by far the most Jeremies I've ever seen in one place.

Leaving a line of dead dinosaurs behind me, I slam into the double doors of the monastery. A raptor chases after me. I aim the ray gun toward him and hear a tiny *splooch*. I'm out of ammunition. I throw the gun at the raptor, but it sidesteps around it. I curse aloud and brace my body for the impact.

The raptor leaps from about three feet away. It lands on my chest and knocks my body backwards onto the ground. Its jaws open with a screech. I hit it in the snout, but catch my hand in its mouth as I scramble back. Teeth scrape the skin of my wrist and arm down to the bone. I raise my injured fist again and punch the raptor in its right

eye. It cries out in pain and leaps back. I search around wildly, blood pouring from my wound. The raptor shakes its head like a wet dog, rattled but not destroyed. I need a weapon. Quick.

I snatch a branch up from the ground and brandish it like a sword. The raptor bends low, opens it mouth and screeches loudly. Three other raptors a little ways behind it look over with interest. Two of them hold a monk while the third punches him in the stomach.

The raptor in front of me is about to charge. I don't think my stick will do much, even if I can get in a good hit. Then someone yells. I risk a glance over my shoulder, and the raptor charges. The call has come from a monk behind the monastery door.

"Get your stupid ass in here!" the monk screams. I sprint toward him. The raptor is gaining. I feel its hot breath on my ankles as I squeeze through the door and help the monk slam it behind me.

"That was close," I say, dropping my stick in the sand.

"No shit," the monk says. He wipes his brow with the foot attached to his left arm and glares at me. "Elder Zohar wants you. Now."

This hostility seems a bit out of character, but I shrug it off. "Where is he?"

"In the temple-tent, fuck brain," the monk snaps, gesturing violently toward the tent before turning back to the stairs up to the wall.

I cross the commons. Monks run

across it carrying loads of ammunition and big cages full of pigeons and squirrels. Fire rains down from the sky. I feel I should have a weapon in hand, but don't think I have time to stop by the armory. Elder Zohar's request seems urgent.

When I enter his tent, I find two elders sitting, praying before the great gold-faced idol. Elder Zohar glances over his shoulder as I enter. He rises onto his fingertips. He lifts one of his lower fingers and cracks the knuckle against the carpet. "Seize him!" he says. The other elder turns around and looks at me. I think he's scowling, but it's difficult to say, as half of his face is a thigh.

I whirl around. Three monks flank the tent entrance. Two of them rush forward, grabbing my arm. The third monk is Oomka. I look to him for help. "Oomka, what's going on? Help me!"

"No one will help you now, traitor," the thigh-faced elder says in a muffled voice, and then, turning to Oomka, "What's wrong with his face?"

"We know where you have been going; we know what you have done," says Elder Zohar, ignoring the thigh-faced elder. "I knew something was troubling you yesterday, but I never suspected this. I thought that killing a few Jeremies would cure you of whatever was ailing you. Now, I know that it is a deep sickness of the mind."

"What?" I say, horrified and confused.

"How could you do this to us?" says Oomka in a quaking voice. I struggle to turn my body to look at him, but the two monks holding me painfully by the shoulders jerk me backward.

"What do you mean? I don't understand what's happening. What do you think I did?"

"It's no use playing dumb, you traitorous nag," says Elder Zohar. "You were seen giving confidential information to a Jeremy." He spits on the floor.

For a second, I'm speechless. I look to Oomka.

"I followed you," says Oomka, his eyes wide and sad now. "I saw you with that Jeremy. I'm sorry. I had to say something."

He *had* seen me, but what had he said? Was Petunia safe? Would the peaceful enclave of trachodons at the top of the mountain be massacred? Panic. It doesn't matter if the monks plan on torturing me or killing me. There is no one to warn the trachodons.

"No, you don't understand!" I shout. "It's not what it seems!" Looking directly into Elder Zohar's eyes, I say as calmly as I can, "They're peaceful; they're a species we don't know about, and they make thoughts, like the monks used to do. Believe me, I've seen these thoughts."

Elder Zohar scoffs and spits again. "Take him to the third tower and lock him up. Don't let anyone in the building."

The two monks who have my arm yank it backward, hard. "And send a group of monks up the south face of the mountain to the top. Let's bomb these fuckers before they come down and join the party," Elder Zohar says to the thigh-faced elder.

Tears. Huge, sloppy, childish tears pour down my face as the monks drag me across the commons toward the third tower. I can't stop the flow.

My giant face welt is still swelling. I feel it pulsing on top of my head. How the hell am I going to reach Petunia? I have to warn the trachodons. I have to save them. I have to save Petunia, burrow down to the center of the earth with her and take refuge on an empty island. It is the only way. We can grow old there, like in my dream, and be free of all this war and bloodshed and sadness.

* * *

From my window, I see the battle raging below. It looks hopeless. The Jeremy swarm the walls, so many of them, piled on top of each other in a rolling mound of spiny, reptilian flesh. My head throbs.

Huge cannons mounted on the tops of plesiosaurs fire giant flaming moths that flap over the monastery, raining fire down on the monks. A blast shakes the tower.

I figure there are a few possibilities now, and none of them sound promising: Either Jeremies break through the monastery walls and kill me, monks kill me for betraying them, or the giant mass on my head expands until it explodes and kills me.

Two tyrannosaurs near the southeast corner of the wall chip away at stone with the huge white femurs of their ancestors. No one protects that corner of the wall. It looks like a flaming moth crash-landed on the section, a twenty-foot circle of ground charred and black around it.

I have to do something. But my head throbs. I sink down under the window, still sobbing unconsciously, although the huge mass, which is now about as big and round as my entire head, prevents my eyes from excreting any real tears.

I try to return to the soft peach place Petunia had created in my mind. But it seems so far off, buried deeply beneath my immediate pain and horror. I reach, swimming through blackness, and there is a teal light above me, and a door with a little gleaming handle in the pupil of an eye. It is Petunia's eye.

I reach for the door and turn the handle. Petunia's eye is furnished like an old Victorian cottage. It looks like the room in which we grew old together, in my dream. I walk to the couch and bury my face in the gaudy floral fabric. It is rough but warm. My face welt has shrunken to a small lump again, and I hear the sounds of dishes clinking in the kitchen, then a soft voice calls, "Will you peel some of these potatoes for me, baby?"

I raise my head and look through the door to the kitchen. Petunia stands in a pink apron, beating eggs. She smiles warmly and gestures to the kitchen table where a little basket of potatoes sits near an empty metal bowl.

Three baby dinosaurs run in and out of the room, laughing and screaming. "Walking feet, boys!" Petunia chides.

I sit at the table and begin to skin the potatoes into the bowl. I watch Petunia, rolling dough on the island. She looks up and sees me watching her. "What's up?" she giggles.

"Nothing," I say, shaking my head and looking at the potato in my hands. "You're beautiful."

She laughs and rubs the bottom of her bill, leaving a little smear of flour behind. I laugh, too.

* * *

There's a huge crash from the battlefield. I snap back to reality and gaze out the window. Jeremies have broken through the monastery wall. Monks flee from the huge tyrannosaurs stomping in at the front. No one fights back. No one shoots. Everyone runs.

A lightening bolt of pain, and the welt on my head cracks open. Screaming, I fall to my knees. White splotches of agony cloud my vision. I try to rush back to the eyeball house, but can't see anything. Everything is washed out. I must be dying.

There is a ripping sound as something huge crawls out of my head. A leathery wing unfolds, covered in sticky yellow mucus. It flips around, and then the whole thing drops to the floor.

It's a pterodactyl.

It looks at me. It cocks its head and squawks.

I rush toward the pterodactyl and clamber onto its back. "Take me to the trachodons; take me to my Petunia!" I tell it.

It squawks obligingly and spreads its wings.

Chapter Eleven
Everyone Holds Hands

We soar through the air, as high as the tower and gaining altitude. The monks below are little mice. The tyrannosaurs are little cats.

We are far above the monastery now. The mice become mosquitoes. The cats become crane flies.

The forest sweeps past beneath us like a soft green carpet. I hug the pterodactyl that sprang from me. It lets out a happy squawk and turns to wink at me. I stroke the bright orange crest on it head. "Thank you," I say.

* * *

The trachodon village is in a clearing like the one where I first spoke to Petunia. Small yellow flowers adrift in a bright green sea. I am reminded of Petunia's eyes. Suddenly, she is running toward me.

There are no monks, no plastic-encased dinosaurs. I let out a huge sigh of relief, but there is no time to rest, no time to hug Petunia with my whole body.

"Quick!" I yell as she approaches. "The monks are coming with guns!"

Other trachodons are listening. Some scream. A mother grabs her child by the hand.

"What's happening? We heard explosions," Petunia says, grabbing me up in her arms and holding me against her chest like she did in my dream. My feet dangle twenty or so feet off the ground.

An older-looking trachodon peers out of a door nearby. "Everyone calm down," he calls across the clearing. Upon his approach, he bends low to peer at me. "Tell us what's going on, young man," he says.

Petunia sets me back on the ground. I tell the gathering crowd of trachodons what is happening at the monastery. My pterodactyl squawks a few times as if to confirm my story. The trachodons nod and gasp.

There is silence across the gathering. They look at each other. The older trachodon looks from Petunia to me. She is crouched down; we are holding hands.

"George," says the old trachodon suddenly to another, "go quickly and fetch the Steve. Everyone else," his chest swells as he looks around the clearing, "the time has come. This is the sign for which we have been waiting. Prepare for battle."

I whirl around. "Battle?" I ask. "And you have the Steve?"

Petunia scoops me up in her arms again and puts me on her back. "I'll explain later," she says, hurrying off in a crowd of trachodons. "Just keep quiet up there for a bit."

Suddenly, trachodons rush toward one building near the opposite end of the clearing from which I entered. They run past us, armed with metal plates and chain mail, carrying spears and swords. Two others push a tall wooden catapult. My pterodactyl follows us on foot. He squawks a little as he runs awkwardly.

"What's going on?" I ask. "Where's everyone going?"

"To the monastery. We're going to help you beat the Jeremy, once and for all," Petunia says.

"We don't stand a chance!" I yell, my throat constricting in panic. "You can't! The monks will think you're on the side of the Jeremy!"

"It's all right," Petunia says, looking around as she hurries toward the armory. "The Steve will help us."

* * *

Petunia and I race down the mountain, surrounded by trachodons in suits of armor, carrying steel swords as long as city buses. Strange creatures of various size and shape run alongside us. I sit, perched above Petunia's shoulder blades. Her head is enclosed in a shiny helmet. She carries a giant mace.

The Steve carry no weapons. I wonder how they will be able to help the trachodons. My pterodactyl, however, was given a samurai sword, his species' preferred weapon. He flies behind us, squawking excitedly. His squawks give me a little more confidence.

As we near the rear of the battle, we see small groups of monks still fighting in the field, but things seem to have gotten worse since I escaped. The monastery is overrun. Buildings burn.

The south fields are so thick with plastic dinosaurs that the trachodons must spread out to weave through them. Once clear, they plunge their swords into Jeremies, taking them by surprise. Luckily, as Jeremies fall around them, the last groups of monks fighting recognize that the trachodons are on their side.

We make our way steadily toward the monastery walls. Jeremies farther up seem to realize something is happening at the rear of the battle.

Trachodons, no longer able to take the Jeremy by surprise, begin to fall under heavy machine gun fire. Blades explode from the guns of the stegosaurs. Petunia ducks, raising her hands to shield me. The blades zip over our heads, slicing another trachodon in three. Petunia doesn't flinch.

Even amidst all this carnage and death, I'm amazed at her bravery.

A stegosaurus—two massive iron cannons mounted on either side of its scaly back—approaches rapidly. Trachodons scatter. Cannons fire. Everything around us erupts into flames. Petunia dives to the side just in time to avoid the blast, but other trachodons are caught in the blaze, screaming in agony as their dinosaur flesh bubbles and burns. My pterodactyl flies ahead of us. He squawks jubilantly as he slices the head from a plesiosaur carrying a long bow. The plesiosaur's paddle-feet twitch on the ground, and my pterodactyl rises

up into the air triumphantly, sounding his victory with a mighty squawk.

I notice, with a rush of anger, that the Steve cower behind the trachodons on the edge of the forest. Assorted furry and fishy faces watch the battle anxiously.

"I thought you said the Steve would help us!" I yell to Petunia. She is grinding the head of a raptor into the ground beneath us.

"They need energy; they're gathering strength!" she calls back, whirling around to throw the mace into an approaching triceratops' face.

Looking back, I notice that not every Steve stands around watching. At the back of the group, several are gathered in a circle. Steves are creatures made of energy. I realize they must need the destructive energy of the battle to act. All the same, I wish they would hurry up. A curious yellow glow seems to encircle them; but maybe I am imagining it.

Suddenly, I feel the need to do something, too. Hiding on Petunia's back makes me feel useless, so I slide down into the fray.

At once, and only inches from my body, a trachodon clubs another triceratops over the head with a battleaxe. Triceratops blood splatters me. The liquid is hot and sticky, and I feel sick. Still, I lunge toward the detached forearm of a fallen monk and grab the flamethrower lodged beneath it.

I whirl around and torch an approaching tyrannosaur. The flames don't stop him. Thick steel plates cover his front and sides. He slashes the three towering spikes strapped to his head at me, catching me in my armless side. I feel a stab of pain as they connect with my spine, and I soar up into the air.

I can do no more than gasp before I land squarely in the arms of a trachodon, who had apparently dove onto the ground to catch me. It is the old trachodon to whom I had spoken on the mountaintop.

"Get back to Petunia," he says.

I decide it's best to listen to him. He drops me into the crumpled wheat stalks of the scarred field, and I search for Petunia.

She's nowhere to be seen. There's only a dense cloud of blood, flesh and severed limbs, dinosaurs and monks flying in every direction.

I scream her name, but Petunia doesn't materialize from the mass. A huge clawed foot stomps down close to me, and I scramble out of the way as three more feet stomp by, leaving gaping holes in the field. It's another stegosaurus, laden this time with one half of a rotating saw-blade apparatus. It runs in a circle, unable to move the machine on its back without a partner. The whirling blade catches trachodons, severing them in half. Monks try to duck under the blade as it passes; some are cut in half as well.

As I watch, holding the flamethrower, unable to move, the stegosaurus spins around and heads back toward me. The glistening silver blade is feet away. I can do nothing but wait, so I flatten myself in the mud, covering my head with the flamethrower. Suddenly, a huge clawed hand snatches me.

The hand throws me up into the air. As I twist around above the battle, I see Petunia beneath me, leaping over the stegosaurus, plunging the sharpened base of her mace into the Jeremy's eye. Then Petunia snatches me out of the air and slams me hastily onto her back.

I can see across the battlefield again. Trachodons are losing ground; Jeremies have overrun the monastery. In the distance, a plesiosaur hangs onto the top of the third tower, waving its green front limbs around in apparent triumph.

My stomach plunges into my toes. We are losing; perhaps we have already lost.

Petunia begins wrestling with a tyrannosaur. I cling on for dear life when, suddenly, finally, the Steve—aglow with yellow light—rush out from behind the trachodons. The lumbering, sprinting animals tear toward oncoming Jeremies through a forest of plasticized corpses. Human flesh and blood-soggy wheat squish beneath their claws and hooves.

Bullets whiz past them. Several make contact, and those bodies fall under the pounding feet of the other Steve.

Ten feet from impact with the Jeremies, a wave of cloudy, twinkling mist shoots from the glowing Steve. Those Jeremies that it hits vomit fireflies into the air, roar in agony and clutch their bellies. They drop their guns and swords and kneel, choking and gasping as the insects crawl out of their eyes and nostrils and tear past their razor-sharp teeth in swarms. Dinosaur flesh rains from the sky as bodies explode from the inside all around the monks still fighting up ahead.

The sparkling firefly mist sweeps over the field. Trachodons follow. The air glows yellow. Fireflies are everywhere. The air is too thick with them to breathe. I am choking on fireflies.

The trachodons race toward the monastery. The mist has hit the walls. Jeremies collapse all around. The Steve charge and climb the walls.

Monks run behind us, cheering and whooping. Monks drop their guns and fall into prostrations. Monks hug each other. Monks wave detached arms and legs.

Monks and Steve embrace each other. Steves kiss monks. Trachodons lift monks up into the air. Monks ride on trachodons. Monks kiss trachodons. Trachodons kiss Steves.

Monks run toward the monastery. Steves run toward the monastery. Trachodons run toward the monastery. The high brick walls of the monastic compound are piles of red-gray rubble. Smoke billows out of the windows of the remaining buildings. Scared-looking villagers crawl out of the wreckage and stare at the ocean of exploded dinosaurs. Meat and intestines cover the south field. Giant pieces of ribcage and twitching dinosaur limbs protrude from the mess. Swaths of skin and chunks of muscle are draped over the plasticized dinosaur statues.

Columns of black smoke curl up into the gray sky.

* * *

In the midst of the celebrating monks, holding one of Petunia's clawed fingers in my hand, I watch a fish-headed Steve walk slowly out of the remains of the temple-tent. The white canvas is draped over the tall idol, obscuring its face.

The fish-headed Steve carries half a monk.

No, it's not just half a monk. It's Elder Zohar.

A long sword protrudes from his chest. The Steve carrying him is crying.

Elder Zohar never went to find the Steve. His face is frozen in anger. His bald head glistens with moisture. His bottom fingers are clenched into fists, and his intestines trail behind the Steve.

Elder Zohar performed Harakiri. He is dead.

It has just begun to rain. Petunia and I are holding hands.

Epilogue
The Myth of the Great Creator

There is a story told by the monks that, at the End of Days, another age will begin. Once the earth has been split up, the pieces that once made the crust and the carpet and the wide, open, cavernous center will rejoin in a new and better order.

In this other age, monks, fireflies,